My Brother Jack

This prize-winning novel about two Australian brothers traces their story from childhood, when their parents (a sapper and an army nurse) return from the First World War to the bitter anticlimax of their humdrum life in a Melbourne suburb. George Johnston brilliantly reanimates dramatic incidents of childhood, adolescence and eventual maturity, depicted against the backgrounds of Dickensian vividness.

And then the brothers — and half the world with them — are faced with the Second World War and the decisions that they, as men, must make. Largely autobiographical in the great tradition of Thomas Wolfe, the book contains, in Jack Meredith, a character who will remain the epitome of everything Australians like to believe themselves to be.

George Johnston

My Brother Jack

Collins
Fontana Books

First published in 1964 by William Collins Sons & Co. Ltd
First issued in Fontana Books 1967
Thirteenth Impression August 1979
Fourteenth Impression September 1981
Fifteenth Impression January 1982

© George Johnston 1964

Printed and bound by
The Dominion Press, North Blackburn, Victoria

FOR MY OWN BROTHER JACK . . .

Fiction there is—and history. Certain critics of no little discernment have considered that fiction is history which *might* have taken place, and history fiction which *has* taken place. We are indeed forced to acknowledge that the novelist's art often compels belief, just as reality sometimes defies it. Alas! there exists an order of minds so sceptical that they deny the possibility of any act as soon as it diverges from the commonplace. It is not for them that I write.

ANDRÉ GIDE

CHAPTER 1

My brother Jack does not come into the story straight away. Nobody ever does, of course, because a person doesn't begin to exist without parents and an environment and legendary tales told about ancestors and dark dusty vines growing over outhouses where remarkable insects might always drop out of hidden crevices.

Childhood, looking back on it, is like this—a mess of memories and impressions scattered and clotted and pasted together like a mulch of fallen leaves on a damp autumn pavement. So the first memory, naturally, is of a childhood we shared together—he was only three years my senior but he always seemed to me to be much, much older—and although it is a memory made up of many parts, distinct and indistinct, mundane and fantastic, coherent and incomprehensible, it is fixed now into a final and exact if distant image of a place once lived in and never to be returned to, like the city seen by the wife of Lot in that last yearning moment before she became the pillar of salt.

With me it focuses most sharply around the small, rather fusty wallpapered hallway upon which the front door opened in that undistinguished house—weatherboard painted dark stone and a corrugated iron roof of sun-faded Indian red—which sat behind a wire fence, privet hedge, small square lawn of buffalo grass, and the name *Avalon* in gilt letters on a blackwood panel in a flat and dreary suburb far away in Melbourne, Australia. "Far away" is meant in a temporal as well as a spatial sense, for not only did all this begin to occur some ten thousand miles distant from where I am now, but this was more than forty years ago, not long after the First World War ended.

The hallway itself, in fact, was far from undistinguished, because a souvenired German gas-mask hung on the tall hallstand, looking like the head of a captured Martian, and the whole area of the hall was a clutter of walking-sticks with heavy grey rubber tips—the sort of tips on walking-sticks that relate to injury rather than to elegance—and sets of crutches

—the French type as well as the conventional shapes of bent wood—and there was always at least one invalid wheel-chair there and some artificial limbs propped in the corners. Our sister Jean, who was the eldest of us four children, eventually married a returned soldier who had had his leg amputated, and this seemed to us, at the time, quite normal and expected. Jack and I must have spent a good part of our boyhood in the fixed belief that grown-up men who were complete were pretty rare beings—complete, that is, in that they had their sight or hearing or all their limbs. Well, we knew they existed, but they seldom came our way.

How this happened ought to be explained, and this can be done only through the figure of our mother, still something of a stranger to us at that time, mostly because of her years of absence from us, but also because she was even then not really an integrated part of the household but seemed only to visit us each afternoon or evening in her starched nurse's uniform or her dark blue, red-collared cape. Usually she carried with her a smell of ether or iodine, or of carbolic. She was head sister in the operating theatre of the big military hospital which was only a mile or so to the north of our house, along Kooyong Road. Twenty years later, when I was a grown man, the hospital was still there behind a black wall of huge pines and a secondary palisade of dustily-mottled plane-trees —the same confused blocks of long low " temporary " wards, much more faded, set amid flowering shrubs and overstuffed beds of wilting cannas, and tired lawns, and scuffed gravel paths. I went there to visit my sister's husband Bert, who was back as a patient having the nineteenth additional slice taken off his amputated leg. By this time the place had become, by official designation, the Cauldfield Convalescent Hospital, although quite a few of the patients were there from that time of twenty years before, already a pretty long convalescence and one which for a good many of them was never to end.

I do not remember the beginning of it, because I would have been hardly three when my father, an electric tram mechanic, volunteered as a sapper in the engineers, and went off to Gallipoli with the Anzacs. Nor do I remember my mother going. It seems that after the brave bungle of the Dardanelles she volunteered as an army nurse, and was shipped off to France, leaving her four small children, Jean, Jack, me, and our two-year-old sister Marjorie, in the care of a pugnacious and diminutive little woman named Emma, who was our grandmother on our mother's side. There were just the five of us in the house, then, Granny and us four kids.

Dad was away at what was always referred to as "The Front" for four years altogether, and Mother for rather more than three. They were still overseas when the Armistice was signed. They both came home in 1919, but not together, because Mother returned, of course, in a hospital ship: an odd thing was that in all the time they were in France together they never once succeeded in making contact with each other. Dad, who had been gassed, but not seriously, near Vimy Ridge, went back to his old job at the tramway depot, but Mother got herself transferred to the operating theatre in the hospital and went on being a nursing sister.

One recollects something of this later phase in a series of vivid little vignettes that are incomplete and scattered, but bright enough, like the fragments of spilt colour I remember strewn on the hall carpet all around the artificial limbs and crutches when the front door slammed in a gusty wind one day and shattered the decorative leadlight side panels of red and green and blue and amber glass.

Almost the earliest and yet the clearest of these images is of the troop-ship *Ceramic*, with her four rakish masts and her tall tilted smoke-stack, coming home to the flags and the festoons of garlands and the triumphal arches and the bands playing Sousa marches on the pier at Port Melbourne. The blue-grey abstract dazzle of the camouflage-painting on the steamer's incredibly long, lean hull, although spectacular, came as no surprise to me, but I do remember being astonished by the bright daubs of red-lead and the more sanguinary streams of rust streaking down from ports and hawse-hole and scuppers, because I had only visualised the ship before in the grey monotone of a mounted photograph which was kept on top of the piano, together with a hard army biscuit on which was drawn with Indian ink a sketch of a camel and the Sphinx and a palm-tree and the Pryamids and the legend *Australian Imperial Forces Cairo New Year* 1915. There was no coincidence in the photograph being there on the piano; the *Ceramic* was the transport that had taken Mother away; the coincidence was that it was the same ship that brought Dad home. Even so, I had not expected the vivid redness of the rust and the red-lead, which to my awed childish imagination looked like blood pouring down the ship's side. Perhaps it had been.

I was seven then, but small for my age, and the day was charged, for me, with a huge and numbing terror. This fear was involved with the interminable blaring of brass bands, and a ceaseless roar of shouting and cheering, and the unending trampling past of gigantic legs. I can only assume that after the beginning of it I became too frightened to look up at the hours-long progression of dark, hard faces under wide, turned-up hats seen against bayonets and barrels that were more blue than black. I seem to retain glimpses of packs and rolled blankets and bandoliers, but the really strong image that is preserved now is of the stiff fold and buckle of coarse khaki trousers moving to the rhythm of knees and thighs and the tight spiral curves of puttees and the thick boots hammering, hollowly off the pier planking and thunderous on the asphalt roadway. The climax of it all came when a strong voice, hoarse with excitement, began to shout, " Minnie! *Minnie!* " and without warning I was seized suddenly and engulfed in one of the gigantic, coarse-clad figures and embraced in a stifling smell of damp serge and tobacco and beer and held high in the air before a sweating apparition that was a large, ruddy face grinning at me below a back-tilted slouch hat and thin fair hair receding above a broad freckled brow, and then there was a roar of laughter, and I was put down, sobbing with fear, and the thick boots marched on and on, as if they were trampling all over me.

Minnie was my mother. She had come back from the war three months earlier than Dad, but she was at the hospital and still pretty much a stranger, and on that day of my father's homecoming it was the familiar, gnarled hand of little Emma, my grandmother, which I tightly and damply clutched all through the overwhelming day.

At home neighbours and relatives had erected a big arch above the wire mesh of the front gate, with " Welcome Home " picked out in daisies and snapdragons and carnations against a background of lily leaves and gumtips and maidenhair fern, and at the party that evening everybody crowded around the piano and sang " Roses of Picardy " and " Mademoiselle from Armentières " and " The Rose of No Man's Land " and " Blighty " and " Pack Up Your Troubles in Your Old Kitbag " and " There's a Long, Long Trail A-winding," and everyone was drunk and hilarious, and I was fed so much fruit salad and jelly that I vomited.

That, for me, was how the First World War ended. It was also, in a way, the beginning of my trying to piece it together. . . .

Because of the differences in our ages, the impression of all these excitements on us four children could not expectably have been the same, but Jack and I must have shared certain similar feelings about the symbolism of the hallway and the constant presence in our house of all the derelicts of war whom Mother brought home to stay, since we had to be turned out of our room, and for years after we shared a make-shift bed on the floor of the sleep-out, which was really only a section of the back veranda partitioned off by flywire screens and a lot of damp ferns. But there must have been a great deal of this sort of thing at that time—being turned out of beds and sleeping in provisional rooms, I mean. Not only in our house or our suburb, but everywhere. All over the world.

There was a lot of mess to be cleaned up in those years of 1919 and 1920, after the war and the Spanish influenza: the bodies of the dead to be located and the great cemeteries set up, and all those military hospitals in France and Flanders and Britain and Italy to be cleaned out of colonial troops so that there would be space in which to try to heal the indigenous maimed. Back to Melbourne then the hospital ships and transports were bringing sick and wounded Anzacs by the thousands, and in the big military hospital where Mother worked temporary wards were added to temporary wards, and beds were shifted out on to verandas or even crowded into hastily erected canvas marquees—there were some parts of the place where one would get the odd impression that a circus or a garden fête was going on—and what had once been no more than an old mansion set in spacious grounds began to have the look of a swiftly developing city. Even so, things finally got to such a pass that any of the earlier patients who seemed capable of existing on their pensions in the civilian world outside were quickly discharged and repatriated to make room for the newcomers. So there were quite a few disabled men, still pretty infirm, who suddenly found themselves demobilised and alone and helpless outside the army organisation which for four years had enveloped every second of their activities, and with no place to go. These were the ones whom Mother brought to our house.

Some stayed a few weeks or a few months, there were others who were with us for years. Altogether I suppose forty or fifty of them must have inhabited our house at one time or another.

The majority of these have now become a kind of diffused composite image—they must have been brave people and cheerful enough in their collective infirmity, because in the composite there are their jokes and their badinage, but not all that much suffering—but there are still some of them who are distinctly preserved in memory, as sharply detailed as an insect sealed in amber.

The two New Zealanders, for example, are there—Aleck, who had been blinded early, at Gaba Tepe, with his polished leggings and his Boy Scoutish hat with the four dents in it: and "Stubby," who was really only a trunk and a jovial red face in a wheel-chair, a German whizzbang having taken both his legs and both forearms at Villers-Bretonneux. At various times we had others who had lost more than one limb, and all the rest were intensely proud of these "double amps" and would boast to their friends about their good humour or their dexterity, but among these victims Stubby was always the doyen. Then there was Bert, the gawky, tow-headed Australian country boy who had been a real "hayseed" when he had volunteered. He had been under age then and had given a false name, but after all that he lost his right leg on the first and only day of action he ever saw in France. And that was only four days before the Armistice was signed —the very day that Kaiser Bill was scuttling off to Holland. Bert was still only about eighteen when he came to our house on a pair of French crutches, there being no point in a one-legged cripple trying to go back to work on his father's impoverished little selection-farm outside Corindhap, which isn't real farming land at all, just quartz country and worked-over gold diggings. In a sense Bert never left us again, because later he got a job working in the Repatriation Department's Artificial Limb Factory at South Melbourne, and then he married our Jean. The nightmarish one in this remembered gallery is Gabby Dixon, because he kept in the background and was never seen much, and I don't suppose he wanted to be seen because he had suffered terrible facial burns with mustard gas and his face was no longer really like a face at all. He used to frighten me with his staring silences, and he is about the only one I remember as a cheerless figure, because sometimes at night through the thin partitions of the wall we could hear him sobbing in his room. I am pretty vague now about all the others, although I do remember Duval, who was French and very dapper and had lost an arm. He used perfume on his handkerchiefs and made high-pitched incomprehensible jokes and upset everybody, even Mother, until he finally took off for Noumea. Nobody who came back from France ever seemed to like the " Frogs " very much.

Those who stayed with us all seemed to go on wearing their khaki uniforms or their hospital blues for a long time, and whenever they were being photographed—and somebody was *always* taking group snapshots on the square of buffalo lawn with everybody carefully placed and grinning around Stubby in his wheel-chair—they would invariably put on their army caps or hats. One of the group would always be holding a crutch up, jokingly.

When they were not posing for these photographs they were a cheerful, diligent crowd on the whole. Stubby had learnt to make string doilies, using his teeth and the leather-padded stumps of his forearms, and blind, taciturn Aleck endlessly knitted balaclavas in navy blue or khaki wool. He knitted very expertly and I never understood why he made only balaclavas, which had been useful enough in the winter trenches of the Western Front but which I never saw a single person in Melbourne wearing. Bert had acquired a kit of shoe-repairer's tools through a grant from the Limbless Soldiers' Association, and at this time he was teaching himself a trade and intended to rent a little cobbler's shop with his deferred pay and gratuity. The others would tease him good-naturedly about this ambition ; his active service had been of such brief duration that his gratuity and deferred pay would hardly have added up to the price of a snobbing bench. (Bert always talked of the trade as " snobbing "; he did become quite adept at it and for years, even after he had gone to work in the Artificial Limb factory, he always kept our school boots and shoes in wonderful repair.)

Sunday was the big public visiting day at the hospital and Mother had made it a practice that Jean and Jack and I should go round the wards selling postcards to aid the Red Cross. The other two used to enjoy this, because they would get sweets and fruit and biscuits, and even little tips of money that were not meant to go into the big cubical Red Cross tins, and Jean liked to put her Sunday dress on and a white bow in her hair, and Jack had a way of cheeking the wounded men he had come to know, and they would always engage him uproariously and then say to their visitors admiringly, " That's Sister Min's kid; he's a real dag, that one!"

I was the one who hated these Sunday commitments. I hated the unending tiring labyrinth of wards, the stretching miles of maimed men in white enamelled cots, the noncommittal doctors in their white gowns moving silently along corridors that smelt of chloroform and cotton lint, the squeaky wheeling of shrouded trolleys, the shapes and the no-shapes that lay hidden beneath the white counterpanes with the red crosses embroidered on them, the lowered false voices of visitors. I was half aware of a formless shadow of disaster that I wanted to shout against or run away from: it existed in the unexpected sounds of pain or delirium that came from behind screened-off beds, it lay across the interminable recession of men's profiles that were always lined and ward-pallid and set horizontally on white pillows, it clung to the changes in occupancy that one noticed from one Sunday to the next without ever knowing, or even daring to ask, whether it was death or healing that had effected the changes.

I don't know when it was that I began to suspect that these desperate Sunday feelings were really only an extension of a terror which I knew to be real, even though I did not understand it, but which was somehow related to the day the *Ceramic* brought my father back, and also to the leather-and-metal, stiff-jointed legs and the claw-like appendages to the artificial arms propped in the corners of our hallway, and to the faces of Aleck and Stubby posing for snapshots beneath their flat-brimmed New Zealand hats, and to Gabby Dixon weeping in the darkness of his bedroom, and to Jack and me in the sleep-out listening to the grown-up laughter around the cribbage-board in the sitting-room or to the more furtive slithering noise which was made by a big creeper vine we called the Dollicus as it moved in the night wind against the screen of flywire.

I never did talk to Jack about these mysterious, disturbing fears. Or perhaps I did and don't remember. (It occurs to me that there is almost no conversation in this story yet, but this is right. One remembers fears first, then things, like the Dollicus, and conversations only much later.) There was always that difference of three years between us, anyway. On Jack, the effect of the absence of both our parents at the war had been to make him wild and adventurous and reckless. He was fighting other kids in the streets, and usually winning. More and more often he would go truant from school—we used to call it " playing the wag "—especially when he learnt to forge Mum's and Dad's signatures impeccably and could write his own excuse letters to his teachers . . . there had even been some minor scrapes with the police. He gave poor old Granny, our seventy-year-old guardian, a terrible time from the very beginning. He regarded me, tolerantly enough but without any mincing of words, as a " bloody sawny little sonk," and it is perfectly true that the period which had turned him into a wild one had made me something of a namby-pamby. Jean bullied me, Jack despised me, my younger sister was a nuisance and a tell-tale, so I clung to my grandmother then as I did later, when the troopship came home. The mischief with which I involved her was always unintentional. Like the terrible day of the Dollicus seeds.

What sort of creeper the Dollicus really was is something of which I have no idea to this day, but that was what it was always called. (Granny had a rare malapropism with botanical names: the rhododendron was the " rota," our pelargoniums became the " paragonia," the hydrangea was always the " hyter." Still, for all I know she might have been pedantically right for once with this creeper, because botanical names often derive from Ancient Greek and *dolikos* is a perfectly good Greek word meaning " long " and this par-

ticular creeper was certainly a fantastically long one and
the seeds it bore were carried in long thin black pods.) It was
ink-dark, huge, dank, and insect-haunted and although it
often scared the wits out of me at night it was useful on rainy
days because it carried thousands of hard pellet-like little
seeds in its pods—in a Daisy air rifle you could use the seeds
in place of BB shot—some of them white and some of them
black, and these I would collect and arrange on the linoleum-
covered floor in a complicated make-believe game which was
supposed to represent battles between the Germans and the
Aussies.

I was doing this one rainy morning when my grandmother
came home from shopping, by which time my private Arma-
geddon had spread from the sleep-out to the vestibule.
Granny opened the back door, shook her umbrella, and
stepped inside. The combination of her wet shoes, the waxed
linoleum, and the scattered Dollicus seeds was too much:
her feet slid from under her, and down she came with a crash
which, considering how frail and tiny she was, sounded quite
awful. But worse than this, her shopping basket went high in
the air, then followed her down, a bag of new-laid eggs falling and breaking in a paste of yolk and albumen exactly on
the grey crown of her aged head. The shock of witnessing and
being responsible for this grotesque disaster plunged me into
immediate panic. I fled through the back door, scaled the
wall of the outdoor privy, from there scrambled to the roof
of the house, clawed my way up the slippery gable to the
brick chimney, and sat myself shivering on top of it.

I stayed up there for two hours, with Granny raging
around the garden below me, threatening me with a bran-
dished tablespoon and a bottle of castor-oil. Eventually it was
my fear of the height that proved too much for me, and I was
cold and wet and desperately unhappy, and I had to come
down.

To my amazed relief she didn't punish me at all, and when
she put her arms around me very tightly and kissed me I
realised she was crying. Perhaps it was the memory of this
that made me clutch her hand so tightly on that later day
when the *Ceramic* brought the soldiers home.

In a sense, of course, I was too young for the war to have

had any direct effect on me, since there was really nothing of it that I could remember. Yet what is significant to realise now is how every corner of that little suburban house must have been impregnated for years with the very essence of some gigantic and sombre experience that had taken place thousands of miles away, and quite outside the state of my own being, yet which ultimately had come to invade my mind and stay there, growing all the time, forming into a shape.

And it went on for years. There was no corner of the house from the time I was seven until I was twelve or thirteen that was not littered with the inanimate props of that vast, dark experience, no room that was not inhabited by the jetsam that the Somme and the Marne and the salient at Ypres and the Gallipoli beaches had thrown up. Stubby sitting by a window tearing with his teeth at the white threads of his doilies; Aleck in another room knitting his balaclavas or fumbling with quick-tapping insectine fingers for his tobacco pouch; the bumpy, squeaky sound of someone in a bedroom testing an artificial leg; the bathroom that everlastingly smelt of antiseptic and ointment and ether and Condy's crystals: and even outside, in the backyard sunshine, there would be Mother's white nursing veils and aprons blowing on the clothes-line in a smell of yellow soap, and underneath the fig-tree Bert sitting on an upturned packing-case, a long leather bib tied around his chest and his empty trouser-leg neatly folded up and fastened by a safety-pin, hammering away at half-soles and heels. There was no radio then, but we always had " sing-songs " around the piano on Sunday nights, with Mother playing, and for years the songs were always the same—the " old favourites " of the war years, " Tipperary " and " Over There " and " Johnny Get Your Gun " and the rest of them.

It was not until I discovered the big deep drawer at the bottom of the cedar wardrobe in my parents' bedroom that I began to sense a form in the shadow that lurked in the wards and the corridors of the hospital, and to give a shape to the faraway experience which had moved in behind the privet hedge to occupy every room and every cranny of our mundane little house. During the years when Mother and Father were away the drawer must have been the repository for all the souvenirs and things they would send back to Granny, or

the things she had preserved herself for their relationship to
"The Front," and to this collection Mother and Dad would
have added their own memorabilia when they returned, for
there was a service revolver in the drawer, and a cardboard
box full of stubby .45 bullets and clips of .303 ammunition
in a leather bandolier and campaign ribbons and various
regimental badges and a German Iron Cross and the citation
that had gone with my father's Military Medal. But also
there were elaborate French silk postcards and innumerable
foreign coins and banknotes and, most important of all, the
full set of weekly parts of the *Illustrated War News* and a
copy of *The Anzac Book* and the three volumes of Louis
Raemaker's cartoons about the German atrocities.

I would steal into the bedroom when Dad was away at the
tram sheds and Mother on duty in the operating theatre, and
I would lock the door and spend hours on the floor in front of
the big drawer. The Raemaker cartoons, at first, were the
dominant fascination.

One knew nothing then about propaganda, so that the cartoons, in my mind, assumed a horrible reality, the substance
of nightmare translated into printed truth. For weeks I was
in morbid thrall to these grotesque, hating pictures of brutal
infernos, of cloven-footed devils wearing Kaiser Bill hats
impaling naked babies and women on their swords, of priests
being mutilated and crucified by the Prussians in front of
sacked and burning towns, of the grinning skeleton of Death
in a Uhlan's helmet wielding a scythe across the shell-pocked
desecration of No Man's Land, of the bestial Huns dis-
embowelling starving Belgian children, and mysterious words
like *Kultur* and *Gott Mit Uns* written across a ruined world
in letters of blood.

But after a time, perhaps because it was essential to reject
the horror that the pictures inspired—for I was unable to
develop a hatred, which, in fact, was the purpose of their
message—I forced myself to realise that these were only
drawings, after all, made, I thought, by some vengeful and
embittered man who must have suffered frightfully at the
hands of the Germans. And as their power to oppress me
lessened, I gave greater attention to the copies of the *Illustrated War News*. For these pictures were not imagined and

drawn out of wrath and vindictive hatred; these were the
real photographs of what had taken place.

Here, across two whole pages, was that treeless, shell-torn
wilderness of mud and barbed wire and duckboards and
craters and broken artillery wheels and abandoned ammunition boxes that was the Somme, " The Front," that No Man's
Land about which they all sang so robustly at the Sunday
night sing-songs. Here, in actual photographs as true as the
Kodak snapshots taken on our own front lawn, were the gas
victims and the blinded and the bandaged tottering back from
Cambrai, and gaunt men in tin helmets squatting in the mud
while the stretcher-bearers carried blanketed bodies along the
duckboards, and the corpses sprawled in muck or drowned in
flooded shell craters or hanging like cast-off rags on the
tangled wire, and the tanks rolling down the trenches, and
the smoke palls across towns, and the steeples hanging upside
down from churches. And one day I suddenly knew that this
was the connection with the things propped up in our hallway and with the shattered men who inhabited all of our
house and half of my mind: for here, in sepia and blue and
black halftone, were Vimy Ridge and Villers-Bretonneux and
Hill 60 and Amiens Cathedral and Gaba Tepe and the burnt-
out Cloth Hall at Ypres, and Bert " snobbing " in the back
yard and Gabby Dixon's face at the dark end of a room and
the smell of chloroform in corridors and the bronchial cough
of my father going off in the dawn light to the tramways
depot.

I was attending State school by this time, and I liked to
walk home by way of the railway viaduct, down past the
chaff-and-grain store where I was sometimes sent to buy bran
and pollard for our hens, and then along the little street
beside the railway line that ran between Ripponlea and
Elsternwick. In this street there was a second-hand-dealer's
shop with a window full of contents that fascinated me. It
was a shabby, rather ramshackle little shop; the whole building would shake whenever the train roared through the clay
cutting opposite. There was always a special enchantment in
this, for once the reverberations sent a stuffed owl toppling
down into a tray of old wedding rings, and several times the
tremors caused crystal pearl-drops to fall from the dusty

chandeliers overhead, and always the shuddering of the building would make the little collection of second-hand glass eyes jiggle around and change their places slightly in the fly-spotted saucer that lay at the front of all the crazy clutter, so that the eyes seemed to wink or glare at me.

Two doors along from this place was the Phœbe Biograph and Cinema Palace which showed episodes of the Pearl White serials on Saturday afternoons, and between the two buildings was a dilapidated, narrow-fronted photographer's studio which had been deserted and padlocked for as long as I could remember. The window was full of dust, dead flies and cock-roaches, and a great many spotted photographs that had been there for years. The sun had faded them to a ghostly, deathly pallor, but they were all of young men in the uniform of soldiers, most of them wearing slouch hats turned up at one side, and all of them with Rising Sun badges on their tunics. They were mostly boyish-looking faces, none of them with the expressions that I had seen at home or in the hospital wards, so that I guessed the portraits had been taken years before, when they had enlisted or just before they had em-barked for overseas.

I was staring in at these photographs one day—really I was only waiting for the signal of the train's whistle on the via-duct, which would be my cue to move on to the second-hand shop window—when a ragged, agate-eyed boy who was at my school but several years older and in the sixth grade, came down the street, kicking a tennis ball before him. He stopped alongside me but said nothing. He just stood there for a long time, right beside me, staring in with me at the pale photo-graphs. Finally, in a flat voice and without even looking at me, he said, " All them blokes in there is dead, you know." He stared at the pictures a moment or two longer, then said, "Well, hoo-roo," and waved to me and moved off and kicked the tennis ball right down to the end of the street and trotted off after it, whistling.

I ran all the way home that day, trying not to cry, because I didn't know what it was I wanted to cry about, but I never after that looked in the window of the photographer's studio or the second-hand shop. From then on, when I went to the Phœbe for the serial matinees or the Harold Lloyd comedies, I would always make a long detour to go the back way.

It was shortly after this that I began to get rid of the contents of the big drawer. I did it quite carefully, a little at a time—I suppose it took me months to complete the job—and after a while I found I could do it with material gain to myself. I sold the books of the Raemaker cartoons and the sets of the *Illustrated War News* to Garcia the greengrocer for wrapping paper, and all the silk postcards and strange coins and odd souvenirs I either sold to kids at school or swapped for marbles or foreign stamps or toodilumbuks. There was a slight shock one day when we had parsley delivered from Garcia wrapped up in some of the Raemaker cartoons, but Granny didn't even notice it.

I left the revolver there, and the bandolier and Dad's medals and things like that, but my parents never went to the drawer in the wardrobe, and I don't believe they ever knew what I had done with all the other things; perhaps they no longer even remembered that the stuff was there.

It doesn't matter any longer, of course, because all them blokes in there really *are* dead now.

CHAPTER 2

The thing I am trying to get at is what made Jack different from me. Different all through our lives, I mean, and in a special sense, not just older or nobler or braver or less clever.

Only the other day, sitting in the sun outside a waterfront coffee-house on a Greek island where I have been hiding for several years, something happened which made me think about this. It was a day of intense heat—that burning Mediterranean summer heat that should be measured in degrees of cicadas. The sort of heat and the sort of burnt-out light that always reminds one of Australia, of the smell of bushfire smoke and dust blowing and the dry tangle of bark-litter beneath the gum-trees.

At our table was a tall, youngish Englishman, a failed aristocrat who had been sent down from Oxford some years before, rather disgracefully, and who had come to this island with the evident intention of drinking himself into a condition of irreparable decay. He was the sort of person who burns easily and the heat had made him despondent and he had been telling us of some of the more lamentable interludes in his life. After he had completed the sorry account he stared broodingly into his wine glass, then shook his head sadly, and said:

"None of you, of course, will ever know what it was like to be the younger son of a younger son."

"No," I replied with sudden sharpness. "And you will never know what it was like to be the younger son of a tram driver!"

The angry way in which I said this startled the Englishman —it rather surprised me, too—and he left the table almost at once, and without paying for his wine.

It did not occur to me until later that my brother Jack, even had he been the younger son, would never have said a thing like that, because I cannot imagine him wanting to carry a grudge against anything, the way I often seem to have done.

My father's name also was Jack, simply because that had been *his* father's name. Jack—never John—was the name always given to the firstborn boy, and Dad had been the eldest boy among nineteen children. Mother differentiated between my father and my brother by calling them Big Jack and Little Jack; when my sister Jean had a son and named him Jack as well, Mother gave a promotion to my brother and from then on they were stepped down as Big Jack, Young Jack, and Little Jack. And years later, when my brother finally had a son after having fathered a whole clutch of daughters, the boy was named Jack without the least hesitation.

How far this goes back I do not know, but there was an even earlier ancestor who had gone to Australia midway through the time of convict transportation, as first mate on a three-masted barque, and his name, certainly, was Jack Meredith. This one was a bad lot. In the Southern Ocean he led a mutiny in which the captain was thrown overboard, then they deliberately ran the vessel ashore near Twofold Bay, and because there was a desperate shortage of general merchandise in the penal settlement at Port Jackson, they salvaged the cargo and began to run it up to Sydney Cove in the ship's boats, expecting to sell the stuff at huge prices. The plot was detected almost at once because a duplicate copy of the barque's cargo-manifesto had already reached Sydney in a naval brig, so this particular Jack Meredith was convicted for barratry and hanged in chains on the gibbet at South Head.

There were odd things like that in the series of developing human patterns which eventually culminated in Jack and I sharing the floor in the sleep-out.

I suppose it was all pretty typical of what happened in Australia in the first century or so of colonial life. One ancestor of ours had been in the naval landing party which first hoisted the British flag over the new settlement at Botany Bay in 1788. Other ancestral connections drifted out there later, mostly from Scotland and probably nonentities.

Mother's father, however, made quite a name for himself. He was a Highland Scot from Sutherland and he got to Australia as second mate on a smart Liverpool clipper of the White Star fleet, the *Red Jacket*, but he and all the crew abandoned her at the anchorage in Hobson's Bay to join one of the periodical stampedes to the goldfields. He later became an officer of the Mounted Constabulary in the man-hunt after Ned Kelly and his gang, and later still prospered enough to own a goldmine and two newspapers, and grow rich and mean and puritanical.

I remember him as a very old man. He was tall, stiff, gaunt, and grey—he always reminded me of a ringbarked tree, and inspired in me something of the same dread which would always fill me when I saw one of those dead, ghostly trees standing alone in a paddock at night—and I don't think he ever spoke to me except to quote some precept from Scripture.

He died as he had lived, in a suffocating smell of sanctimony, and left most of his fortune to build an enormous and incredibly ugly Presbyterian church. At his funeral a good many men who had worked for him, in his mine or on his newspapers, lined the driveway of the big, proud, inhospitable house he had lived in, and I remember that one of these men spat on the coffin as it was being carried out to the hearse.

It was not until long after his death that it became known that this pillar of righteousness had kept his private secretary as his mistress for over twenty-five years. He left her a small annuity. Nobody but his wife, Emma, had even suspected his secret infidelity with Miss Throckmorton. My grandmother had, in fact, been aware of it from the beginning; she had then left her husband and never went back to him again in forty years, but she never betrayed his sin to a living soul and died with her secret intact. It all came out, ironically enough, from Miss Throckmorton herself, who by this time was senile and old, and boasted of her sexual adventures, partly because she felt she had been treated parsimoniously by her former paramour and partly because she hated to be thought of as an " old maid."

Emma herself, who was to be the custodian of our infancy, was a very singular character. Her mother had died in giving birth to her, somewhere along the Clyde, in 1847, and her father, a roving Clydeside engineer, took charge of her. Her first infant years were spent with him in Spain, where he was engaged on the construction of the earliest Spanish railways; then he went back to Greenock and supervised the building of one of the first small paddle-steamers to be designed for the Australian coastal river ports. and took her out to the Grafton River, in the colony of New South Wales, with his daughter aboard. The ship, which was named *Grafton*, carried only enough coal for forty-eight hours' steaming, so there was a fine departure down the Clyde under an impressive black plume of smoke and enough coal left in the bunkers to make a majestic appearance off the little river port of Grafton, twelve thousand miles away. The passage out around the Cape was made under sail and took 266 days, during which time the ship was twice dismasted and eleven members of the crew died from scurvy. Granny, who would have been about ten at that time, never forgot this experience, and in the final years of her life, when she lay in our house, crippled and bed-ridden, she often recounted the story to me. This provided me with my first opportunity to practise real deception.

I had become an apprentice in an art studio by this time, and an art student, so as a birthday gift to the old lady I expertly forged a " contemporary " water-colour painting of the *Grafton* in the exact mode of the marine painting of the time, " aged " and faded and spotted it meticulously with chemicals and smoke, had it carefully framed, and presented it to her with the statement that I had picked it up in a Melbourne antique shop. She identified it at once as the very picture which had hung in the ship's tiny saloon over seventy years before. Poor Gran. Still, it became her most valued possession, and never left the wall above her bed until she died in that stuffy little front room smelling of senility and lavender water, when, in accordance with her deathbed request, it was put into her coffin and buried with her. The unqualified success of this deception delighted me for years, less for the pleasure I had given my grandmother than for the testimony it provided of my own cleverness.

Her father had stayed in command of the *Grafton* for some years after sailing her out, but in the late 'sixties, when news came of a great gold strike in Otago, New Zealand, he hurried down to Melbourne, invested his savings in a decrepit old Williamstown ferry steamer, loaded her up with mining machinery, and sailed off to cash in on the big bonanza. It was just as well that this time he left his daughter Emma at home, for the overloaded vessel struck a gale in the Tasman Sea, and ship, crew, and my great-grandfather were never seen again.

Emma, now twenty-two, and bewitchingly pretty if the daguerreotypes of the period are any witness, thus became an orphan in a strange city without a penny to bless herself with. She took a job as a barmaid in a Melbourne saloon, and fought off drunken admirers, for the gold rushes of the 'fifties and the still-remembered exploits of Lola Montez had given to the Bourke Street pubs a reputation for raffish excess which they were loath to relinquish: and from there she gravitated to the rich goldmining city of Bendigo, lived precariously under canvas with the Chinese diggers, married a feckless Irish gold-fossicker named Duthie, and gave him seven children before he abandoned her. I never found out what happened to those seven Duthie children, although I remember, as a child, that there were cryptic and vaguely shameful references to them from time to time: and it is my impression that my grandfather, who detested them, paid them to keep away, once Emma had married him.

By her second husband Emma had only three children (Miss Throckmorton having occurred during her pregnancy with the third), and Minnie, my mother, was the eldest. From the wealthy, sheltered, and respectable life into which they were born, all three children for the rest of their lives steadily and conscientiously descended on the social, economic and perhaps even on the moral scale, probably because of the fact that the reckless Emma had a more profoundly vital influence on them than their stern, staid, and distressingly dull father.

Emma must have had a complete understanding of my parents' patriotic abandonment of their children during the war, because many years before, if not for the same reason, she had done precisely the same thing herself, for the moment her last baby could be entrusted to a wet-nurse she walked out, leaving her husband to the tender solaces of Miss Throckmorton and her children in the care of the servants. It is impossible to say now whether this action was taken as a genuine moral protest against her husband's indiscretions, or whether she found him so insufferably dull that she simply seized on this as an excuse to get free of him. Anyway, for many years she cheerfully wandered alone around the world —she had a curious passion for spas and thermal springs and places where she could take curative mud baths; we once had an enormous collection of stereoscopic photographs of these places—and quelled her happy wanderlust only when it became necessary to look after us children.

During her travels her own children separately began their declines from grace. My mother was the first to slip. Having grown up with governesses, pony-carts, riding instructors, music-teachers, and private lessons in oils and pen-painting, she fell out of the provincial *petite-bourgeoisie* and clean into love with a tall young tram driver called Jack Meredith, who was physically attractive but socially beyond the pale, since he lived with a horde of ragged brothers and sisters in what was virtually a slum hovel on the fringes of Chinatown. He was a big-built, blond, athletic young man who had taught himself to play the violin, rowed stroke in a racing eight on Lake Wendouree, and was the colony's amateur single-sculls champion. The match was categorically disapproved, not only by Minnie's father, but also by old Meredith, an embittered, fiery Orangeman who had suffered great inequity on the question of mining leases, struggled constantly to keep nineteen children fed and shod, had become a rabid

socialist, and loathed everything which, in his mind, my
mother's family stood for.

In this impasse, my mother and father took the only course
possible to young lovers. They eloped, were married by a
young parson who happened to be the cox of Jack Meredith's
racing eight, and fled to Melbourne.

Unfortunately, this happened in the 'nineties. The great
land boom had collapsed, banks had closed their doors,
depression had swept the colony, and half Melbourne was
unemployed. For three whole years my father was unable to
find work, except for occasional odd jobs, so during this time
Mother went out as a charwoman or took in washing. When
Dad finally found work as a mechanic in the tram sheds,
Mother sold her mangle and bore him a son, which died a
few weeks later of spinal meningitis, before it could be
christened Jack.

Two years later Jean was born, later a boy came along
and survived long enough to be called Jack, Dad kept his
job in the tram sheds, I was born, then my sister Marjorie,
Mother joined some organisation that was giving courses in
home nursing, and in due time the war broke out and the
Kitchener posters were up on the hoardings. During these
years we lived in a pretty slummy neighbourhood and Mother,
with a good grace, allowed her decline to continue. Except
for the *First-Aid Manual* and her text-books on nursing, she
never opened a book after coming to Melbourne, and from
all her careful grooming by governesses and private tutors
she retained very little that was " genteel " save a continuing
interest in oil-painting—nothing original, of course, but careful copies made from oleographed prints of still-lifes, birds,
flowers, and scenes, which were published for this purpose
and distributed through the art stores. This hobby of hers
was later to prove of significance to me, although this is really
connected with what happened to her younger brother, who
was my Uncle Davy (the one born at the time of the Miss
Throckmorton incident).

He had been trained on one of Grandfather's newspapers
and had turned out to be so brilliant as a journalist that he
was actually editing a newspaper in Melbourne when he was
still only in his middle twenties. Alas, the seeds of decline
were in him also. He made the mistake of falling in love with

a red-haired barmaid at the Saracen's Head Hotel, drank to excess just to be with her, lost his job, lost the barmaid also, and sank into obscure poverty.

The brother in between Mother and Uncle Davy, who was my Uncle Stan, sank even farther. He became involved in a variety of sharp practices, then took up with a circus, became a sideshow barker and pitchman, and eventually began to run his own "attractions" at the agricultural fairs which were then—and for all I know still are—always taking place somewhere or other in Australia. In an attempt to buy a costly new entertainment called The Whip, which was then being a great money-spinner in America, he heavily insured his "Speed Palace" of Miniature Dodge-'em Cars and set fire to it in the early hours of a Sunday morning, his intention being to buy the coveted Whip when he collected the insurance money. Unluckily, he miscalculated the amount of petrol necessary for the conflagration and in the ensuing holocaust two adjacent shops and three houses were burnt to the ground as well as his Speed Palace. Poor Uncle Sam was apprehended in Brisbane, where he was living under an alias, and died later in the Bogga Road Gaol, probably of a broken heart, a year before he would have completed his seven-year sentence for arson.

It was through this uncle that I was first introduced to a darker and seamier side of life than any I had known up to that time, for one of my earlier memories is of being taken on a furtive Sunday afternoon visit with my parents to see Uncle Stan and his wife, who was my Auntie Gert. (It was then, and to a large degree still is, an inviolate Australian practice to make contractions of all personal names longer than one syllable and to expand those that are monosyllabic. So that, for example, while John almost invariably became "Johnno" and Jack "Jackie," names like Minnie, David, Gertrude, Emma, and Elizabeth were only used in their shortened forms of Min, Dave, Gert, Em, and Lizzie. Every relative I had as a child was an Ern, Marj, Dot, Steve, Tom, Stell, Fan, Bert, Gin, Alf, or Bill.)

There was something excitingly sordid about this particular visit—I suspect it was to do with money having been borrowed, or some trouble that involved Uncle Stan—because Mother was very subdued and Dad was furious. Uncle Stan at that time lived in one apartment of the first block of flats ever seen in Melbourne. It was in St. Kilda Road, and of red brick, with leadlight windows. The novelty of this type of communal living was regarded in the somewhat staid city of Melbourne as having distinctly immoral qualities, and I remember how we entered the lobby with Mother holding my hand very tightly and speaking in a hushed forced voice, and Dad looking grim and disapproving and making it quite obvious to somebody that he was being forced into doing something to which he was strongly opposed.

My own participation in this visit was very restricted, for it was not long before I was sent into a bedroom and the door was closed on me, and for an hour or more I nervously listened to the muted sounds of altercation or shivered at the persistent memory of the brief glimpse of depravity which reluctantly had been permitted me. It had been, to me, a startling scene of a smoke-filled room with the electric light burning, for the window shades had been drawn against the afternoon sun and over-curious neighbours, and around a beer-slopped table several hard-faced men in their braces had been playing poker for a scattered pile of sixpences and shillings. Torn-up racecourse betting tickets were littered on the carpet. Also in the room were three big-breasted women in blouses, who were sprawled in a kind of abandoned way in the Genoa velvet arm-chair or on the sofa, and they were all smoking cigarettes and drinking beer and making loud, laughing comments about the men, but the men just squinted through the cigarette smoke at their cards and took no notice at all. The women all were rouged and lipsticked, and one of them, my Auntie Gert, had dyed red hair worn very crinkly with the new Marcel wave.

Uncle Stan hardly looked up from his cards to say, "Well, strike me lucky, it's Min an' Jack! Hang on till we finish this hand; Ed's just opened the jackpot."

Auntie Gert, who seemed to be tipsy and who stank of Californian Poppy, embraced us all affectionately enough, but then looked at me and burst into a shrill peal of laughter, and said, "For God's sake, Min, why do you keep dressing him up in them there velvet collars? The kid looks a real little sis!"

Mother mumbled something, and I saw Dad's face grow

even darker, and then I was escorted to the bedroom. I never heard what the visit was all about, but on the way home my parents would not say one word to each other, and that night I could hear them quarrelling violently in their bedroom.

Probably Jack and I had been moved out of the sleep-out by this time and given beds of our own in the tiny room we shared opposite the kitchen.

The reason for this was that the character of the house had changed again. Mother had finally taken her discharge from the hospital and had given up nursing—professionally, at any rate—and Stubby and Aleck and Gabby Dixon and all the others had gone away, and all that remained to remind us of the war were Bert, who stayed on with us because he was engaged to Jean, and his crutches and artificial legs, and the German gas-mask on the hallstand, and albums full of snapshots, and Dad's bronchial cough.

With Mother's return to civilian life, Granny had gone back to her travelling—I think she was in New Zealand at this time, on some mysterious business concerned with the Duthies —and the second bedroom was now occupied by two old spinster sisters of my father. We accepted as quite normal the fact that they were invalids. As a result of cataracts, Aunt Lizzie had become totally blind and she also must have been in a condition of near-paralysis for she seemed to spend most of her waking time between an invalid wheel-chair and a depressing toilet-commode, and Dad always had to lift her in and out of bed when she had to sleep or get up. Her sister was Auntie Gin. (It was axiomatic in the fixed nomenclature of the family that one was Aunt and the other was Auntie. I never realised, until I read her funeral notice in *The Age*, that Gin stood for Virginia.)

She had been born a deaf-mute and suffered from arthritis. She could do nothing much about the first affliction, but for the second she always wore little bands of grey flannel sewn around her wrists, and when the pain in her joints was really severe she taped lily leaves around her legs, which bulged and wrinkled her black lisle stockings and gave her an extra-ordinary appearance. But she never worried about how she looked. She was always cheerful and gay. She taught me the deaf-and-dumb language and to read her own flying, flickering fingers, and we had long pointless conversations together. They were pretty unobtrusive, the two old ladies, and eventually they both died in our house, but I cannot recall which of them went first.

I do know that they were both alive when Granny returned to us, because this involved yet another rearrangement of domestic space and Jack and I had to move back to the sleep-out.

Emma had really intended only a short visit, because, although well into her eighties by this time, she was still very spry and considered that she had years of globe-trotting ahead of her. Unfortunately, on her return from New Zealand she jumped off a tramcar while it was still moving. I had often seen her do this, very blithely, at Kooyong Road corner—she detested the convention of waiting for the tram actually to stop—but this time she was carrying a portmanteau in her hand, and it must have affected her balance for she came down heavily and fractured both thighs and her pelvis. An ambulance brought her from the hospital to our house, but as she was eighty-four when this happened she never walked again.

To the very end I was the only one she would always send up to Grimwade's sweet shop for her daily bottle of lemonade. It was sold then in bottles that were stoppered by small glass marbles, which had to be pushed in with the thumb. I would do this for her and she would nod and say, " Thank you, Davy. Ah well, it cuts the phlegm," she would say, " it cuts the phlegm."

More than seven years after her accident she was finally carried from our house in a silver-mounted coffin, with the forged picture of the *Grafton* in her custody, and a pleased smile on her shrivelled little monkey face.

Jean, by this time, had married Bert and moved into a house, almost the twin of ours, which faced us from the opposite side of the street. Jack and I were back in a bed-room.

For the first time since I had been born, the house called *Avalon* was occupied solely by the Meredith family.

CHAPTER 3

During this time, of course, one was becoming more and more aware of an overpowering exterior world that existed beyond the house and those who occupied it. This world, without boundaries or specific definition or safety, spread forever, flat and diffuse, monotonous yet inimical, pieced together in a dull geometry of dull houses behind silver-painted fences of wire or splintery palings or picket fences and hedges of privet and cypress and lantana ; and all these sad, tidy habitations had names like *Sans Souci* and *The Gables* and *Emoh Ruo* (which I always took to be a Maori name until I learnt that it was only " Our Home " spelt backwards) and *The Rest* and *Nirvana* and, of course, other *Avalons* beside ours, for this was a very popular name which would occur once in very nearly every block. Most of the streets were named after long-dead councillors of the municipality or for battles in the Crimea or Boer wars. All the way through to the city proper there was nothing to break the drab flatness of this unadventurous repetition except the club flags flying over the grandstands of some football ground or other, or a particular factory smokestack that impressed by its height or shape or the amount of reek it gave off, or the grimy brick wall of the Rosella Jams and Pickles Factory with the cloth-capped girls working and chattering behind the railway-sooted windows.

A lifetime later I went back there and the horrible flatness of it all was just as real as ever, but far more depressing, since one no longer had the child's exaggeration of scale to help it out. In that earlier time it was always possible to invent what in reality did not exist. There was a public golf links about two miles away from where we lived, and in the middle of it an ugly grass-grown mound that could not have been more than thirty or forty feet in height. Yet we would walk there often, through the unmitigated melancholy of those suburban streets, simply for the adventure of scaling its sides and playing at Everest mountaineers and pretending we had toboggans.

It must have been only very occasionally that we could experience a true adventure, like the day when Jack and I had gone down to collect mussels for old Granny from the piles of Point Ormond pier, and from the little jetty we saw the great storm which was to become known as the Brighton Cyclone charging towards us across the bay in a whip of white horses below a tumult of bruised purplish crepuscular cloud. Coming across the sea, the cloud would tear off in downward strips that would begin to gyrate madly and scoop the harbour waters high into the air. It was the first time I ever saw waterspouts. There were some scruffy allotments just inland from the pier, and on one of these were a number of big cement pipes, four feet in diameter, which were waiting to be sunk for side drains out of the Elwood Canal, and Jack and I hurried to one of these and crawled inside to shelter from the storm.

When the wind struck the whole earth shook, but neither of us really appreciated the violence of the cyclone (we found out only much later that it killed and injured quite a number of people) until we saw a T-model Ford, which had been parked beside the kerb without its hand-brake on, moving along the road with nobody inside it, just rolling along quite slowly and steadily, propelled by the violence of the wind, and we could see huge branches tearing off the trees and red tiles from the roofs of seaside houses flying against a ragged wet sky that screamed at us. Just then the big cement pipe we were hiding in began to move, trundling very slowly at first, then gathering momentum down a slight incline, so Jack hauled me out, and somehow we were able to get to the big kiosk-restaurant behind the point. It was packed with frightened people, and the proprietor, whom we had never thought of as a kindly man, was handing out free cakes and ice-cream to everyone, and bags of boiled lollies to the children. Then all at once there was a terrible noise and the whole roof of the kiosk vanished from above us, and the rain and chips of wood and stone and plaster pelted down, and everybody fled, jostling each other and shouting. It was just as well they did, for within ten minutes the whole kiosk was a flattened ruin. (The kiosk had been very Late Victorian, with imitation turrets and spires, and one of the spires remained

for months in the top of a pine-tree, a hundred yards away
from where the kiosk had been!)

Going home was difficult because the canal had over-
flowed and the roads were flooded torrents wherever the
ground was low and the wind kept knocking us off our feet,
but Jack, even so, pushed me in behind a huge rusty steel
boiler that looked as if no power on earth could shift it,
while he crawled along the gutter of Glenhuntly Road to
where an Oldsmobile tourer was parked with the hood gone
and the isinglass side-curtains torn away by the wind. After
a great deal of effort, because he kept getting knocked flat by
the wind, Jack managed to force the car door open, and then
I saw what he was up to.

He released the hand-brake and crawled back to me on his
belly, and we crouched side by side in the lee of the boiler and
watched the Oldsmobile begin to move. It slowly gathered
speed and went rolling away down the road, and lurched over
the tram lines. It must have been doing fifteen miles an
hour by the time it collided with a telegraph pole.

Looking back on those times, I find myself more and more
impressed by the " pot luck " quality of life in general and
growing up in particular, at least as far as it applied in
Australia. Although very likely it would have been much the
same everywhere at that period of broken or changing values.
Everything seemed so hopelessly unorganised: you just grew
up and took pot luck on your chances.

I suspect that Jack was aware of this from the beginning.
The first brief homily I ever remember his giving me went
something like this: " Listen, nipper," he said—when we were
schoolboys he never addressed me as David or Dave or Davy,
but only as " nipper "—" Listen, nipper, you got to have a
go at it. Even if you know you can't bloody win you still got
to have a go. You'll always be pissin' into the wind, but that
don't mean it isn't worth givin' it a burl."

Cynicism thrived then in the prevailing climate of disillusionment. People had found that it's easy to smash down
old standards, but a lot harder to build new ones in their
place. Much bitterness had built up out of the war, and by
the time I was about thirteen all the returned soldiers we
knew had come to see the whole conflict as a monument of

disorganisation and waste and political chicanery. They had had their years in the trenches but the world of mufti to which they had returned had hardly become a place fit for heroes. Life, in their own words, was " a fair cow." The war profiteers had grown richer than ever. Usually it was the man who had dodged the war who was now the boss. Returned Diggers were always coming to the door in those days selling shoe-laces and matches. The soldier settlers who had wanted to go on the land usually found that the grants they were given were Mallee desert or backbreaking Gippsland scrub or acres of ringbarked trees that would take years to clear or scoured blocks around the dead shafts and mullickheaps of the old gold diggings.

People then in those years of the mid-'twenties did not appear to have much faith left in anything at all. Neither the Church of England nor the Y.M.C.A. had emerged from the war with particular credit—the Salvation Army people seemed to be the only ones the soldiers still respected, so they would always buy the *War Cry* from the bonneted " Salvo lassies " who went around the pubs on Saturday afternoons—and in Melbourne even the forces of law and order had come to be suspect as a result of the great police strike, which laid the whole city open to licence and anarchy.

My father and Bert both joined up as " Special Constables," and each night after supper they would march off together, with Bert's wooden leg squeaking, looking rather sheepish with their white armbands and the truncheons they had to carry, and with Mother's final shouted injunction stinging in their ears :

" Now don't you two silly idiots get yourselves knocked about ! "

Jack, who professed to be on the side of the looters and the smashers of shop windows and the hoodlum gangs who had taken advantage of the lawless situation all through the city, deeply resented the " Specials," and when Bert came home one night after a street riot with his skull split open by a chunk of road metal, Jack said to me, " Serve him right, the bloody crawler ! Pity the Old Man didn't cop one too ! "

The violence and disorderliness continued long after the police went back to duty. It was a wild time for the young. There seldom seemed to be much importance attached to

education then, and one never heard anything about child
guidance or the parental example. The State schools—the
ones we went to, at any rate—were crowded, inefficient, and
pretty brutal in their methods. We had a fifth-grade teacher
who sent three boys of my class to hospital by hitting them
across the head with a steel ruler, one because his tone was
wrong during the part-singing of "The Harp That Once in
Tara's Hall." (Eventually this teacher was sacked by the
Education Department, but of my class eight ended up as
gaolbirds—two with life sentences—one became an internationally known "con" man, one committed suicide, and
one, after a hectic career as a mobster in Squizzy Taylor's
gang, was hanged for murder.) The main aim was simply to
get children through to the Qualifying Certificate, so they
could get out to work at the age of fourteen. Nobody ever
seemed to know what sort of job the "Qually" qualified you
for. There seemed to be more truant-officers than teachers
and the truant-officers were thought of—by parents as well as
by boys—as a kind of corps of pariah-bureaucrats with about
the same standing as the despised municipal catchers of stray
dogs who went about with their whips and nets and caged
carts.

Large feuding gangs of young hooligans roamed everywhere
around Melbourne looking for trouble. The two big rival
gangs in our part of the suburbs were the Grey Caps and the
Bludgers, each of them sixty to eighty strong. They were
always attended by satellite groups of much smaller boys,
who would set fire to cypress hedges or smear paint on gates
or push blazing wads of oily waste into the post-boxes or take
down their pants and do their excrements on the footpaths to
show how bold they were. When the two gangs confronted
each other there would almost always be a fight, and these
attendant urchins would retreat to the rear to scream encouragement and to "keep nit" for the approach of the
police.

The gangs fought occasionally with razors, but more often
with sticks and stones. There was one evening when these
two forces came to grips almost in front of our house, and
they ripped every wooden picket from the fence of Jean's
house across the street and began to belabour each other
with the billets, and when Bert came out on to his front porch,

to try to get to the house next door so that he could telephone for the police, he was hit on the head for the second time with a piece of road metal.

What baffled me for a long time was Jack's real attitude to all this violence. He loved conflict as much as he hated authority, and he was about as undisciplined and pugnacious as any boy I ever knew, and at the time of the police strike he had certainly seemed to be on the side of the lawless. Yet he had nothing but loathing and contempt for these big, wild gangs that roamed the streets.

Once, in front of the entire Bludgers gang, he caught one of the show-off smaller children who was emptying his bowels on the pavement outside Cleland's grocery shop—where Jack sometimes earned money as a casual delivery-boy—and he took the kid by the scruff of his neck and rubbed his face in it. Then, with his hands in his pockets, he calmly walked right through the crowd of sixty hefty young hooligans who were glowering at him. Not one of them lifted a hand.

Not so very long after this the Grey Caps deliberately pitched a half-brick through the plate-glass window of a dressmaker's shop which employed a girl whom Jack at this time was " taking to the flicks "—his amorous life began very early—and next morning Jack played truant from school and went to the brickyard where Dud Bennett, the leader of the Grey Caps, was working as a hod-carrier and stacker. Bennett was a stocky, thickset young tough, not appreciably taller than Jack but about six years older.

" You're the king-pin of that push that bashed in Miss Fogarty's place last night, aren't you?" Jack said to him.

" An' wot if I am?" Bennett put down his hod.

" Miss Fogarty never did you any harm, and she got her big window smashed in."

" Yeah!" Bennett grinned. " Someone chucked a brick."

" There's nothing smart about chucking a brick," said Jack. " Have you and your gang of apes ever tried to chuck a punch?"

Bennett grinned again and spat on his hands and they squared off at each other, but Bennett never landed that punch. Jack landed three. The first bloodied the hod-carrier's nose, the second blackened his left eye, and the third, a straight left, knocked him out. Jack brought him round by throwing him into the brickyard's horse-trough, dragged him out again, hauled him upright, steadied him, then knocked him out all over again.

The foreman of the brickyard took a hat around among Bennett's workmates and the five shillings and sixpence he collected he gave to Jack.

Jackie Meredith was beginning to get quite a reputation around our neighbourhood, and it was not long before both gangs were making overtures for him to join, but he paid no attention to them at all.

What was so terrifying about these suburbs was that they accepted their mediocrity. They were worse than slums. They betrayed nothing of anger or revolt or resentment; they lacked the grim adventure of true poverty; they had no suffering, because they had mortgaged this right simply to secure a sad acceptance of a suburban respectability that ranked them socially a step or two higher than the true, dangerous slums of Fitzroy or Collingwood.

In this world Jack and I were left pretty much to our own devices for a few years. Apart from seeing that we attended school, did our homework, ate everything that was placed on our plates at meals, minded our table manners, had butter on our bread or jam on our bread but not both, and never answered back, Dad and Mother seemed to pay very little attention to what we did. Occasionally Jack would be thrashed for fighting or coming home late, or I would be snapped at by Dad for " always having your damned nose in a book," but otherwise there was little control of us and no guidance.

It was a long time before I understood the extent of their own preoccupations.

Mother was often sick and suffered a great deal from migraine—one realised only later that it was the time of her menopause—and I suppose there must have been a racking psychological malaise with it, an aching nostalgia for the importance and the brave excitements of her nursing days. For all those vanished Sunday night sing-songs when she had sat at the piano and her devoted Digger friends had roared out the chorus of " The Rose of No Man's Land," and smiled

down at her and lifted their beer glasses in a toast when they
came to the lines:

> 'Mid the war's great curse
> Stands the Red Cross nurse:
> For she's the Rose of No Man's Land.

. . . and when she had put on her best starched uniform and
gone to the Garden Party at Government House to receive
her medal . . . when our house, in fact—and perhaps more
than we ever realised of Mother's entire being—was cemented
in the solidarity of a great and mutual experience that could
only be expressed in such songs as these, and in badinage
exchanged in bad soldier-French, and in the interminably
repeated and curiously esoteric jokes about saps and support-
trenches and furphies and bedpans and whizzbangs and
entrenching tools.

But what I realise now, although I never did at the time, is
that my father, too, was oppressed by the intimidating factors
of fear and change. By disillusionment and ill-health, too. As
is often the case with big, strong, athletic men, he was an
extreme hypochondriac, and he had convinced himself that
the severe bronchitis which plagued him could only be attri-
buted to the German gas he had swallowed at Vimy Ridge.
He was too afraid to go to a doctor about it, so he lived with
a constant fear that his lungs were decaying, and that he
might die at any time, without warning.

In his state of mind one can only suppose that he must
have been darkly and profoundly disturbed by the years-long
procession through our house of Mother's " waifs and strays "
—those shattered former comrades-in-arms who would have
been a constant and sinister reminder of the price of glory.
And glory itself had curdled in the tram sheds. With him, the
edge had long since worn off war-time camaraderie, and
although he still occasionally attended club meetings of the
Returned Soldiers' League his sarcasm and pigheadedness
always got him into arguments and he invariably came home
drunk and irritable.

Moreover, he was frustrated by his failure to have made
anything of his life—he could see no possible advancement in
his trade beyond the position of depot foreman, which involved very little more pay but a great deal more responsibility

—and this had made him morose, intolerant, bitter, and violently bad-tempered. Most of his displeasure and resentment he focused upon Mother. He had altogether lost patience with her role of Florence Nightingale to the halt and the lame, even though two of the three who were in our house at this time were his own sisters. My memories of the period all have the tint of nightmare.

One must allow for time's foreshortening, but I can hardly recall a night when I was not wakened in panic by the stormy violence of my parents' quarrels. Often Mother would run from the house in the dead of night, swearing never to return, and there was one specially terrible occasion when Jack and I were awakened in the sleep-out by the sound of Mother, who was outside in the rain and the darkness, whimpering like an animal as she tried to crawl into hiding beneath the Dollicus. A few moments later the sleep-out door was pushed open, and my father peered in. He was muttering to himself and grunting, a gigantic black silhouette against the dim diffusion of light from the vestibule—he was six-feet-three then and weighed over sixteen stone—and in his hand he had the service revolver from the drawer in the bedroom wardrobe. He stood there for a few seconds and then he closed the door and went out into the back yard, and we listened to him stumbling around and cursing near the woodshed and behind the sycamore-tree. We could still hear Mother sobbing very softly, for she was really only inches away from us on the other side of the flywire screen, but Dad failed to see her crouched beneath the black, dripping creeper, and he came inside again, and we could hear him searching through the house and knocking things over.

Across from me on the thin mattress Jack was grinding his teeth and swearing under his breath, and once he muttered, " One day I'm going to *kill* that bastard!"

Then we heard the front door slam. I was too paralysed by terror to move, but Jack got up from the mattress and went out and made Mother come inside. I heard him take her into the kitchen. She was sobbing and choking. I kept my face buried in the pillow and my eyes tightly closed.

Everything finally grew quiet, and the vestibule light went out, and Jack came back to bed.

" What was the matter?" I whispered fearfully.

"Ah, it's him," he said. "That bastard, the Old Man. He frightens her to death. She says she's goin' to run away. She was goin' on in there about she's *got* to run away. She won't, though."

I just lay there, shivering.

"I cooked her up some cocoa an' made her go to bed," he said. "She'll be all right in the mornin'."

There was a long silence then, and I thought he had fallen asleep, but he must have been still thinking about it because after a while he said:

"Ever thought how *little* Mum looks when she gets worked up like that? You know? Remember when she used to get herself all togged out in them nurse's clothes of hers, with all that white starch over those big tits? She looked so damned huge then, after old Gran, I mean . . ." His voice trailed away reflectively, and then he said, "I suppose it's just we're growin'."

It would have been about this time that I began hiding myself in the big sea-chest—supposedly a relic of my grand-father's days in the *Red Jacket*—which stood next to the pianola in what was variously called the Big Room, the Front Room, or the Dining-Room. I would climb into it and pull the lid down and try to work out ways of murdering my father without being found out or getting Mother into trouble.

The pianola, a big rosewood Aeolian Stroud, had replaced the piano during one of my school holidays, and although it was very impressive it never really dominated the room the way the old piano had with its curly brass candle-holders and its parapet of photographs and the lace fringe hanging over and all the crowd around it, singing. The last of Mother's genteel attributes vanished with the coming of the pianola, because by this time she had given up her painting and once the pianola arrived she seldom played for us. The pianola effected other changes, too. The army biscuit from Cairo had been placed inside the glass dome which contained the decora-tions from various wedding cakes and other things like that and this collection had the place of honour on top of the pianola. New photographs—school groups and Jean's boy friends and portraits of those who had "passed on," like Auntie Gin and Aunt Lizzie—had replaced most of the older photographs. Sóme were still there: Dad as a young man at the oars of a racing shell, and the family group which had been taken before he went away to Gallipoli (Jack looked truculent in a lace collar, and Dad in his sapper's uniform, and me with a head of golden curls: the picture was hand-tinted, of course); but the picture of the *Ceramic* had gradu-ally been pushed farther and farther to the back, and one day it dropped off and fell down behind the pianola and nobody ever bothered to retrieve it.

The front room was the formal room of the house and we children were never encouraged to use it. Long before, it had been the gay setting for the Welcome Home party and the Sunday night sing-songs, but those days had gone. Al-though it was referred to as the dining-room we never ate there, and I was always glad of this because it had come to be a rather intimidating apartment. It had bay-windows sealed off by heavy cretonne curtains and a long sofa across which no play of sunlight ever moved and a big sideboard cluttered with the cut-glass and E.P.N.S. of innumerable gifts and all the walls were crowded with Mother's paintings of flowers in vases and landscapes she had never seen—snow scenes and Swiss lakes and thatched cottages.

In the centre of the room was a huge table covered by a fringed cloth of heavy autumnal pattern, around which Sunday afternoon visitors were stiffly seated, and upon which the dead in their coffins were laid out in state. I remember being taken in to meet embarrassed relatives in their Sunday best—" Say hallo to your Cousin Stell," I would be im-patiently commanded ; " Go on, don't just stand there!"—and I also recall the forced and frightening intrusions to pay final respects to the bloodless dead faces of Emma and Aunt Lizzie and Auntie Gin. (I saw my father, dead in his coffin at last, on that very table, but this was not until many years later, for he lived to seventy-three, having died, not of German gas, but of a heart attack.)

The big table was reversible: one side was the dining-table but it could be turned over to make a half-size billiard-table. It had been bought at an auction sale to try to keep Jack out of the sordid billiard-saloons and pool-rooms along Glenhuntly Road. It was not very successful, for in these dens of iniquity Jack had achieved considerable skill with a cue, and once Dad realised that Jack could always give him a start and still beat him at billiards, snooker, or pin-pool, it went back to being a dining-table.

I suppose there was a sort of masochism in my going into this depressing room simply to experience the claustrophobic privacy of the old sea-chest, but I was obsessed at this time by a very real terror that Mother would be brought to such a point of resentment of her husband's tyranny that she really *would* run away and leave us all. The prospect of such a thing happening was so firmly established in the chamber of uncertainties that seemed to be the dominant area of my mind that I felt any desperation would be justified if this could be prevented. In the stuffy, suffocating darkness of the sea-chest I would try to imagine what it would be like to be left unprotected against his ragings and injustices. Jack cursed and threatened, but he was still too small to do anything. There was no David against this Goliath, so I tried to work out other means. Nothing came of it, except that, in recent years, there have been several critics who have wondered why in all my books there is invariably some more-or-less symbolic cave scene.

I don't want it to be thought that Dad was always brutal or that Mother was always weeping. Through all these images there is a scatter of improbable brightness, like raindrops falling through sunshine. There were Sunday mornings in the kitchen, or Saturday afternoons if there was to be a party, when Mother and Jean and Marj would be endlessly baking —scones and sausage-rolls and sponges and cream-puffs and rock cakes and queen cakes, and sometimes a tray of lamingtons specially for me. Mother would be at the gas stove, doing the roast and the pies and the queen pudding, and the girls would do their baking in the big black one-fire-stove which burnt box blocks we would order from the timber yard by the hundredweight. Jack and I were allowed to lick the mixing bowls. There were always curling-tongs heating on the top of the kitchen range, and somebody would be ironing underwear or dresses, and the two girls would have their hair in curling papers. Enmities and prejudices were forgotten and there was always a lot of joking and laughing and singing of popular songs; these were good days.

Even Dad would join in sometimes. There were odd strange

days when he would surprise us all by getting out his old
violin, and in a dusty haze of flying resin would play Irish jigs
for us or the strange songs he liked to sing, like "Working
With The Hot Asphalt" or "McGinty's Goat."

He had a mania, also, for new popular fads. Crossword
puzzles obsessed him for a long time; when this palled he
became a fanatic about radio, first with the crystal-sets he
used to build and then with valves and rheostats and super-
heterodynes and blueprints of new circuits. When he was
engrossed in these pursuits he was much less severe with us,
but even in these good times I always seemed to be unlucky.

I was twelve when the crossword puzzle mania hit Australia.
There was a joke that went around the school: "a ball-bear-
ing mousetrap in six letters"; the answer was "tomcat." I
didn't see the point of the joke at all, but that night, to
ingratiate myself with my father, I told it to him. "You filthy
little swine!" he bellowed, and dragged me to the bathroom.
I didn't know why I had been thrashed until Jack came
home that night and explained it to me.

Exactly when, or why, Dad introduced his system of
monthly punishments I no longer remember. We had always
had summary punishment, of course, for offences immediately
detected—a cuffing around the ears or a slash with a stick or
a strap—but Dad's new system was to punish for the offences
which had *escaped* his attention. So on the last day of every
month Jack and I would be summoned in turn to the bathroom and the door would be locked and each of us would be
questioned on the sins which we had committed and which he
had not found out about. This interrogation was the merest
formality; whether we admitted to crimes or desperately swore
our innocence it was just the same; we were punished for the
offences which, he said, he knew we *must* have committed
and had to lie about. We then had to take our shirts and
singlets off and bend over the enamelled bath-tub while he
thrashed us with his razor-strop. In the blind rages of these
days he seemed not to care about the strength he possessed
nor the injury he inflicted; more often than not it was the
metal end of the strop that was used against our backs.

This went on for several years, and God knows what damage it did to me psychologically. I remember that from
about the twentieth of every month I would behave with the

innocence of a saint and the sycophancy of a French courtier in a desperate attempt to prove my rectitude. It made no difference. I was beaten anyway.

It must have been this cruelty that really launched Jack on his fighting career. By this time it had been decided that Jack and I would have to " learn a trade " so that we could both get out to work and bring money home. We were sent to a technical school for this training. Jack, it had been ruled, would be a plumber. And Mother vicariously satisfied some ambition in herself by decreeing that I should become an artist. I had a certain aptitude for tracing and copying things, and this certainly qualified as " art " according to the standards of Mother's training in oils and pen-painting, and I was written down accordingly for special courses in " commercial art," which largely consisted of lettering, the drawing of solid objects, and the slavish copying of selected travel posters and advertisements in the *Saturday Evening Post* and *Ladies' Home Journal*.

Although at class and in examinations Jack was really the cleverer of the two of us, he was only a year ahead of me at this school, although three years my senior, he having fallen so far behind at the State school we had attended because of his truancies, insubordination, and general wilfulness. At the technical school we did part of a basic High School course—mathematics, algebra, geometry, English, chemistry, and so on—and the rest of the time we devoted to our " special classes." I would go to the commercial art school and Jack to the plumbing, gasfitting, and sheetmetal workshops. Neither of us had much interest in these special courses.

Jack was far more concerned with sport. He was an opening batsman in the school cricket eleven and a member of the football eighteen—we played a curious and immoderately rough game of football known as " Australian Rules "; there were eighteen players in each team, the game was played on a huge oval and was divided into four quarters of twenty-five minutes each—but his real interest was in boxing, and at about this time he had decided to enter for the school championships. He used to practise " shadow boxing " in our back yard, and he bought himself a punching-ball and gloves, and then he began to use me as his sparring partner.

There was a very great disparity between us at this time. I

was still small for my age, chubby, soft, pink and fearful. Jack was fairly tall and rangy, with blue eyes, a beaky nose, and disorderly cornsilk hair ; the sort of hair which hinted at premature baldness. His mouth was wide and full, but it could set in a hard, tight line when he was angry, like the jaws of a trap. He had ears which, in his own words, " stuck out like jug handles." There was a gawky, awkward look about his bodily movements, but it was dangerous to bank on this for I never knew anybody as fast on his feet or as quick with his hands in a boxing ring or a street brawl. He was wiry rather than strong and there was a savage, whipping sting to his punches. He always spoke slowly, with his eyes on the person he was addressing, as if his words and phrases had to be shaped according to the effect he was producing.

As his sparring partner I was hopeless. At first he used to treat me gently enough, only tapping at me with his gloves, and chiding me for my cowardice or my lack of skill or my obtuseness in not following his instructions, but eventually he must have felt that I needed to be toughened up, because every now and then he would really hit me. Often he brought blood from my nose or made me realise what it was like to be winded by a right jab, he loosened a tooth, he blackened my eye, and once he knocked me unconscious with that vicious straight left of his. I began to dread the Saturday mornings of sparring practice almost as much as I dreaded the end-of-the-month appointments with Dad in the bathroom.

I doubt if I contributed much to his boxing career, but he did win the school lightweight championship, and then a fool of a sports master decided that the winners of the separate divisions should fight an elimination series to determine the " School Champion." It ended up with Jack matched for the finals against the best school heavyweight, Snowy Bretherton, a giant of a senior, six feet tall and virtually a grown man. This bout was fixed as the highlight in the programme of School Exhibition Week, when parents were invited to see the students' work for the year.

Mother, who detested fighting, had not been told about the bout, and Jack had delegated to me the task of keeping her occupied during fight time. She was in the commercial art room proudly examining my exhibit—a " poster " for Palm-

olive Soap which I had traced and copied very carefully from
a full-page advertisement in an American magazine—when a
woman neighbour of ours, Mrs. Gillon, came rushing into the
classroom screaming blue murder. " Mrs. Meredith!" she
cried. " Mrs. Meredith, they're killing your boy Jack! Come
quickly, Mrs. Meredith! They're killing *your* boy!"

They were midway through the seventh round when Mother
reached the boxing ring. Jack was still upright, but his
chest and stomach and legs were red with blood, and he was
practically out on his feet, although still weakly throwing
punches, and Snowy Bretherton, grim-faced and merciless,
with a black eye and a split lip, was coldly circling him and
cutting him to pieces. Mother climbed right into the ring,
and with her umbrella attacked both Bretherton and the
idiotic sports master who had instigated and was refereeing
the hopelessly unequal fight. The bout ended at once in
pandemonium and immense confusion, and with Jack unconscious on the mat. My shame and humiliation at my mother's
behaviour were almost overwhelming.

Six months later Jack tackled Snowy Bretherton again on a
vacant lot behind the timber-yard, and this time he knocked
Bretherton out.

There were fights then—usually without benefit of the
Marquess of Queensberry's rules—almost every day. In the
streets, on the vacant lots, in the school yards. I would avoid
them whenever I could. The only fight I ever won at school
was on the football field one lunch recess.

It was against Harry Meade, who had become the butt of
our form partly because he was a tale-bearer, but mostly
because his parents would keep sending notes to the teachers
pointing out that the boy was " delicate." Occasionally he
would throw fits and froth at the mouth. None of us then
knew anything about epilepsy: we regarded these paroxysms
as a deliberate act which Meade would put on to prove this
ridiculous business about his being " delicate."

I no longer remember the cause of our quarrel, but I do
know that the fight that ensued was an absolute victory for
me. Meade had no idea of boxing at all. He would blunder
up with his arms flailing and his eyes tightly closed, and all I
had to do was to step to one side and hit him as he staggered

past me. I hit him and hit him and hit him until his face was covered with blood and he had fallen whimpering and twitching to the ground. His fists never once touched me.

As I was standing there in the circle of boys, flushed with triumph, I saw Jack approaching. I looked across for his approbation, but his face was hard and set.

He pushed through the ring of boys, looked down for a long moment at the disgraced sprawl of the loser, then came across to me.

"Why did you have to fight *him*?" he said.

"Well, *he* started it . . ." I began to protest.

"That kid's crook, you knew that," he said. "You could have killed him."

"I tell you he started it."

"Why didn't you just hit him once then?" he said fiercely. "That poor little bastard couldn't fight his way out of a brown-paper bag! What the hell do you think *you* were trying to prove, you dirty stinking little tike, going after him like that!"

With that he slapped me right across the face, very hard, and turned on his heel and walked away. The boys began to disperse, sniggering a little shamefacedly, and I just stood there looking down at Harry Meade, while two of his mates brought water from the tap and washed his face.

There was a curious little sequel to this. About a week after the fight Harry Meade gave me a present of a silver trumpet. Well, that was what I called it, but it wasn't a trumpet really, and it wasn't silver; it was nickel-plated and it was part of one of those bulb-horns they used on the old motor-cars. I was very proud of it, partly because you could blow tunes through it and partly because it was, symbolically, Harry Meade's truce and tribute to me.

Two nights later we were playing in Carlingford Street and I lost the trumpet in the soft earth at the verge of the road: it was after nine o'clock at night when Jack came and found me. It was pitch dark and I was on my hands and knees, weeping, crawling round in the loose earth, feeling for the lost trumpet. I never found it.

Not long after this, Jack had his showdown with Dad. He went into the bathroom on the last day of the month to take his belting, and without a word of protest he shed his shirt

and singlet and bent over the bathtub and accepted his
punishment. When it was done he straightened up and faced
Dad and said:

"All right, Pop, that's the last time you're goin' to whale
into me like that. You try to lay that strop across me next
month, an' we're goin' to fight it out, see."

Dad never thrashed him again.

When Jack told me about this later I said, "Did you tell
him he had to stop hitting me, too?"

He looked at me very carefully, then said:

"Christ almighty, nipper, you can fight your own battles,
can't you?"

But I couldn't. My beatings continued, more ferociously
than ever. They only ceased because one day my father went
too far; he lambasted me so savagely that I fell unconscious
into the bathtub, and the welts across my back made by the
steel end of the razor-strop had to be treated by a doctor.

Mother called in Doctor Sheridan, who was on the panel
for the Ancient Orders of Foresters' Lodge, and who had
been on the Western Front with Dad, and attached to the
same division, and it was because of this old link they had that
he didn't make a police report. But he did warn Dad that if
he was called in again he would have to go to the police about
it, and Mother took a stand, too, and told Dad that she
would ring for Doctor Sheridan the moment the bathroom
punishments were resumed, whether I was badly hurt or not.
So that was the last time it happened.

CHAPTER 4

I never finished my last year at that technical school. I could
never grasp more than the simplest mathematics and I was
failed for the Intermediate Certificate, so unless I repeated a
year and sat again for the examinations I was precluded from
moving on to any higher form of education. In a way I half
hoped that I would be given this second chance, but by this
time I had turned fourteen and could legally go out to work.
I accepted, passively enough, my parents' decision that I

should be apprenticed in commercial art to a lithographic firm in the city.

I had almost no interest in art then, commercial or otherwise, and remarkably little talent for it, and I am not sure that I even knew what lithography really was, but evidently there were no other applicants for the job, so I began work with the firm of Klebendorf and Hardt, a printing company which had been established by Germans seventy years before and still occupied its original premises in a tall, semi-derelict warren of a gaunt granite building in a narrow city lane opposite a pub which was supposed to be an exact replica of an old English coaching-inn (or so I always believed until I saw an old English coaching-inn).

My father signed indentures for six years' apprenticeship, beginning at a wage of fifteen shillings a week, with annual rises of a similar amount, which would ensure that I would reach manhood earning five guineas a week, presumably as a skilled poster-lithographer, decorator of jam labels, and occasional designer of advertising showcards or tram-bills.

From my first earnings I had to buy my lunches, which I was able to reduce to a wholemeal bread-roll and a banana or two, and my " worker's weekly " railway ticket. Apart from two shillings, which I was permitted to keep, what was left over went into the family housekeeping. " Worker's weeklies " were a shilling or so cheaper than the ordinary " business weeklies," but they were not supposed to be used by white collar workers and thus were not valid through the barriers of the city railway stations after ten minutes to eight in the mornings. So I was always at work an hour too early, before the lithographic studio was unlocked, but except on the cold winter mornings I never minded this much because something was always happening in the narrow lane. There would be down-and-outs scrounging through the rubbish-tins or searching along the gutters for cigarette butts, and I loved to watch the council rat-catchers at work with their strings of little fox-terriers, or the trucks unloading bales of paper or drums of litho-ink, and office windows opening, and very often there would be shirt-sleeved club servants grumbling to one another as they hosed the vomit off the pavement outside the ornate portico of the Savage Club.

Jack, of course, had been pushed out to earn money long

before I left school. He had been sent to work with a suburban plumber named Fred Foley, whom Jack detested and
resisted; if I was prepared to accept my destiny passively,
my brother certainly was not. He learnt something of the
trade, because he was quick at picking up things and he liked
to learn, on the principle that " You can never tell what might
come in handy one day "—years later he could expertly fix
drains or leaking taps or " wipe a joint," and his soldering
was something to see—but the impression he gave at home
was that all he was learning was how to get drunk with his
workmates on Friday pay afternoons and various ways of
driving old Foley to the point of a nervous breakdown.

Jack was never really sure at this time exactly what it was
he *did* want to be, but a plumber certainly it was not. Sometimes he thought of himself as a sailor in the merchant
service, going around the world in tramp steamers, or as a
boundary rider on an outback cattle station, or as a patrol
officer rounding up head-hunters in New Guinea. He talked
vaguely of joining the French Foreign Legion—everybody
then was reading *Beau Geste*—or of going into boxing as a
professional (a year or so later he did, in fact, win a State
amateur lightweight championship), or of pushing off on his
own as a gold prospector. Nothing came of these vague
ambitions; he got his fun even out of plumbing, and, in any
case, by this time his real interest was girls.

I was still attending school on the day he lost his job as a
plumber, but I was in my room that afternoon trying to
understand logarithms when he came in almost splitting with
laughter. He flung himself on the bed and kept clutching the
pillow and choking and roaring and it was several minutes
before he could even tell me that he had " got the boot." I
had a clutch of panic wondering what Dad would say when
he came home from the tram depot, and I asked him, rather
nervously, how it had happened.

" We had to clear the upstairs WCs in that big house of
Britling's down Ripponlea way," Jack explained chokingly.
" One of the maids must've dropped an apple down, because
three of the dunnies were choked. I had to take the taps and
dies down to that silly old galoot Foley, and when I got there
I saw that the stupid goat was standing with his head right
under the open downpipe, looking up it to see what was

wrong. Well, as it happened I *was* a bit caught short at the time, so I shot along to the top dunny like a rat up a rope, and had a bog, and pulled the chain, and, nipper, she was the bloody beautest bull's-eye you've ever seen. The old bastard got it all over his face—the lot, bum-fodder and all, and a cigarette butt thrown in for good measure! Jesus, was *he* ropable!"

He had a variety of jobs after that—I cannot recall what they all were, but I know he never went back to plumbing, and then a few years later he left home to work on a wheat farm in the Wimmera.

But until that happened he added a frightening new dimension to my uncertainty, an abrasive torment that it took me years to get over. Sex . . .

I never knew anybody at that time who had read or even heard of Sigmund Freud. There were no Penguin editions or paper-backs then, and Freud's was hardly the sort of information that would percolate through those picket fences or hedges of golden privet, or even find its way to a suburban panel doctor of the Loyal and Ancient Order of Foresters; and even some years later when I listened to people talking about complexes, inhibitions, frustrations, repressions, wish-fulfilments, and the libido, they seemed to be quoting an outlandish gibberish.

Jack had never heard of Freud either, but he saw sex early and clearly. It had no complications for him. It was merely another part of the adventure and hazard of living. He liked girls. And, what was perhaps more important, they liked Jack.

This was not only because of his reputation as a boxer, or a " sport," or even as a " character." At seventeen he was not much taller than he had been at school, although he was only an inch short of six feet, which was tall enough, but his body had filled out and toughened, and he had lost the awkward look he had once had. He had become a light, graceful dancer, and he walked well. Yet mostly, I think, it was his irrepressible audacity that captivated the girls. Anything he tackled was tackled with immense gusto, almost as if he had to eat life in huge gulps . . . while his appetite was strong . . . or before they cleared away the table. He seemed to meet everything full on ; side-stepping was something he kept for the boxing ring. There were times, I am sure, when he carried his challenge to a point almost of flagrancy as a deliberate way of shocking the smug, the prim, the reproving. He seldom spoke a sentence to anybody without colouring it with the most extravagant slang and often with memorable images. I treasure some of his sayings even now, thirty years later. He would describe somebody as being " as silly as a two-bob watch " or " dreary as bat-shit ": of a notorious bore he said, " every story the bastard tells is as long as a wet week-end " or, alternatively, " he's just about as funny as a dead baby's doll." After the flat-chested flapper figure had become *passé* his succinct comment on poor Gwen Taidmarsh was, " She wears a sweater like it's been hung on a nail twice." Still my favourite is the comment he made once when he was convinced that Dad was trying to victimise him over something. " If the Old Man had to saw Jean Harlow in halves," he said bitterly, " he'd damn' well see that I got the half that talks!" He never wrote me a letter until after he had gone to the Wimmera: I remember being astonished by it: it was written in a near-copperplate hand, in an almost mid-Victorian prose style, and with hardly a hint of a colloquialism.

As with his vocabulary, his appearance was almost blatantly offered for public consumption. He was an upstanding, good-looking youth, but he would plaster his hair down with cheap brilliantine and part it in the middle, and sometimes he would favour sideburns and a hairline moustache, and he began to wear white ties with a black shirt, and pearl-grey Oxford bags, and ox-blood or two-tone shoes. Part of this sartorial masquerade, possibly, may well have been his calculated incitement to riot.

" Yeah, I know I look like a two-bob lair decked out like this," he once admitted to me cheerfully, as he trimmed his sideburns in the broken vestibule mirror. " But let me tell you something, nipper. This is the only rig-out that'll always get the sheilas in. Let me tell you another thing—once they see you with a sheila, walkin' around like this, there's always some touchy pissant who gets all worked up about it and wants to knock your block off!"

Jack's first tentative explorations of the feminine *mystique* had been completed before he was twelve—at which age, incidentally, he had stopped smoking " tailor-made " cigarettes, on the ground that they were effete, and had taken to rolling his own—and he moved into the world of more advanced sex with a whole heart and a totally open mind. The prospect of " landing a sheila " would fill him with the same kind of gluttonous rapture as a second or third helping of his favourite food, which continued to be Mother's steamed jam roly-poly.

My feelings and attitudes were so totally opposed to his in every imaginable way that I would sometimes catch him looking at me and shaking his head in an utterly mystified way. At first he tried to be tolerant or amused, but there were times when I would infuriate him to such a degree that I think he might have punched me but for the fact that he knew very well that for all my priggishness I was the only person who was loyal to him. I never told tales. Yet he still regarded me as a " bloody little sonk," and for the next few years he continued to shock me with a ruthless consistency which I realised was deliberate only very much later.

He deplored the puritanical views I held about smoking and drinking, but it was on the question of girls that he most resented me.

" You're growing up to be a real bloody little wowser," he would say with an angry contempt, and I would blush to the roots of my hair, for in Jack's bawdy and colourful lexicon wowser was the most despicable form of human or animal life. The wowser was the man who saw fleshly sin in every simple pleasure, who believed in the total observance of the Sabbath, who regarded sport as a device of the Devil, who grew apoplectic at the thought of males and females dancing together, who imagined the fiery pits of hellfire and brimstone yawning for all young people who smoked, drank, sang, or even laughed together.

I would writhe under his scorn—that there was more than a germ of truth in the charge made it no easier to bear—but I could do nothing about it. A girl could reduce me to an almost pathological state of dread and shyness. I would flush if one so much as glanced at me. I would become pink and stammering when a comfortable middle-aged housewife approached me in the street to ask directions to a city store or advice on a tram destination. Either of my two sisters could provoke me to the point of tears by deliberately baiting me until they could scream triumphantly:

"Look! Just look at him! He's blushing! Just look at him blushing!"

In the twelve months after I left school a dreadful, phenomenal thing happened, and in that year I grew eleven inches, and my grotesque skinniness, with the pimples that came about this time, made everything immeasurably worse. I stopped going swimming that summer because I was convinced that everybody on the beach was pointing out my skeletonic shape, that every giggle or guffaw or whisper was directed at me. I began secretly to buy physical culture magazines, but cancelled the order after I had taken three issues because the comparisons were so shattering. I saw myself as the perpetual figure captions " Before," never as the muscular Hercules captioned " After." (This thin physique to some degree has remained with me; I still value a foreign correspondent's licence which years after this was issued me in India. My physical description for some reason was to be entered on the card as " tall and gangling " but a *babu* clerk typed it in as " tall and dangling.")

Jack, untroubled by any such inhibitions, spent almost every night prowling the city like a tomcat. And the city was fiercely generating a life of its own that was exactly in key with his wild, gay, rebellious outlook. The Jazz Age had reached its crescendo: the wail and boob of saxophones, the twanging of ukuleles, and the mad jumping of the Charleston had even begun to invade the hitherto inviolate stuffiness of our suburbs. Beyond our neat hedged perimeters, the world suddenly seemed transformed into a jungle of iniquities, of violence, sex, flaunted revolt, alarming uncertainties. The newspapers reprimanded in editorials the wayward follies and excesses of the young, quoted hair-raising legal reports of teen-age girls who carried contraceptives in their handbags, spluttered about " companionate marriage," lifted their circulations with shocking stories of scandalous goings-on in parked coupés and sedans, and screamed for the banning of books. Along St. Kilda Esplanade and in the open parks policemen and Peeping Toms prowled with torches at the ready to catch flaming youth in the very act of burning. Swaggering through it all, with their heads held high, went the

slim, flat-chested, emancipated, waistless girls wearing rouge
and lipstick and with shingled hair—or, worse, the Eton crop
—their skirts above their knees and their stockings rolled
below. And in eager, effervescent pursuit, went my brother
Jack, with brilliantine on his hair.

Dad had bought a second-hand Chevrolet, but he was a bad
and hopelessly nervous driver, and this created a curious and
paradoxical situation. Jack, who had driven the utility for
Foley the plumber, could handle a car very competently, and
he had nerves like steel. Dad liked to go by car to race
meetings or football games on Saturday afternoons, but since
the heavy traffic and the problem of finding a place to park
would have torn his nerves to shreds he would make Jack do
the driving. In return he was obliged, reluctantly and not too
often, to allow Jack to take the car out on his own at night.
Whenever this happened he would work himself up into a
terrible state wondering what Jack actually *might be doing*
in the car. He usually found out when he was cleaning the
car on Sunday mornings, and he would come snorting in from
the shed he had fixed up for a garage, his face a study, gin-
gerly holding in his fingers some object which he had found
on the floorboards or wedged in behind the seat cushions—
hairpins or a rouge compact or a lipstick or a suspender torn
from a girdle. His stormings and rantings never seemed to
perturb Jack. Certainly they failed to discourage him. The
trophies became still more spectacular. A silk stocking was
found in the glove-box. A girl's corselet was dragged from
behind the back seat. And the day Dad found a pair of black
rayon scanties trimmed with coffee-lace, a jazz garter of
yellow and black silk, and an S.S.W. brassière, all stuffed
together into one of the side-pockets, I really thought he
would have a stroke.

Jack just grinned. " Trophies," he said, and there was a lot
of pride in the way he said it. " You know, Pop, I really
brought them scanties home for you. I said to myself, you
know, they'd be just the thing for Pop for wipin' down the
windscreen."

A week later Dad nearly had a stroke again. We had
visitors on Sunday afternoon, some of Dad's friends from the
Lodge, and they were taken, of course, into the front room.
And there, under the glass dome on top of the pianola, with

the old army biscuit and the wedding decorations, Jack's
trophies had been tastefully assembled—the garter and the
brassière and the rayon scanties.

Whether Jack was out in the Chev or prowling afoot, he
would always come home long after Dad or Mother had
locked the house and gone to bed. I would hear the side gate
furtively opening, then a scratching rustling through the ferns
would herald the silent removal of the outer flywire screen,
and Jack would crawl through the window and switch on the
light and sit on the bed and give me a detailed account of his
adventures. The more he shocked me, the better he was
pleased: there was a fiendish implacability about what he
regarded as vital indoctrination.

There was always a post-mortem next day, when Dad
would try to determine what time he had come home, but the
formula was unvarying.

" You were damn' late in last night, weren't you?" would
be Dad's aggressive opening.

"Late? Oh, have a heart! I got in just a minute or two
after you went to bed. I saw the front light go off just when
I was comin' down the street."

" Funny I didn't hear you," Dad would say sarcastically.

" You? You wouldn't have heard a thing. You must've
dropped off like a log. You were snorin' like a trooper when
I came in. Dave remarked on it. His light was still on. He
was in bed reading."

Jack would turn to me blandly, I would nod endorsement of
the lie, and, more often than not, Dad's spleen would be
transferred to me.

" You and your blasted books!" he would snarl. " All
you're doing, my lad, is muddling your mind and ruining
your eyesight Why the devil don't you get out and *do*
something."

" Just what I keep telling him," Jack would say. " He ought
to go out and pick up a sheila."

" At *his* age. What damn' good would *that* do him?"

" Well, it'd be better than sitting around a bedroom all
night with those sonky mates of his."

This was one of the root sources of Jack's hostility. My
" sonky mates " were three boys who had been in my year
at the technical school ; we were united by the double bond of

being uninterested in girls and of all having failed to pass for the Intermediate Certificate. Jack had no time for any of them. Bob Hawkes wore his hair too long—" like a sissy "— took violin lessons, suffered from asthma, and was interested in classical music. Bill Bardswell played with model electric railways and didn't believe in sport. Ronnie Curtis sang in the St. Catherine's church choir, still collected cigarette cards, and lisped. Since I already had crazy ideas about everything which Jack regarded as normal and necessary, and because I was always reading books, my brother's dread was that this companionship would turn me into a homosexual. It was entirely *his* dread: I was not aware at that time, nor for years afterwards, that homosexuality existed. (The scurrilous jingle on the subject which was current in those days was known to almost everybody in Australia, but it happened to concern a certain aberrated musical comedy and vaudeville singer, so that for all my adolescence and youth I firmly believed that " homosexual " was only a fancy word for a female impersonator.)

For quite a while the four of us stuck together anyway, in spite of Jack's hostility. They would come round on their bicycles every night after supper, and we would go to my bedroom and shut the door. There was a sad, desperate innocence about it all. We shared a deep guilt at having failed at school, we had all been sent out to jobs in which we were barely interested, we had no idea where we were going, but somehow it seemed imperative that we must try to " better " ourselves, and it seemed to us that this could be achieved only by groping for some sort of education that had passed us by. Since there was nobody to guide us we would contend with each other in " discovering " important authors —Ibsen and Chekhov and Tolstoy, Balzac and Flaubert, Gibbon and Defoe (never Shakespeare or Keats or Milton, crucified victims on the three crosses crowning the Golgotha of Australian education), and everything we read was above our heads. But it excited us. We went on groping and pretending.

Gradually, however, a secret desire began to germinate in my mind. I wanted to write. It began with poems, but they were very strange poems to emerge out of the Melbourne suburbs, because I had read *Heimskringla* and become ob-

sessed by the Viking sagas and I filled whole exercise-books
with bad verses about berserk fighting men and beaked longships filled with corpses:

> *Wildly they rolled, tightly locked on seas riven,*
> *Bound in war's embrace, the black ship and red:*
> *Corpse-ring was theirs, for the raven, unshriven,*
> *Had croaked in the night for the Skardaborg dead.*

I kept the exercise-books hidden in my mattress, in case
Jack should find them. I knew that as poetry the stuff was
worthless, yet the exercise-books represented a privacy which
I felt to be important . . . too important to survive Jack's
derision.

It never occurred to me that Jack, for all his crudity and
insensitivity, might have been right, and I wrong. I could not
have realised then that I was beginning to fabricate a pattern
which I would continue to work on for years to come, a
pattern of evasion, where I could establish my own sense of
belief and of security only in some area of the imagination
that was as remote in time and place as the Norse longships,
and as dissociated from the troubling present that existed all
around me. Fumblingly, hardly even conscious of what I was
doing, I was setting out to try to side-step a world I didn't
have the courage to face.

But Jack still refused to side-step anything, even the baffling
nature of his own brother.

" You've got to get rid of those sonky bloody cobbers of
yours," he said to me one night. " The way you lot are
heading you'll end up a bunch of tonks. Why the blazes don't
you get out and chase a tart or two?"

" Because I don't want to."

" It wouldn't hurt you just to try."

" You know I can't stand girls. I don't want to try."

" Oh, don't come the raw prawn with me! How can you
say you can't stand 'em when you've never even touched one!
Jesus, they're not going to *bite* you!"

" Leave me alone," I pleaded miserably.

On this I remained stubborn. That was easy enough. I
had my pimples to consider and my awful lankiness. I was
a clear inch taller than Jack now, but thirty pounds lighter,
and I would go scarlet just thinking of the girls sniggering
about me on Elwood beach. I had still to grow body hair,

and at intervals my face would blotch unpleasantly with nerve rashes. I was constantly humiliated by the teasing of my sisters. All I asked was to be left alone.

And Jack had no intention of leaving me alone: the more stubborn I became the more brutally he would force his indoctrination on me. He made me read *Beckett's Budget*, a sordid weekly newspaper which had rocketed into prominence almost overnight on its scandalously detailed stories of sex and crime and violence. Sometimes he was funny with it, like the night he moved around the bedroom pretending to be doubled up like a sufferer from lumbago. When I asked him what was the matter he said:

"I got an attack of Coopay Crouch, that's all."

I just looked at him, not understanding.

"Don't you know what Coopay Crouch is?" he asked.

I shook my head.

"Well, it's when you're with a sheila in the front seat of a coupé, see, and you've got to get out in a hurry, and then you find you've buttoned your waistcoat to your fly. That's Coopay Crouch, see."

But usually there was nothing funny in his methods. He would ostentatiously show me the contraceptives he always carried in his wallet, explaining the technical difference between Sphinx brand and Black Cat. He would buy sets of dirty French postcards, not because of any element of pornography in his own character, but simply to shock me into some realisation of what it was all about. He would deliberately lecture me on the use of sea-water as the only effective solvent for semen stains on one's trousers. I grew more and more appalled. That must have been the only time in my life I ever came to hate my brother Jack.

CHAPTER 5

The obvious escape was at work, and for a time I accepted this without questioning it.

Apart from two incredibly old Germans, all the artists employed by Klebendorf and Hardt, whether "creative" or reproductive, worked in one huge studio. It was a grimy, high-ceilinged room with sooty windows on the western side overlooking the lane. The other three walls were lined from floor to rafters with pulpboard, so that the big twenty-four sheet posters we were printing could be pinned up there, for colour checking and matching.

A kind of strange exotic beauty had been imparted to these walls by a semi-accidental montage of overseas posters which for years had been pasted up on the pulpboard, presumably as outstanding examples of commercial art, and had since become exquisitely textured by the prickings of a million pins. I never realised then that there were museum pieces among them—one of Toulouse-Lautrec's " Jane Avril " bills, and two by the Beggarstaff brothers, and some of the powerful huge lithographs of Brangwyn and Joseph Pennell —because most of the posters were from the British railway companies, Great Western and London North Eastern, usually by Fred Taylor or Frank Newbold, and from the very beginning it seemed wonderful to me to be working in that grubby, crowded, utilitarian place with the vision always before one's eyes of Tintern Abbey and the front at Scarborough and the stained glass of York Minster and the chalk cliffs of Dover and the Welsh mountains and the fishing trawlers bucking out of Grimsby.

There were ten of us in the room, seven seniors, a journeyman lithographer just out of his indentures, and another apprentice as well as me. Each of us worked at a huge, sloping table, large enough to take the sixty-by-forty zinc plates which were used for lithographing the posters, and solid enough to support the heavy, smoothed, oatmeal-coloured stones on which the finer work was done. We sat on very high counting-house stools.

There was a rough division in that the best lithographers were all down the front, near old Joe Denton the head artist, and we two apprentices were down there also, so he could keep an eye on us and give us things to practise on. The other apprentice was his own son, " young " Joe, who had also come from a technical school and who had just completed his first year. The places at the rear were occupied by those more concerned with the " creative " side, which meant the designing of a new poster for some product, or labels for jams or canned fruit, or showcards commissioned by some client for his patent medicine or his oatmeal, or, when times were slack, "spec" designs for posters or leaflets or cutouts which the company's travellers would try to hawk around the town.

It was more a practical division than a hierarchical one—any of the designers was a perfectly capable lithographer, either on stone or zinc, and those around Joe Denton could always get away from the smell of gum arabic and Korn's litho crayon and turn out a good original poster. It was just that each person had one little speciality that he could do a bit better than any of the others. With Barney Druce, the journeyman, it was lettering, with Paul Klein it was the human figure, with Tom Middleton it was an uncanny control over the Ben Day stipple screens, with old Joe Denton it was a miraculous, meticulous tidiness and a gift for judging and blending colours, which, after all, is the real wizardry of reproduction. Even Young Joe, with only a year's training, had developed quite a skill in squaring up from the small original poster sketches the huge charcoal key-drawings on the twenty-four-sheet walls, which would then be rubbed down on to the separate zinc printing plates. In all the time that I was there I never came to be specially good at anything, but they were kindly people and not one of them ever deliberately made me feel my inferiority.

The grouping was mostly a convenience, because there was always a necessary interchange of basic materials—sponges, gum arabic, litho ink, and crayon at one end; poster colours, T-squares and matt board at the other—although no artist would ever lend his own brushes or stippling pens or hand-rest: they were most superstitious about their personal tools, and I doubt if any one of them would have trusted his favourite sable or No. 2 Gillott pen to Rembrandt himself.

All these things were in the smell of the big room, and the smell was locked forever inside those high grimed windows, the crayons and inks and colours and gum and T-squares and rat-dirt and acids and charcoal and stale bread and damp pasteboard and Jane Avril with her toe pointed and the black barges under the Brangwyn bridges.

The two artists excluded from the big room were both Germans. They seemed so incredibly old to me that I thought at first they must have been survivors of the pioneer establish-

ment of seventy years before and that they had inhabited their
frowsy little crannies from the day the building was completed. They were very much alike. Both were tiny, both
had soft white whiskers and thin white hair, and pale pinkish
skin, rather like the flesh of baby mice. Their eyes were so
pale that they seemed to be almost washed away. They
seldom spoke except to one another, either in German or in
halting English, and their voices sounded like rubber squeegees
sliding on glass. Their separate cubby-holes were not only at
opposite corners of the building but were on different floors,
yet they would always meet to eat their luncheon sandwiches
together in the sunshine on the step beside the lorry-bay.
They would chew on their Pork Fritz or liverwurst and never
pay any attention to what was going on around them—it was
usually just the printers, with square newspaper-hats on their
heads, playing wall cricket with a tennis ball or football with a
tied-up bundle of reject quad-crowns, or the boys from the
paper store flirting with some of the girls from the packaging
department or the calendar room ; they would just sit there
side by side, like two tiny creatures out of a fairy-tale, talking
to each other in sleepy nodding squeaks.

Yet these two frail old men were the true hierarchy of the
place, old craftsmen from some other time that was still
revered. Ludwig Steiner, a tempera painter, had been brought
out from Düsseldorf fifty years before ; Fritz Richter had
come from Munich a year or two earlier with a shipload of
lithographic stones from his own native Bavarian quarries.
(These were the stones that Klebendorf and Hardt still used
for the high quality work ; decades of polishing and re-polish-
ing had made them somewhat thinner than they were, but they
had a silky, sensuous texture, and there was any number of
good labels or Christmas cards in them yet.) Steiner only
worked on very special commissions ; otherwise he devoted
his time to rich, incredibly detailed tempera paintings for
calendar pictures. They were stereotyped subjects—women
and children, animals, snow scenes, flower pieces, young
lovers, autumn landscapes—but they were quite beautiful in
their way, and in the attentive detail of their soft, glowing
surfaces more closely related to Van Eyck or Botticelli, really,
than to Claude Cranston who ran the calendar department.
Steiner's paintings were never sold outright. Cranston would

select the best of them and they would be reproduced in four-colour half-tone and printed up in tens of thousands " on spec " and then sold in small lots all over the country, usually to rural or suburban stores or grocery shops or wood-yards or chocolate manufacturers. A blank space would be left be-tween Steiner's picture and the place where the calendar-pad was pasted, and this, at no extra cost, was the area where the buyer's name and advertising message would be printed. Something like *Moran and Cato for Sacrifice Values* or *Consult J. J. Hiddlestone On All Pest and Vermin Problems.* It seemed sad to me that Steiner's pictures were always spoilt in this way.

Fritz Richter was more a craftsman than an artist. He made etchings on copperplate and pulled them up on an ancient handpress which was a miracle of cast-iron curlicues and lions' heads and eagles, and sometimes he did steel engravings, but mostly he was engaged on the very finest lithography, and he always worked on the choice stones he had brought from Bavaria more than half a century before. There were hundreds of these limestone slabs stored in the loft, but Richter had them all numbered and he knew exactly what each separate stone was best for. He would go round with a feather duster once a week and dust them down and pat each one, and he would always grind and polish and clean the stones himself when they were to be used, and he had his own secret mixtures for gum and acid and *torsch* and asphalt and chalk. He was quite fantastic at fine work and subtle stipplings and delicate gradations of colour. With his left hand he would hold a magnifying-glass over the stone, and work beneath it with a camelhair brush as fine as a needle--no more than two or three hairs—and although he would keep this up for nearly eight hours a day his fingers would never tremble, although in the lunch-time break he could barely hold his sandwich for the palsy in his ancient hands.

The big studio and the separate crannies occupied by the two old Germans were the cells of " art " at Klebendorf and Hardt, and everywhere else except for the business offices and sample room on the ground floor was " The Factory "—a great roaring and thundering and clattering and swishing, a bedlam of giant rotary offsets and racketing flatbeds, of lino-types and monotypes chattering their nervous messages to

slugs of antimony, or slobbering ink ducts and grinding
guillotines, and rumbling conveyers from the varnishing
machines, and the gabbling of the girls, and the everlasting
slap-slap-slap-slap of printed sheets.

It was never my intention to defect on the people at Klebendorf and Hardt, and there were times later when I came to
regret the way I had gone about it, but as it all happened
there never really seemed to be any particular point of decision. It was just a kind of drifting thing.

They were a warm-hearted, gentle, considerate crowd in the
big studio, and like most true craftsmen they had a serenity
and dignity that I seldom saw later among those who would
profess to be "serious" artists. To this day I harbour suspicions of bohemian ferocities.

All of them balanced their work with other interests. Old
Joe Denton grew exhibition dahlias, Tom Middleton played
the 'cello in a string quartet, Barney Druce was an amateur
photographer and secretary of a canoeing club on the River
Yarra, Paul Klein painted water-colours for a commercial
gallery and made ship models for his own joy. The studio
must have provided some cross-fertilisation of interests, because every one of them was a fanatical Savoyard, and at any
hour of the working day would be as likely as not to burst
into a chorus from *H.M.S. Pinafore* or *Yeomen of the Guard*
or *The Pirates of Penzance*, then everyone would join in and
the whole studio would rock to Gilbert and Sullivan airs until
old Klebendorf would open the door and peer in and shake
his head wonderingly and go away. (The first time I ever
dined out in my life was at Paul Klein's house, to which I had
been invited to meet his wife and to hear the score of *Ruddi-
gore* played on the Victrola ; the first time I ever visited a
theatre was when the whole studio made up a party to go to
Iolanthe.)

Although work was the paramount endeavour in the big
studio, there were certain formal levities which old Joe
Denton condoned. The singing, of course, was one of them,
since he could quote by heart every libretto that Gilbert ever
wrote. But he also, surprisingly, permitted the dart-play and
the practical jokes with turpentine.

In lithographing on the big sensitised zinc plates the artist's

hand or any other part of his flesh must not come in contact
with the plate; he works with mauls and hand-rests, moving
around his table, seldom seated on the high counting-house
stool, more often than not bent over, as Jack used to say,
" head down and ass up, like a sandpiper." The " turps
game " and dart-play were both related to all this. Each
artist had his own collection of home-made darts: little
feathered blocks of wood pointed with used phonograph
needles which would be aimed with considerable force at the
backside of the artist who stooped too temptingly over his
work. There were many times when I got home to find my
underpants spattered with blood and my buttocks fiery with
pain, but one had to take it all in good part and try for
revenge. The turps game demanded more finesse. Our high
stools had circular concave seats; the idea was that while the
artist was engrossed a pool of raw turpentine would be spilled
surreptitiously into this concavity; when the artist at last sat
down to rest his aching arms and back, the turps would soak
through his trousers to the infinite agony of his private parts.
I have seen the whole studio convulsed with laughter while
Tom Middleton, clutching his balls, went roaring through
the factory like a maddened bull.

I think from the very beginning old Joe Denton, and perhaps all the others too, must have known that I was really not
very good potential material for Klebendorf and Hardt, that
I would never have the total aptitude or the sense of dedication, or even just the willingness and patience to persevere,
that would ever bring me to even the basic standards of
craftsmanship which the studio demanded. It must have been
the fact of Young Joe being an apprentice too that saved me
from the castigations I deserved. Joe Denton was enormously
proud of his son and he knew that the boy was potentially a
first-class craftsman, and I am sure this made him lean over
backwards not to be thought of as favouring Young Joe
against me. It was always his son who got the occasional
rough edge of his tongue, never me.

I was not envious of Young Joe in the beginning; I only
grew to be jealous of his skills later, when I began to suspect
that he might be carrying tales to his father about me.

Old Joe, of course, had no doubts that, given any sort of
co-operation at all, he could train us on the technical side:

beyond this to be a successful commercial artist one would need only two more things—a high standard of skill in lettering and the ability to draw the human figure. Barney Druce gave us our training in lettering—hours of trying to do, to his satisfaction, a Roman or sans-serif alphabet with a No. 1 camelhair brush in letters an eighth of an inch high with no part of one's hand or arm touching the exercise board—and for training in the human figure we were sent to the drawing and painting school at the National Art Gallery. We went first to the Antique School, drawing in charcoal from plaster casts, then to Life Class. Each of us, Young Joe and I, were given two afternoons off a week to attend the classes, and we had to do five nights a week at night school. We took different afternoons off, because there always had to be one apprentice in the studio to run the errands.

Later I was glad of this, because there was nobody to know that I was cutting the lessons, but when I began skipping the night classes as well it became more difficult, because Young Joe must have known what I was doing, even though he was way ahead of me and up their doing oils in monochrome from nude models while I was still struggling in fine charcoal on Michelet paper, with the " Apollo Belvedere " or detail from the " Laocoön." At first I used to skip only an occasional class, then I would stay away from the school a full week at a time; finally it came to the point where in a whole term I attended only on the night when one signed the students' book and got an easel place.

I lived in mortal fear of Young Joe telling his father. It would have been very difficult for me explaining to old Joe Denton that, while my artistic ability might not have shown any noticeable improvement, I had completed a record of the homeward passages of every wool clipper sailing out of Melbourne between 1860 and 1890, and that by a diligent study of the *Papyrus of Ani* I was teaching myself to read and write the hieroglyphics of Ancient Egypt. I need not have worried. Young Joe never told tales either.

It was Paul Klein, really, who moved me on the tangent. There was a thing of the past making an arabesque of this, too, for Paul had been a patient in the Caulfield Military Hospital and had known my mother.

"Of course I knew her," he had said to me once, then added, just to please me, I think: "Everyone who was in the war knew Sister Min." Anyway, the night we went to *Iolanthe* Mother came too, as his guest.

Paul had been involved in a skirmish at Rabaul, in German New Guinea, but he had got a bullet in his leg and a good scar and walked with a limp and a cane, and there was something about this combination of the tropics with the military exploit that made him, to me, far more glamorous than the victims of the commonplace savagery of the Western Front.

It was Paul who introduced me to the waterfront.

There was an interest then in marine painting, and his gallery had suggested he do a series of water-colours on dockland subjects. Melbourne's river wharves were still picturesque then. There was an anachronistic little quay—in fact it was actually called The Little Dock—which to the despair of the municipal traffic people butted right in among the city tram lines and the stamping dray-horses and the confusion of the Spencer Street railway viaduct, where the timber schooners and ketches from Tasmania always tied up, schooners like tht *Joseph Sims* and *Alma Doepel* and the big ketch *Defender*: they would be there with their patched sails drying among the warehouses and business offices and the ship chandlers and the overhead power lines and the smoke from the goods trains, with an ancient clipper-bowed steamer called *Edina* warped in behind. (Years before we had always gone to Portarlington or Geelong in the *Edina* for the annual tramways picnic.) And farther down river at the timber berths along Lower South Wharf there generally would be three or four big square-rigged sailing-ships unloading sawn planks from the Baltic—four-masted barques usually, either Scandinavian like the *Beatrice* and *C. B. Pedersen* and *Herzogin Cecile*, or American like the *Moshulu* and *Tonawanda*, although if they were American ships they would usually be swinging out Oregon building timber from Seattle or Portland.

After I had been working in the studio a few months Paul began to take me around the docks during the lunch-time breaks. We would chew on our food as we walked about looking at the ships and the unloadings and the tugs and lighters at work, he with his sandwiches and me with my bread roll and bananas, and Paul would make quick little sketchy notes of things in sepia wash on a small block he carried in his pocket.

It was on Saturday afternoons that he would do his more finished paintings, and eventually I began to go with him, because I rarely had anything else I wanted to do at weekends. I remembered how surprised I was when he set up his paints the first time because the subject he chose seemed so drab and ugly. It was an old coal-hulk which was tied up alongside one of the Howard Smith coastal steamers. All along the lower Yarra and in Victoria Docks they used these grimy old hulks to load coal into ships' bunkers—motor-ships were only just beginning to come in then—and this particular hulk, the *Garthsnaid*, was not much more than a low-floating rusty hull supporting three stumpy masts which gave purchase to the loading derricks and a squalid little deck-shack for the vessel's watchman. As it happened, directly across the river a Finnish full-rigged ship was berthed alongside Sharpe's timber yard, and the crew was aloft bending the sails on the yards, and it seemed to me that this romantic and beautiful thing should be the subject for an artist and not a grimy old hulk half awash in a garbaged stream.

" But why are you going to paint this?" I wanted to know, and asked him why we didn't call the ferryman and get him to row us across to Sharpe's wharf. Paul just smiled, and then explained to me that " pretty-pretty " subjects like the Finnish square-rigger were best left to the calendar painters, and he tried to show me the things of pattern and shape and colour and form which he saw in the squalid hulk of the *Garthsnaid*.

" And you just look at what beautiful lines she has," he said, with the reverence of a man who respected ships and made patient, loving models of them. " You see, David," he went on, " all the old coal-hulks they use around the docks here used to be clipper-ships, or most of them, anyway. This one was a Scottish wool-clipper called the *Inversnaid*. She was a full-rigged ship, too, just like that one over there at Sharpe's, only a lot prettier. One day she got dismasted in a storm out in Bass Strait, and they towed her in here, and instead of breaking her up and selling her for scrap they chopped her down to her lower masts and used what was left of her yards for derricks and made her into a coal-lighter.

But in a way," he ended musingly, " you can still see what she *was*, can't you? I mean, she's still beautiful, don't you think?" He nodded to himself. " She really *is*, you know."

It is on observations as ordinary as this that the very tangents of our lives are changed.

I began to leave home in the mornings an hour earlier. This carried with it the disadvantage of having to eat breakfast at the same time as Dad, but now instead of sitting on the steps in the lane waiting for the studio to be unlocked, I could go wandering around the waking wharves, and for the first time in my life I came to be aware of the existence of true beauty, of an opalescent world of infinite promise that had nothing whatever to do with the shabby suburbs that had engulfed me since my birth. The fine floating calligraphy of a tug's wake black on a mother-of-pearl stream in the first glow of a river dawn, the majesty of smoke in still air, the pale and tranquil breath of river mist and morning steam, the rising sun picking golden turrets out of derricks and samson-posts and cranes and davits, the coloured smoke-stacks and the slender gilt pencillings of masts declaring themselves little by little against the dark haze-banks that always in this waking time veiled the river flats, the faint images of ships far down the stream, coming in from Gellibrand, looming out of dew and light and sea mist, and then, at every bend and twist of the river, changing the shapes of beauty like a rare vase turned in the fingers of a connoisseur.

It filled me with an excitement, almost an exaltation, that I could tell nobody about. I did not see it then as a way out of the wilderness, for the stuff of this material was too fragile to be considered as something which might be *used*, but I was quite sure that something important had happened to me. I moved through this newly-discovered world breathless and alone, like Adam in a new Eden, and I felt almost as if I had to walk on tiptoe wherever this shining place extended.

It was not very long before I began to visit the wharves on Sunday afternoons, too. I would go alone, taking a sketch-block and my water-colours, but I seldom made a drawing and for a long time I never talked to anybody. The river world was very different on these Sunday afternoons. There was practically no activity anywhere, because Sunday work meant double-time for the wharfies or dock hands or tugboat crews or lightermen, so that the ships which made port on a Sunday would usually stay at an anchorage off shore and save port dues and not come up the river to discharge their cargoes until early on Monday morning: and because of the labour costs there was rarely any cargo-handling on those ships already at their berths.

So there would not be much to see on Sunday afternoons apart from an occasional police car slowly patrolling the deserted dock roads, or Customs men walking around, or the shipping companies' watchmen tapping dottle from their pipes and talking together around the silent cargo sheds, or the little bands of bold frizzy prostitutes plying their trade from ship to ship, or a drunken seaman lurching back to his boat from one of the illegal " bogedas " around Dudley Flats.

One Sunday afternoon the coal-hulk which Paul Klein had painted, the *Garthsnaid*, was tied up at the gas company's coal wharf, underneath the dead silent black gantries that took the conveyer belts up and over the wharf to the plant in front of the big cylindrical storage tanks. The wharf was thick with soft black dust, and amid this an old crone was pottering around. All the longshoremen knew her as " Snotty Sal," and she lived in a rags-and-rubbish hovel in the wasteland behind the docks and drank methylated spirits. There were quite a few " metho " drinkers living around Dudley Flats at that time. The old woman was stooping around with a frayed basket muttering to herself while she gathered lumps of coal that had fallen from above. She never made a fire with this coal: she would sell it and buy " metho " with the money. The gasworks foreman knew this and he had a soft spot for Snotty Sal and just before the knock-off whistle blew at midday on Saturdays he always made a point of seeing that the upper conveyer belts were jolted around a bit so that a hopper or so of anthracite would go spilling down on the wharf below.

The only other person in sight was the *Garthsnaid*'s watchman, who was sitting in the sunshine outside his little deckshack, in a black litter of coal-dust and stacked baskets, boiling a billy of tea over a tin brazier. He was a thick-chested, stumpy man wearing patched trousers and a grey flannel undershirt.

I do not know what impulse it was that made me overcome my shyness, and clamber up the dirty gangway and go aboard the hulk, but the old watchman seemed very pleased at the prospect of company and offered me tea in a filth-encrusted tin pannikin. He was not at all prepossessing at close quarters, for he had only one eye and a big puckered scar down the left side of his face and his cropped grey bullet head was a mass of extraordinary little bumps and dents, and he had no teeth and kept wiping away brown spittle on the back of his hand.

But he was a friendly, good-natured man, and he must have been starving for any sort of companionship, because he soon became quite loquacious.

" Years back, son, I used t'be sailmaker in this 'ere ship," he told me. " Yeah, that I was, son. Old Sails they used t'call me. When she were caught in that westerly gale off'n King Island an' lost 'er sticks, there I wus an' there we all were, son, caught 'twixt a shit an' a shiver, an' a lee shore howlin' at us so close you c'd damn' near 'ear the shingle crunchin'. We wore 'er off, but it wus a friggin' close shave we all 'ad, me boy, an' once we'd got the old 'ooker safe inter port and we'd come ashore to the Sailors' 'Ome over there in Williamstown I said to meself, ' Well, Sails,' I sez, ' it's 'igh bloomin' time yer swallered the anchor!' Which I did. Jest like that. Then 'Oward Smiths bought the old ship, or wot wus left of 'er, an' made a lighter out o' 'er, an' they gimme the job 'ere as watchman. Suits me, son. The work ain't 'ard, and gen'ally speakin' they leaves yer alone."

" Did you sail in her when she was the *Inversnaid*?" I asked him.

" Well, spare me days, boy, 'ow would *you* know 'bout that?" he said in wondering admiration. " No, no, she wus the ol' *Garthsnaid* when I knew 'er, an' that's the bloomin' name she'd 'ad fer donkey's years. Rigged as a barque, she wus ; she'd got into some trouble years before out in the nitrate roads at Antofagasta, an' they never put the square yards back on 'er mizzen. She wus a bloomin' pretty ship though, even cut down like that. Rounded the Horn five times in 'er, I did. I wus in pretty near all the ships o' the Garth Line—bein' a sailmaker, like, it wus best t' stay with one crowd, yer know . . . oh, all of 'em, yeah, the *Garthpool, Garthwray, Garth Castle, Garthglen* . . . nitrates from Chile mostly, or timber or wheat, an' sometimes guano from Peru, but this one was the sweetest of 'em all. She wus the littlest ship in the fleet, too ; she was older than all the others . . . she's iron, see, an' they wus all steel, big thick boogers, four-mast barques most of 'em, jest built as carriers, like . . . no lines at all. . . ."

After this I used to look to see where the *Garthsnaid* was tied up on Sunday afternoons, and through the old watch-man, whose name I never got to know, I heard a lot of stories about old sailing-ship days, and quite a bit of the history of the other coal-hulks that worked with the tugs up and down the river and across to Williamstown. They were grimy, rusted, derelict things, black with filth and coal-dust, but there were romantic stories about almost all of them. One of them, a wooden lighter called the *Success*, had actually been a convict ship that had sailed out to the colonies even before my ancestor, that earlier Jack Meredith, had been hanged for barratry. Another had trimmed her stunsails against the *Cutty Sark* in the tea races from Foochow: and there was a sad, hog-backed wreck almost rotting away in a backwater near Williamstown that Joseph Conrad had once been first mate of.

It was while I was walking back from the coal wharves one Sunday evening—I remember that there was a big mob of gamblers playing two-up on the vacant area outside Sharpe's timber yard, with their " cockatoos " posted all around to keep watch for the police—that the enlightenment came to me. It hit me so suddenly that I had to stop to catch my breath, and one of the " cockatoos," a young, rat-assed tough with a cloth cap pulled down over his eyes, must have thought my sudden halt was suspicious—perhaps he felt I was loitering around as a pimp for the police—because he slouched across and jerked his thumb for me to get moving.

I nodded and went dazedly along the wharf. By the time I had reached Little Dock I had walked out of my wilderness. For the first time in my life I knew exactly what I wanted to do. Going home in the corner of a second-class compart-ment on the Brighton Beach train I was stupefied by dreams and was over-carried three stations beyond my suburb.

In the bedroom that night I began to write it down. I called it " The Glory That Was . . ." and because of a shy shame that overcame me I could not bring myself to put my own name to it. I signed it " by Stunsail," and gave my real name on the covering letter and sent it off to the magazine editor of the *Morning Post*.

Two months later the newspaper printed the article in its Sunday magazine section—they had assigned a staff photographer to get photographs of the coal-hulks I had written about—and a few days after this they sent me a cheque for five guineas with a letter saying they would be interested in reading more of my contributions.

I was torn between a lofty exultation and a blushing shame, and I cashed the cheque secretly and told nobody, and I was choked with relief that whatever was being done was being done by " Stunsail " and not by David Meredith. I kept the money in my pocket for a week or so, wondering what to do with it. The magnitude of the sum was overpowering. I would have to work forty-eight hours a week for seven weeks at Klebendorf and Hardt to earn as much! Or—and this was ever more startling—the money in my pocket was precisely the amount I would be permitted to keep from my earnings for a whole year.

Eventually I spent it all at a sale of second-hand library books in Coles's Book Arcade. I bought the four volumes of Basil Lubbock's histories of the old sailing-ships, *The Colonial Clippers, The China Clippers, The Blackwall Frigates*, and *The Western Ocean Packets*, and a rather battered three-volume set called *Wonders of the Past*. This was concerned with ancient history and archæology, and I didn't quite know why I *had* bought it, except that it had wonderful colour-plates on the finds in King Tutenkhamen's tomb, and I was surprised that none of the eager, grasping bargain-hunters at this book sale seemed to want it.

Perhaps I bought it because, like the coal-hulk *Garthsnaid*, it was an unsuspected cog in the ratchet of my destiny. But this, even now, takes us on to impossibly difficult ground, and certainly there was nothing of that sort of thinking in my mind then. All I knew was that the readings in my bedroom, the exercise-book of poems stuffed inside the ticking of my mattress, my stubborn rejection of Jack's alarming indoctrina-

tions, had all come together at last into the semblance of a
path that would lead somewhere. I was fifteen. And I was a
writer. Lonely and secretive, and desperately anonymous, but
still a writer.

CHAPTER 6

The National Gallery School, for all its high-sounding name,
was really only an enormously long tin shed, heavily raftered
under a roof of corrugated iron, which was a kind of shabby
annexe to both the Art Gallery and the National Museum.
Three-quarters of its length was used as the Antique School, a
bizarre, tunnel-like recession of intimidating chiaroscuro, filled
with innumerable chalk-white plaster casts of antique Greek,
Græco-Roman and Roman nude statuary posed under bare
electric bulbs against the blackness of the shadows. It was
an unnerving, jolting sort of place, because nothing really
agreed with anything else, and one had no sense of harmony
or of proportion or of perspective; one's eyes would move
uneasily from dwarfed foreground figures to gigantic shapes in
the far distance, because some things were half-lifesize and
others were lifesize and some were twice-lifesize: some stood
at floor-level, others posed on high pedestals, many were suspended from the roof girders. To this disconcerting confusion
were added other hazards to visual balance—the strange
palisades of the assembled easels, the scatter everywhere of
dismembered fragments, severed heads, amputated hands or
feet (usually still shod with sandals), and limbless torsos, the
blank white staring of sightless eyeballs, the startling contrast
of the girl students in their floral smocks moving with indifference beneath the uncoloured fig-leaves of naked gods.
    Here the first-year students worked with charcoal on paper,
choosing their own subjects, moving from acanthus-leaf to
sandalled foot, to bust, to stele, to standing figure, working
always closer to the Life Class door. Erasures were permitted,
but only with stale bread kneaded into pellets. The stale
bread attracted mice, which infested the shadowy places
behind the pedestals.

The Life Class was up at the top end of the long shed, behind a baize-covered partition and a closed door bearing a painted sign, SENIOR STUDENTS ONLY. Here students of both sexes worked from nude living models, at first in charcoal, then with oils in sepia, and, in their final year, with a full oil palette. So that tonal values might remain constant the big classroom was windowless, and lighted by electricity even in day-time. The walls were lined with framed figure paintings, the exhibition submissions of former students who had won travelling scholarships to Europe. These works were almost always greatly disparaged by the incumbent students. Although the models usually were either very old men or very young boys, or fat and wrinkled women—for old Barnaby Stanton, the master of the class, had laid it down that " you are not here to make pictures for chocolate boxes or the covers of the magazines ; there is more art in getting a wrinkle right, or a sagging muscle, or the bony unreadiness of an adolescent, than you'll ever find in Theda Bara's breasts, or any other vamp for that matter ! "—the fact remains that most of the boy students passed through that Life Class door to be confronted for the first time in their lives by the spectacle of a naked woman. This had become the formal moment of initiation : the other students around the circle of easels would wait for it, watching the novitiate while he nervously procrastinated with eyes sedulously averted from the model throne, arranging and rearranging the legs of his easel, his charcoal, his wad of bread, his sheet of Michelet paper, his drawing-pins. Then, when the moment could no longer be delayed, the newcomer would run his tongue over dry lips, take up his selected stick of charcoal, turn to face the model ; and inevitably his hand would go down to adjust the crotch of his trousers. The instinctive embarrassment would produce a roar of delighted laughter from the attentive circle, in which the girl students would join as loudly as the men, for this was the nineteen-twenties, the age for youth to prove new freedoms and equalities, and these young people at their easels were, in the Melbourne of that time, the representatives of bohemia, the intellectual *avant-garde* of an era still waiting to be proved.

There was only one entrance to the school. Students had to go up the steps past the equestrian statue of Joan of Arc and beneath the towering granite columns and through the main doors of the museum to check their names in the students' book at the inquiry desk. Then they could find their own way through the long halls and rooms of the Oceania ethnological collection. This was all right if it was Day School, when the museum was open to the public, but for Night School it was a different thing, for the ethnological rooms were always empty and in darkness and I never once went through them without feeling a little scared. The door leading out of the museum lobby would close behind me with a kind of hissing whisper, and a slow soft slap, and there in front of me would be the dim checkerboard of the tiles and the queer gloom-gleam of glass cabinets, and the awful distance stretching ahead that had to be covered through a smell of musty decay and dry death, with the hollow ring of my heels striking and echoing from the marble tiles, and the terrifying shapes of things that peered out at me from the dimness, the idols and totems and fetishes from New Guinea and the Pacific Islands, shrivelled heads hanging from hanks of stringy hair and grinning skulls and fearsome masks with the eye-sockets plugged with pipeclay or ochre. It was always a relief to reach the end door and push through into the bright, bustling, bizarre nightmare of the Antique School.

I had no particular friendship with any of my classmates. I was far too shy to speak to any of the girls—if one of them came to draw the cast of the Donatello head that I was working on I would move my own easel somewhere else—and none of the men students seemed specially interested in me. Now I can see why. In the first place, there was my lack of real competence: the standard of my work was not high enough to provide an element of competition. And since I was not rivalling them for the attention of the girls I offered nothing that was challenging. To them, I think I must have been very dull. But there was something even deeper than this. All the other boys and youths and young men who were there were passionately interested in Art, and they, unlike the men in the big studio at Klebendorf and Hardt, spelt it with a capital A. Whether their passion was genuine or whether it was no more than an expression of the hot, intermittent fevers of the young I do not know; not one of my classmates, so far as I know, ever made any sort of name for himself. But then they would dress extravagantly, as if initiation into the esoteric world of Art carried with it the right to wear a uniform; they would be forever flinging their prejudices and beliefs and opinions at one another: they would plagiarise their own gods, and defile the gods of anyone else. They lived according to some constantly changing creed of noisy controversy.

I never got myself involved in their interminable arguments. I never took out an art book from the gallery library. I never collected reproduction prints of the works of Renoir or Degas or Picasso or Matisse or Turner, or whoever else happened to be the fashionable deity of the moment. My shyness only partly explains my isolation from all the other students; instinctively I must have known that I was just as ill-fitted for Art with a capital A as I was for the quieter and more dignified craft that was practised in the big studio of Klebendorf and Hardt. Isolation turned into withdrawal, and withdrawal finally became total rejection. But that was not until much later.

It is really quite surprising, now I come to think of it, that I should have known Sam Burlington at all. I cannot even remember how or when I first met him, although it must have been through Young Joe, because he, like Burlington, was in Life Class, and in the normal course of events Life Class men would seldom have anything much to do with the plodding riff-raff of Antique.

What makes it even more difficult to understand is that Burlington was the outstanding personality of the school at this particular time. He was a very talented student, and, although he was only about eighteen then, he was generally considered a certainty to win the coveted Travelling Scholarship. He was the authoritative rebel on " modernism," his family was wealthy, he was unique among the young students in having his own apartment and studio in Spring Street, he had publicly led an abortive students' demonstration outside the Customs House after some Government bureaucrat had banned the importation of a print of Modigliani's " Red Nude " (only strong pressure by the more conservative students had prevented him from carrying a placard defending " The Public's Right to the Pubic!"), and it had been he who, at the time of the annual inspection of the school by the elderly, stodgy trustees of the Gallery, had dressed all the lifesize casts in ridiculous old clothes. The " Venus de Milo " wore a sleazy evening gown and a fur tippet and a jewelled toque, the " Diana of the Chase " looked anything but virginal in a bead-fringed cocktail dress and a cloche hat. The " Apollo Belvedere " wore frock coat and bowler hat and although he lacked trousers he wore coloured jazz-garters, carried an umbrella, and affected a posy of artificial violets over his fig-leaf. " Antinous " would have shocked the Emperor Hadrian, since he wore a Richmond football jersey and shin-pads ; the writhing figures of the " Laocoön " all wore jockstraps ; and a bust of Cæsar stared grimly out from beneath a swagman's wide hat hung with corks on strings.

This was the sort of thing that Sam Burlington thrived on, and he always had the effrontery to get away with it. Later, when I was in Life Class with him, he was always up to something. One night when the model failed to arrive Sam stripped off all his clothes and mounted the throne. Another time when the same thing happened he raced down to one of the brothels which were functioning then in Little Lon and hired a notorious prostitute known as Condy's Clara. He paid the fee out of his own pocket, since Clara's rate was considerably more than the fifteen shillings which was the standard modelling fee.

Although Sam Burlington was always friendly enough to me even when I was in Antique Class—perhaps because of my aloofness from the controversies which he considered juvenile and ludicrous—my association with him didn't really develop until just after my sixteenth birthday. In the meantime I had gone on secretly writing my newspaper articles, still using the pen-name of Stunsail. The articles were always about the old sailing-ship days, and this, of course, helped me to side-step other issues which I was not prepared to face. Very often there would be facts I would have to check in the yellowing newspaper files of the previous century, so there would be many nights when, instead of turning through the doors of the ethnological collection, I would walk straight on to the Newspaper Room or up the broad marble stairs to the reading-room of the Public Library.

Both these places stayed open at night for the same period that the painting school was open, so that unless Young Joe

Denton noticed my absences and told his father there was nobody to know of my duplicity. I began more and more to neglect the school. I had now decided that I wanted to write a book about the wool clippers that had once traded to Melbourne, and this meant going through the shipping intelligence columns of every newspaper published between 1860 and 1890, and I was frantically busy filling note-books with the accounts of these clipper-ship voyages and getting material for the Stunsail articles.

It seems almost unbelievable now, but the *Morning Post* took every piece I submitted. With the money I received I either bought books or I sent remittances to a nautical photographic agency in London to buy prints of old photographs of the ships I intended to write about. (I was lucky to get a picture of the *Garthsnaid* in her heyday as the *Inversnaid*, hove-to off the Downs under topsails: the old watchman had been right—she really had been a beautiful little ship.)

This was a strange and furtive period, filled with secret elations and fearful guilts, and an agonising sense of the pressure of time. In the studio I had the feeling that Joe Denton and Young Joe and all the others were talking about me when I was not there; I thought they were watching me out of the corners of their eyes, quizzically, aware of my defections and simply biding their time. Yet on the surface of it they were just as patient with me as before, and they kept on trying to teach me the craft.

The day had to come when I was entrusted with the job of lithographing a client's order all by myself. It was a fairly simple single-sheet poster in four colours for Kiwi Boot Polish. Joe Denton obviously should have given it to his own son to do, but it was passed over to me, I think to try to build up my self-confidence. I did the drawing-up all right and the tracing down, but I made rather a mess of the key-plate by carelessly spilling some gum arabic, and then running over here and there with the *torsch*, so that part of the plate had to be pumiced out and cleaned and re-sensitised. This always means a ragged finish to a job, and I expected a reprimand at least, but Joe Denton passed the plate without any comment.

Next morning I was out at the ink slab with George Rosevear, the litho printer, checking rubbings for the yellow underprint, when one of the stone hands came up with the prepared key-plate and began to bolt it on to the rotary drum.

He called me across to examine it, and to my pleased surprise I saw that all the edges were clean and sharp. I ruled in the register marks with great confidence.

"Well, it came up pretty good, didn't it?" I said to George Rosevear, and my relief must have made me sound a little cocky.

He looked at me out of his red, craggy, printer's face through steel-rimmed spectacles below a square hat made of newspaper.

"An' so it effing ought to!" he snorted. "Joe Denton an' that boy of his stayed back three hours last night an' did the whole effing plate again! An' they didn't sign the overtime sheets neither!" He worked his mouth at me as if he was going to spit and then picked up his roller and bent over the ink slab.

I felt as if I wanted to be sick. It was the first time I recognised the feeling of being shut out. Quite shut out.

Neither Joe Denton nor his son ever mentioned what they had done, and I could never let on that I knew, because that would have made the position impossible for all of us. When the poster was finished Joe Denton pinned it up on the wall and sent for old Mr. Klebendorf to come up, and said, "The Kiwi order, Mr. Klebendorf. Incidentally, young David there did this one, right from scratch. It's the first he's tackled on his own. Pretty good, don't you think?"

Klebendorf only nodded and grunted, the way he always did, but he patted my shoulder as he was going out, and I felt as if a door had closed behind me, closed very quietly, with the clicking of a lock.

In childhood and adolescence there can be hardly anything more destructive, anything quite as defeating, as a knowledge of an inferiority, of an incapacity to reach standards imposed not by oneself but from outside. The feeling of being shut out, which I had felt in front of George Rosevear, moved with me now into the studio. I realised with a sickening finality that I did not *belong* to these kindly, simple, consider-

ate people, with their fixed integrities and the honesty of their
beliefs and the truths of the things they prized. I wasn't good
enough. I never could be good enough. . . .

The situation had suddenly been reversed. Now it was only
at home that I could escape. Nothing was as real or as
important as the privacy of my room, the mounting pile of
journals and note-books, my swelling library, the heart-
thumping secrecy with which I had to work. I was hardly
conscious any longer of Jack's comings and goings or his
scornful observations, or of Mother's sadness, or even of
Dad's surly moods and intermittent brutalities.

The deception here, of course, was just as profound as at
work. My family took it for granted that I was an excellent
apprentice, that I was succeeding with Klebendorf and Hardt
where Jack had failed with Foley the plumber. So far as they
knew, I was at night school most of the week, I spent my
week-ends sketching, and I enjoyed my job so much that I
would get up in the mornings hours earlier than was necessary
just to get to work. I did not disillusion them; indeed I lied
barefacedly about the progress I was making, in lettering, in
lithography, in figure drawing. I took home the Kiwi poster,
of course, but I would also bring printed samples of work
that Tom Middleton or Barney Druce or Young Joe had
done, and say that I had lithographed them; I discovered
some old rejects of Steiner's tempera pictures, and I stole two
of them and took them home and pretended they were my
paintings. Mother admired them so much that she had them
framed and they were hung with her own paintings in the
front room. They were still there on the wall, to my shame
and horror, thirty years later.

Oddly enough, I think there was one moment during this
curious period of double-deception, when a fairly normal
adolescence might have been possible. It was Dad who prevented it, although this was not really deliberate. His antagonism towards Mother still continued, although it was less
directly violent than before, and had spread into a kind of
sullen general misogynism, and on top of this he had begun
by now to hear disturbing reports of Jack's nocturnal escap-
ades from several frightened suburban parents. He knew
that Jack had slipped beyond his control. He was positive

that he would get some girl into trouble and bring shame to the Meredith name, to say nothing of the possibilities of a court order or a shotgun marriage. Like many a weak man before him, he saw the temptation as the source of the evil, and women became his anathema.

It was about this time that a boy I had known at school, Jerry Farley, had his sixteenth birthday, and I was invited to attend his party. I was allowed to go, since it was a Saturday night, but Dad had lost at the races and was in one of his bad moods, and he made a point of warning me that I was to be home no later than ten o'clock.

Apart from Dad's "Welcome Home" and the Sunday night sing-songs, which didn't really count, I had never gone to a proper party, so I walked up to Royal Parade in a kind of excited trepidation which turned into intense nervousness when I saw the crowd that was there, and there seemed to be as many girls as there were boys, and some of them were dancing together, doing the Charleston and the Black Bottom and the Varsity Drag. Farley had four sisters. Moira, the prettiest, was about a year older than Jerry, and she came across the room to where I was sitting, with her friend Helen Midgeley, who was older still, and they began to talk to me because both of them were at an art school in Praham, studying fashion design, and they were interested in me because I was actually working in commercial art. I was embarrassed at first, but they wanted to know about lithography and the studio and after a time I found that I was explaining things without any self-consciousness.

Helen Midgeley was a tall, fair-haired girl with very pretty legs and she was wearing a straight, plain-coloured dress where most of the other girls were frilly in party frocks, and she had an air of cool, sort of sexless friendliness which had the effect of making me feel, for the first time in my life, at ease and warm and eager in the company of the other sex. Moira was more volatile and more challenging, with a sort of wild impetuosity in her talk—flinging at me her passion for Rembrandt, her adoration of Whistler, her admiration of Russell Flint, almost as if they were accusations—but it was the cooler balance of the older girl, her genuine curiosity, her obviously more mature intellect, which really captivated me. I had never in my life known anyone so beautiful and so

poised and so clever. When Moira eventually was dragged
away to dance, Helen stayed with me, talking.

"I don't know that I'd ever want to make a career of
fashion drawing," she said. "Unless it would take me to
Paris or London or somewhere, where one could *be* somebody. You're going to the Gallery school, is that because of
commercial art, or do you want to be a real artist?"

"I want to be a real something," I said. "I don't know
about an artist."

"A real what then?"

"A writer, I think. In fact, I think that's exactly what I
will be. A writer. I'll be a very famous writer." I had a
desperate wish to tell her that I already *was* a writer, that the
best newspaper in the city published everything I sent in, but
I was terrified that she would disbelieve me, or laugh at the
pseudonym I used. But she just gave me a slow, cool,
interested smile and said, "When you *are* famous I promise
I'll buy all your books. David Meredith. I'll remember the
name."

After that we talked for a long time about books and about
writers, and she didn't seem interested in the dancing or the
games, and I enjoyed her company so much, and the sweet
strange smell of her, that I forgot about the time and it was
already past ten when I took my leave, and out in Royal
Parade beneath the stars and the wind-swing of the pepper-
trees I had a feeling of immense happiness and I ran almost
all the way home, slapping at the tree trunks and the picket
fences and talking to myself.

When I came to the corner of our street a great black
figure sprang out at me from behind Gillon's cypress hedge
brandishing a thick wooden stick. It was Dad. He chased
me the rest of the way home, beating me across the back.

"There were girls there, weren't there?" he kept shouting
at me. "You were chasing the girls, weren't you? That's
why you disobeyed me, eh? Ten o'clock was what I said!
Ten o'clock! Take *that* for your girls! And *that*! And
that!"

Everything finally came to a head on the evening after my
own sixteenth birthday, which occurred not so very long
after I had graduated to the Life Class.

I only just scraped through; in fact, if I had been honest about it they would have failed me. In spite of my repeated absences it was easy enough to qualify on attendances as these were checked off from the students' book at the main inquiry desk of the museum, and I would always sign the book whether I was going to classes or to the Newspaper Room. The real snag was the three submission drawings that had to be shown to Barnaby Stanton. I had made one pretty good study of an acanthus frieze, but I knew my figure work was weak, so I stole two good studies from Young Joe's folio of the previous year, which he always kept at the factory studio, and submitted all three drawings as my own. I felt guilty and ashamed about it, but I just could not afford to be failed, because this would have meant a report to Klebendorf and Hardt, questions by old Joe Denton, and complete exposure of my defections. Nobody ever found out. Old Stanton looked at me in some curiosity—understandably enough, since I was almost totally unfamiliar to him—but anyway he wrote me for a pass.

Then came the incident of my birthday. Birthdays were never particularly celebrated in our house, and presents were seldom given—and then only new shoes or socks or shirts or handkerchiefs, useful things which would have had to be bought anyway—but this year it was different. It happened that Granny and I had birthdays in the same zodiacal sign, so that it was only a week or so since I had given her the forged picture of the *Grafton*. Mother was pleased that I had graduated to the Life Class, because this to her meant painting instead of drawing. She had no idea what Life Class really was—because of Dad I never told them anything about naked models—and I think she had it confused some way with Still Life, but she knew that it was a senior class and that I would need oil paints. So she and Granny clubbed together and gave me a present of a five-pound note. With this I was to buy my box of artist's oil colours.

I got permission next day to leave work half an hour earlier, so that the art dealer's store in Little Collins Street would still be open, and I knew exactly the box of paints and the shape of the palette I wanted, and I had decided in my mind on how many sable brushes would be needed and how many hogshair, but fate again took a hand in my affairs, because there was a narrow little shop right next to Dean's art store that was having a sale of reconditioned second-hand typewriters, and right in the very front of the window display was a huge, old-fashioned Remington standard typewriter with a carriage about two feet long, and a card resting on the keyboard which said, *Good Working Order Guaranteed —£5 Cash or Considerate Terms.*

It was then only ten minutes off closing time, so I hardly hesitated at all; I handed over the £5 note and they gave me a receipt and a printed guarantee and the big typewriter. They offered me a waterproof cover too, but that would have cost an extra half-crown and I didn't have the money, so I just took the Remington as it was.

It was an uneasy, muggy evening with a storm brewing, and the Remington seemed to weigh a ton, and the width of the carriage, which kept sliding and ringing the bell, made it very awkward to carry, and by the time I had staggered as far as Swanston Street the shops and offices were closing and it was the rush hour, with everybody pushing and jostling for the trams. The sultriness had made people irritable and nobody had much patience with me and my cumbersome burden, and it was quite some time before I was able to struggle aboard a Darling Road tram, and even then I had to stand with the typewriter still in my arms. We were crossing Prince's Bridge when the conductor elbowed his way through the straphangers. The weather and the crowds had given him a fine temper too, and he began to make a tremendous fuss when he saw me and wanted to kick me off at the next stop.

" All the damn' room yer takin' up!" he snapped. " Why doncher 'ire a van fer that there thing?" In the end he made me get out and stow the typewriter on the greasy, slatted floor in the rear motorman's compartment. This gave my arms a rest but every time the tram lurched or clattered over points or junctions I thought the old Remington would fall to pieces.

Anyway I got it undamaged to our stop at the corner of Kooyong Road. By this time I was flustered and aching, and the weight of the typewriter seemed to increase with every step, so I put it down on the wooden bench outside Cleland's shop while I rested. Then a funny thing happened.

A depot tram coming home from the city pulled up and a

middle-aged man got off. He was well-dressed and looked like a solicitor or a chartered accountant, and he carried an attaché-case and an umbrella. He began to step off briskly down Kooyong Road, but when he caught sight of me he looked over curiously and stopped and came across to the bench. Then, without saying a word to me, he opened his attaché-case and took out a sheet of note-paper that looked like a business letter and turned it over and rolled it into the carriage of the typewriter, and then with two fingers he picked out: " *Now is the time for all good men to come to the aid of the party.*"

" Hmm, yes, it has quite a nice touch," he said, and smiled at me, and then, " It's beginning to rain, you know," he said. " Which way do you go?"

I told him where I lived, and he said, " Well, come on, let's get along. That's my way too. You don't want to get that thing wet. You should have a cover for it by rights. Come along, I'll hold this umbrella for you."

The rain fell first in soft warm dots, as big as shillings, then turned into a steady drizzle as we walked down, so he took me all the way to our gate and left me with a cheerful good night. The curious encounter with this kindly stranger had made me forget all my discomfort and embarrassment, and I had such a joyous excitement tingling through me that I decided to surprise Mother by presenting myself at the front door.

Unluckily, Dad, who normally never answered the door, happened to be in the hall; as soon as I saw him I could see that he was in one of his bad moods.

" You," he said curtly. " Why didn't you go round the back way?" Then he saw what I was carrying and frowned. " What in the name of God is *that*?" he said suspiciously.

" Oh, it's only a typewriter," I said, as I eased it out of my aching arms and set it down very carefully on the rug. I tried to make it sound nonchalant ; I still felt proud and happy, but it had twisted somehow, being confronted by Dad instead of my mother.

" Min !" he shouted. " Min, just come and see what this damned dolt of a son of yours has brought home now !"

I see now how impossible it was for me, at sixteen, to have had even the faintest glimmerings of the corrosive forces which lay behind the scene that was to follow. I was familiar enough with the patterns of violent physical tyranny in my father's character, but it would be years before I could expect to understand the darker currents that obsessed him— the virulence of the acid thing inside him that was always biting blindly . . . to accuse, to blame, to find other scape-goats for his own failures and failings. (Even ten years or more later, when strong acids were eating at my own charac-ter, and when I behaved with as much violence and cruelty and injustice to my own wife, I still had not learned to understand it.

Yet the clue, I think, was in that shout to my mother, this deliberate use of the phrase, " this son of yours," for I remember now, repeatedly in their quarrels, how blame was fixed by him always on some presumably malevolent influ-ence for which Mother was responsible. " I hope you're proud of that worthless damned son of yours!" he would say to her, or " They get it from *your* side of the family," or " I'd watch that daughter of yours if I were you." Mother was the source of contamination. From her side of the family came all the rank seeds of rottenness and failure.

Perhaps the warp in his mind went all the way back to that crowded hovel on the edge of Chinatown where he had grown up with his resenting, furious, victimised Orangeman father. But there at least, rowing on the lake, playing his fiddle at the Saturday socials after the regattas, he would have thought himself to have *been* somebody, and I am sure he had come genuinely to believe that his defiance of his own father had been the point where he had gone wrong. His father had warned him against involvement with a family he was con-vinced was parasitical and rotten and corrupted, and he had flouted this advice and eloped and run away, and nothing but bad luck had followed.

There had been years of unemployment, of casual labour, of hardship, his first child had died, he had escaped into the adventure of war and got nothing out of it but chronic ill-health and had come back to the same poor job as before with four whole years of his life wasted. As his bitterness and resentment increased, it focused more and more sharply upon his wife and her family, and there were many things upon which his rancour might feed. He had not asked her to go galloping off to France after him, abandoning and neglecting her children, allowing them to grow up like savages . . . then coming back and wasting years of her life, and his, on her pet soldier-boys. Her skinflint father had died, leaving her not so much as a shilling. Her bedridden mother had been a burden on them for years. And her two brothers—one a drunken waster and the other a sponger and a crook.

Gradually the poor self-persecuted man must have come to see his own family failing as he himself had failed, and this he could attribute only to the contamination spreading from the poisoned source. His eldest child had been able to do no better for herself than marriage to a maimed country bumpkin, one of the soldier-pets they had had to support for years . . . his eldest son had turned into a young larrikin who would end up in a cell at Pentridge or get the whole family smeared all over *Beckett's Budget* . . . and he would have seen me, I am sure, as some sort of furtive spineless weakling with that same taint in me that would take me down the drain with all the rest of them. . . .

Mother seemed to come very slowly up the passageway to the hall, and my heart sank when she pushed through the heavy curtains. I realised there must have been a row before I got home ; she looked pale and ill, and her eyes were swollen behind her glasses. Dad just made a sweeping contemptuous gesture at the Remington, which now looked huge and ugly and useless against the frayed, faded square of Axminster.

" David, what have you got that for?" Her question shivered a bit, on the verge of shrillness.

There was something in the way she spoke that unsettled me, and when I opened my mouth to explain no words would come. I could not understand how a quite ordinary thing like a second-hand typewriter could upset them both the way it seemed to, and I had a bewildered sense of being forced out beyond what I could explain into a wilderness of baffling terrors and prejudices which had nothing to do with me at all. Mother kept staring down at the typewriter with a blankness in her eyes, as if she was doing it only so that she would not have to look at Dad or at me, and she was quite still except for her hands which kept clenching and unclenching.

" All right, get that infernal blasted contraption out of my

sight!" he ordered roughly. "Go on! Get rid of it!" I
began to make some sort of protest but he cut me short.
"This minute, do you hear me. Get it right out of the house.
I know what you're damned well up to, so you get rid of it."
There were thick veins, like pale worms, throbbing at his
temples. I tried to explain, to protest, to plead with him, I
even began to stammer out my confession about writing
articles for the *Morning Post*, but his rage had turned almost
icy and seemed to be directed at Mother rather than at me, at
the source of contamination:

"I told you this, didn't I?" he said to her. "I told you
the sly young devil was scribbling all that muck in his room:
hiding it away in his mattress! We sacrifice everything to see
he gets an education. We try to bring him up properly. We
work our fingers to the bone to make sure he learns a trade.
But he has his own ideas, doesn't he? He's decided he'll
follow in the footsteps of his wonderful bloody namesake . . .
that brilliant writer . . . his clever Uncle Davy! That waster
of a brother of yours who's drunk himself and his family into
the poorhouse! He's to become just like the rest of that
damned, worthless, rotten, stuck-up family of yours. . . ." He
was almost beside himself now, ranting and cursing and
spattering spittle everywhere, and Mother was backed into a
corner of the hall, sobbing, and God knows what else he said
because I was caught in a dark whirlwind of hopeless bewildered misery, but I do remember him shaking me furiously
and shouting, "Get that infernal bloody contraption out of
this house, this minute, you, and either come back without it
or don't come back at all!"

And then I was outside in the street beyond the wire fence
and the privet hedge, with the huge Remington in my arms
and the rain beating down upon my tears.

It must have been about half past nine by the time I got to
Sam Burlington's studio in Spring Street, above the doctors'
surgeries, and I don't really know why I went there, except
that I couldn't think of any other place to go.

I had to ring the door-bell four or five times, but I knew
he was home, for I could hear the subdued sound of voices
and Ravel's "Bolero" playing softly on a phonograph.
When he finally did come his sandy hair was stuck out in

sharp funny spikes against the dim light in the passageway and all the orange-and-black décor, and his shirt was unbuttoned.

It must have given him a shock to see me standing there on the porch landing with the big typewriter all glistening with rainwater, and my hair plastered down over my forehead, because I was soaked to the skin by this time, and he must have known I had been weeping, from exhaustion as much as from misery, but he didn't really show much surprise. He looked more pleased than anything, really, but then he was always happiest when things occurred outside a range of expectation. He tried to make a joke of it at first.

"Well, well, well, so our distinguished young confrère Meredith has gone into commercial travelling," he said. "Alas, dear Meredith, I have inherited a Corona portable from a deceased great-aunt of mine. So I am not in the market for this excellent linotype machine you offer in your palsied hands. Now, had you been peddling illegal narcotics, good drummer, or autographed photographs of Clara Bow, or——" But he broke off at that, seeing the expression on my face, and he was silent for a moment, watching me, and then he stepped back from the door and said, quite casually, "Come on in and tell me the news."

There was a girl in the studio sitting on the edge of the sofa, a pretty blonde whom I remembered seeing once or twice in the Antique Class. Her hair was loose and she was fastening the buttons of her blouse.

CHAPTER 7

Sam Burlington put me up that night on the sofa in his studio. The sofa had a smell of Evening in Paris, and a disturbing musky scent I didn't recognise at that time.

The blonde girl went away soon after I arrived. She and Sam talked together for a while in the passageway in low voices, with a lot of smothered giggling on her part, and I heard her say, "But it's high time I went home anyway, after the way you've been carrying on, you devil."

Sam came back into the room and went over to where I had

put the typewriter on the table where he kept his art books and folios and old copies of *The Studio* and *The Lone Hand*. A puddle of water had dripped on to the table and he wiped it off with the sleeve of his shirt. The sheet of note-paper was still in the carriage, by this time all rain-blotched and cockled, and Sam bent over to work out what the man with the attaché-case had typed, and then let out a short snorting laugh and with his own two fingers awkwardly typed out *The quick brown fox jumps over the lazy dog*, then *S. J. Burlington . . . Sam, Sam, pick up thy musket*, but at that point the keys went through the soggy paper and it ripped off the carriage in wads of pulp.

" Better get some oil into this thing or it'll rust up inside," Sam said, and then he turned to me and straddled a chair and said, " Well, what is it all about?"

So I told him what had happened. Not only at home, but everything that had led up to it. Exhaustion had collapsed the last of my defences; it was like the drawing of a bung from a charged barrel; the contents, so long sealed up, poured out in a flow that couldn't be checked. He listened intently. He never questioned or interrupted. I don't think his eyes ever left my face. I can still see him, sitting there in his unbuttoned shirt watching me, his arms across the back of the chair, his little soft chin mounted on the back of his wrist.

Sam Burlington was shorter than I and built rather slight, and his very immobility came as a surprise, because there was always a perkiness and a quickness of movement about him that gave him a kind of skittery, bird-like quality. He was not really attractive at first sight because his skin was sallow, almost pasty, and he had somewhat protuberant honey-coloured eyes—the sort of eyes my mother would always define as " goitrous "—and his sharply pinched nose and recessive chin, together with the way his nondescript feather-coloured hair would never stay down but fly into spiky little crests, enhanced the avian look he had. The odd thing was that after you had been with him a minute or two you quite forgot what he looked like and he became personable and charming.

Gradually, as I talked, I began to feel less unhappy. I could see that the story gave him pleasure. His eyes would glitter with satisfaction as I recounted each of my defections, gleam with an impish and whimsical delight at the absurdities of the *Garthsnaid*, my theft of the Steiner paintings, the pieces in the *Morning Post*, my history of the wool clippers. I don't think he was at all interested in my ambitions, but he relished the unorthodoxies of the situation.

"So, not to make a pun of it, you have cut the painter, young Meredith," he said when I had finished. "And you are now adrift in the great big world . . . a useful analogy this, old boy, since you appear to have seen your destiny in watery things. Coal-hulks and clipper-ships and hoary old shellbacks, eh?" He rubbed his hands together delightedly. "'Stunsail' I like, I honestly do," he said with his sudden explosive honk of laughter. "I think I shall have to call you Stunsail, it somehow suits the bold absurdity of your cause!" (Sam Burlington adored talking; he handled words with the comic skill of a vaudeville juggler tossing Indian clubs; he loved to play with puns and flowery phrases and ludicrous images; he had that overflowing confidence in words, in verbal sleight-of-hand, which, a few years later, would have been a rich asset had he wanted to be a radio commentator, instead of sinking himself in seclusion and growing roses, the way it finally worked out.)

His face suddenly was serious, his forefinger lifted in admonition, his voice grew stern. "Stunsail," he said, "stay away from home!"

"Well, yes, that's all right, but . . . but where can——?"

He stopped me with a grand gesture. "To-night you will rest your caravan here," he said. "Your infernal machine, in fact, you may lodge here indefinitely. I may practise on it myself. You can come here to write your epics and in emergencies you can present yourself for beggarly hand-outs. On wet nights or when you feel defeated I dare say we can always find a *gunyah* for you in some odd corner. You will, naturally, sometimes have to avert your eyes from our scenes of licence and depravity. Otherwise, Stunsail old cock, you will test your abilities now on the great big world. You will sleep on park benches, pass out in doss-houses, be ritually arrested on vagrancy charges. I shall arrange meetings for you with accommodating harlots who are both cheap and clean. I shall show you a place for down-and-outs in Russell

Street where you will be able to get sausage-and-mashed, roll and butter, and two mugs of foul but hot coffee for fourpence-halfpenny. For a mere fourpence-halfpenny, my dear Stunsail, for a handful of coppers, you can stay alive and round Cape Horn with a muse of fire! Do you not find this challenging and marvellous? The world will be your oyster—likewise a creature of the salty deeps. Stunsail, your great chance has come!" He flung his arms wide. His laughter snorted. "Now," he said, "you get those bloody wet things off and go and have a shower, and I'll make you up a shake-down on the sofa."

This happened early in the Australian autumn of 1928, and I did stay away from home almost until winter settled in. My brother Jack found me two days after I had left home. It was at night, and I was alone in Sam Burlington's studio when he came.

"So I tracked you down, eh?" he said, without any other greeting, and pushed past me into the passageway, his shoulders forward a little and his mouth set aggressively. Sam had gone out half an hour earlier on a sudden impulse to round up friends for a party, and since my role in the impending function had not been made by any means clear, I was even more dubious about what he would think of somebody like Jack calling there, because Jack stank of brilliantine and he was wearing his widest Oxford bags. (Sam was careless but conservative in his dress. Clothes were one of the things he was never excessive about, and he detested the art students who wore floppy black bows and beards and their hair long, and his own hair was always clippered "short back and sides" the way the Richmond and Collingwood footballers wore theirs.)

"You on your own here?" Jack asked curtly.

"Yes," I said, and closed the door. "Well, I am for the moment. Sam's gone out to bring some friends back."

He had gone ahead of me down the passageway, walking a little stiffly and with a kind of studied swagger that told me he had an unsure feeling about his surroundings, but he had balked at the studio door.

"You better go in," I said awkwardly.

"I dropped in to that Art School place," he said, talking ahead of himself and not looking back at me at all, "and there was some peroxided sheila told me where you were." He went into the studio with his hands in his pockets. "I reckoned that was where I might find *you*," he said. "You weren't among those present, eh?"

"Well, no . . . I stayed here to-night. There was an article I wanted to write."

He glanced across at the big typewriter, and my unfinished article on the Hobart Town whalers, and nodded disapprovingly. Already the room was heavy with the smell of his brilliantine. I was suddenly shocked to think of Jack going to the Gallery School, and asking questions.

"You been going to Klebendorf's?" he said.

"To work? Of course. I was there yesterday and to-day."

"I would've looked you up down there, but I didn't know what the lurk was, see, and I didn't want to put you in. Do they know?"

"No."

"Well, that's all right." He was looking at me now. "Mum wanted to get the police when you didn't come home," he said.

I just stared at him, waiting.

"Yeah. She and Pop were at each other hammer and tongs half the bloomin' night. Pop didn't want to have a bar of the rozzers and started to shout the flaming place down, so I thought I'd better come out and try to find you." He was nosing round the studio now, picking things up and putting them down in distaste, and making it very clear that he strongly disapproved of the place where he had found me. "Listen, what sort of a frigging joint *is* this you've got yourself into?" he asked.

Looking back, I can see Sam Burlington's studio quite clearly, but now it is difficult to set it in its time, and quite impossible to visualise it as Jack must have seen it. The predominating colour scheme was orange and black—" tango style " it was called and it was all the rage then in Melbourne —and there were a good many fringed " Spanish " shawls tossed about and parchment lampshades which Sam had decorated either in flat geometrical shapes or in the swirly, elongated, prancing and pirouetting nudes of *art nouveau,* and there were the books that everybody then was making such a fuss about—*The Green Hat* and *Private Lives of Helen of Troy* and *The Sun Also Rises*—and lots of prints pinned up on the walls—some Picasso reproductions and Modigliani's illegal " Red Nude " (you could always be perfectly certain that Sam would have anything that had been banned by the Customs Department), and a Conder fan and a whole collection of the naughtier Norman Lindsay prints and some Aubrey Beardsley illustrations torn from old copies of the *Yellow Book.* On an easel in the corner was a large stretched canvas of a not-quite-finished but extremely frank female nude which Sam was working on. There were also some bronze incense-burners and pink jade horses and a New Guinea totem drum which Sam, for a joke, had stolen one night from the museum's ethnological collection and had never been able to smuggle back and a Mexican straw hat.

Jack just walked around among all this, looking and poking at things and grunting and hating it all. Suddenly he whipped round at me and said, " Listen, is the codger who owns this place another of your bloomin' tonk friends or what?"

" Sam? Oh, don't be idiotic, Jack. He's very nice."

"I didn't ask whether he was very nice. I asked if he was a poofter."

" Listen, Sam's my friend. He's at the Gallery with me. He's——"

" Yeah!" He pulled a face. " I met some of them coves at the Gallery to-night. Bloody bunch o' stuck-up bastards if ever I've seen 'em, with those effing ties they wear, and some of 'em with their hair longer than the girls'!"

He was glowering now at Sam's canvas in the corner.

"Who did *this thing*?" he wanted to know.

" Sam," I said.

" Cripes! it don't leave much to the imagination, does it?"

" Oh, stop this stupid business, Jack," I said impatiently. I was growing more and more aghast at the thought that Sam would return and find him there. " It's Sam's place, and this is the way *he* likes it. It's nothing to do with you. Why don't you sit down for a minute and tell me what *I* should do and what Mum and Dad have been saying?"

"What you should do?" He turned away from the easel and examined me. "Well, I'd better see this mate of yours first, hadn't I?"

That made me chew on my lip. "Well . . . yes," I said evasively. "He shouldn't be much longer, I suppose. Or, if you like, we could go down the street to a café and talk about it there." I suggested this eagerly, hoping he would agree. But it just added to his truculence.

"Oh, no," he said. "I'm going to see this mate of yours, don't make any mistake about that. That's one of the reasons I came up here." He turned away to resume his examination, and said, "Have you moved in with him here?"

"Yes . . . no . . . well, I don't know. He let me stay here last night and the night before . . . just while I'm working things out."

He nodded without any pleasure or approval and said, "Wonder it hasn't given you the willies! You know, the way he lives I reckon he must be a poofter of some sort." He spoke with undisguised disgust. "Just take a dekko yourself. This looks like a tart's place! Smells like one too!" He made a business of holding his nose, although by this time the reek of his own brilliantine had conquered every other smell in the studio, even the pungency of Sam's oils and turps. "And what's he do with all the slinky shawls, and that Rudolph Valentino muck over there? And those dirty pictures on the wall?" He moved over to the end door and poked his head into the little bedroom and recoiled and said, " 'Struth! Stinks like a mick church!"

I felt suddenly sick of the whole business.

"I think we'd better go, Jack," I said unhappily. "I'll go back home if you think I should."

He obviously hadn't wanted me to say this, because it made him sit down, and he looked me over very carefully as if he were studying me for visible marks of decadence.

"That's going to depend on this codger, though, isn't it?" He crossed his legs more comfortably and took out his tobacco tin and his Zig-Zag papers and began to roll a cigarette. "If he turns out to be another of these poofter friends of yours I wouldn't let you stay here for all the tea in China." He licked the cigarette, twirled it in his fingers, bit off the loose shreds of tobacco, and spat them on the floor. "Or you *want* to go home, is that it?" he asked causally.

"Well . . . I don't know." I looked at him uncertainly. "I didn't run away, did I? It was Dad who kicked me out, wasn't it? How do I know what they're saying even? I told them I wanted to write things and now they know and——"

"Ah, that flamin' house is no good for anybody!" he cut in with sudden startling ferocity. "I'll be getting out of it myself any bloomin' day from now." He struck a match and lit the cigarette. "It's Mum, though, isn't it?" he said in a quieter tone.

I nodded dumbly. He kept slowly turning the lighted match in his fingers, staring at the flame, and the blue tobacco smoke trickled slowly from his nostrils.

"You see, I got the boot to-day," he said. "I didn't do anything this time, but Crebbin sold that storeroom place to old Kinross because they're going to make a garage, and he decided to close down half the workshop and lay eight of us off. We got a week's screw instead of notice. I was going to try it up the bush for a while, the Wimmera or the Mallee or maybe those fruit places along the Goulburn, but now . . . well . . ."

"But now what?"

"Well, it kind of depends on what you're going to do, don't it?" He squinted at me through the scribbles of smoke. "That's the point, isn't it? We can't very well just leave Mum there with *him*, can we?"

I could feel my tongue drying, but I swallowed a bit and said, "Well, I can go home if you want to try the bush."

"Yes . . . well, I don't know, Davy. . . ." He studied the cigarette carefully, and picked another shred of loose tobacco from the end of it. "You know, now that this has happened I been thinkin' about it, and I reckon it might be the makings of you to have a go at it on your own for a while. I mean, just to get out of that bloody rotten house for a bit . . . that bloomin' smell of pisspots and lavender water and old women dying. . . . And all those flaming rows!"

"But if you've lost your job . . ."

"Ah, there's a ton of yakker about. I can pick up something else. I don't mind hangin' around if you want to give it a go. You wouldn't be giving up your job at Klebendorf's?"

" No. I couldn't, anyway. The papers are signed for six years."

" Yes, well I could meet you somewheres Friday nights and take your pay home to Mum. Or you could buy a postal-note and send it to her."

I nodded. " I was wondering about that. She'd still need the money, of course."

He gave a short mirthless laugh. " They're not John D. Rockefellers, are they? They still got the house to pay off. And the Chev. And that bloomin' pianola. And God knows what else besides."

" That's right." I had a sudden feeling of miserable empty worthlessness. There was not one single thing that I had thought about. I had not thought of somebody being with Mother, nor of their needing the pay, nor of Jack's responsibilities. I didn't even seem to know any longer how I had got myself into the situation . . . now it had turned into just another part of the drifting and the dodging, and even the decision as to what I was to do evidently was not mine to make. Jack had come looking for me, and Jack would decide.

" We can talk about that after, though," he said, as if he knew exactly what I was thinking. " First we got to take a dekko at this poofter mate of yours, don't we?"

Just then I heard the click of the key in the door lock, and a good deal of chattering and laughter, and there was a sound of heavy things bumping and a chinking of bottles out on the porch landing, and then over it all floated Sam Burlington's clear, gay cry:

" Fife and drum, Stunsail! The fun begins!"

" My bloody oath it does!" Jack muttered to himself with a kind of grim pleasure. He had got up from the chair. He was standing with that slight stoop forward that I knew so well, his shoulders loose, and his feet placed the way he always had them in the boxing ring.

Even Sam Burlington's sang-froid and love of the unexpected were not proof against the spectacle of Jack standing there in the studio, and for a long interval he was arrested in the doorway, his mouth open, utterly speechless, with the questioning faces of his friends crowding up behind his own mask of astonishment. I realised with a sudden accumulation of shame that Jack had Saxe-blue godets inserted at the ankles of his pearly-grey Oxford bags!

Then Sam pulled himself together and came into the studio, wrinkling his nose and sniffing at the air, and said, " So we have company, Stunsail," and his friends pushed in behind him with crates of drinks and a nine-gallon keg of Victoria Bitter, and among them was the pretty blonde girl who had been with Sam on the night I arrived. She took no notice of me at all, but to my surprise she looked at Jack in a cool, half-mocking sort of way and said, " Hallo, so you did find him? " and Jack nodded, still very watchful and poised on his feet, and Sam swung around and said, " Now what the devil *is* this all about, Jess? " and she shrugged and turned away and suddenly I knew that " Jess " and the " peroxided sheila " at the Gallery who had told Jack where I was were one and the same person, and I clawed through my humiliation and shame to say, " It's all right . . . I'm sorry . . . this is my brother—this is my brother Jack," and then everybody was pushing into the room and making a lot of noise as they put down their burdens, and staring with amused curiosity at Jack, and Sam was saying, " But my dear Stunsail, I never knew you even *had* a brother. What did you say his name was? Jibboom? Topgallant? My dear Stunsail's brother "— he held out his hand—" welcome to the Spring Street Saturnalia. Your name doesn't matter. Whatever we are now, we shall be under jury-rig before the night is out! "

Jack was still tensed and watchful, but I could see that he was a little bewildered too. His handshake with Sam was cordial enough. And Sam beamed at him. Sam liked to meet things full on, too. He tossed an instruction over his shoulder —" For heaven's sake, Jess, do open a window or two; the place stinks like a tarts' shop! "—and then he clapped Jack on the shoulder in the friendliest possible way and said, " You just make yourself absolutely at home, Taffrail old cock, while the rest of us organise the orgy."

" His name is Jack," I said in a thick hoarse voice.

Sam's laugh snorted out. " Jack, Taffrail, Jibboom, what does it matter? " he said expansively. " Does he know how to broach a niner and get the bung in, that's the point? " He waved at the nine-gallon keg of beer, which had been propped up on the sofa.

" My bloody oath he does! " said Jack enthusiastically.

Had I been a little older or a little wiser I might have known that Jack and Sam Burlington would have got on famously with each other. They were only total opposites superficially; their impulses were similar and they shared the same extravagances.

It was not many minutes before Jack, with the nine-gallon keg working efficiently and the pots filling, was making apologies for his intrusion. " I was just looking for me young brother, see. That's all I came up about. I didn't know you were going to have a bit of a rort here. I mean, I had no intention of pratting in, if you follow what I mean."

The extraordinary thing was that the others all seemed to like Jack, too; they were fascinated by his slang, the tricks he had in rolling a cigarette, the superb self-assurance with which he handled the beer kegs and the pots—he had volunteered himself as " barman "—the stories he told. They seemed not even to notice the smell of his hair nor the absurdity of his clothes. Even so, I was relieved that the girl called Jess was the only one I recognised from the Gallery School. The others—five young men who gave the impression that they lived in good houses in Toorak or South Yarra, and three quite pretty girls—were strangers to me. They remained so. Nobody was ever introduced to anybody else, so I never did learn who they were, and after that night I never saw one of them again. So it didn't matter, anyway, what they might have thought of Jack, although this is not the sort of thing one thinks of at the time.

The opening stages of the party itself are a lost thing now, although fragments linger like flecks of old paint caught in crevices of wood. I remember Jack's puzzled inquiries, and Sam's gleeful explanations, about the name of " Stunsail "; and my own discomfiture at the disclosures, even though only Jack seemed to be at all interested. I remember my alarmed revulsion at the shameless exposed way the girls sat on cushions on the floor, with their knees carelessly apart in their short skirts and the shadowy disturbing gleam of naked thighs above their rolled stockings. I was shocked by their casual acceptance of drinks and cigarettes, by the candour of their conversation, by their abandoned submission to kissing and petting.

I cannot be sure now whether my withdrawal from the party was because of all this, and voluntary, or whether Jack had some hand in it. Up to a point he had entered into the spirit of the occasion, but he was still watchful, and I think he remained suspicious for quite some time both of his surroundings and of the company he was keeping; it is possible that these suspicions, imposed upon his voluntary guardianship of me and his earlier opinions of Sam and his studio, set up a curious paradoxical grimness in his own mind, and that it was he who, feeling that I was too young and too inexperienced to be a participant in a festival which even he was not too sure about, tactfully suggested my retirement. I do remember that when one of the girls chided me for not drinking it was Jack who said, quite firmly, " He don't touch the stuff, and he don't smoke, and he don't have a thing to do with sheilas."

Whatever the reason, I found myself in the little bedroom with the door closed against the gradually mounting hubbub of wild conviviality. It is a troubling and sometimes alarming thing to have to follow the course of a party through a closed door; the perspectives of behaviour get hopelessly out of true; the conclusions drawn tend to be over-dramatic. Wrong inferences are read into overheard fragments of conversation, and even wronger ones into the gaps of silence. There is no validity in trying to follow with cold logic the uninhibited course of other people's gaiety; a sober person is always hopelessly out of depth at a drunken party, and if he is there behind a closed door, so much the worse for him.

After a time I stretched out on Sam's bed and tried to sleep, but a jangling discord kept me tense and vigilant. I was racked by nerves, by panic, by shame, and, it must be admitted, by an overwhelming curiosity. At one moment I would be fiery with shame wondering what errors of taste or manners my brother was committing; the next moment my brain would be reeling with the pictures of the debaucheries my imagination would fashion. There was no harmony nor even continuity in the sounds that drifted through the closed door. They were separate discordances, each with its own implicit and alarming meaning—the sudden slamming of a

door, the sharp high-pitched scream of a girl, inexplicable
jets of uncontrolled hilarity, the crash and tinkle of breaking
glass, the shrill racketing gabble of dispute, thickening voices,
grown hoarse and louder, all talking at once, the wailing of
the phonograph suddenly cut off with the rasping croak of the
needle sliding across the grooved wax, questions uncompleted
and answers unheeded, the sound of a girl hysterically sobbing, the rhythmic shaking of the floor to the Charleston
beat . . . " *Yes, sir, that's my baby ; no, sir, not just maybe ;
yes, sir, that's my baby now . . .*" Jack's voice singing in
vaudeville cockney, " *They've dug up Father's grave to lay a
sewer . . .*" Claps and thunderclaps of undisciplined laughter,
the sound of a bottle rolling, the thud of a piece of furniture
overturning or of a body falling. . . .

It must have been hours later when I realised that the
raucous bedlam had changed into something else a duo-
logue, quite muted, slow-voiced and thick, and as I strained
my ears to listen I realised it was Jack and Sam Burlington.

They were obviously talking about Sam's painting on the
easel, because Jack was saying, slowly and carefully, as if each
word had to be chosen with great particularity: " That's her
there, though, isn't it, in that picture of yours?"

" Jess? Yes." The words came from Sam's mouth as
" Jesh " and " yesh." There was a long pause before he spoke
again, now with a melancholy intonation. " Shavagely dish-
appointed, ol' cock," he said. " Shavagely. Shall put a
palette knife through damn' thing firsht thing t'morrow.
Will, y'know. Don't believe in likeneshes, Taffr'l, ol' cock.
No good. Y'knew it was Jesh, eh? No good. Pity."

" 'Course I haven't seen her in the buff like that," Jack
said. He spoke thoughtfully and even more slowly than he
usually did, but his words came out without much slurring ;
he seemed to be standing up to it better than Sam. " You
mean t'tell me," he went on, " she strips off an' sits around
starko and lets you paint her like that, without a stitch?"

" Nasherally, ol' cock. Nasherally. Quite 'nother matter in
bed. Quite different. Art is art, o' cock. *Arsh longa vita
brevis.* Latin tag. 'Propriate. Art is long, o' cock, an' life
is short. An' Jesh is Jesh. Yesh, sir, thash my baby. Jesh.
Look at her over there, eh. Jush *look* at her ! Beau'ful girl.
Talent too. No morals. Wassit matter? She'd sleep with

you. Me. Anybody. *Arsh longa vita brevish.* Mushn't de-
ceive ourselves, Jack o' cockalorum. Mush pull ourselves
t'gether. Too friv'lous. Tha's it. Friv'lous. 'S-where you'n
me are wrong, Taffr'l ol' cock. Too friv'lous. Need purpose.
Earnestness . . . tha's it. Tha' brother o' yours got the right
idea, y'know? Not friv'lous, see, not friv'lous. . . ."

" Sonk, though," said Jack thickly.

"Dishagree," slurred Sam. " Dishagree categorically.
Categorically," he repeated as if surprised that he had been
able to pronounce it.

My face was burning as I tiptoed to the door, and very
quietly opened it an inch or two. They were seated side by
side, cross-legged on the carpet amid a litter of bottles,
glasses, ash-trays, spilt puddles of beer, broken glass, the
upended keg, and the unconscious bodies of all the other
guests, who had passed out in the chairs, on the sofa, on the
floor and even under the table. Jess was sitting bolt upright
against the wall, with her head back against a door hinge and
her eyes tightly closed. Jack and Sam looked like the two
survivors of a massacre. Both had empty beer glasses. They
were holding them very stiffly in front of their faces, peering
at them with owlish intensity.

" Been a sonk ever since he was a kid," Jack said to his
glass solemnly.

Sam in turn addressed his empty, froth-encrusted glass.
" But not friv'lous anyway," he said. " Not like ush. Wasser
matter with him?"

" Nothin'," said Jack. " Kid's all right. Jus' sonky, that's
all."

" What d'you care?"

" He's my brother, isn't he?"

" What d'you care?" Sam repeated.

" First sheila he goes out with," said Jack, " he'll either
pick up a dose, or he'll get her up the duff, or she'll march
him up the altar quick as a rat up a rope. Either that or he'll
end up a tonk."

" *Arsh longa vita brevish,*" Sam said profoundly.

Although there were many nights when I slept on the sofa in
Sam's studio, that first party evidently established a tacit
precedent, and whenever Sam gave a party, or was more

privately entertaining Jess or one of his other girls, it was unmistakably conveyed to me that I should remove myself. On these nights I would sleep on a park bench in the Fitzroy Gardens.

After the first few days the whole adventure proved dismally unsatisfying. I resented the discomfort and inconvenience, and with every day that passed I grew more homesick. The typewriter remained in Sam's studio, but I found myself unable to concentrate when I was there and the article on the Hobart Town whalers, which I had begun with such confidence, remained unfinished. I no longer went to the Newspaper Room or the Public Library, and I stopped visiting the wharves. At Klebendorf's I worked without much spirit but more conscientiously. I regularly attended the Life Class but my work gave no satisfaction either to Barnaby Stanton or myself.

Jack, who had got a job delivering on a baker's round, would meet me once a week in Fitzroy Gardens—he never visited Sam's place again—and I would give him the money to take to Mother, and we would talk for a while or go to a newsreel theatre, and although I always prayed that he would suggest I go back home he never did, and for some reason I never dared suggest it myself. Not to him. After a while I found myself hoping that Mother or somebody in the family would become seriously ill, or have an accident, or that some terrible domestic calamity would happen which would necessitate my returning. But nothing like this occurred and Jack seemed to treat my exile in the most off-hand way.

I was unable to come to grips with any single aspect of the situation in which I found myself. Sam's ebullient prophecies had curdled and soured. I did sleep on park benches and occasionally I did eat sausages-and-mashed at his café in Russell Street, but I met no harlots and visited no dosshouses and wrote no epics and was not arrested for vagrancy. After a while I suspected that I had become something of a bore and a nuisance to Sam Burlington, and so I began to visit the studio less and less frequently, but this left me with that much more time in which to savour, bitterly and morosely, my own loneliness and misery.

The only thing of importance that happened concerned the *Morning Post*. They had two of my earlier articles, which they had accepted but had not yet published, and since anonymity had by this time lost its point I wrote to the magazine editor suggesting that the pseudonym of "Stunsail" should be discarded in favour of my own name. The articles appeared on two successive Saturdays under the name of David Meredith. A week later Jack brought me a letter which had been delivered at home. It was from the newspaper, and signed by a Bernard Brewster, magazine editor. There was a subject, the letter said, which he would like to discuss with me and nine o'clock on a Wednesday night would be a good time if it suited my convenience.

I presented myself at the inquiry-desk in the impressive marble lobby of the *Morning Post* building. A man wearing a green celluloid eye-shade telephoned my name, nodded, and directed me to the lift, and when I got out at the third floor a boy of about my own age was waiting to escort me to Mr. Brewster's office. We went down a long corridor smelling of linoleum-wax and ink and paper, broken by many doors of frosted glass. I could hear the faint, distant rumble of machines and the familiar chatter of linotypes. The smell of wet ink became more heady.

The boy knocked on one of the doors of frosted glass, opened it, and motioned me to enter. I walked into a big room lined by books behind glass. A broad-shouldered fat man sat in his shirt-sleeves behind a huge glass-topped desk littered with books and papers and proofs on spikes. He had a shock of white, silky hair and a ruddy face with heavy dewlaps folding into his several chins. He wore thin mauve braces.

He looked up, frowned at me and the other boy, waved an impatient hand, and growled, "Later. Later, boy. Not now. I'm expecting a caller."

"This is Mr. Meredith, sir," the boy said. "He has an appointment."

The fat man's hand sank very slowly to the desk. He stared at me so fixedly, and for so long, that I could feel the hot blood colouring my face as ruddily as his. His neat chubby fingers stroked gently backwards and forwards along the edge of the blotter. I heard the boy go out and close the door behind me.

" Are—you—Stunsail? " he said at last, spacing each word carefully in a thick, growly voice.

" Yes, sir," I managed to get out. " Well . . . I . . . I'm David Meredith, sir." I tried to smile, and immediately wished I hadn't. He bent his head and began to stare very intently at the edge of his desk. He had brought his hands up in front of his face, and his fingers were slowly stroking at his temples.

" How old are you? " he asked, without looking at me.

" Sixteen, sir," I said.

" Take that chair there," he said. " Sit down." He lowered his hands to his thighs and tilted his head back, and stared hard at something on the ceiling.

" Largely because of an article you wrote for us," he said, addressing whatever it was he saw up there, " the *Post* has decided to organise a kind of annual race between these rather picturesque Bass Strait timber schooners and ketches which you dealt with in that—er—that piece of yours." He rubbed tiredly at his eyes. " We—er—we thought you might be able to help us. Preliminary articles and so on."

" Yes, sir," I mumbled nervously.

He squirmed his fat body as if his underwear was pricking him. His head came down slowly, almost reluctantly, and he fixed me with a soft dazed gaze from eyes that were moistly brown. " It was our impression," he said mournfully, " that you were a retired sea captain. A sailing-ship man. An old shellback."

I felt there was nothing I could say to this. I felt guilty and uncomfortable. I reddened again under his dismal appraisal.

" And you are "—he cleared his throat carefully—" you are sixteen, you say? "

I nodded dumbly.

" Fascinating! " He said the word as if it were an obscenity. But it seemed to clear some cloudiness and despair from his mind, because he suddenly smiled at me, and his face immediately was amiable and friendly, but this was only for an instant for he folded his arms across the blotter and sank his head on them, and his shoulders began to shake, to shake more and more convulsively until his whole body was shuddering like a huge jelly, at first silently, and then with great choking gasps of laughter mixed up with racking fits of coughing. When he finally lifted his head his eyes were streaming and his cheeks were shining-wet and there was a damp patch on the blotter. It took him a minute or more to get his breath, and then he said, " Tell me, boy, why—why did you . . . call yourself . . ."—and he seemed to choke trying to get it out—" *Stunsail?*" he exploded.

" I—I don't know, sir," I said disconsolately.

" Stunsail!" he repeated in a tone of wondering amazement.

In stricken silence I watched his face go redder, but although a spasm or two shook his body he was able to control himself and gradually the kindly expression settled back on his face.

" Anyway, Meredith," he said in a tone that was suddenly brisk and pleasant, "you seem to know a great deal about ships and shipping. Even if you are not the Ancient Mariner I had envisaged, the old shellback! Not even a *young* shellback, eh? What do you do, boy? Are you still at school?"

" No, sir. I work in a lithographic studio."

He gave me a long, searching look, as if he was convinced that I was lying. " How long have you been there?" he asked.

" Almost two years, sir."

"Like it?"

" Well . . . it's—it's all right, sir."

Again he gave me that long careful scrutiny.

" You write well, boy," he said. " For a youngster you write very well. I enjoy your pieces, even if you do have a weakness for splitting the infinitive. Have you ever considered journalism as a career? I mean as a full-time thing, not just as a contributor?"

" Well, no . . . not really . . . I don't——"

" Think about it," he said crisply. " Clearly you have a bent for it. We could start you off here on the *Post*. On the shipping round would be your place, obviously. Sixteen, eh? Hmm, it *is* a little young, unless you began as a copy-boy. In the normal course our cadet-reporters are older. We like to take them from one of the public schools, or the University. Two years, you say? Good heavens, you started work at fourteen then? Fantastic! Tell me about it."

"I—I couldn't come here to work, sir, because I'm apprenticed, you see," I told him, "and it'll be another four years before I get out of my time."

"Hmm." He put his fingertips together and studied them thoughtfully. "Quite a long time. Your father, of course, could buy you out of your indentures. Would he want to do that, do you think?"

"I don't think he would, sir," I said, trying to imagine it. "He—he doesn't approve of my writing."

"Really? How extraordinary." He put his thumbs behind his mauve braces and adjusted them more snugly across his shoulders. "Well, the matter can wait, there's no urgency about it, since you are still only a boy. And if at some later stage you feel like working for us you can always get in touch with me. In the meantime just keep on with the articles. On the educational side, a public school education or a university degree are not strictly essential, however desirable. Legally we can only insist on the cadet having his Intermediate Certificate. You took your Intermediate, of course?"

"Oh yes, of course, sir," I lied.

"All right. You think about it. And now, Mr. Stunsail Meredith, supposing we get down to our muttons and talk about this Bass Strait race of ours. . . ."

When Jack and I went through the gate into Fitzroy Gardens I knew that I was beaten. The southerly had dropped but the cold wet air it had swept in seemed to lie on the lawns and in the still puddles on the paths. The park benches, wet from the last shower, looked grimly cheerless: little pearly drops of rain were still running from the wood and falling to the soggy trampled mush of fallen leaves that smeared the asphalt with red and golden stains. The tall poplars lining the paths were almost bare, grey and scratchy against a colourless, washed-out sky, and the damp air had flattened the smoke from the smouldering mounds of autumn leaves so that all the distances of the park were concealed behind an opaque blue haze. The smells of wet earth, decaying vegetation, and pungent smoke combined towards a chilling sense of melancholy and finality. I knew with a sudden certainty that I would not spend one more night in Sam's studio, nor one more night on a hard, cold bench.

"Let's go back the other way," I said to Jack. "I want to have a look at something up in King Street."

"What! That's right over the other side of town!"

"It doesn't matter. Come on." When we were out of the park and into the street I said, "How's the job with the baker?"

"It's a fair cow," he said. "Got to be at the bakehouse at four o'clock, two hours before the bloomin' sun comes up. Got to clean the stables, wash down the van, load it up, harness up the laziest flamin' mare you've ever seen, then run in an' out of houses with a basket that weighs a bloomin' ton until your legs nearly drop off. He's such a mean stingy bastard he'll only pay two carters an' we don't get through our rounds till four in the afternoon. Twelve hours a day, six days a week, he pays you four lousy quid, no overtime, and he docks your money if you pinch a yeast-bun!"

We went to the shabby top end of King Street, where there was a whole block of sordid little shops which served as rural labour exchanges. The window of each shop was smeared over inside with streaky whitewash; the outside surface was covered with a peeling skin of glued-up squares of coarse wrapping paper on which was crudely scrawled the details of jobs available in the country districts—jobs for shearers and shearers' cooks, for general farm-hands, for timber-cutters, fruit-pickers, wheat-lumpers, drovers, boundary-riders, general rouseabouts, married couples, farm domestics, sleeper-cutters, mine workers, engine hands. Outside every shop a greasy paste-pot stood on a packing-case, and at intervals someone would come out from one shop or another and slap up another announcement, or sometimes to mark a big red cross on an earlier announcement to signify that the job had been filled.

There were a good many seedy, shabby men all along the seedy, shabby block, propped against the telegraph poles and walls and doorways, morose individuals or apathetic groups that talked desultorily or rolled cigarettes or borrowed "the makings." The impression they gave was of a kind of mass idleness, the way seamen look outside a shipping office or wharfies waiting for a pick-up, although these men all looked shabbier and there was something in their pinched, suspicious

faces that seemed deliberately to exclude hope. There was a
constant movement among them, not hurrying, a shuffling up
and down the block to check on each deletion and there would
always be one among them to offer some curt observation
about the condition of the shearing-sheds at Yackandandah
or the state of the roads around Mount Elephant or the way
the fruit-pickers were treated at Shepparton. There was a kind
of purpose in it, though, because every now and then one of
them would see something to his liking, and he would slouch
into one of the shops in a studiedly casual, off-hand way, and
a few minutes later he would come out stuffing a paper into
his pocket and he would walk off down King Street very
quickly, and another cross would be marked across one of the
still-damp sheets.

They don't hire rural labour that way any more, of course,
because all the grubby little shops were swept away a couple
of years later when the depression struck, and there were no
spare jobs going up in the bush or anywhere else, but that was
the way it was then.

"What's the bloomin' big idea?" said Jack. "What are
we doin' up here?"

"I just thought it was time you looked around for another
job," I said. "What you're doing now doesn't sound much.
What about the bush?"

"Eh?" He glanced at me sharply.

"I think it's time you tried it in the bush. You can't stand
the job you've got, and you say you're sick of living at home.
Well? You see, Jack, I think it's about my turn to hold the
fort."

He thought about this while he rolled a cigarette.

"You still *want* to go up the bush, don't you?"

"Wouldn't mind," he said, and licked the cigarette paper.
"Be a change from that flamin' bakery round." He spat out
the tobacco shreds and said, "What about you, though?"

"I'll be all right. I said I think it's my turn."

He nodded. "You'd be all right at home now, you know.
I keep on telling Mum you're all right, and she still thinks
you're staying at the Y.M.C.A., but she misses you a bit, I
think. And things are different now, you know. She thinks
the sun shines out of you now they're printing those things of

yours in the paper. She's always over the back fence skiting
to Mrs. Gillon or Mrs. Hatrick about you. You'd think you
were the bloomin' editor the way she goes on."

"Yes, but what about Dad?"

"Ah, he just wanted to know what you were doing with
the money they pay you. I told him you were keeping a
chorus girl from the Tivoli. He nearly had a blue fit! So I
took pity on him and said you were saving up to buy a
steam-yacht, and he damned near knocked my block off! Oh,
I wouldn't worry about the Old Man. Anyway, he's building
himself a new wireless, a great big six-valve superheterodyne
thing, and most of the time he's got his bowels in a tangle
over that." He nudged me suddenly. "Look there's not a bad
one." A hard-faced man with broken veins all over his nose
had just finished pasting up a grey, glue-sodden sheet. Jack
read it aloud: "Wimmera District. Wheat farm, two thous-
and acres, small mixed stock, unmechanised, six-team com-
bine. Young, sober, industrious general rouseabout wanted.
Separate quarters, Sundays off. Four-pounds-ten a week, all
found. Twelve miles from Dimboola railway station. Second-
class rail fare provided. Starts June first."

"You've always wanted to try the Wimmera, too," I said.

"Wouldn't mind givin' it a go."

"And better money than you're getting here."

"With keep chucked in. So I could still send Mum *her*
money and have enough for smokes and a schooner or two
and five bob each way on the nags of a Saturday. You know,
I think I might give it a burl."

Neither of us was aware of it at the time, but that was an
important ratchet in Jack's destiny. It was that job in the
Wimmera that closed the door upon his youth forever, that
gave him the woman who was to become his wife, that eventually would move him into days of disaster.

When he came out of the shop his face was one big grin.
"Thanks, nipper," he said.

"For what? It's my turn, isn't it?"

When we got to Young and Jackson's pub he insisted on
taking me into the bar and bought a pot of beer for himself
and a glass of sarsaparilla for me, and cracked jokes about the
big nude painting of Chloe, and his happiness was so obvious
that I began to feel good about what I had done; although

up to that point an uneasy guiltiness had nagged at me
because the whole thing had been done on a kind of false
basis. I'd made him sign up for the Wimmera job only
so that I would have an excuse for going home. Not because
I wanted to accept responsibility at home or do Jack a good
turn, but only because I could no longer face a continuance
of discomfort and inconvenience and cold and loneliness.
June the first interested me far less because of its being the
day when Jack would begin working on a farm than for
another reason; it was also when a Melbourne winter would
begin.

Jack wanted to go on drinking so I left him in the bar and
I picked up a Yellow Cab and went up to Sam Burlington's
studio and got my typewriter.

CHAPTER 8

The months that immediately followed Jack's departure have
run together in a peculiar way; they have the dimension of
experience but not of time; what remains is a sort of luminous, enduring calm unrelated to days or weeks or the markings on a calendar. I am reminded of a long summer afternoon that Cressida and I shared on the grass beneath the
elms at Bray, not far from the lych-gate of the church, from
where we could still hear the soft slow dip and splash of
punt-poles along the Thames and the parties picnicking on
the banks, or we could watch or not watch the white figures
at the cricket pitch and the fieldsmen on the green and the
crowds in indolent movement around the pavilion. It was a
still, golden day that seemed to extend itself in an endless
tranquillity towards no gloaming; even the darkening of the
shadows and the movement of the rooks were only variations
on a theme of peace; there was no commitment to a possibility of night.

So it was in that curious time that stands exactly midway
between two wars. The world was so sure of itself then.
Everyone was busy, prosperous, snug, complacent, convinced
that nothing could disturb security or the solid reassurances of
progress. The golden afternoon of benevolent certainties

would be forever protracted. Dusk could be held off indefinitely. There would be no night. Not even in the wilderness
was there any prophetic voice to give foreboding that within
two years the underpinnings of an entire world would brutally
be wrenched away.

So if I was lulled into a false sense of security in that
period, I can hardly claim uniqueness. Complacency is one
of the more insidious forms of self-deception, and I think it
is this that explains my error of judgment. I saw as something
profound and permanent a change in my life which, in fact,
turned out to be both superficial and temporary; the thing of
telling significance, which would mark my career forever
and leave a cicatrice upon my soul, I never saw at all.

After Jack went to Dimboola we moved his bed out into
the sleep-out, and I had the room all to myself at last. I
bought a long work-table and put it where the bed had been,
and on it I set out the big Remington and all my note-books
and papers. Nothing had to be concealed any longer.

Jack each week from his pay sent mother a postal money-
order for two pounds, but except for the one letter he wrote
to me nearly a year later he sent no news of himself.

The house was quieter now and I was able to work with
undisturbed energy. There had been a kind of tacit agreement
about not discussing in any detail my absence from home.
Justification had proved to be on my side. Dad, I think, was
secretly ashamed of his part in the affair; with the earnings
from my writings I had bought a new wireless-set for the
house and I had paid for the old Chev to be re-ducoed, and
Dad's hostilities, if he still harboured any, were well concealed. Mother was relieved and happy to have me back, and
about her only references to my exile were in the form of
remarks like, " There, I bet you didn't get a pudding like *that*
at the Y.M.C.A. canteen," or " Heavens, Davy, who did you
have to *pick up* after you at that Y.M.C.A. hostel? " (Jack
had done his work well; she was perfectly sure that I had
spent all my time away as a guest of the Y.M.C.A.)

My visit to Mr. Brewster, at the *Morning Post*, had had
splendid repercussions, and he would often commission special
articles from me. With these, plus my own contributions,
there were few Saturday editions of the *Morning Post* that
did not carry some feature or other by David Meredith.

In my new standing an aura of benevolence seemed to extend almost everywhere. At work my articles were discussed and approved—Paul Klein saw me as his protégé and was quite puffed up about it—and even old Joe Denton held me in a curious kind of mystified respect. An odd thing is that this new self-esteem generated in me a greater humility in other directions; I tried much harder at Klebendorf's and the standard of my work improved very distinctly; I became more conscientious about the Life School classes. Unfortunately, I had never really got over the excruciating embarrassment of my initiation to my first nude female model, even though she had been a grotesquely unappealing middle-aged woman who had lolled revoltingly on the throne with two leathery, pendulous breasts sagging to a wrinkled little pot-belly. Even so, unless I knew in advance that the exercise was to be a study in the draped figure, I generally skipped classes when a girl or a woman was modelling. In fact this often suited me, for another diversion around this time had given me unusual new interests.

The fact was that all my writing had not been as successful as my things for the *Morning Post*; in other directions there had been a couple of disconcerting setbacks. My book on the history of the wool-clippers had been completed, sent off to a publishing house, and curtly rejected. A novelette which I had written about the South Seas blackbirders, called *Pearls of Maiëta*, received equally unflattering treatment. I saw suddenly, with some dismay, that in the sailing-ship theme there might be a bottom to the pot. Escape, I began to think, might lie in a totally different direction. With a glib audacity which I now find quite surprising I reached back more than four thousand years in time. I decided I would be an Egyptologist!

My imagination had been greatly fired some time earlier by the accounts of the opening of King Tutankhamen's tomb which were printed on one of the three volumes of *Wonders of the Past* which I had bought at Coles's book sale with my first cheque from the newspaper. Gradually I had come to dream of an occasion when some eminent archæologist, Sir Flinders Petrie himself perhaps, would come visiting Australia on a desperate search for a brilliant youthful assistant, and in this dream—for the dreams of the young have this quality of a lingering sadness—I saw myself shyly but confidently offering my services. My lack of education would be brushed aside. What would an Intermediate Certificate matter? . . . here was a young man trained in drawing and painting and copying, skilled in wrĩting, who could also *read the hieroglyphics of Ancient Egypt*! This I saw as the crucial asset, overriding every other consideration, and much of my spare time was now devoted to the specialised reading-annexes at the Public Library to which enrolment as an art student gave one privileged access. Here I pored over scholarly monographs or diligently studied the facsimile they had there of the ancient papyrus of the scribe Ani known as *The Book of the Dead*. (It is within the frame of time that our attitudes are shaped: two minutes away from where I sat I could be repelled and terrorised by a shrivelled head in a glass display-case or by a sexless old lady apathetically naked upon a model throne, yet in the gruesome rites of Ancient Egypt, in the foulness of the embalming practices and the nightmare grotesqueries of its Pantheon, I found only beauty and wonder and delight!)

Within six months I *was* able to read and to copy the strange language of that long-dead civilisation, but, alas! neither Sir Flinders Petrie nor any other eminent Egyptologist ever did visit Australia on such a quest, and after a time I went back to my sailing-ships.

These various activities, however, occupied almost every moment of my time in this long brimming period of treacherous stability. Without Jack there to goad and prod me I gave no thought whatever to girls or to going out. Nothing disturbed my complacency. Within the safe, comforting shelter of the wire fences and the privet hedges, I could find everything I needed in the times of an earlier century when ships moved in eternal beauty under pyramids of canvas, or in the infinitely more remote and thrilling world of lotus columns and stiff staring pharaohs and mummy wrappings and funerary boats on a great strange river. . . .

The world then, as I have said, was poised exactly midway between two disastrous wars: I see now that I, too, stood in a kind of self-created vacuum exactly in the middle of two balanced points of experience. The First World War had ended ten years before, and ten years later the Second would begin. I had been born seventeen years before; it would be exactly another seventeen years, and I would be thirty-four, before I would be able to even partially disentangle myself from the toils which, all unwittingly, I was already beginning to fashion for myself.

I was not prepared for it. In a special sense I was not prepared for anything. I had turned seventeen and I had not taken a girl out, even to the local cinema. I would not have known how one went about it. My familiarities extended beyond the reach of true time and I was intimate with shadows, and the shadows had the heads of ibis and jackal and hippopotamus and cat and crocodile and cobra, and their names were Anubis and Thoth and Set and Sekhmet and Bast and Isis. . . .

My recall to the realities of where I was came with the shock of a sudden, unexpected blow.

I know it was a Saturday morning, because I had bought my copy of the *Morning Post* at the Kooyong Road tram stop, knowing that one of my articles was to be printed that day. I turned at once to the magazine section, and read it with smug pleasure.

It was the format of the newspaper that postponed the shock. The *Post* was a broadsheet of conservative, old-fashioned type, and the front page carried only classified advertisement columns, mostly Deaths, Births, Funeral Announcements, and In Memoriam notices. These last I always liked to read because they were often very funny, for the bereaved advertisers would usually accompany their memorials with short verses of their own composition, which were regarded as more " original " than the stereotyped and succinct prose tributes like " *Still Missed*," or " *An Empty Place In All Our Hearts*." This trivial detail recurs to me most vividly—and I can even remember the verse that tickled my fancy on this particular morning:

> *Gabriel blew his trumpet,*
> *St. Peter shouted, " Come!"*
> *The Gates of Heaven opened*
> *And in walked Mum.*

Amused at the picture of Mum moving into Paradise, firmly corseted, wearing sensible shoes and her best felt toque

and a fur tippet, and carrying her shopping-bag on her arm,
I turned to the centre section of the newspaper, and there, on
what was always called the " cable page," two half-tone
blocks, one above the other, arrested my attention, for staring
out at me from the grey columns were Sam Burlington and
his girl-friend Jess!

There is always a sense of incredulity evoked by this sort of
thing, when the taken-for-granted anonymity of a newspaper
is fragmented. The world of half-tone blocks is peopled by
strangers: the kidnapper, the murderer and his victim, the
absconded embezzler, the jilted sweetheart, the unscrupulous
financier, all these are people *we* never know. So it was a
long moment before I could take it in: as if the machinery
of cognition had slowed down to deliberately postpone com-
prehension. Yet the bald captions on the blocks left no doubt
as to identity. The single-column block said " Samuel Burlington "; the three-column block above it, showing a pretty,
nymph-like girl in a striped bathing costume, with long fair
hair blowing in the wind and a canoe paddle in her hand, was
marked " Jessica Wray." And at the top of the page, across
what for the *Post* was the sensational splash of a four-column
headline, the black Cheltenham Bold capitals said: STUDENT
HELD FOR QUESTIONING ON JESSICA WRAY MURDER, and below
this, in smaller type: *Intimacy Admitted: Startling Studio
Disclosures.*

I was appalled . . . I felt dazed and, sick and stunned. I
hardly remember getting off the tram; with my fingers
clenched around the unbelievable newspaper I walked to the
railway station as if in a dream. Legs moved to the crisp,
creased whip of trouser-cuffs, the freshly polished shoes of a
working morning mounted the wooden footbridge, shook a
dead match from a crack, crumpled underfoot a Capstan
package, descended, rang metallically on chaffy asphalt;
through a hundred flickering images, a fluttering scatter of
discarded tram tickets, through legs, shoes, a white clock
embroidered on a burgundy sock, the ferrules of umbrellas,
attaché-cases, a strapped bundle of library books, a fluted
Thermos-flask, through the mad jump of mundane things
the placards screamed at me from the station bookstall:
STUDENT HELD IN MODEL SLAYING . . . GIRL MURDER SENSATION
. . . " WE WERE LOVERS " SAYS ART STUDENT . . .

It was not until I boarded the train that I began to feel the thing turning in and beginning to invade me. An infinite distress possessed me. The carriage rocked and clattered through the flat suburbs; the shouting of the porters was echoed by the wheels and the name of every station seemed to clang from the steel rails along which we were rushing headlong into horror . . . Elsternwick, Ripponlea, Balaclava, Windsor, Prahran, South Yarra . . .

I was in a second-class smoking compartment. Women never rode in smokers in those days, and at each station more men would get in, and they were all discussing the murder, some of them with gravity, but mostly with coarse jokes and comments, and with lechery in the hard bulging eyes that seemed to roll along the headlines, and across the grey-black stippled facsimile of the girl I knew as Jess. Their words, lively and seditious, jumped from door to window, twined around the smoke wreaths and the chipped mahogany and the string mesh of the luggage-racks and the dead matches and empty cigarette packets beside the cuspidors and the old blotched tourist photographs of Porepunkah and Toolangi. "They arsk fer it, these young ones, the way they carry on. It's no bloomin' wonder . . ." "Wouldn't 've minded if she'd arst *me*; I could've given 'er an inch or two!" "Ha, ha, ha!" "Spare me days, she sounds as if she was a real *one*, though!" "You know wot t'expeck wiv these bo'emian types, though . . ." "Humdinger, I'd say, didn't mind strippin' it off, neither . . ." "Yea, but jist fancy a pretty sheila like that . . . dunno wot the world's coming to, fair dinkum I don't . . ." "These days they think they kin git away wiv anythink, that's the trouble . . ."

The train clattered on through the grimy deserts of suburban rectitude.

The pain of all these memories I set myself deliberately to revive almost a year ago when I came back here to the island from Provence. In the huge old trunk which Cressida once christened "our portable attic" I found the newspaper clippings tucked away inside some old dog-eared note-books, and these yellowing scraps of coarse paper from more than thirty years age are beside me as I try to set this down.

I had not seen an afternoon newspaper on the Friday, so

the story of what had happened had come to me as an absolute surprise. One of the clippings I have preserved (*why*, I wonder?) is from that Saturday morning edition of the *Morning Post*, and this is what had happened:

At some time in the early hours of the previous morning, Jess—I do remember that I could only think of her then as " Jess ": Jessica Wray in an odd way was not really the same person, or was perhaps only a half-tone block after all, and not really a person at all—Jess, then, had been criminally assaulted and strangled to death in a desolate area of sub-urban parkland. Her body had been found by a night-shift worker taking a short cut home behind the St. Kilda football ground, up towards Albert Park Lake. (In this clipping Jess is described as a " slim, beautiful 20-year-old art student, the only daughter of a Camberwell bank manager.") The victim, it was alleged, had spent the previous evening in the company of a fellow art student, Samuel Justin Burlington, aged nineteen, of Spring Street. They had gone to the theatre to see *No, No, Nanette!* Burlington, questioned later at Russell Street police headquarters, admitted that the girl had accom-panied him after the performance to his studio apartment, which is close to the theatre. There they had had " a drink or two," but had quarrelled. According to Burlington's testi-mony he had wanted to " patch it up," but the girl insisted on leaving, saying that she intended to spend the night with a girl friend who lived at St. Kilda. Burlington walked with her to the Flinders Street railway station, saw her through the ticket barrier, and walked back to his studio. He went to bed but was still awake at 12.35 a.m., when, according to his account, Miss Wray telephoned him from a public call-box at St. Kilda. " She felt mean about our quarrel," Burlington stated, " and now it was she who wished to patch it up." By this time the last train had gone but she suggested taking a taxi-cab and returning to Burlington's apartment. She added that she was also a little worried and frightened because she thought a man who had been in the same compartment on the train from Flinders Street was following her. Burlington said that by this time he had become " rather impatient and irritated with her." He told her she was imagining things, and advised her to go to her friend's place for the night and they would " talk about it later."

Here there was a cross-heading in bold black type, POSED NAKED, and below this was printed an alleged admission by Burlington that "he had been intimate with Miss Wray over a period of some eighteen months." He also confessed to having used her "on a number of occasions" as a nude model for his paintings. She had, he alleged, posed naked for other artists as well. A large portrait in oils of the victim, completely unclothed, was found by police in Burlington's apartment, together with a number of obscene pictures and publications.

The story ended with: "Burlington is being held at police headquarters for further questioning."

As I remember it now, it was the awful plausibility of the situation that began to assail me through the chilled numbing sense of horror and disgust with which I read the account through the coarse and callous chorus of the men around me —"Well, if you want to be the village bike, you've gotter expect to be ridden!" "Ha, ha ha!" And with this came a disturbing niggle of thought about my own participation. The world which these men in the swaying compartment gibed at and condemned was a world in which *I* was involved . . . this youth and this girl who were the pivotal figures of scandal and tragedy were friends of mine . . . I had slept in that very studio, commented on that very painting! It was not at this point that I began to feel my own security disintegrating, but it was here, I think, in this shadowy sense of involvement, of being invaded from outside by dangerous forces of association, that my moral corruption began.

I know that before the train reached Flinders Street a taint of nightmare began to intrude into my thoughts. I was staring out through the carriage window and against the white rush of movement I saw only Jess. The image kept changing. I saw a half-mocking smile amid a crowd of faces; a girl on the edge of a sofa, buttoning up a blouse; I saw a thoughtful young student's face behind a falling wing of soft hair halflighted by the reflection from a sheet of paper pinned to a drawing-board; a pretty, lolling, flaxen-haired doll drunkenly asleep with its head against a door-hinge. . . . It was at this point that the texture of nightmare trespassed on my thoughts. She was there, walking ahead of me, half seen in the shadows and lamplight and the windy movements of a deserted night, and mine were the soft and stealthy footsteps that pattered along behind her, down the midnight-emptied pavements, beneath the mottled black splashes of the eucalyptus, furtively across the coarse onion-grass of an empty park towards the cavernous secrecy of the trees. (Perhaps I only like to think this now; that I have made this up to show that I knew of Sam's innocence from the very beginning. Yet the night of that Saturday was the first time I remember having erotic dreams.)

Yes, of course I believed in Sam's innocence. I *must* have done. For it was only the sense of *invasion* that was so disturbing then.

In the studio that morning there was, naturally, much discussion about the case, but to my intense relief it was to Young Joe that they turned with their questions about Sam and Jess; assuming, I suppose, that being younger I would not have known them as well. The discussion in the studio was quite a different thing from the men talking in the railway compartment. These were all decent, respectable people, and there were elements of the tragedy that obviously shocked and disturbed them profoundly. Yet they kept the thing in some sort of balance. They saw nothing shameful in the fact of a girl posing for an artist. There was nothing of prurience in their observations; they were concerned for the proprieties, but not for the hypocrisies.

I ate lunch in the city that Saturday, and then walked along Flinders Street to wait for the first editions of the afternoon papers. The headlines, of course, were bigger. With the crisper, tauter approach of afternoon-paper journalism, the case had become "The Jessica Murder." The victim was referred to as a "nude model" and no longer as an art student, Sam Burlington was a "young bohemian painter." "Our special reporter" was given a whole column in which to describe Sam's studio: "One sensed in these flamboyant and almost fœtid surroundings the atmosphere of the seraglio and a taint of young depravity and irresponsibility that seemed to bear no relationship to the decencies and dignities of Australia's proudest city."

A new and dramatic element had entered the story. It was printed in a separate "box" under the heading *Call-box Riddle*:

Burlington, under police interrogation, continued this
morning to maintain that Jessica had telephoned him
from a public call-box in St. Kilda at 12.35 a.m.

Detective-Inspector Graham Craik, of the C.I.B., who
is in charge of the police investigations, revealed to-day,
however, that for the past six weeks, in the St. Kilda
area, as a check on larrikinism, gang operations, and
housebreaking, all telephone calls made after midnight
from public call-boxes in the district, have been monitored at the exchange.

There was no record, he added, of any call having
been made to Burlington's number from any public
telephone in the municipality.

It is believed that police may ask for Burlington's remand in custody at the City Court on Monday morning,
pending the coroner's inquiry at the City Morgue, to
where Jessica's body has been moved.

Investigations continue meanwhile at the scene of the
tragedy.

Even with this, the storm did not burst in its full fury until
the Monday.

Melbourne then had no Sunday newspapers, and I was
trapped in the terrible hiatus of waiting and not knowing. I
spent as much time as possible away from home, for I was
frightened that Dad or Mother would ask me questions. I
must have spent hours and hours in aimless walking; or perhaps subconsciously there was a kind of guidance in it, a sort
of symbolic " night journey," for I remember standing alone
on the end of the jetty at Point Ormond, from where Jack and
I had watched the cyclone approaching, and crossing the
vacant allotment where we had sheltered in the cement pipes,
and walking up past the new concrete café that had replaced
the old kiosk, and then along through endless blocks of dreary
streets to the golf-links where we had climbed the little knoll
and tobogganed down the onion-grass and talked of Everest,
and where, eleven years later I was to see Cressida for the
first time in my life, cleaning 3.7 shells in a gunpit.

I kept assuring myself that I was safe enough from any
possibility of involvement. I had never told my parents anything about Sam Burlington or the studio in Spring Street.

And journalistic colour had begun to move the picture away from mere art students into a presumably more depraved world of " nude models " and " bohemian painters." There was no reason for alarm. There was nothing that could affect *me*.

What I failed to take into account was the effect of the story on the staid, stiff attitudes of conservative Melbourne. It was as if a vent had opened in the very structure of society, out of which suddenly exploded the violent antagonisms and resentments and prejudices which had smouldered and intermittently spluttered for almost a decade. The whole rebelliousness of youth in conflict with the embitteredness of an older generation was only, I think, a part of it. There was also, I believe, something faintly hysterical in the indignation of the worthy and the virtuous, as if by the very loudness of their cries they might silence their own guilts and conscience in the matter ; as if by concentrating their angers on this target suddenly exposed in all its brazen implications they might find in a clamour of self-righteousness some substitute for lost values and discarded standards. And they resented the intrusion of ugliness into the long, golden afternoon that was to continue forever.

Exposed suddenly before their outraged eyes was the whole inimical world of " young bohemia." Here were the obscene graffiti of the Jazz Age scrawled all over the solid, dignified grey stones of " Australia's proudest city." Here, in shameful exposure, were naked girls posing for depraved young men not even old enough to vote. Here were barefaced admissions of sexual intimacies, of almost Parisian immorality and profligacy and decadence, culminating, as if God had shown his righteous wrath, in the raw brutalities of rape and murder.

In the newspaper of that Monday there was very little that was new to add to the case, but the headlines were inflammatory, and every newspaper fulminated in editorials against youth's lascivious betrayal of its responsibilities. With sickening bad taste, one of the more sensational weeklies devoted half its front page to a reproduction of Sam's painting of Jess naked, giving the last loathsome touch of obscenity by masking out the pubic area of the picture.

Curiously enough, the police, at the formal hearing, asked for an adjournment but no remand in custody, and Sam

Burlington was allowed to go home. I stayed away from Life
Class that night, but I heard later that Sam did not attend
either—nor ever did again. He must have spent the night in
his studio, because somebody told me next day that for half
the night there were press photographers waiting in cars all
the way along Spring Street.

At supper my father was strongly aligned with the virtuous
accusers. Sam Burlington, as far as he was concerned, was
already convicted. " That vile murderous young brute " was
the way he referred to him, and he fed his misogynism on Jess
as a " loose dirty little trollop who deserved everything she
got." I pushed my plate back and began to leave the table,
but he fixed me with a hard, suspicious look.

" You're not mixed up with that sort, are you?"

" For heaven's sake, do I *act* as if I am?" I said.

" You better not be, that's all. It'll be the end of you if you
get yourself mixed up in disgusting carryings-on of that sort."

" I'm not getting mixed up in anything."

" Didn't one of the papers say this young brute goes to the
same art school you go to? The girl was there, too, wasn't
she?"

" I think so."

" What do you mean, you *think*? You either know or you
don't." He glared at me. " Do you know this Burlington?"

" No. Oh, I've seen him occasionally in the classes. He's
in his final year. The seniors don't mix much with us."

" What about that girl?"

I just shook my head and turned away, but as I went out
the door he called after me: " You stay right away from that
sort. Touch pitch, you'll be defiled, remember that!"

Nothing was said about it at breakfast. The alarm clock, set
as always at twenty minutes fast, ticked along among the
canisters and knitted tea-cosies on the kitchen shelf ; Mother,
round as a ball in her shabby red dressing-gown and with her
greying hair loosely pinned up, looked sleepily dishevelled as
she pottered around the stove in a reek of frying bread ; a
crusty tin loaf and the bone-handled bread knife were on the
oil-cloth in a scatter of crumbs: a fly delicately treaded the
beaded doily that veiled the big brown milk jug ; Dad, morose
and taciturn as on any other morning, sat in his braces and his

grey flannel undershirt, noisily sipping, as he always did, his
second cup of tea from the saucer, champed on his food,
looked up resentfully, growled, " Get a move on, Min, for
God's sake! " and Mother said, as she had said on every
morning I could remember, " You're all right, that clock's
twenty minutes fast." She forked the bread, clattered plates
in the sink, moved over to the boot-box to polish Marj's
school shoes. A blowfly, activated by the kitchen warmth,
buzzed and pinged at the window-screen, and Dad rose with
a scowl and pulled down the blind and with his thumb against
the stiff material crushed the insect's life out against the wire,
and the dead fly dropped to the window-sill and lay on its
back with its legs stiff. Dad knocked it along the sill and on
to the floor with the handle of the bread knife. The certitudes
of another morning surrounded me, definite and unchanging
and reassuring.

It was about ten o'clock when old Klebendorf came up to
the studio. " De boy iss being vanted," he said to old Joe
Denton in his thick, gruff German accent, and turned to me
with a heavy sad face and said, " Come. Dere iss somebody
vants to see you."

I was aware of all the others looking at me curiously as I
followed him from the studio, for it was seldom that any of
us was summoned down below. The ancient lift in its battered
iron cage came clanking up like a ghost dragging its chains ;
the old man, standing beside the shuddering wire cables, did
not speak to me as we descended through the roar and
clatter of machines. He took me past the business office and
along the corridor to the travellers' sample-room, opened the
door and motioned me to enter. " Dey vill speak to you," he
said, and shuffled back along the corridor grunting to himself.

There were two men in the room, both wearing belted
gaberdine raincoats. One was a middle-aged, thickset man
with a brown snap-brim hat ; his teeth were clenched on a
stubby, diamond-stemmed bulldog pipe and the heel of his
right hand was grinding plug tobacco in the cupped palm of
his left, and he was looking around with a kind of dull curiosity at the display of posters and showcards and cut-outs and
labels and Steiner's calendars. His companion wore no hat.
He had thin receding black hair slicked back like a shining

caul against his skull. He was tall and thin and youngish and he was staring out at the lane through the barred, sooty windows. At my appearance he half turned his head, gave me one long up-and-down look from a hard brown face, then turned his eyes back to the window. He said nothing then nor at any time later, and I don't think he even looked at me again.

The older man had the big reddish nose of a vaudeville comedian and a heavy but good-natured face, although his very light-coloured eyes gave him a kind of hard, intense look with it.

" Ah, Meredith, is it?" he said amiably, and nodded at me and began filling his pipe.

I waited with an anxious expectancy, but he tamped away at the bowl very carefully, and took two matches to light up properly, and said nothing until the pipe was drawing to his satisfaction. His companion went on staring moodily into the lane.

" This is—not—in any—sense "—the older man spaced the words jerkily through puffs of blue smoke—" an official call. We are from Russell Street," he said without any emphasis. " I am Detective-Inspector Craik. Criminal Investigation Branch."

He paused there, as if for effect, and the effect on me was to keep the words echoing in some dark area of desolation that was cold and treacherous and hostile.

" You'll probably guess what this is about," he went on calmly. " You've been reading the newspapers. Pretty rotten business, eh? That poor wretched girl! You knew her, didn't you? And this chap Burlington, you're a friend of his. Right?"

I tried to say something but my mouth had gone dry and I could only stare at him.

" Don't be frightened, son," he said soothingly. " You mustn't get worried. I said this wasn't in any way official. We aren't involving you, or trying to implicate you in any way, in what is, after all, a thoroughly unpleasant business. You don't even have to answer any questions if you don't feel like it. But there are certain things we're trying to find out, see, and it's just possible you may be able to help us a little. Do you follow me? What do you say, Meredith?"

"I . . . well, yes, of course. I mean, I'll help, sir . . . if I can. But—but he isn't *really* a friend of mine. And I—I hardly . . . well, I hardly even knew—er . . ."

"Jessica Wray?" he prompted me gently.

"I hardly knew her at all, sir."

"We were given to understand, though, that you stayed for quite a few weeks with Burlington. You lived in his studio, didn't you?"

"Well, I didn't. . . . I mean, it wasn't exactly *staying* with him, sir. It was——"

"Now, wait a minute, son." His smile was kindly, his voice reassuring. "You're getting yourself all worked up over nothing. Let me repeat that we're not trying to *involve* you in this. But you see, my lad, you seem to be the only person who has spent any time at all with Burlington in that Spring Street studio place of his, and so——"

"I'm only saying I didn't really *stay* there, sir," I cut in desperately.

"Hold on a sec. Just let me finish what I wanted to say. We thought you might be able to give us some sort of picture of what went on up there. What was *your* impression of the place? For example, was this chap Burlington in the habit of throwing lots of wild parties?"

"I don't know, sir. I don't remember any."

"Were you ever in the place when Burlington and Jessica were there together?"

"I . . . think I was once, sir. I'm not sure."

He smiled at me. "Oh, come on now," he said. "You would have remembered that, I think. She was a very pretty girl, wasn't she? Did you find yourself attracted to her?"

I flushed and shook my head.

"It seems there were a number of young chaps who were," he said and smiled faintly at his pipe. "You say you slept there, but . . . Well, let's put it this way: you haven't really made it clear how it was that you were staying there and yet you were *not* staying there."

"Well, I mean if they had parties or——"

"You said you didn't remember any parties."

"I—I mean if there was company, or she was there with him, I . . . well, I'd be sent away, you see, and——"

"Kicked out, sort of? Eh? Well, then where would you go?"

I looked at him blankly.

"I mean where did you stay on these occasions? Did you go home? Or to a hotel?"

"No, sir."

"Well, what?"

"I—I used to sleep in the Fitzroy Gardens, usually."

"You used to sleep *where*?" He glanced at me sharply.

"Fitzroy Gardens. Oh, and the Y.M.C.A. I went there a few times, too . . . when the weather was bad."

"But otherwise the Fitzroy Gardens? On a park bench, do you mean?"

I nodded miserably.

"But that's where all the down-and-outs go, and the metho drinkers. Didn't it strike you as a funny sort of place for a youngster like you to be? You could have been picked up there, and charged as a vagrant, do you realise that?"

I mumbled something.

He moved his shoulders beneath his overcoat, then turned his back on me. He seemed engrossed suddenly in a mounted display of canned fruit labels. "Did you resent this?" he asked, without looking at me; he was running his forefinger over a Del Monte pineapple label to feel the gold embossing.

"Resent what?"

"Well, being kicked out and made to sleep on a park bench while this very pretty girl and this friend of yours were canoodling up there." He turned slowly and stared at me and his face was no longer amiable. "Didn't you ever wish it was *you* doing the canoodling and not Burlington? That the positions were reversed, so to speak?"

I opened my mouth to protest, but his eyes were pale and frosty and hard and he went on talking at me:

"Listen, son, we have to look for motives in a crime like this, and in the case of this chap Burlington there's a bit of a snag about the motive. You see—now I'm only trying to explain something, do you understand?—you see, in your case we *could* find a kind of motive. If you were secretly in love, say, with this girl and she kept stalling you off, and if on this particular night you were resentful that you'd been kicked out again and made to sleep on a park bench with the drunks and dead-beats, well what would there be to stop you hanging around in Spring Street until the girl came out, then following her home, and taking your revenge?"

"But—but it's months and *months* since I was there!" I gasped in horror. "At the studio or Fitzroy Gardens or anywhere! It's almost——"

"Calm down, son, calm *down*!" He chuckled. His eyes were twinkling and his face was good-humoured again. "I used that as an explanation, that's all. What I'm trying to point out is that in your case there would be a motive for the rape as well as for the killing. Do you follow me? Now Burlington's a slightly different matter. It's possible that if the quarrel they'd had had been a really passionate one he might have followed her down to St. Kilda, and maybe resumed the quarrel, and then in a fit of blind rage he might have strangled her. Would that sort of violence be compatible with his character, do you think?"

"I don't know."

"But then that wouldn't really explain the rape, would it? It seems to me that a chap who's getting all the skirt he wants from his girl-friend, and has been getting it for a year or eighteen months, is hardly likely to think in terms of rape— well, not so far as that particular girl is concerned, anyway. Unless, I suppose, there was something very peculiar in their relationship, or this quarrel they had was a specially violent one. Tell me, Meredith, what did *you* really feel about this relationship they had? Did you feel that they got on well? Or did they quarrel a good deal? Try to remember, son. Did you ever hear them squabbling together? Any threats? Physical violence? Or would you say that they struck you as being genuinely in love with one another?"

"But I *can't* answer these questions, sir!" I said wildly. He had me almost at the point of tears. "I—I just don't know. I tell you he wasn't really a friend of mine. This is the truth! Look, sir," I said desperately, "the other apprentice here, Joe Denton . . . he knows Sam Burlington much better than I do . . . they're in the same class and——"

"Is that so? Well, we may want to have a word or two with him as well later. Did he stay with Burlington too?"

"Well . . . no, I don't think so. But——"

"Ah, well that's really the point we're interested in, isn't it?" He sighed. "I'm sorry you can't help us more. You seem to have got it into your mind, somehow, that we're trying to tangle you up in this. Well, tell me just one thing more, though, Meredith, and then I think we can call it a day. What is your own personal opinion of Burlington. Be frank about it, son. Don't be afraid. What I'm driving at is this . . . would you consider him the sort of person who would follow a girl into a deserted park in the middle of the night, criminally assault her, and then murder her in cold blood?"

"No, sir . . . well, I don't know . . . I mean, if I don't know him really well how is it possible for me to say? I honestly wasn't as friendly with him as lots of others and——"

"All right, son." He cut me short with a wave of his stubby pipe. "You don't have to get upset about this. You're not involved. If the necessity arises we can get in touch with you again, but I shouldn't think that will happen. You can trot along back to your work now. Off you go, son."

The interview had shaken me to the core, so I did not take the lift back to the studio, but went out through the paper store and down the length of the factory to the fire-escape steps at the rear of the building. It was no use the detective telling me I was not involved, because I *was* involved. I was involved in the awful plausibilities of the situation, and I could feel around me the disintegration of everything that I had taken to be secure. I knew that I would have to get a grip on myself before facing the others in the studio, so I trod the circling iron gratings of the steps one by one, very slowly, the way old Steiner and Richter always climbed them, and with every hesitant step another question would assail me. Should I have reported to old Mr. Klebendorf? What should I tell Joe Denton? Were they even now calling Young Joe down to question him, too? And there were more abstract questions that were more terrifying. Would the detectives also go to my home to ask my parents about me? Would the newspapers report the fact that they had come to talk to me? . . . "Detectives of the C.I.B. who are investigating the Jessica Murder to-day questioned David Meredith, aged 17, an art student who was a friend of the murdered girl. Meredith, who works as a lithographic apprentice with a city printing firm, is believed to have harboured a grudge against Jessica, police allege, because he was secretly in love with her and . . ." The imagined possibilities filled me with horror.

Perhaps even now they were suspicious because I had been evasive in my answers. Might it not have been simpler just to have told them that Sam and Jess had been very devoted to each other? . . . that Sam himself was a gentle, kindly, whimsical sort of person who wouldn't have hurt a fly, who would be utterly incapable of raping or strangling? But there had been this panic of denial . . that was it, *the panic* . . . it was this that had jolted me . . . this sense of being invaded and struck down by some blind and heedless force. I was aware of a shape of unsolicited disaster that imperilled me everywhere—at home, at work, in all the securities I had established, in my own soul. And they wanted to tell me that I was *not involved*!

My ordeal was not yet over.

There was an undisguised curiosity in all their faces when I got back to the studio, and Joe Denton said, " What was it? Were you on the mat?"

" No, Mr. Denton." I shook my head. " As a matter of fact, it was a detective. From Russell Street." This made them all sit up. " They're just checking with some of the Life Class students on Sam Burlington."

" But why pick on *you*?"

" Ask me another," I said, and shrugged. " I suppose they just took some names at random from the students' book, and they're checking around them."

" That sounds pretty hit-and-miss, I must say. What did you tell them?"

" Well, what *could* I tell them, Mr. Denton? I just said I thought Sam Burlington was a pretty decent sort of a chap. And I said the girl was his . . . well, you know, they were very fond of each other and all that. I said I didn't think he would do a thing like *that* to her."

" Well, he jolly well wouldn't, either! " said Young Joe loyally. " There's something pretty fishy about all this, if you ask me. It *couldn't* have been Sam."

" Yes, well it's up to the police to find that out, isn't it? " his father said, and that seemed to close the subject.

But about half an hour later the telephone rang on Joe Denton's desk, and he took off the receiver and said, " Who? Yes, he's here. Half a mo." He pushed the telephone to one side. " David, it's for you," he said, in a tone of faint surprise.

I moved in behind his stool with a sinking heart.

The voice was thinned down and faraway, but I recognised the brisk, growly tone: " Ha! is that you, Meredith? Brewster here. Brewster of the *Post.* I'm ringing you up, Meredith, because a thought has just occurred to me. How would you feel about dashing off a quick feature for us?"

" About what, Mr. Brewster?" I asked nervously, acutely conscious of the fact that Joe Denton was only six inches away from me and that his stippling pen was quite motionless in his fingers and that there was not a sound in all the big studio.

" Well, I know you are a student up at this art school. You're in the Life Class, isn't that so? Well, this is the point. I realise this may seem rather off your familiar beat, but it mightn't be at all a bad thing for you to get your teeth into something altogether different. Are you there, Meredith?"

" Yes—yes, I'm listening, sir."

" Briefly, then, you must be perfectly aware of the enormous public interest which this terrible Jessica Wray thing has stirred up. Not so much the crime itself, which is a matter for the police-roundsman. I am thinking of the whole question of how you young art students live, your nude models, bohemian parties, your attitudes to moral values, all that sort of thing. This has suddenly become a subject of immense public concern. Nice subject for you to have a stab at. Am I getting through to you?"

" Yes, sir."

" You should keep it absolutely impartial, you know. We don't want to jump into sensation for sensation's sake, in the way, I am very much afraid, some of our reptile contemporaries have done. Frankly, I can't really believe you youngsters are as despicable as people are trying to make out. There must be work done, dedication, a sense of purpose, genuine beliefs. Give us all that. Let us try to get to the truth of the picture, eh? Don't you think a good, balanced, colourful twelve hundred words from you could make a really excellent feature? It would have to be rather a rush order, though, Meredith. We should need the copy by six to-morrow afternoon at the latest. Now did you get all that?"

"Yes. Yes, I did. But—but I don't think I'd be able to do it for you, Mr. Brewster. Not in the time."

"Ah, that *is* disappointing. Most disappointing. Hmmm. Let me think, now. Well . . . at a pinch we could give you until, say, nine to-morrow night."

"I still couldn't do it, sir. I'm sorry. You see, we've had some rush orders here and we're all working overtime to get them out. I'm sorry about this, Mr. Brewster."

"Well, your work comes first, of course. Naturally. Although it's a great shame, really. You see, the trouble is that this particular feature is dead if it's not pegged to the news. Well, never mind, it was a thought. I dare say we can get one of the staff writers to tackle something. Deadlines are deadlines in this business, eh? 'Bye for now, boy."

I put the receiver down and Joe Denton gave me a slow sideways look and said, "And what, may I ask, was *that* all about? And what's this business of us all working overtime on rush orders? We're slacker than we've been for months, and you know it."

"Oh, I just said that, Mr. Denton," I said, flushing. "I had to think of something to say. It was the man at the *Post*, the magazine editor I write things for. He wanted me to do an article for them in a hurry."

"What about?"

"Well . . . as a matter of fact, it . . . it's tied up with the murder story. He wanted me to write an article about the way art students live and all that sort of thing."

Joe Denton took up his stippling pen and tested it on the back of his hand. Below the knuckles the skin was covered with a mass of fine black pen marks like a mat of tiny hairs.

"Well," he said, "you really seem to be becoming quite a figure in the case, don't you?"

The final turn of the screw came next day, when the post brought that curious stilted letter of Jack's that I have already mentioned. It was written in a round, careful, copy-book hand—not a childish calligraphy, more the mastered meticulousness of an account-keeper or a public scrivener—on a sheet of faint-ruled paper torn from an exercise-book.

Dear David,

I take up my pen to write to you in connection with this trouble your friend Samuel Burlington has found himself in. I have been very shocked to read what they have been saying in all the newspapers. It is a very sad and awful thing about that girl we met because she seemed to me to be a nice person and there weren't any hard feelings in that direction that I could make out.

Your friend Sam struck me as a rather peculiar young fellow but he was decent enough and he was very kind to you on that occasion when you were up against it and both of us know that he is not the sort of chap who could do a dirty thing like that. I would have written to him myself to tell him this but I cannot remember the address. Anyway I know you will be seeing him to cheer him up and give him moral support, because he will need all his friends at a difficult time like this, so I would be very much obliged if you could just tell him of my sincere feelings in the matter. He may not remember me of course but it might help him to know that even a fellow he hardly knows is staunchly and loyally on his side.

Generally speaking life up here is pretty good. There is a nice girl who looks after the three kiddies because the man who owns the property is a widower and I have been going steady with her for about six months. A sheila called Sheila ! ! ! We take the buggy every Saturday and get into Dimboola which is a fairish sort of town and we either go and see a picture if something good is on or attend one of the Old Time Nights at the Mechanics Institute.

I am becoming quite an expert at the polka and the valetta and the parma waltz and the Highland schottease (is that how you spell it?) and of course the old favourites like the barn dance and things like that.

Please give my best regards to Mum and Dad and the rest of them. And don't forget to tell Sam Burlington

when you next see him that your brother Jack is on his
side. I will lay down my pen now with kindest regards,

I remain,

Yours sincerely,

Your affectionate bro.

Jack

But it was not until the following Saturday that I went to see
Sam. As far as the Jessica Murder Case was concerned he
had dropped out of interest the day before.

Just after dusk on the Thursday evening, a twelve-year-old
schoolgirl had been attacked and assaulted in the same park
not fifty yards away from where Jess had been murdered.
The newspapers were full of a new sensation: SEXUAL MANIAC
AT LARGE? In all the excitement of the new hue-and-cry, the
story of Sam's exoneration hardly received any attention. In
fact I think the *Morning Post* was the only newspaper to
publish the item, and even then it was buried away in an
obscure paragraph at the end of all the rest:

Selwyn Grant, an employee on the switchboard at St.
Kilda telephone exchange, yesterday testified that on the
night of the Jessica Murder he monitored a call made
from a public call-box to the number listed for Samuel
Burlington at 12.34 a.m. Grant was to begin his annual
holidays at the end of the shift. Inadvertently he wrote
the data on a slip of paper, which he put into his pocket,
intending to enter it in the log before knocking off. He
forgot to do so. The following afternoon he left with a
party of friends to spend a week camping and trout-
fishing. It was some days before he saw a newspaper, and
remembered the report which he had overlooked. He
communicated the information to police at Buxton when
he visited the township to buy provisions, and Russell
Street C.I.B. was informed accordingly.

I called on Sam in the middle of the afternoon on the day
after this appeared. It was between acts of the *No, No,
Nanette* matinée, and there were crowds of people laughing
and chatting around the lobby of the theatre, but otherwise
the street had a forlorn, emptied-out, Saturday afternoon
look, and the surgeries and office buildings were closed, and

chaff and bits of theatre programmes were blowing along the gutters.

I was appalled at the change that had taken place in Sam. I felt about him something of what I had felt about the street outside—he looked shrunken, forlorn and emptied-out, drained of busy-ness and importance. He was like this from the moment I set eyes on him, as if my knock on the door had frightened him.

At intervals during my visit he would make an attempt to rally, but it didn't really work. He was dispirited and uneasy, yet I felt he was appreciative of my call. "Thanks, Stunsail," he said with a kind of twisty little smile. "None of the others have bothered to look me up. Only you. Isn't that funny?"

He was very restless, but there was no quickness in his movements any more, and no . . . well, no *light* inside him, if I can put it that way. The studio seemed different, too. It looked drab and artificial, like a backdrop from a failed stage-play. The portrait of Jess had vanished, and other things seemed to have gone as well, although I could not quite identify what they had been. Everything had changed, anyway. . . .

He sailed from Australia three weeks later—it was months before I even knew he had gone—and he never went back. Well, I have never been back either, if it comes to that, but perhaps the ties that so precariously bind us to our alien world are not of the same weight and substance. What I do know is that in some queerly special way we are both tied inextricably to the events of that long-ago time in Melbourne. The things that happened in that week were to go on having a profound effect on both of us, more directly on Sam, of course (he never painted again, for instance), but perhaps more insidious and more finally damaging on me. It's always hard to tell with these things, though.

When I saw him last year he was pottering around among his rose-bushes in that same slow, rather spiritless way, a bald, paunchy little man in pale, washed-out Provençal farmer's clothes and a battered straw hat. He is doing well enough with his cut flowers for the Paris market, but he is still a bachelor and I think lonely. He has a passion for operatic music, which gives him an interest.

We sat in the courtyard and drank some of his own wine, which was a bit sharp but pleasant enough, and reminisced about this and that. The place he has is small and austere and rather beautiful in its way, of grey stone, with a little pointed tower and an arched Romanesque gateway and the poison-ous-looking blue stain of the vine spray splashed on white-washed walls, and the walls are low so that you can sit on them and look down over the rose gardens and across the speckled landscape to the hills. I had the impression that he never would go back to Australia. The man who killed Jess was never apprehended, you see, and I think there is some terrible worm of stark terror that keeps crawling around in his brain, behind that bald, brown, ordinary little face with the hurt bulging eyes and the sunken jowls.

When I was taking my leave of him, he squeezed my arm and grinned, and for the flash of an instant, gone almost before it could be recognised, the old Sam was there. " You're wearing pretty well, old Stunsail," he said affection-ately. " Much better than I am." He glanced ruefully at his paunch. " Well, *tant pis*. It's the way it happens to us. You know, life's a pretty funny business when you come to think of it. I remember a talk I once had with that brother of yours. I told him then that you were the only one of us who had the right idea." He squeezed my arm again. The air was sodden with the smell of roses. " Well, good for you, Stunsail," he said warmly. " Good for you!"

CHAPTER 9

It was after that week of the Jessica Wray case that I began to become a master of dissimulation. Among his aphorisms Kafka quoted a phrase that seems to have greatly haunted and intrigued him—" but then he returned to his work as if nothing had happened "—and I suppose this can be applied to me. Kafka was acutely aware, of course, of the boundless field of conjecture and implication involved in the statement.

Mother, whom I loved, and my father, whom I still de-tested, knew virtually nothing of what I was doing. I imagine that to them I had become a queer, separate kind of creature, too puzzling to be understood and by this time too removed from their ways and views to be prudently corrected. I used to do everything in my power to preserve this sense of isolation. I lived, if I may employ a cliché, a life of my own, and this was not disturbed until Jack returned from the Wimmera with his sheila called Sheila.

They arrived at the house unannounced fairly early one Sunday morning, having come down from Dimboola on the night train. Jack looked brown and hard and grown-up, and thinner than he had been, and there was a vaguely anxious careworn look about him which I did not understand at first. Sheila Delaney was an exceedingly pretty girl, but she seemed rather pale and ill, and it was not until I heard why they had come to Melbourne that I saw the reason for Jack's expression and the sick look she had.

She had just recovered—in fact was still recovering—from a severe attack of double pneumonia, and since Jack had lost his job on the farm because of a sudden sharp slump in wheat prices, he had decided to bring her home so that Mother could look after her.

We never suspected at that time—and, anyway, the fact would have been lost sight of in the angry tumult that almost immediately was to follow—that the sudden fall in wheat prices and the loss of Jack's employment were the first hint of the disaster that was coming. There was much dust in the air in that year of gorgeous sunsets, and not many people realised that the dust was half the world's security blowing away. . . .

I must tell first about Sheila Delaney. She was Roman Catholic and an orphan. Her Irish father had been killed at the Gallipoli landing when she was a child of seven, and her mother had died two years before she met Jack in the Wimmera. She was about the same age as Jack, a month or two older, perhaps, I can't remember, but she had had a good convent education and was well-read and well-spoken and obviously better educated than Jack. She was slim and yet rather rounded and womanly with it, and not very tall, and although there was a quality of quietness about her she could be bold, too, in a way. I should try to explain this. Perhaps it was something Irish in her, but she insisted on being accepted as she was, and not as people thought she should be. It was this aspect of her character, I think, even more than her religion, that riled Dad almost beyond endurance. (One saw this later, when in the face of his obstinate injustices, she refused, just as stubbornly, to move even an inch towards placating him.)

She had a pretty rather pointed little face with short, jet-black, soft-curling hair and the bluest eyes—very Irish, in fact, that face of hers—and she would look very squarely at everybody and not appear diffident or downcast. She would smoke her cigarettes, or take a glass or two of beer, in front of anyone without seeming to be brazen or trying to prove something ; she had the prettiest legs, and she wore very short tight skirts and she would sit with her legs crossed and parts of her bare thighs showing, and she wore thin blouses that were always cut rather low, and all this may or may not have been intentional—for she was well aware of her own strong sexuality—but I know she had a way of disconcerting me and of driving Dad almost to a point of distraction. She was very much in love with Jack. And he with her.

The first day passed off all right. There was the excitement of having Jack back, and the girl was so obviously unwell that there was a good deal of solicitous activity on Mother's part with barley-water and soft-boiled eggs carried on trays to the bedside and the loan of a pink crocheted bed-jacket, and my desk had to be moved out and Jack's bed brought in from the sleep-out, but even during this time I could see that Dad was under some strain he found difficult to suppress. Perhaps it was that for quite a long time he had not had a target that he could define or see in the frame of familiar prejudices. Jack, also, was abstracted at first and clearly so concerned for Sheila's well-being that he probably did not even notice Dad's uneasiness.

At any rate, it all blew up the following afternoon with the sudden violence of a summer thunderstorm.

I was in my room working on an article for Mr. Brewster, and I heard Dad call Jack into the kitchen, and their voices came to me clearly across the narrow vestibule.

" This here woman you've brought into the house," Dad began the argument without concession to politeness, " how long do you propose to keep her here?"

" Well, she's sick . . . at least she's been sick, and she's still pretty crook," I heard Jack say, in a tone that betrayed some surprise. " So I just thought she——"

" You *thought*! Look, hasn't it ever occurred to you that there's a right way and a wrong way of going about a thing? There's no by your leave, is there? . . . you just land her on us whether *we* want her here or not! "

" Well, where else would I take her? I came home because I——"

" Has it occurred to you that she probably needs a week or ten days in bed? That's what your mother says she needs."

" I know. She was pretty sick up there and——"

" That's it. Who do *you* think has got the time to run around after her? Your mother hasn't got a dozen pair of hands. Don't you think she's got enough to do in this house without——"

" I don't see you doing much running around!" Jack retorted angrily. " Isn't it for Mum to complain if——?"

" It's me who runs this house, not your mother. It's *me*, see! And you just put that in your pipe and smoke it, my boy! And I'm running a house, d'you understand, or trying to, and not a blasted convalescents' home!"

" What the hell are you *getting* at?" Jack's voice was subdued and very taut. " What've you got against her?"

" I just don't like her attitude, that's all. I've seen these lah-de-dah ones before who have to be waited on hand and foot. The way she talks, and those stuck-up airs she gives herself. Who does she think she is? Lady Muck?"

" You don't bloody well know what you're talking about!" Jack snapped.

" Don't I?" (Even in the words I could see the sarcastic twist to Dad's mouth.) " Then I'd better tell you what else I think, eh? I think she's nothing but a cheap little trollop, puffing away at her damned cigarettes and sitting there with her skirts up showing all she's got! And she's a mick, too, isn't she? Sheila Delaney! You've only got to look at that face of hers . . . as Irish as Paddy's pig . . . and that bloody cross thing she wears on a chain round her neck. . . . Go on, answer me, you! She's a mick, isn't she?"

" She's a mick, yes," Jack said in a voice that hurt, even across the distance of the vestibule. " What's that got to do with it?"

"What's that got to *do* with it!" Dad stormed. "Are you out of your wits? We're Protestants in this house. *Protestants*, do you understand! This is a decent, Godfearing house. And I want no confounded Roman Catholics under this roof whether they're sick or they're not sick!"

"What are you trying to tell me, Pop?"

"I'm trying to tell you that no house of mine is going to be overrun by tykes, that's all."

There was a long, tense silence after this, and I sat on the edge of my bed in rigid trepidation, but when Jack spoke his voice seemed steady and controlled, although every one of his slow-spaced words seemed to cut like a knife.

"Listen to me, Pop," he said. "I don't care whether she's a mick or a Protestant or a holy roller. She happens to be my girl, see, and if it interests you I happen to be in love with her."

"*You* in love . . ." Dad began to splutter.

"As far as being a trollop, that's for me to say. She's a respectable girl, and nobody knows it better than me. As for being stuck-up, and Lady Muck, that's just because she speaks nice . . . because she's got a better education than you have, or than you ever damn' well gave to me. She——"

"You—you ungrateful swine! We've worked our very fingers to the bone for——"

"Suppose you let *me* have a go, Pop," Jack cut in with terrible coldness. "You just stand back and let the flamin' dog see the rabbit. You're the one who brought this up. Well, let me say *my* piece now. You wanted to know why I brought her here. I brought her here because she's sick and Mum's a trained nurse and I thought she could take care of her for a bit while I look around and pick up another job. I thought——"

"You and your jobs! You've never been able to hold down a job for two weeks in a row, you're so——"

"Listen, don't give *me* that! I've been in one job for close on two years. And let me tell you something. I've kicked into this house from every pay I've ever earned. You can't say I haven't given my whack, can you? For the last two years you've been getting two quid a week from me regular as clockwork. Is that right? And I'll tell you something else while I'm about it. Ever since I've been knee-high to a grasshopper, this damned house of yours has been crawling with your bloomin' convalescents, with bloody men with their legs chopped off and their arms chopped off, with no eyes and no lungs . . . and when *they* haven't been here there've been dotty old women dying all over the flamin' house! And the place stuffed with crutches and wooden legs and enemas and bedpans and piss-bottles, and you couldn't get a game of snooker because there was always a bloody coffin on the table! Jesus, Pop, don't you stand there and tell *me* about this—this undertaker's parlour you've been running for the last ten years! Do you realise that young Davy and me knew all about an artificial leg or an abdominal truss or a frigging chloroform mask before we knew what a see-saw was or a Meccano set! We——"

" Don't raise your voice to me, you——"

" For Christ's sake, your own daughter's just over there on the other side of the street married to one of your damned convalescents! *He* got a bed here, didn't he? *He* got looked after. Yes, while young Davy and me had to sleep on the floor in that sleep-out for donkey's bloody years so there'd be room for the cripples and the corpses! And now—stone the crows! this is a beautiful turn-up for the books, isn't it?—now, when I want to bring someone to my own home—someone I happen to be in love with: someone *I* intend to marry, this time—I'm suddenly in all the bloody strife in the world. Ah, to hell with it! Whenever you come back here you run into strife!"

" Nobody asked you to come back."

" No? Well, I came back, didn't I? And I brought my sheila with me, didn't I? And I——"

" You brought an R.C., that's what you brought. You brought a tyke! And I won't have one of that sort staying under this roof."

" Well, you can bet your bloody life you won't have to. As soon as she's well enough to go we'll be getting out of here, don't make any mistake about *that*!"

" The sooner the better then," said Dad. " And good riddance!"

They stayed for several days, though, because Mother put her foot down about Sheila being moved, and then Jack came

into our room one night and took off his jacket and tie and
looked around as he began to unbutton his shirt, and said,
" You know, Davy, you've made this place look real nice.
The shelves there, I mean, and that panelling, and the books
and things. Although it was better when that desk was here
instead of this old bed. You've done it jolly well, just the
same. You've made it into a sort of study, really. You look
the real bloody old absent-minded professor, don't you?" He
grinned at me and looked around for his pyjamas and said,
rather casually, " Well, you can put it all back to-morrow just
the way it was. We're clearing out."

" But why should you?" I spoke firmly, to ride myself
over a little twinge of guilt, because his words had evoked
in me an involuntary inward sigh of relief that peace of mind,
the securities, the established values of my isolation might
yet be restored.

" Ah, it's the Old Man. He goes on, needling away, finding
fault with everything, trying to pick another row every time
he talks to me. I'm just fed up with it, that's all. Trouble is
I've walked my jack off to-day, and not a flamin' job in sight.
I bought *The Age* this morning, Davy, and you wouldn't
believe it, but there was less than half a bloomin' column of
Situations Vacant, and *seven* bloomin' columns of Situations
Wanted. And a queue of about a hundred blokes at every
job that was going. It's a fair cow at the moment, I tell you
straight."

" Oh, well, something will turn up. But what about Sheila?"

He sat on the edge of the bed in his pyjama-bottoms and
rubbed away at his toes.

" Well, he don't want her here, that's it. He's made that
clear enough, hasn't he? Davy, what the devil's wrong with
Pop? Mum and Sheila, they get on like a house on fire, they
do, you know. And anyway, you know Mum. She's only
happy when she's got someone to look after. She's all right.
It's *him*. Davy, what *is* wrong with him? He just don't want
anything. Remember when we were kids? . . . he was always
kicking Mum out. You come home here with that bloomin'
typewriter of yours, and he kicks you out. I bring my girl
back here, same bloody thing. What the hell's *wrong* with
him? It just seems like he . . . well, as if he can't stand anyone else to have anything at all." He kept rubbing away at

his toes while he talked. " You know, when we were coming
down in that train from Dimboola sittin' up all night, I
thought of this place as a kind of . . . well, you know, a sort
of place of sanctuary—that's a jaw-breaker isn't it?"—he
chuckled self-consciously—" have you twigged how I slip into
long words now? . . . being with Sheila's done that . . . she's
got quite a . . . an extensive vocabulary "—his head was
down over his feet and his shoulders were shaking, laughing
at himself—" and when we get here we're treated like we're
a couple of flamin' lepers. Why does he *have* to go on like
that? Mum's tickled pink. And he's like a bear with a sore
head. It beats me."

" Jack, he doesn't really have anything against Sheila. He
doesn't mean this about her being a Catholic and all that.
It's just that he has to have something to rant and rave about,
so he can prove *he's* master of the house."

" I don't think it's just that. You know what I reckon,
Davy? I think he just can't bear that other people should be
able to do what they want to do. All Mum wanted to do
was nurse people and look after 'em. All you wanted to do
was write. All I want to do is to get Sheila well and then get
spliced to her. I suppose he feels he's never been able to do
what he's wanted to do himself, so he has to take it out on
everybody else. Mind you, in one way you can see the Old
Man's point of view . . . I mean, he must be sick to death of
seeing his house being run as a kind of a—a sanatorium, or a
charity institution ever since he landed back from the war.
Although I'll bet the old bugger was glad of their disabled
soldiers' pensions, or their old-age pensions, or the two quid a
week I kept sending him all the time I was away. But if he'd
only try to be *human* about things, that's all."

" If you go away from here, what are you going to do?" I
said.

" Oh, I'll do something. I can look after myself."

" And Sheila?"

" Don't worry about her. She's my responsibility. You
know, that's another thing I just don't understand about him.
He's been at me for years about how irresponsible I am, and
the first time I come back with a girl I'm tracking square
with, I get hoisted! *He* knows she's not just another piece of
skirt I'm chasing. I've told him that in two months' time I'll

be twenty-one, and I'm going to marry her, and nobody can stop me. Makes no difference at all. Jesus, you can't win, can you?"

"Jack," I said, "there's a very good nursing home up in Glen Eira Road. Why don't you take Sheila there? They'd look after her while you found yourself a job."

He looked up at me. "And what do I do for money? By the end of this week I won't have a brass rahzoo left."

"I can give you the money," I said. "I've been saving the money I get from those articles in the paper. I can let you have fifty pounds."

"*Fifty quid!*" He stared at me as if I were mad. "Are you pulling my leg? Fifty quid's a lot of money!"

"I can give it to you. Honestly. It'll take care of Sheila for a couple of weeks, and it'll keep you going until you find some work. You can have it, Jack."

His head was down again and his face hidden from me, and he was rubbing away at his toes. For a long time he was silent. "I'd pay it back, you know," he said at last in a low troubled voice. "You'd get it all back."

"Well, we needn't worry about that now. But Sheila would have proper attention, and you'd feel independent about things."

"Thanks, nipper," he said, but he kept rubbing at his toes and he didn't look at me.

They left next morning and I returned to my work as if nothing had happened, and to this day I do not know whether I did it out of generosity and my love for Jack, or whether it was just the price I paid to have the house peaceful again and my own life free from invasion.

It was like a great river flooding or changing its course, the way the Depression came—the insidious creeping movement of dark, strong, unpredictable forces, the flow of hidden currents, a clod falling and dissolving, a slide of earth, the cave-in of an entire bank, a sudden eddy swirling around a snag, tilting it over, sweeping it off into a black oblivion.

Even when the disaster had spread everywhere and its destructive menace understood, something unfeasible remained. The work trains, to me, going to my job at the same hour on the same days, seemed just as crowded, the same people pushed at the ticket barriers with the same impatient roughness, the shops were as full as ever of their desperate enticements. It was out in the suburbs mostly that one gradually came to see it.

They brought in the dole, and then the dole became "the sustenance," and around this time they unlocked the Defence Department warehouses and out of the mothballs they took the old surplus greatcoats and tunics and they dyed them a dull black—all that brave khaki of 1914-18—and against the contingency of a Melbourne winter issued them out as a charity to keep the workless warm. So that as the unemployed grew in number the black army coats became a kind of badge of adversity, a stigma of suffering.

One would see the shabby figures shambling along the suburban streets, carrying a loaf of bread and in a cloth bicycle-bag their meagre handout from the Sustenance Depot of tea and sugar and flour and potatoes, and a wisp of tobacco. Or there would be a queue of men the length of a block, most of them in the ill-fitting, shameful black, in apathetic competition for half a dozen casual jobs. As the situation grew worse desperate attempts were made towards alleviation, and the "black coats" moved then in the more regimented bands of the "sustenance-workers" and you would see them with their brooms and picks and shovels and council tip-drays working in slovenly unison on pointless municipal projects. Every now and then one would recognise a familiar figure among them—Dud Bennett, the one-time leader of the Grey Caps gang, driving a council dray laden with gravel, looking small and shrunken now: and Snowy Bretherton in a black greatcoat top-dressing the strip of lawn outside the local town hall. It was a time of a sad and terrible human degradation for which there seemed to be no remedy.

This was the time, too, of the first trickle in from Europe of that other human flotsam, Jews mostly and refugees from a new malignancy, and this, also, was misleading at first for the trickle had become a flood almost before one realised what was happening. Even the language of suffering, of course, had to be Australianised. The refugees became the "Reffos," just as the sustenance-workers had by this time become the "Sussos."

Dad by now was depot foreman so he kept his job at the

tramways running-shed, but Bert, who had been " retrenched "
from the Repatriation Department, put on his uniform again,
although this time the tunic and the greatcoat were dyed a
dull black, so he must have had a different feeling about it
from the time, fourteen years before, when as a hayseed kid
from Corindhap he had gone away with an assumed name and
bright badges and a sense of glorious adventure to have his leg
blown off in France. He went back to casual snobbing to eke
out the sustenance. By this time he had three children to
keep.

In our suburb there was a constant, unnerving movement of
these pathetic and yet somehow oddly sinister figures in their
black tunics and greatcoats. Sometimes they would come to
the door asking for an hour's work to cut the hedge or to mow
the lawn or to stack firewood or even to run errands . . . or
sometimes more bluntly just to ask for a handout of food or
money. A few of the more resourceful among them had made
themselves crude little hand trucks which they would push
clatteringly around the streets, collecting old newspapers or
scrap-metal or unwanted clothes, or with coal or kindling-
wood to sell.

I remember the evening when Dad came into my room and
said: " I want you to print me up a sign. You do printing at
Klebendorf's, don't you?"

" Lettering things, you mean? Yes."

He handed me a bevelled oblong of hardwood, and said,
" This is for the front gate. The carpenter at the sheds fixed
it for me. I want you to paint a sign on it. Can you print
this up for me?" He passed over a crumpled slip of paper
on which he had crudely printed out the words: BEGGARS,
HAWKERS, AND CANVASSERS WILL BE PROSECUTED.

I lettered the sign for him in white on black, but then he
made me take it out and screw it to the front gate. I wanted
to protest but his face was so stern and implacable that I said
nothing. While I was attaching the sign to the gate two
middle-aged men in black greatcoats came across and stood
there watching me. When in my nervousness and humiliation
I dropped one of the screws one of the men stooped over and
picked it up and handed it to me, but neither he nor his
companion uttered a single word. When the sign was firmly
fixed against the gate they just turned away and shuffled off

along the street muttering to each other. It was not very long
before these signs—or something like them—were on gates all
over the suburbs.

At Klebendorf's the terror moved into the big studio in a
different way. Advertising appropriations were cut and orders
petered out, and there were long slack times when we all
worked feverishly on "spec" designs, but there were very
few orders that seemed to come from them. Out in the
factory half the machines were silent, and the flatbeds and the
big rotaries were covered over with spoiled sheets of double-
quad printing paper, like the drapes over furniture in an
unoccupied house. Finally there was the surprising day when
old Klebendorf came up to the studio. I say surprising,
because the old man, whom I had never known to do more
than grunt out a gruff sentence, or just grunt, had called the
art staff together to hear his careful set speech. That was the
only time I remember the two old Germans, Steiner and
Richter, coming to the studio together, like two timid mice.
Perhaps it was their presence that made old Klebendorf
sound more German than ever, or maybe it was only emotion
that twisted his speech.

"You vill all know," he began after a good deal of coughing and threat-clearing, "that der printing indusstry iss not
now in a condition of equitableness. We have been standing
off thirty men from the factory already. Thirty goot men!
It iss not goot. Nein! But "—he clenched his fist—" it iss not
as bad, my frients, as our oppositional firm of McIlwraith
und Todd, which has its doors closed, pouf!"—he spread his
pudgy hands in a queer little quick gesture—" und every man,
every goot man at that place is a job without. This iss bad.
Ach! The times are of great difficulty. Here at Klebendorf
und Hardt we have the good company and the good staff. Ve
will act mit honour. Ja! But the orders they are not, and the
overhead is of a cost phenomenal, und there must be taking
place a changement. So! There will be suffering, but we vill
spread the suffering. We will spread it so that no man he iss
hurting too much. Ja! There is no man here who iss losing
his job. Nein! Not vun! I have talked together with Mr.
Denton, und he vill tell you our prosement. Vot ve think
iss best for all of us. Our difficulties ve will share, eh? Mein
Gott! Mein Gott! it is of such difficulties the vorld over at

this time! I have preoccupational matters very great. *Mein* own land is suffering also, and many of my own people are coming so far to seek assistance, and them I must be helping a little also. You understand? It is of great difficulty. Something bad it happens in this world . . . I do not know vot it iss. . . ."

As I listened to the old man, his gross, flabby face crumpled in a mask of concern and anxiety and embarrassment: his thick guttural accents groping to express some vital message of mercy and loyalty and consideration and humaneness, my mind turned back to an image of a child in a locked bedroom rummaging in a wardrobe drawer. Was this the Hun of the Raemaker cartoons? This ludicrous little fat figure with the heavy gold watch-chain looped across the burgomaster belly, striving for a " condition of equitableness " in a world where economic disaster had sprung out like a beast from the shadows—was this the hateful figure of German *Kultur*? His voice had thickened even more as he struggled to get hope and conviction into his words:

" It vill not last. *Ach Gott*, it cannot last! It is a phase, no more. There will come another changement, this it iss sure, *und* for the good. *Ja!* We vill ride it out, eh? We vill all share the difficulties, *und* so we vill ride it out. . . ."

After he had finished Joe Denton put the situation crisply. " What we've worked out is this," he said. " There's not enough work here to keep us *all* busy, we all know that. So instead of chopping staff we'll try a system of rationing. Each one of us will take it in turn to stand down for two weeks without pay. *Without* pay, remember. We'll see how it works out. Everyone will be in this, apprentices and all. If things continue to get worse it might have to be a month off without pay, or two blokes off together. We'll have to see about that. It depends how things go. I don't think I have to tell you that there aren't any jobs going anywhere else. Here at Klebendorf's we're probably better off than any other place in the city. One of the apprentices will take his time off with every alternate senior man. I'll be taking the first lay-off myself, beginning to-morrow, and Young Joe here will come with me. You, Paul, will run the studio while I'm away. That's all. Any questions?"

There were no questions. The rationing went into effect.

Old Joe Denton returned after the first two weeks and made a big thing about what a marvellous time he'd had, staking up his dahlias and labelling them and doing all the odd chores around the house that he'd been putting off for years. Paul Klein went off, and I with him. For me it was a wonderful two weeks. All the time I would have spent at Klebendorf's I was able to devote to my work-table, writing. Mother would bring my lunch in on a tray. I wrote articles, sketches, stories, paragraphs, and I sent them to newspapers and magazines in other States, and even overseas. (I got rejection-slips, of course, but later, when I was able to add up the tally of that time, I found that I had made in those two weeks seven times the amount of money I would have earned in the same period at Klebendorf's!)

For the others, though, it was a bitter, anxious time. The Depression steadily grew worse. The rationing became a month off without pay, then two men would go at once, and still there were not enough orders coming in to really keep busy those who remained. There were no more practical jokes with turpentine, no more playing of the darts game, and nobody any longer would lift his voice in a chorus from Gilbert and Sullivan.

Many of the factory floors were quite silent now for hours and even days at a time, and through them Mr. Klebendorf would wander, a solitary, head-shaking ghost of himself, grown ten years older and stooped under the weight of his anxieties, grunting and clucking and snuffling through the ruins of a lifetime, trapped in an endless nightmare of liquidation and broken faith. He hardly ever spoke to anybody. He could seldom be found in his own managerial office. He would just shuffle around, haunting the static floors of his business ; one would come across him in the most unexpected places—standing alone by the dusty deserted ink-slab where old George Rosevear had once put me in my place, stooped over and curiously jabbing his fat little finger into a dry ink duct, sidling down the length of the disused varnishing-machine, his hand gently moving along the coarse canvas of the conveyer-dryer as a child might run a stick along a picket fence, staring for five minutes at a time at a covered monotype machine or an idle guillotine, or walking around in the rat-infested loft among the racks of limestone slabs that had

come out from Bavaria. And wherever he went there would
be other eyes watching him in unspeakable apprehension: a
girl in a blue smock standing at a wrapping table, a mainten-
ance mechanic oiling cog-wheels, a printer in the jobbing
department dusting powdered silver on the wet print of a
batch of wedding invitations, Claude Cranston standing behind his stacks of unsold calendars.

Towards the end of that year the old man had a stroke.
Two of the stone hands who were still employed found him
crumpled up below the feed platform of the big rotary-offset
that took the sixty-forty sheets. One side of his face was
twisted up and his left eye rolled around loosely. They carried
him into the studio, because we had an old couch there, and a
telephone with which a doctor might be summoned. He
remained fully conscious for sixteen hours, and while we
were waiting for the ambulance to come he sent down for his
son, Werner, and made a rather pompous, disjointed little
speech, handing over the business as if it were all in the flush
of its prosperity. That night a second stroke took him off.

It was old Klebendorf's death, I am sure, that finally drove
home to me the appalling irony of the situation I found
myself in.

I was conscious suddenly of the agonising insecurity of
every other person in the studio. Being skilled craftsmen,
they had become the victims of their own craft skills and
specialisations: there was nothing else they could do and
nowhere else for them to go. Half the lithographic studios in
the city were running on the barest of skeleton staffs or had
closed down altogether.

They no longer made jokes about their " time off." They
were loyal and brave and they shared every adversity with
scrupulous fairness and without complaint ; but in every face
the eyes were haunted by an embedded shadow of disaster:
each man, seeing his lay-off time approaching, would grow
more and more silent under the afflicting dread of its con-
sequences. One noticed trivial things ; they all looked less
spruce, even almost shabby, in the mornings ; there was no
money to spare for dry-cleaning or new ties or a better suit,
or even for the absurd extra things like the buttonhole that

Paul Klein would buy every morning from the old woman
outside Spencer Street railway station—frangipani or gardenia or a red carnation—when he used to come to work
dapperly limping and swinging his cane. Tom Middleton's
string quartet was disbanded. Barney Druce gave up his
photography and resigned from the canoe club. Just little
things like these that sat in their eyes like cold stones. One
knew, of course, that they were all beginning to fall behind
on their payments towards the securities which represented
the absolutes of their being, their house mortgages and their
insurance policies, a Baby Austin, a block of land in a
" better " suburb, a sandy allotment at Dromana where one
day a holiday " week-ender " might be built. There was
murmured sombre talk of second-mortgages and the Credit-
Foncier and the surrender-value of insurance policies.

Among them all, only I was secure. I, who had to a great
degree betrayed their kindliness, who had defected on all the
honest standards in which they implicitly believed, I was the
only person who had a way out of the dilemma, who had
security, who had a second string to his bow.

I gave the matter very careful thought, and then one day I
approached Joe Denton, without any previous reference to
Mother or to Dad, and I asked him if he would consider
waiving the last fourteen months of my indentures. I explained that I thought I would be able to live by my writing,
that if I was out of the way it would give that much more
latitude to Young Joe, that there was really not enough work
any longer to justify two apprentices. He thought about it
for a long time, rubbing away at his chin, and then he looked
up at me and said:

" Well, it might be a practical solution, David. You're
pretty hot stuff with this writing of yours. You probably
would do better there in the long run. Yes, I'll put it up to
Werner if you want me to. Your parents would have to agree,
of course, and one of them would have to come in and sign
the waiver. For my part, I think on the whole I'd be in favour
of it. You're quite right, too, it *would* be a help to have the
pressure eased a bit. I think Young Joe would be grateful to
you. None of us knows how long this state of affairs is likely
to last."

Before talking to him I had, of course, taken the pre-
caution of telephoning Mr. Brewster. At the end of that
month I joined the editorial staff of the *Morning Post*.

While all this was happening Jack had been engaged in his
own personal battle with the Depression. So at this point I
must retrace some ground. . . .

After Sheila came out of the nursing home they took a bed-
sitting-room in a back street in Windsor, because the rent was
cheap and it was not far from Chapel Street, where Sheila
had found a temporary position as a salesgirl at Maple's.
Jack could get no regular employment, but he picked up
casual work from time to time, relieving on a baker's round,
some pick-and-shovel jobs, delivering briquettes, driving a
contractor's truck, peddling Tattersall's lottery tickets. Things
like that.

Although I was absurdly embarrassed by the fact that they
were obviously " living in sin," I would go down to Windsor
every week or so to see how they were getting on. It was an
even sadder street than the one we lived in—facing rows of
identical little duplexes, sitting behind picket fences and small
desiccated garden plots filled with geraniums and laburnums
and pigface, and the whole street had decayed in a shabbily
respectable way, so that the prim little duplexes were lined up
like regimented rows of faded spinster sisters assembled to be
praised for their virtuous endurance. It was the sort of street
where children played along the gutters at marbles and hoops
and cherrybobs and tipcat and hopscotch, because there was
nowhere else to play, and at regular intervals down the pavements unkempt oleanders and dusty pepper-trees grew out of
crumpled wire guards, inside which chaff had gathered and
discarded matchboxes and the dried turds of dogs. All the
houses had door-knobs that were brightly polished, and
coloured glass leadlights, and names on their gates. The one
where Jack and Sheila lived was called *Rose of Sharon*.

They had the front room, which was larger than one might
have expected, but it was so filled with huge clumsy things—a
dining-room table and a sideboard as well as an entire ven-
eered bedroom-suite in figured walnut—that it was not really
very spacious at all. They had a gas-ring and a shilling
meter in the corner, and to get to the toilet, which was only

an outhouse, they had to go down through the duplex and way up to the end of the backyard, where a paling fence concealed a lane crowded with battered dust-bins. There was honeysuckle growing over the outhouse because the place was unsewered and a sanitary truck came twice a week to collect the cans. Their Irish landlady lived in some rear part of the other half of the duplex.

Still, Jack and Sheila seemed very happy there . . . or they were at the beginning, at any rate.

From the first, Jack fought the Depression on his own terms and in his own way. He refused implacably to take the dole or to have anything to do with " sustenance work." " If *you* think I'm going to stand there holding my hand out like a flamin' beggar, you've got another bloody think coming!" he would say. Or: " Catch me lining up for a handout with all those bloomin' black crows!" It was not bravado. He genuinely believed it was " the Susso " that was the crushing evil of the times, that the very fact of living on an artificial succour would rip the spirit out of a man, that by donning the dyed black coat you gave in, and accepted the humiliation of defeat without " giving it a go."

He would involve himself in strange ventures to prove his convictions. If he could find no job in the city he would take himself off to the country for weeks at a time on rabbiting expeditions and scratch out a meagre subsistence by selling the skins. But the price for rabbit skins dropped to nothing, and then it was gold " fossicking " that captured his desperate imagination.

" Remember those Christmas holidays from school, Davy?" he said to me excitedly, during one of my visits. " You know, when we'd go up to Bert's father's farm near Corindhap. All those worked-over gold diggings . . . d'you remember? Well, listen, I'm going to give it a go up there. There must be heaps of gold still left around you know. Jesus, when they were workin' the place up there they were having gold strikes every-where, and they'd just tear through a place like snit through a blanket. Don't you remember Berringa? . . . that dead town where everyone walked out when they struck it bigger some-where else . . . all those locked houses and the mullick-heaps and the poppet-heads . . . or that long tunnel the Chinese miners opened up through the mountain near Dereel? I bet you, Davy, there's a ton of stuff up there still, if you can only get your bloody hands on it!" He chuckled and slapped my shoulder. "It'd be a turn-up for the books if *I* struck it rich, wouldn't it, eh?" He rubbed his hands together. "Like that parsimonious old bloody wowser of a grandfather of ours! Jesus, he *owned* a goldmine, didn't he?"

He was away for weeks on this quest, and I can imagine him now, looking back on it, more movingly than I did then, for there were times when I considered him a stubborn fool who should accept the situation and take the dole as everyone else was doing. I see him quite differently now. I see him as a proud, lean, solitary figure, with his blanket-roll and his billy and his wash-pan and his few things, searching through the streets of silent, uninhabited houses and the long-abandoned workings of an Australian " ghost town," or, with a stub of candle in his fingers, cautiously exploring the dangerous tunnels and the caved-in shafts and diggings of generations before, or washing the sandy gravels in the quartzy beds of shallow streams. Making his lonely camp fires, too, under the scraggy gums, cooking his damper in the ashes, playing to the heedless night for his own solace the mouth-organ he always carried in his pocket.

Jack, I realise now, was a character born for ardent adventure. (The stage was never big enough.) He was hamstrung by circumstance and, in another way, by his own innate nobility. He could have acted out some passionate Conradian drama, in South America say, or on some unnamed island, of which he would have been king. Looking back now, down the years which gave adventure to me and denied it to him, one likes to think this. The circumstances were against him. But circumstances are against all of us. One way or another. . . .

He came back from his gold-fossicking gauntly thin, and, with an attempt at self-justification and pride which turned into a joke against himself even before he had finished speaking, he showed Sheila and me the results of it all—one small oval-shaped aspirin bottle not quite filled with gold dust and tiny glittering chips. " Never mind, Sheil'," he said, with that undaunted grin of his. " It was still worth givin' it a go!"

One thing was sure, seeing him with Sheila. Jack was mated. Their characters, in fact, were much alike—they had the same loyalties, audacities, obstinacies, prides, the same strong and frank sexuality. Whenever I visited them at Windsor I would ask if they needed help, and it would always be Sheila who would say, " No, we're all right, thanks, Davy. We're managing fine."

It was during these visits that Sheila began to exert on me an unsettling fascination. With her return to health she had become quite extraordinarily attractive, with her colour and vitality and the sparkle of her personality, and she was well aware of this, and with me she played a game that was deliberately coquettish, but not cruelly or wickedly: more in a kind of bold, joking way. It was unmistakable, all the same. She would deliberately assert her physical magnetism, in a roguish glance, a way of moving, in a " leg show " or a trick of leaning against me: she would leave the top button of her blouse undone so that one could see the rich, creamy top curve of her bosom or the delicate lilac shadow of the cleft. It was almost like a teacher taking a child through its first primer. " Look," she was saying in effect, " this is a woman. This is a real woman." She would challenge me with good-natured sexual teasing. When I was leaving she would always embrace me tightly and kiss me and rub herself against me and sigh, *Mmmm-mmm-mmm!* in an amused parody of sexual ecstasy. I realised that Jack had put her up to this, perhaps as a more effective extension of the indoctrination he had unsuccessfully tried to force upon me years before, for when he was away she never conducted herself like this at all ; she was just pleasant and nice and friendly to me.

Yet her indoctrination was far more successful than Jack's had ever been, or perhaps it was just that I was older: I know that I would walk up to the Windsor railway station stupefied by a swirl of strange, disturbing sensations and aching with a queer hunger I had never known before.

One day I called at the house to find that Jack had gone away again. " He left the Thursday before last," Sheila said to me. " Somebody told him there were better chances of finding a job up in New South Wales, so he decided to give it a try. He got a lift in a lorry as far as Tocumwal, but I've not heard from him since."

" Well, how are you placed?" I asked. " Do you need anything?"

" No, thanks, I'm all right, Davy. I can manage fine."

She kissed me good-bye, but dispassionately, and I think it was no disloyalty to Jack that I found myself wishing she had been more warmly provocative.

Several weeks passed before I went back to Windsor. In the right-hand front window of Rose of Sharon there was a hand-printed card which said, ROOM VACANT. *Apply Next Door (No.* 21*a*). I went out again and in at the other picket gate and rang the bell and the landlady appeared. She was a big, scary-eyed woman who looked as if she lived in a perpetual state of seige behind the intimidating ramparts of her breasts. Her handshake had the limpness and the slightly clammy, unpleasant touch of a used church candle.

" Them in there?" she said. " Oh no, dearie, 'e went away some little time back, an' she left 'ere las' We'nsday. No forwardin' address, dearie, no, nuthin' like that. Not the least idea, ducks. No, she jist paid up proper-like t' the end of the week, an' orf she went with 'er port', down t' the station, I suppose. Left the place nice an' tidy though, I must say. An' that's the main thing, ain't it?"

It was a long time before I saw either Sheila or Jack again. I assumed that Jack had found work in New South Wales and that Sheila had followed him: it meant nothing that one had no direct news of this: during his two years in the Wimmera Jack had written only that one letter home. With their absence the Depression seemed to drop more into the background of our lives. Behind the sign on our front gate we were secure and comfortable. The men in black coats no longer bothered us: Dad had his job and I had mine. The recurring crises at Klebendorf's affected me only as an enhancement of my self-esteem, and later there were the excitements of my new job with the *Morning Post*. (There was much to write about for the city was beginning to plan the festivities which would celebrate the centenary of its foundation—" This is the place for a village," John Batman had said—and one of my roles in this was to arrange for the restoration of one of the old coal-hulks as she had been in the time of her pride to act as a nautical museum. The sufferings and hardships of the Depression gradually had come to have a blurred, out-of-focus quality of a film background.)

Jack came back one wild winter evening in July, with hard squalls of rain blowing in on the southerly, and Dad and I were sitting by the gas-fire reading the papers and waiting for Mother to bring supper in from the kitchen, and she came in wiping her hands on her apron and said, "Wasn't that somebody at the front door?"

She fussed off up the passageway to the hall, and we heard the front door open, and then there was a strange, strangled cry of "*Mum!*" above the slash and slap of rain against the window, and immediately after this a heavy crashing thud. Dad and I rushed up to the front of the house, and there was Jack flung unconscious on the hall carpet in a dark spattery stain of rain water, and the hallstand fallen across him and Mother kneeling there beside him and staring down and trembling as if she had seen a ghost.

It was the sight of Jack's feet that shocked me first—the broken uppers of his boots hanging in strips of wet leather, and his soles a mass of blood and torn flesh and the wet threads of ruined socks, all pulped into a horrid wet paste: and then I saw the white wasted face lying there on the faded Axminster in a tangle of pale wet hair, and I pushed out through the door and raced through the pelt of rain to Gillons' house to telephone the doctor.

For three weeks he hovered precariously between life and death, and for most of that time he was either in a coma or delirious with fever, so that it was not until much later that we found out what had happened.

It appeared that after he left Windsor he found that conditions were just as bad in New South Wales as in Victoria, if not worse, so he had worked through the back country all the way to Sydney, enduring God knows what hardships and privations, and when Sydney proved as useless as anywhere else he had shipped as a deck-hand on a Chilean freighter bound back for South America. How he got his papers I never found out, but anyway the ship was laid up in Chile for want of a cargo and Jack was paid off. He got work for a few months as a labourer, helping to lay an oil-pipeline across the Chilean Andes, but then that project, too, failed because of the Depression, and Jack must have been in pretty desperate straits by the time he was shipped out of Valparaiso as a

" Distressed British Subject " in a tramp steamer bound for Sydney.

He landed back in Australia sick, exhausted, and virtually penniless. Not knowing where to go to be given help—or perhaps too proud to plead for it—and without any money for the fare, he set out to walk home to Melbourne. The way he went, with detours in search of work, was a journey of over seven hundred miles, for he had worked it out that the chances of finding odd jobs and occasional meals and shelter for the night would be better on the coastal road. He was wrong. Doors were closed, there were few hand-outs, even places of shelter were infrequent and far apart, and it was the dead of winter. Through the long, lonely stretches of the eastern forests he should, by all the standards of reasonable chance, have perished of starvation, of exposure, of exhaustion—yet somehow he survived. Once past Eden and Twofold Bay (where an earlier Jack Meredith had put a barque ashore), even the points of settlement were dangerously separated and the grim wet forests of Cape Howe and East Gippsland bitterly inhospitable. And still he survived. There were, of course, occasional kindnesses. A timber-splitter near Cape Disaster fed and sheltered him in his crude bark humpy for nearly a week: the lighthouse-keeper at Gabo Island looked after him for a day or two: near Orbost a dairy-farmer's wife gave him a bed and hot food during a storm that lasted forty-eight hours. But after Bairnsdale, which was still a long way from Melbourne, he never remembered anything of his journey home. Somehow the bloody pulp of his feet and the indomitability of his spirit carried him on.

I shall never know for certain what honing instinct it was that brought him back to our house. Was it only that he was ignorant of where Sheila was living? Or was it that in the blind delirium through which he moved this was, after all, the sanctuary to which those who were flagging always come for help? . . . the maimed and the sick and the ruined and the failed and the dying? That one terrible choking cry when the door was opened, " *Mum!*" insists to me that this was the prime and powerful force that urged him on.

Dr. Sheridan came and made his examination and gave little or no hope of survival. "Do what we can," he mumbled grumpily. " 'Fraid the poor devil's pretty far gone. Bad case.

Malnutrition, pneumonia, total physical debilitation, considerable loss of blood—those feet of his, really shocking state, you know!—can't tell what else besides. Do our best. Don't want to hold out too much hope, though."

"But shouldn't he go to a hospital?" I asked.

"Do just as well here. Have to be sat with, day and night, every minute. Get better care here, I think. Your mother is a first-rate nurse, after all. We can give the medical attention. Only be a matter of luck, anyway. Game's up if we try to move him at this stage. Better off here. Lap of the gods now."

Even Dad, although he was mumbling and grumbling all over the house, was deeply affected, and he offered no objection when Mother and I insisted that we should try to find Sheila Delaney. I was able to get small paragraphs inserted in two of the newspapers, and 3LO, the wireless station, put over police broadcasts at intervals for two successive days—"Would anyone knowing the whereabouts of Sheila Delaney, last heard of at . . . the matter is very urgent."

On the third day Sheila came from Moonee Ponds, where she had been sharing a room with her cousin. She brought her portmanteau with her. She seemed pale and anxious, and thinner than I remembered her, but she looked Dad squarely in the eyes and his own glance wavered and fell and he took the suitcase from her and said huskily, "You'd better go and see him. He's in there. I'm afraid he's—he's pretty crook." Dr. Sheridan was no more optimistic than he had been. But Jack was still alive.

She came out of the room after about ten minutes. Her distress was obvious—she was white as a sheet, and her hands were shaking, and I could see that she had been crying—so I led her down the passageway to my bedroom.

"But he looks ghastly, Davy," she whispered hopelessly. "He looks *terrible*! He—he didn't even know I was there."

"He hasn't been conscious since he came here," I told her awkwardly. "The doctor's been putting things into him with tubes. We—we've been trying to get you for two days," I said. "What on earth are you doing out there at Moonee Ponds?"

"I've been there almost a year," she said. She had wiped her eyes and was getting control of herself. "It—it was convenient. June helps me with the baby. Well, she's looking after it now."

"Baby?" I looked at her quickly. "Whose baby?"

"Jack's baby, of course. Whose would you think?"

There was a long pause before I could say, "A boy?"

She shook her head. "A girl." A faint smile touched her mouth and vanished. "I've called her Sharon," she said.

"Does Jack know?"

"No." She bit at her lip. "No, he doesn't know. He never wrote. I—I didn't know where he was."

"I suppose he didn't write because . . . well, if things were going badly with him he wouldn't want to worry you. He—he's not much of a letter-writer at the best of times."

"That's right," she said, and tried to smile.

"Would you have told him if you *had* known where he was?" I asked her.

She thought about this. "It would have depended, I suppose," she said. "I don't know, really. I would have told him if I thought it would have helped him. So I'm glad I couldn't tell him, I think. I don't see how it would have helped him to have known."

I rubbed at my knuckles and said, "Sheila, why didn't you get in touch with *me*? I could have helped you. You must have been having an awful time."

"Oh, we managed," she said.

The perspective of time has fused the anxieties and the tense pain of those interminable days and nights into a bearable recollection, yet there is one particular night that stays vividly with me. It was probably some time between midnight and three in the morning, because this was when I would usually take my turn to sit by the bedside. Jack was running a high fever that night, and off and on was raving in delirium about somebody who had cheated at two-up, or gabbling on about some racehorse that had "run dead," or trying to sing strange, slangy, ridiculous old football club parodies of years before:

> She barracks for Richmond I bet you a zac,
> Because her bloomers are yellow and black:
> Face like a dragon, bashed in by a waggon—
> That's Peggy O'Neill!

Probably it was the song that started me off, because it took me back at once to the school days we had shared, although there seemed no connection at all between the raving emaciated face on the white pillow and the cocky little Jackie Meredith of those earlier years. It occurred to me suddenly that this was the first time in his life that Jack had had the privilege of occupying the double-bed in the front room. The thought at once filled me with unspeakable horror; I stared aghast at the rumpled violet-patterned eiderdown, at the white-enamelled rods and columns of the huge contraption rising to the balls and acorns and crazy curlicues of brass, and behind all this in the shadows of the corner of the room was the toilet-commode that Aunt Lizzie had used, and suddenly the whole room in the weird dim glow of the night-light was dancing with the apparitions from a nightmare. They were all there, gibbering around that big bed in which most of them had suffered and some of them had died— Stubby and Aleck and Gabby Dixon, my grandmother Emma clutching her picture of the *Grafton*, Aunt Lizzie and Auntie Gin and all the rest of them . . . and now my own brother was there among them, colourless as a corpse on a starched white pillow, with a glaze of sweat on his wasted face, stretched out in a dreadful dying smell of rosewater-and-glycerine and stale talcum and sweat and iodine and chamber-pots . . . that old familiar smell of death in a closed room . . . and then I found myself out in the hallway, shaking like a leaf, and beating on the door, and calling, " Mum! Mum! I think you'd better come!"

She came in her shabby dressing-gown and took over with her cool, practised efficiency, and I saw that Jack's fever had passed and he was lying quite still and breathing fairly evenly, and Mother was dabbing his temples with cologne and smoothing down the sheets and putting things to rights on the medicine-table.

She gave me a tired smile as she went back to her own bedroom, and as soon as I heard her door close I moved across to the chest-of-drawers and reached for the bottle of medicinal brandy. That was the first drink of alcohol I had ever taken. I pulled the cork out and drank from the bottle —one choking, scalding gulp to burn the pain out.

Jack recovered. Dr. Sheridan shook his head almost in disbelief it seemed, and mumbled something about " constitution of an ox, by Jove!" and Sheila went out to Moonee Ponds and came back to the house with the baby Sharon, six months old and beginning to be very pretty. (A few years back they sent me the catalogue of her first show of sculpture; I was very sad that I was not able to attend the opening, although I did buy one of her pieces, a small bronze " Lucifer," which is up there now on the ledge in front of my desk.)

As Jack's health began to mend, Dad showed a very definite inclination to pull down the flag of truce and resume hostilities—he had got hold of some handbooks on freemasonry to reinforce his arguments—but Sheila Delaney had her man and her child now as well as her own spirit, and Dad was no match for her. About two months after Jack's return they rented a little house at Black Rock and went away.

In the meantime I had telephoned Joe Denton. Things were beginning to pick up at Klebendorf's, he told me, and all the artists, except old Steiner, who had died, were back to full-time work. I told him what was in my mind, and he promised to do what he could; I imagine he felt under some deep obligation to me because of what I had done to help Young Joe. At any rate he telephoned me that same afternoon.

" Yes, I talked to Werner Klebendorf about it," he said. " There's a job going as storeman in the paper department. At the moment it's only temporary. Old Jamieson's still there, of course—we can't very well put *him* off, after all these years—but he's really too old now and too weak to lift the bales. Tell your brother he could start next Monday if it suits him."

Jack took the job and a month later old Jamieson died, and Jack got a permanent job as storeman-packer in the Klebendorf and Hardt paper store, so he rode out the Depression, after all, without ever having taken the " Susso " or put on the dyed black coat.

It was at this time that I took my savings out of the bank to help Mother and Dad redecorate the house, which was looking pretty down-at-heel because nothing much had been done to it since the end of the war. I bought three-ply panels and cedar battens and new wallpapers and various paints and everything that was needed, and we dug out the old Dollicus and tore its vast clinging dark haunted bulk away from the sleep-out wire, and although I remember ripping it down very savagely, it was not until I was in the front hallway hammering up the new panelling that I realised what I was doing.

I was trying to hammer out all the past, trying to seal it off forever behind a skin of polished veneer—the crutches and the wooden legs and the wheel-chairs and the smell of funerals and the comings and the goings, and Mother weeping in the night, and a boy standing with an old-fangled typewriter in his arms and Jack's body sprawled there on the faded wet carpet.

All through the afternoon I worked, silent and intent, hammering on the cedar sheets and the panel strips, battering away at childhood and boyhood and youth, desperately driving nail after nail after nail through the treacherous emotions of a tiny suburban history.

CHAPTER 10

The way in which Helen Midgeley came back into my life was quite fortuitous, really, and perhaps it would never have happened had I not gone to work with the *Morning Post*.

There were formalities to be observed when I first joined the newspaper. I was obliged to begin as a first-year cadet, which meant that for the second time in my life I was working for fifteen shillings a week (in my case, however, the normal four years of cadetship eventually were compressed into eighteen months), and for many weeks I was kept on what were called " day rounds."

Much of this was rather dreary routine work, like checking with the principal hotels to collect paragraphs for the " Personal column," or picking up the mimeographed Stock Exchange and market reports, or compiling the daily Shipping Intelligence lists of arrivals and departures and working out tide-tables and making up the directory of where ships were berthed in the port. All this was presumed to be part of a training in the accuracy of compiling and presenting facts. The *Post* was rather a special sort of newspaper (it was swallowed up a few years back in some big company merger, and promptly " killed," after a century or more of always reputable and sometimes distinguished journalism), and it went to great pains in the training of its cadets. They were members of what was always called the "Literary Staff," and this was not entirely as high-falutin' as it sounds: the paper's editorials were used as English lessons in some of Melbourne's best public schools at that time, and a cadet who used a split infinitive even in a "personal" paragraph would risk a week's suspension, and any chronic mutilation of syntax might even lose him his job altogether.

In addition to the routine work, I would be assigned on three mornings a week to cover the inquests at the City Morgue. These would be only the run-of-the-mill inquests, of course, because a senior man would always be sent down if a hearing looked sensational or if it seemed likely that old Lewis, the coroner, would have to bring in a finding of murder or manslaughter. Otherwise a cadet would be there at the press table for the drownings and suicides and accidents and misadventures that cropped up day after day and never made the news columns, on the off-chance of picking up a freak story, or if old Lewis, who had a sharp sense of publicity, sounded off in his summing-up with one of his always highly printable outbursts on drunken drivers or the dangers of household mishaps or the laxity of controls on potentially lethal drugs. But mostly, I suspect, the cadets were sent along to be toughened up, to have their natural sensitivities rubbed into professional callouses against the raw, stark facts of life and death. A coroner's court is the place for this.

(Often since then I have thought of those mornings at the morgue in Melbourne, of the enormous scope and range of human disaster in a big city too hackneyed or too unimportant to justify even an inch of column-space in a newspaper—the despairing struggles, the fruitless aims, the base endeavours, picked out on two fingers by a constable clerk, folded up in the sheets of a typed deposition, and filed away forever with a pink tape around the folder. . . .)

The morgue at this time was very much a part of a great change in my life. Although I still lived at home, Jack's return and the panelling up of the front hall had dislodged me finally from that house in the suburbs called *Avalon*. I had moved out at last—or had I, perhaps, been moved out?—into a world which for years I had been doing my utmost to evade. There was no way of side-stepping it at the City Morgue—it stared down at you from the high bench in the grey compassionate unhardened eyes of the old coroner, it played across the nervous, frightened faces of the witnesses, it bubbled out through the incomprehensibly gabbled testimonies of old Cartwright, the Government pathologist who did the autopsies. It was almost as if life were presenting to me its darkest and most macabre face simply to sever me irrevocably from my complacencies.

The *Post*, as I have indicated, was an old-fashioned and very conservative newspaper. It never ran a suicide story. It would never print the name of a woman if in any way her reputation might be imperilled. It never publicised abortion. But nonetheless one had to sit the cases through—the cold cross-examinations, the exposures of sordid desperations and pitiful surrenders, the grisly analyses of criminal abortions shabbily conducted in shabby parlours, with all the talk of furtive appointments and slippery elm and knitting needles, and the coarse frightened faces . . . the grimmest of the facts of life summed up in that most poignant of all phrases— " death by misadventure."

Sometimes, between the cases, I would have to walk down to the bank of the Yarra, just to get away from it, just to reaffirm other values of life and beauty: and there would be a pair of black swans and one white one floating beneath the arches of Prince's Bridge, or two of the public schools eights practising for the Head of the River, or an old woman feeding crumbs to the doves, and one would be able to return refreshed to the grim building that looked out across the slow river to the trees and the green roll of the parklands and the proud flag flying over Government House.

Yet after a remarkably short time one got used to it all, and would even affect a bored cynicism at the dullness of the day. By this time, admittedly, I had modelled myself to fit into the new challenge. I had bought a gaberdine trench-coat (which I painstakingly soiled) and a smart brown pork-pie hat, I had begun to smoke, and I would take a daring glass or two of beer in the pubs with the other young reporters. I began, I think, to grow very cocksure. It was one thing to be a lithographic apprentice, it was something altogether different to be a newspaper reporter! I had a sense of being somebody.

I had a frame around me. I was nourished by the flowing sap of green years.

And it was in this immensely vulnerable state that I met Helen Midgeley again. . . .

An enormous " escape " thing had developed out of the Depression, a yearning desire among people to be distracted from the miseries and fears of the times—even in the darkest " Susso " days you had to queue for half a block to get into a Ginger Rogers-Fred Astaire film—and among the urban effects of this were the proliferation of innumerable little coffee-lounges where in dim lights one could talk terror away, or intellectually invite it into safe surroundings, and a fantastic flourishing all through the suburbs of the threepenny lending-libraries.

Along the main street in our suburb there must have been at least a score of these libraries at that time, and although most of them were tiny little shops run by elderly bookish spinsters who were forever recommending Jeffrey Farnol or Georgette Heyer or Ethel M. Dell, one of them, the largest, was part of a suburban chain owned by a sly, asthmatic little shrimp of a man called Perce Parkinson. Each of his libraries was managed by a young and attractive girl, partly to invite custom and partly because Perce lived in a permanent and vain delusion that he would be able to overcome his asthma sufficiently to exert a successful *droit de seigneur* over his pretty hirelings.

" Day rounds " at the *Morning Post* seldom ended before seven or eight at night, or sometimes even later, but I had got into the habit of walking up to Kooyong Road from the railway station, instead of taking the tram, because it seemed to be a way of prolonging the excitements of the day. One spring evening when I was on my way home I stopped to look at the books on display in the windows of Perce Parkinson's library, which stayed open until nine-thirty so that subscribers could come down after their supper and select their reading at leisure, and I glanced inside and there was Helen Midgeley sitting at the desk. A man was standing beside her. She pressed down on a date-stamp, giving it a firm little wobble, fingered through a filing-cabinet, entered something on a card, said " I'm sure you'll like Mowrer—he has something to say," flashed a quick cordial, workmanlike smile at the man, and handed him his books. He came out, and I went in.

"Good heavens," I said, "what on earth are *you* doing here?"

For a moment she looked at me without recognition, and then she smiled. It was an entirely different smile from the one she had offered her customer.

"David Meredith!" she exclaimed. "Well, for goodness' sake!" She looked me up and down. "You've changed," she said, and I was pleasantly aware of a note of admiration in her comment.

"So have you," I said. "Well, it must be nearly four years. . . ." I wanted to say something very clever, but all I said was, "People *should* change in that time, I suppose."

She had grown very pretty. Her hair was much blonder than I had remembered—a gleaming metallic paleness that seemed to pick up light from everywhere, waved very smoothly to the nape of her neck, and then curved up into two heavy glittering sausage-like rolls that came forward to touch her cheekbones. Her eyebrows, which were much darker than her hair, brown almost, were plucked to the finest of arches.

She was dressed very smartly, or so it seemed to me. A navy-blue linen skirt that was fitted to just below her knees, then swirling out around her calves in hundreds of small pleats (skirts were getting longer) and a fine white rayon blouse with navy-blue coin spots, and big Spanish-looking sleeves puffing out from a small curved bolero of the same material as her skirt. Her small waist was cinched in with a red leather belt, and under the neat collar of her blouse she wore a floppy red satin artist's bow. Her lipstick was of the same red—dark and daring. It seemed to me to be a very striking costume, and in spite of the surroundings of battered library books and ink-pads and glue bottles she looked immaculate.

I suppose it was the smartness of her dress and the fact of the artist's bow that prompted me to say, "So whatever happened to the fashion-designing?"

"There's been a Depression, didn't you know?" she said and made a mouth at me. She stood up then. She was almost as tall as I was, and so slender in the tight waist and skirt that her hip-bones projected in two tiny peaks below the red belt, and her long lean legs in flesh-coloured sheer silk had the colour and fragility of the legs of some graceful wading-bird. All her bones were fine—ankles, wrists, jaw-bone, nose. To-day we might have thought of her as having a kind of mannequin elegance: what I remember from that time is a swift fugitive thought, almost a regretful one, that she was prettier than Sheila, but I qualified it by thinking that she was somehow not as warm-looking.

I remember being startled at the improbability of her smartness and her obvious self-confidence in that rather dreary suburban setting, for I was too naïve then to realise that the great suburban artifice is to be smart on nothing, and all of this impressed me so profoundly that I was lost from the very beginning.

"I'm just locking up the shop," she said. "Would you like to stay and have a cup of tea or something?" I accepted with an almost hungry eagerness.

I examined the place curiously while she was tidying things away. The two side walls were shelved from floor to ceiling and subdivided into sections marked off with printed cards—ROMANCE, ADVENTURE, WILD WEST, DETECTIVE, GENERAL, TRAVEL, JUVENILE, NON-FICTION. ("ROMANCE" occupied by far the largest space.) There were tall stands by the windows with big bowls of Iceland poppies, and apart from these the only furnishings were the desk and filing-cabinet, two leather arm-chairs, and a huge, high-backed couch covered with rubbed Genoa velvet. At the rear of the shop, between high narrow shelves respectively marked NEW ISSUES and AUSTRA-LIANA, a curtained doorway presumably led to some private apartment.

This almost at once was to be revealed to me, for by this time she had locked the outer door and switched off the shop lights, and by the dim, secret glow filtering in from the street lamps she led me through the curtains into a pair of very small rooms, divided by a folk-weave curtain of the same material that draped the doorway.

The larger of the two areas was obviously a workshop where books were rebound and had their covers attended to. The air was oppressively heavy with the stinging pungent amyl-acetate smell of quick-drying clear lacquer. There was a small handpress, under which six books were flatly squashed, and a long, zinc-topped bench on which glue and lacquer had congealed in a brittle, peeling, transparent film, and paste-pots and white ink and labels and a stack of book-jacket covers and " blurbs " cut out ready to be pasted on to the covers before they were lacquered over.

The smaller area was a kind of tiny sitting-room, not much more than a box, really, but very neat and feminine, with a cane arm-chair and two straight chairs and a little cupboard which was covered with a patterned oil-cloth with scalloped edges. On top of this was a gas-ring, a tray of cups and saucers, a small willow-pattern set of teapot, jug, and sugar-basin, and a very shiny aluminium kettle. Miniature pots of small cacti were ranged neatly along a wall shelf, and above this was a framed Marie Laurencin print in pale pinks and faded blues and greys of a girl who bore a singular if fortuit-ous resemblance to Helen.

A narrow book-shelf to the left of the gas-ring harboured a selection of volumes which, had I been a little older, instantly might have afforded me some clue to Helen's character. A number of them were from the thin, lobster-pink editions of the Left Book Club, and *Das Kapital* was there, and Veblen's *Theory of the Leisure Class*, and *42nd Parallel* and *Three Soldiers* and *Ten Days that Shook the World*.

From the workshop section a door led out into a small over-grown garden where there was a toilet and a poky wash-room. The broken brick path in the garden was set with big rat-traps.

After all this time it is interesting—and very sad, too, in a way—to draw on memory in such careful detail as to present in fair proportion the setting of one's downfall: to this day that sharp sickly smell of amyl-acetate will often set me wondering about the strange bowers which modern civilisation generally provides for our initiations into the holiest of nature's rites. It did not happen, however, on that first night that I visited Perce Parkinson's threepenny library.

" Will you have tea? " she said. " Or would you prefer a glass of beer? "

" No, I'd love a cup of tea," I said. She put the kettle on, and from the cupboard she took a bottle of lager and a glass for herself, and I was sorry then that I had not asked for beer.

We sat and talked together for more than an hour. I told her what I had been doing, and she gave me an account of her own experiences since that night of the birthday party in Royal Parade. She was still friendly, it seemed, with Moira and Jerry Farley. Jerry was a salesman of tractors and farm machinery, and doing well for himself, but Moira's ambitions to be a great artist evidently had also curdled, for she was now a salesgirl in the lingerie department at Myer's.

"So you're the only one of us who did what you said you were going to do, aren't you?" she remarked. "You always insisted you were going to be a writer. And now you are."

"Well . . . sort of." I wanted to sound modest, but her obvious admiration gave me a tingling feeling of warmth towards her.

"You know, I'd give anything to be a journalist," she said vehemently. "To have the chance of *doing* something. To be able to champion the causes."

"What causes?" I asked.

"Well, you know . . . *everything*!" She spread her long-fingered hands in a gesture of eloquent despair. "The whole world is falling to pieces in front of our very eyes, and nobody cares. Nobody *does* anything. Except to try to crush the working class and sabotage everything that's decent. Just look what's happening in Europe! Mussolini, and that beastly Hitler . . . yes, and you watch Spain, too . . . and the way they're all winking an eye at Fascism just because they're terrified of Russia. David, it makes me want to puke, it really does!"

"Oh, all that, yes," I said, without very much enthusiasm. One heard quite a bit of this sort of talk in the reporters' room, too, mostly among the younger ones, but I had never paid much attention to it. Listening to Helen—because she talked on about the disaster of the Depression and the way the capitalists were trying to keep the masses in their places —I had no great wish to go crusading or to champion causes about which I really knew very little, but that hour in the back room of Perce Parkinson's library was my first intro- duction to Political Woman, and I must admit that it was heady stuff.

Helen Midgeley, after all, was four years older than I, and I was greatly impressed by her sophistication, by her intellectual qualities, by her balanced maturity, and in that neat little annexe where the sharp tang of amyl-acetate was subtly softened by a smell of women's cosmetics and the faint moody odour of the perfume she used, her smart cool beauty was somehow immeasurably enhanced, and I thought of the sofa in Sam Burlington's studio and the queer musky smell that poor Jess had left there, and so I said, " What sort of perfume do you use?" and the *non sequitur* cutting clean across her political tirade obviously delighted her because she smiled with a touch of coquetry and said, " Lenthéric. D'you like it?"; and partly it was the pleasure I felt at my conversational adroitness, and partly a stinging sense of joy that she used Lenthéric and not Evening in Paris (although I could not for the life of me have told the difference), and partly the unmistakable expression in her cool grey eyes that finally sealed my captivation to her.

I called at the library again the following evening, but Perce Parkinson was there, watchfully suspicious, and Helen was very crisp and efficient, and I contented myself with entering my name as a subscriber, and paying the deposit, and taking away two books dealing with European political affairs which Helen recommended.

After that I was a regular caller, and I would make a point of getting there as late as possible, so that Helen would be locking up the shop and I would be asked out into the back room.

I was there on a warm evening towards the end of the second week when she excused herself and went through the curtain and out the back door into the garden. I reached over and took down Thorstein Veblen and I was idly turning his pages when something made me look up, and Helen was standing just inside the parting of the curtain, with one hand on her hip and the other holding back the drape, and she had taken all her clothes off! She just stood there, not four feet away from where I sat rigid in the cane arm-chair, looking down at me with the tiniest suggestive smile at her mouth, and the only adornment to her slender startling nudity was a heart-shaped gold locket on a chain around her neck.

That much I remember. Her overpowering loveliness, that smile beneath the casque of golden hair, the long lean flanks of her nakedness, youthful sensuality imaged for me for the first time. My reaction to this was ludicrous. I must have leapt up from the chair and pushed right past her in a blind panic of embarrassment and fright. I remember nothing really except the slam of the shop door behind me, and then I was running, with pumping arms and jerking legs and whistling breath, running beneath the blue dip of the overhead tramway lights; running along beneath the verandas of dark locked shops and through the mad quick pursuing echo of my clattering heels; running along the blank hedges and the blind borders of the walls, past drifts of fallen peppercorns and peeling posters that flapped and scratched in the night wind, and I must have run for almost a mile before I reeled to a standstill, gasping, and brought my knee up to take the pain out of the " stitch " in my side, and then there was nothing else to do but to face my own hot pained confused self, but it was still early and there were people walking around the streets, so I cut across to the Hopetoun Gardens and went in and sat on the carriage of one of the old Boer War cannons and tried to examine my anger and mortification and shame. It must have been quite some time before I worked it out that whatever it cost me in humiliation I would have to go back to the library anyway; because my hat and raincoat were there and my books and some papers I needed for work.

I could have saved myself all the mental agony. When I finally did walk back the padlock was on the shop door and Helen had gone home.

Yet the following evening it was as if nothing whatever had happened. Helen did mention my having left the hat and the raincoat, but quite casually, as one mentioned someone having left an umbrella long after the rain has stopped. Once the shop was locked she took out beer and two glasses instead of making tea, and we drank some in a deliberately drawn-out way, and then she came and sat on my knee and she kissed me and moved her fingers over me, and when she was ready she led me out to the old couch in the dimly-lighted shop.

I suppose it was a better initiation than I deserved, really. Helen Midgeley was—and while I knew her remained—a neat,

clean, expedient, safe lover rather than a particularly expert
or a particularly passionate one, and she always seemed to
get about as much satisfaction out of it as she ever really
wanted, but at least she was kind about it and patient with my
ineptitudes. (I clumsily slipped off the couch and bruised my
knee painfully on the floor! I had ghastly images of everything being drenched in blood; it was not until some time
later that it occurred to me that it was only *my* virginity that
was being taken!)

It is a wonderful and fearful experience, that first physical
communion with a woman . . . the feverish fumbling, the sad
inexperienced groping for those complex and eternal mysteries
that are harboured in a woman's body, those wobbly intrusions into the perilous poetry associated with a hundred
bewildering new sensations of both the flesh and the spirit:
no matter how many women we may enjoy later nor how
adept we become in the practices of sex, there is probably no
other moment in life that ever repeats itself with such an
excitingly exact mixture of alarm and ecstasy; fear and
frenzy; doubt and intoxication; delight and dread. In a first
seduction, I think, however foolish or naïve or ridiculous,
there is some wistful breathless magic which preserves forever—even if the preservative be sadness or regret—some little
memorable trace of a great wonder and a great loveliness . . .
Perhaps. I grappled with Helen Midgeley on a Genoa velvet
couch in a darkness that seemed too dark and yet not dark
enough, and I desperately tried to remember the things my
brother Jack had told me years before.

Yet that first night must have been satisfying enough in its
way, because it established a kind of pattern for the strange
relationship that was to continue for several years. The
centre-piece of this experience continued to be the huge old
Genoa velvet couch. As we grew bolder we would take off all
our clothes in the back room, then one of us would peep
through the curtains to make sure the coast was clear, and
we would scamper out in the pale illumination which filtered
into the shop from the lights on the overhead tram wires, or
flashed more brightly from the headlights of passing cars, and
like two pagan lovers in a play of moonlight we would fling
ourselves together on to the couch. The couch normally faced
towards the rear of the shop so that once we were coupled

together upon its rubbed resilient velvet its high back would effectively obscure our activities from the street and from passers-by who might chance to peer in through the big plate-glass windows. But one night when I came I saw that Helen had turned the couch the other way around, so that it was directly facing the front of the shop and the plate-glass windows, and when she was stacking the last of the books away I asked her, "Why is the sofa this way?"

"I just thought it might be fun, darling," she said eagerly. "I mean, there's hardly a glimmer of light *really* comes in, is there? Don't you think it'd be marvellous to lie here, the two of us together, making love, and watching the crowds walking past coming home from the pictures!" She giggled suddenly and put her hand over her mouth . . . "And none of them even suspecting we're here at all!"—she giggled again. "Well, if they did see they wouldn't believe their eyes . . . they'd just think they were imagining things!"

"Not for me!" I said firmly. "Oh, no, not on your life! What if one of them has a torch and flashes it in? Or suppose it's the local constable on his rounds, checking? He always shines a torch into the shops, doesn't he?" I took hold of one end of the couch. "That'd really give him something for his note-book! You just grab the other end of this and let's get it back the way it was!"

"I must say you're not very adventurous," she said with a little pout, although she didn't really seem upset by my firm-ness, and later when we were making love she began to giggle again and said, "My! it *would* give them a shock if they looked in and *saw*, wouldn't it?"

One night I asked her what she kept in the locket she always wore around her neck, and which I would often encounter when I was caressing her small high breasts. "You'd never guess in a million years," she said.

"Then I shan't try and so you'd better tell me."

"Oh, no, I'll show you," she said agreeably. We were in the back room at the time, dressing, and she snipped the catch of the locket and bent over me, still half-naked, to show me tiny facing photographs (clipped from a halftone magazine illustration) of two swarthy, intense-looking men, sealed within tiny ellipses of glass.

"Who are they?" I asked.

"The martyrs," she said, rather melodramatically. "Sacco and Vanzetti."

"Oh, come on!" I exclaimed. "You mean those two Italian bolshies who got electrocuted years ago? In America? You're not serious!"

"Yes, the martyrs." She nodded and closed the locket reverently and began to fasten her brassière.

"But isn't that a . . . well, a funny kind of a thing to keep in a locket?" I said, still not quite believing that she could be serious.

"Why funny? It's a reminder," she said stoutly, "of man's inhumanity to man."

"Yes, but you can be reminded of that a million different ways," I said. "You don't have to hang it in a gold locket around your neck, do you? Shaped like a heart, too. I'd have thought you'd have kept a picture of your mother in it, or a lock of hair from when you were a baby, or something like that. . . ."

"Well, it happens *I* like to keep my martyrs," she said determinedly, and pulled her stockings up along her thin, graceful, elegant legs. Later she made me read *Boston*, the Upton Sinclair novel about the Sacco-Vanzetti case, but it didn't make much impression on me, and often afterwards when I was making love to her, or just fondling her, my fingers would come across the little golden locket with the dead radicals inside and I would very gently caress this tiny receptacle that was the casket of political martyrdom—as warm from the life of her own breasts as if the electrocuting charge had just burnt through it—and waves of silent inward laughter would threaten to choke me, and when this would happen I would deliberately rub her pinky-brown nipples with the Sacco-Vanzetti locket until they swelled into hard little columns of sexual erection. . . .

When, a little later, the *Morning Post* graduated me to general rounds, at night, I was able to see Helen much less frequently. But she was usually there on the occasions when I did need her, and she was always accommodating and never demanding. Of her family life, indeed of any life she lived outside the library, I knew virtually nothing at that time. She was a member of some suburban tennis club, I gathered, and I think she would go to its socials and dances, and she was too pretty not to have boy friends, but I knew nothing about them; in all those years I never once took her out at night, and I never even really knew what she did with herself at week-ends. For me she existed only as a part of Perce Parkinson's threepenny library, and the little rooms at the back and the cups of tea and the smells of gum and amyl-acetate and Lethéric, and the old big couch of Genoa velvet that had come to have the smell of the sofa in Sam's studio after Jess had been there.

It was an odd arrangement (I imagine it could have gone on for years and then petered away into nothing, and probably would have except that my importance became important to Helen) and the very oddness of it, of course, suited me down to the ground. Here I was with my own secret mistress, who was beautiful and clever and kind and who asked for nothing, it seemed, except my occasional attentions. She left me free of social obligations and at work I could press my ambitions without distraction. I felt myself to be in an enviable and singular state of grace. It did not occur to me then that one day I might have to pay for all these special dispensations.

CHAPTER 11

There is a useful clue to that time—for a good deal more was happening than these late awakenings of sexuality or the beginnings of a kind of maturity—in the importance we used to attach then to the Monday morning arrivals of the incoming mail steamers, the Orient Line or the P. & O., from London and the European ports: it was always my regular assignment on these days to meet the ships and to interview the more important passengers before they went ashore at Port Melbourne. I would be up long before dawn and would board the ships far down Port Phillip Bay from the launch that carried the customs officers and the port doctor and the harbour pilot and the man from Thomas Cook's with his leather bag of currency to change.

We would see the faint blur of lights down the beacon-flashing curve of the South Channel, and then the big lean graceful shape would emerge out of stardust and darkness and the ground-scum of morning and mist patches brushed across the flat sea and the dark awakening shore of Rosebud and Dromana and Mornington. To the west, the Werribee marsh-flats would remain dismal and forbiddingly black, with only a faint forlorn light from some building on the sewage farm, and even when the sun did come up it would just turn the line of earth dismally and forbiddingly grey instead of black. But by this time we would usually be aboard the big liner.

There would be a wait, tossing in the launch, until the great ship declared itself in the whiteness of superstructure, in the clarification of masts and Samson posts and the orderly array of lifeboats, and the elegant yellow smokestacks and house-flags and pennants and signal-hoists lit dramatically by the floodlighting, and we would hang on a line in a rush of foam below the .jacob's-ladder until the doctor gave medical pratique, and then we would climb aboard into a strange confined warm sea-smelling humming world of sleepy-eyed officers yawning over greetings, and stewards buttoning jackets, and seamen in bare feet sloshing water about with squeegees in lighted alleyways, and a few dishevelled pas-sengers in bathrobes shuffling to the shower blocks with towels and toothbrushes, and through all of this there would be the clang of bells and the throb of power through the muffling decks and the faint changing cadence of the engine vibrations until one would know that the liner had cleared the channel and the big tugs, the *Taronga* and the *James Patterson*, were making the great manila hawsers fast to their towing-bits.

The purser would take us down to the empty dining saloon for breakfast, and he would give each of us a copy of the captain's report of the voyage and a mimeographed " pro-minent passenger list," and after we had had breakfast we would try to hunt them out in their cabins. There were times when the passengers, anxious to pack and get ashore, would be angry at our intrusions, but generally they liked being interviewed.

So far as Australia is concerned, this, of course, was a very old tradition which newspapers like the *Morning Post* had continued to keep up, because being so far away from the rest of the world, twelve thousand miles, in fact (this was the figure they always liked to give for Melbourne: " After all, we *are* twelve thousand miles away from these events!" they would say in apology, or as an explanation, or to waive responsibility), and before the time of radio or submarine cables, this had been the only way for generations that the people of Melbourne had got any news at all of the outside world, by shipping reporters meeting ships coming through The Rip and up the South Channel—the old-fashioned square-rigged steamship packets and the fast sailing clippers—and talking to passengers and bringing ashore copies of English and sometimes even Cape Town newspapers (even the " latest " news therefore would be anything from a month to three months old by the time it got to Melbourne, so that " news," rather than being something that actually was happening *now*, had more the quality of the light of a distant star, in that the cognition of the light had no true relationship to the moment of its emission, but there was nothing else to go by.)

I think this sharp and almost traditional sense of isolation from the things that were happening in Europe—which in a subtle way is still very important to the average Australian mentality—was most profoundly felt in the 'thirties. I do know that right through almost until the time of Munich the meeting of those Monday morning passenger liners continued to be of great importance, and each week, ritually, parties of reporters and photographers would go down the dark bay and climb the jacob's-ladder and expect to find in a two-berth cabin some revelation or oracular presence or mystical enlightenment which, in bringing truth from far away, might help explain the dissonance of the world.

By this time we had our cable services and our radio broadcasts, of course, yet it still seemed that whatever was happening in Europe, the spiritual truth of events, I mean, could be given reality only by the fact of somebody *talking* about them.

He had to be there, right there in front of us, sitting in a tasteful cabin with the louvres faintly whistling, describing the smoke pall above the Reichstag, or the massed banners tossing on the Tempelhof or the endless torchlit tramplings of the Brownshirt columns down through the Brandenburger Tor and along the Unter den Linden and the Wilhelmstrasse . . . or telling of the night-rappings, the shots in the streets, the forced arrests, the marks on walls, the brandings, and the whispered rumours of Sachsenhausen and Buchenwald and

Ravensbrück . . . or scoring the grim comic-opera of Mussolini ranting from his balcony. . . . Only then did it all move out of the pages of the lobster-pink editions of the Left Book Club that were on Helen's bookshelf; only then did it become part of the true and terrible dissonance of the times.

Once, in one of these early morning ships riding up out of the South Channel off a dawn-gilded Luna Park, a great theosophist came, and his followers then were hailing him as the " New Messiah," but we caught him in his shower and he hid his ascetic nakedness behind an Orient Line bath towel and shook his gentle beautiful face very sadly, and he had no solutions to offer nor any explanations of why Brazil was throwing the coffee crop into the sea or America was burning its wheat or Hitler torturing Jews or Mussolini bombing Ethiopians. There was no answer, he insisted, except love . . . Christian love. That, for some reason, didn't seem enough.

Dissonance is a good word for that mad little era, I think. It was a time of dissonance. People were looking at their own problems so closely and so bitterly, and with such total confusion that it was very hard for them to see much else. I think most reasonably intelligent persons were aware that something of awful importance was happening—even if it *was* twelve thousand miles away—but nobody could define it with any sort of precision at all, because the discordances rang in their ears instead of truths, and everyone was inclined to push away the things that were too complex and *new*, and so the strange terrible forces that were forming were still being assessed by old ideals and prejudices and judgments— like Helen with her clichés about the down-trodden masses and her childish belief in the symbolic magic of the martyrs in her locket; or like Dad turning his back on it all by having a sign screwed to the front gate—and what *is* incredible is that out of all this woolly thinking true causes *did* begin to take shape: and although I have been told often enough since by the new clutches of young intellectuals that the arguments were weakly based and were blind to the deeper problems, the fact remains, I think, that that was just about the last time the world did have true, pure causes to believe in. Or thought it had.

It certainly created a particular generation. They belong to me even though I defected on them, and I can pick them now with my eyes closed, just by the way they talk—they are all well into their forties now, or older—and although I don't know one among them who is an idealist any longer, and in fact most of them seem to be rabid cynics about most things, there is still a sort of soft patch of belief in them somewhere, and they all have a little weakness in their hard-shelled armour about that time of the 'thirties when the world had causes. It always gives this queer faint flavour of pessimism to their words.

What was even more curious in a way was that the greater the defections and the political betrayals, the more powerfully valid these causes grew, so that even after the way we would betray Haile Selassie or connive with Hitler or play along with Mussolini there were any number of these eager young idealists more ready than ever to take sides on Spain. The Germans had an odd system operating at this time because they were desperate to get foreign currency into their country, and so they were selling very cheap passages to Europe through their Reichsmarks, which meant that you could get all the way from Melbourne to a port in Europe for only about twenty Australian pounds, and so this was the way most young Australians would travel if they wanted to get to Spain and fight against the Fascists.

Two of the young shipping reporters on the other newspapers, Johnny Drew and Noel Grantham, who were close good friends of mine, both bought Reichsmarks tickets for Rotterdam on a Norddeutscher-Lloyd ship, the *Aller*, and this was a strange thing in a way because Johnny had been one of the real leftist radicals at the University, and he was going to enlist in the International Brigade, and Noel Grantham was a fervent Roman Catholic and he intended to join Franco's forces. They were the best of friends and remained that way. They shared a cabin going over, with lots of political arguments but no quarrels, and travelled from Rotterdam across France together and then parted at the Spanish frontier. They never saw each other again. Johnny died of gangrene in a Franco prison. Noel was wounded but got to London, where he worked as a police parole officer at first, and then he went back to newspaper work and later became a war correspondent. I suppose the 'thirties was the last time in the world when that sort of thing could have happened, when people could still take political sides without prejudice to personal feelings.

The real point about all this is that in the original arrangement I was supposed to go with Noel and Johnny—I had even bought my Reichsmarks and pencilled my booking on the *Aller*—but then Helen stepped in at the last minute and stopped it all. After all her talk of " causes " and political commitment " it was a little disconcerting to find her so stubbornly insistent that I should stay at home.

The *Aller* was delayed for a couple of weeks by some stevedore's strike, and this made things rather awkward for me with Johnny and Noel, although they never reproached me when I cancelled my booking, and when I said to Helen, " But I feel so bloody guilty about it: I should give them a *reason* why I'm pulling out! " she just smiled and said, " Nonsense, you've just got to tell them you've fallen in love and you're engaged to be married, that's all. Besides, you're far too useful in other directions, although you don't have to tell them *that*."

In fact, to be perfectly honest, it was rather a relief to me that she did take this stand, and once she had put her foot down I didn't really try to challenge it. (To this day I do not remember that I actually proposed marriage to her, although perhaps I did, since a date for it was fixed and the church settled.) I had never been caught up in the causes the way Johnny Drew or Noel Grantham had been, for one of them really had a political conscience and the other was a devout and militant Christian, and I had been taken along willy-nilly in something that I was never at all clear about. What I had come to blindly sense through the long pattern of the shipboard interviews was something to do with human suffering that I felt a kind of responsibility to try to understand . . . not necessarily to *do* something about, but just to try to understand . . . and these baffling questions seemed to me to belong more to the Dollicus and the wardrobe drawer and the things in our old hallway than to Helen's tracts and catchcries, but I could never see them clearly enough to grasp at them. They were just shadows, the shadows of carnival balloons or of crucifixions, they were the echoes of running feet fading down long empty corridors, they were the sound of subdued voices heard from the other side of high blank walls, they were erasures in an anonymous letter. They were a burden of troublesome images that defied elucidation. (Jack had a quite straightforward attitude to all these things: when I told him I had booked aboard the *Aller*, he said: "You ought to have your bloody head read! What d'you want to go away fighting for a lot of wops and dagoes for? There's plenty to do here, isn't there?")

I remember the first time a German ship came in flying the new Swastika flag of the Nazis. She was the *Stassfurt*, one of the regular old Hamburg-Australia Line ships which had been calling at Melbourne for years. There had already been some publicity about the new flag and a bunch of leftists were lined up on the end of Victoria Docks carrying placards and shouting slogans and even throwing lumps of coal. But the passengers aboard the steamer were either Australians or European businessmen or German-Jews fleeing from Hitlerism, and even under the new Swastika flag flying right there at the masthead they talked quite openly about the evils of Nazism, while the neat German steward brought out Bock and lager in tall beaded steins, and all the passengers, even the Jews, agreed that they couldn't have been treated better on the passage out from Hamburg.

Yet the queer thing is that not one of the German ships was ever the same after that day. They were the very ships that I had watched in and out of the docks for years, the long graceful four-masters of the Norddeutscher-Lloyd, the *Main* and the *Aller* and the *Neckar* and the *Mosel*, and the spotless, stumpier Hamburg-Australia ships like the *Stassfurt*, and they were even the same jovial and efficient captains I had known for so long, but once they all started coming in under the Swastika a kind of sinister stain seemed to brush off on them, and one never went aboard them again without being oppressed by a feeling of uneasiness, of eyes watching, of mouths opening to ask a question, of jackboots rapping on the steel plates at the far dim ends of alleyways.

Now all this was quite probably imagination, and all of us I think shared these unclarified doubts, but where Johnny and Noel did go away to find some answers for themselves, I was perfectly content, at the end, to have Helen find the answers for me. She loved my coming to her with this first-hand news from Europe, and she would pass the information around among her friends (whom I never knew but who seemed to be active in the Communist Party or the New Theatre or around the Trades Hall or at union meetings), larding it with her own comments and opinions ; and since these opinions were ready-made and pat enough I gradually got to accept them as my own. So I am sure it was Helen, mostly, who was responsible for the falsity I began to attach to practically everything political. (There is a passage somewhere in E. M. Forster where he talks of the " vast armies of the benighted, who follow neither the heart nor the brain, and march to their destiny by catch-words," and Helen certainly was one of these.)

Some of the shipboard interviews continued to move me deeply and strangely, and in a way incomprehensibly. When I would tell Helen about them she would make them seem perfectly understandable and clear, although even then I had the feeling that she would deliver these explanations as if human understanding was a commodity that came in a package with instructions for serving, as if Europe was splitting apart according to a set of tested recipes. I knew that her careful clichés were falsifying it all, but I would still accept her versions of the dissonance gratefully enough as an alternative to the hopeless task of trying to examine and analyse the confusion of multiplying shadows for which no explanations could be found at all

So I had only myself to blame, really.

It is impossible to say precisely *when* Helen Midgeley decided to make me her husband—certainly it was one of the reasons why she kept me from crusading off to Spain—but it is not at all difficult to understand *why*. She could see that I was beginning to cut something of a figure in the world of Melbourne journalism ; I had standing, a good salary, a developing reputation, a political malleability which she would find much pleasure in working on ; I was in every way eligible, and I was exactly the partner to share her own potential expansion, socially, intellectually, politically, and economically. . . .

I had by this time long since passed through my cadetship, and I had graduated from the general and more senior rounds to the élite minority of the newspaper's " special writers." To appreciate the significance of this advancement, one really has to remember the old *Morning Post* as it was, and it is almost as hard to remember a newspaper of thirty years ago as it is to remember the fashions of thirty years ago.

Everything about the *Morning Post* was deliberately and publicly arranged to suggest dignity, grandeur, omniscience, infallibility, and a privileged standing in the community, as if the front page masthead, with its lion and its unicorn and the curly riband emblazoned *Dieu et Mon Droit* and the name in Olde English lettering had conferred some special Royal distinction on the newspaper and its staff. Indeed, it always seemed to me that something of the Royal Palace influence had crept into the architecture of the building, for much marble had been used in the entrance foyer and the lower parts of the façade, and there were impressive doors of studded bronze opening on to the Back Dates Department and a hall decorated with a tremendously large mural all worked out in gold and coloured mosaic of " The Spirit of Communications "—the spirit being a buxom nude woman with bolts of lightning playing from her fingertips who waded Gulliver-like in a shallow sea amid an armada of small ships of various types. A severe storm seemed to be threatening this Lilliputian fleet, for there was an encircling nimbus of thunder clouds, in which sat telegraph operators, astronomers, mathematicians, natives with signal drums, men in solar topees, and white-jacketed scientists with microscopes and test-tubes and Bunsen burners. As an allegory it seemed to mystify most visitors, but they were always very impressed by the fact that it was all created out of tiny chips of gilded and coloured stone, and those on the staff would be very proud to point out that it had been designed by an Associate of the Royal Academy and had cost a cool twenty-five thousand guineas. This also impressed people, because it was more than twice as much as the prize money for the Melbourne Cup.

The *Post* building was ten stories high, being at that time one of the tallest, and certainly among the grandest buildings in Melbourne, and on top of everything else sat a greenish, copper-sheathed cupola upon which was airily poised, on one foot, a gilded representation of Prometheus, which the reporters generally referred to as " Promiscuity Defying Convention." This golden Prometheus held in his hands, of all things a flagpole, upon which one might have expected a Royal Standard to be unfurled on special days, or at least something dashingly heraldic, but the flag, in fact, was rather a drab thing of maroon and green and white which said *Morning Post Classified Ads Give Best Results.*

Between the mosaic Spirit of Communications in the entrance hall and the gilded Prometheus reaching to the sky were a few floors containing offices which were rented out, mostly to advertising agencies, and the rest of the space was devoted to the company's various publishing activities. Although the daily paper was the spiritual core and the financial strength of the business, Prometheus was right to flaunt that banner: it was the endless pages of the classified ads, the death and funeral notices, the births and christenings, the lost property and the land offers, the weddings and the In Memoriams, the legal notices and the business announcements, and the property and employment notices, which formed the inexhaustible Eldorado that was the delight of the counting-house, and on the mundane mass of this revenue the *Morning Post* could well afford all its literary snobberies and proud conceits.

Yet behind the glitter of the mosaic, the sheen of pink marble, and the gilded flanks of allegorical statuary there were warrens of little rooms and airless cubby-holes divided by frosted glass and mahogany, where pinched Dickensian creatures sat with black celluloid cuffs over their shirt-sleeves, and green celluloid eye-shades over their foreheads, and these anonymous troglodytes were forever computing, tabulating, classifying, indexing and invoicing. They were as far removed from our proud and gentlemanly world of the Literary Staff as denizens on some other little-known and underprivileged planet. There was a secondary group of more-or-less weevil-like creatures who did have certain links with us, even though they, too, were hidden away in curious places in rooms beyond rooms or rooms within rooms and rooms around the ends of corridors Among these were the printers' readers, who checked copy and proofs for errors of fact or spelling or typography, and the people concerned with other publications.

The company printed quite a number of strange little magazines that one never saw on bookstalls and could never quite imagine anyone reading—they were to do with crocheting and tatting, or bee-keeping, or gladioli culture, or radio circuits, or house decoration: there was one called *The Christian Parishioner* and another called *Cage Birds* and an *Almanac of Astrology*—and these publications were each of them put out week after week by two or three oldish people in back rooms who seemed not to have names and certainly had no physical features that one ever remembered. The principal of all these subsidiary publications was a weekly called the *Rural Record*, which was aimed at the agricultural world of the Victorian farmer and was crammed with advertisements—the money that poured in from the manufacturers of castrating-tools and sheep-dip preparations and reapers-and-binders and chemicals to kill white ants and stump-jump ploughs and grubbing equipment!—and I think there is some significance in the fact that this journal had to be printed on a thin type of cheap newsprint, because one of the big factors in its circulation was that it could be cut up into squares and used in country privies and when they tried glossy paper for the covers and a centre pictorial section the sales dropped almost immediately.

In a big newspaper organisation there is always a lot more behind the scenes than the marble and the mosaics and the statuary. Since there were fewer than a hundred on the Literary Staff it came as a bit of a shock to realise that there were almost two thousand people on the *Post* payroll who worked in that building. There were the floors of the counting-house, the women's staff, the photographic section with its darkrooms and studios and its etching rooms blue-lit and flickering as if summer lightning had been trapped there, the machine floor and the linotype batteries, the artists' department and the map rooms, the arcaded stores for the great rolls of newsprint, the morgue and the illustrations library, the board-rooms and the conference-rooms, and heaven knows what else in that labyrinth of rooms, floors and corridors. The topmost floor always interested me in the bold shamelessness of its sub-divisions, for there was a central kitchen there, and to the right of this was the Literary Staff's dining-room, with starched tablecloths and good cutlery and napery and flowers in vases on every table, and at the end of this was a small private dining-room (with a cocktail bar

installed) where the directors occasionally gave private lun-
cheons to distinguished guests. On the opposite side of the
kitchen was a very much bigger area and this was the staff
cafeteria, with hard wooden benches and a painted concrete
floor and long wooden tables of scrubbed deal, where all those
other than the Literary Staff or the directors or the chief
executives of departments could buy self-service meals or tea
or coffee in thick china mugs at much cheaper prices. The
place was always crowded and usually there was a warm fug
of tobacco smoke and food smells and the insidious stink of
printing ink and wet newsprint, and in this place you could
hear good talk and real laughter that was quite different from
the discreet amusement which was the most that was ever
permitted in the staff dining-room on the other side of the
floor.

The real heart, in a way, of the whole of this complex
organism was, none the less, the literary department, and this
was located on the third floor, midway between the offices of
the various editors and the noisy floor of the compositors
and the linotype batteries. It was divided into two main
rooms on either side of the chief-of-staff's glassed-in box ;
nearest the editor's sanctum was the sub-editors' room, with
fifteen subs around a huge elliptical table, all wearing green
eye-shades and stooped over, in shirt-sleeves and waistcoats
and braces, as if they were all slightly cowed by the basilisk
presence of Mr. Farnsworth, who had been there as chief sub
for as long as anybody could remember. He sat always on a
chair that was slightly larger than all the others, and raised a
few inches higher, and he had a row of lead-based spikes in
front of him, and to his left the teleprinter and the gawping,
faintly hissing mouths of the pneumatic tubes. Mr. Farnsworth had a series of grunts which the other sub-editors all
understood, as they understood the cryptic markings he would
make on copy or on proofs, and the subs' table worked
efficiently enough to these directions, for it was only very
seldom that old Farnsworth would open his mouth to make
any verbal comment. For all the apparent confusion of spikes
and proofs and copy paper and wire baskets and scissors and
reference books and glue-pots and blue pencils and lay-out
sheets that littered it, the subs' table at the *Post* was one of
the best and most efficient I ever knew.

Mr. Farnsworth was very tall and spare and grey: the word that defined him best was aquiline, for he looked like a very old eagle, rather moulted, who has given up soaring and swooping, and just sits on his high rock staring down at the world below. He became too old later for the pressures and the tensions of the night subs' table, and they made him chief day sub so that he could work only in the mornings and afternoons, sorting early cables and going through spiked copy. He dropped dead in his chair one day around noon, but just sat there staring down at the copy in that basilisk way he had, so that it wasn't until the early night sub, Wally Graham, came on at five-thirty that anybody realised the old fellow was no longer alive, and in fact was already stiff with rigor mortis.

Swing-doors of cracked glass led from the subs' room to the reporters' room, which was a huge high-ceilinged chamber furnished with rows of square tables and chairs. There were varnished maps on the walls and some photographs of early editors, but the room generally speaking was austere and functional. At either end of the room were two lectern-like fixtures, one supporting the duty-book, in which each day's assignments were entered, and the other a huge leather-bound dictionary. There was a rack for coats and hats, a cupboard filled with ink and copy-paper and carbons and stationery, slotted frames for the reading and cutting files of various newspapers, a framed manifesto on the ethics of journalism quoted from some obscure and long-forgotten editorial in the London *Times*, a collection of obscene typographical errors pasted upon a partition, and not much else.

There were only three full-time special writers on the *Post* and I was the youngest of them and the only one who worked in the reporters' room—Gavin Turley, who was young, too, but several years older than I, had an exceptional analytical mind and as he wrote second editorials as well as feature articles, and book reviews as well, he worked in a little room that was an annexe to the editor's office: and "Gunner" Bannister was a crusty old man in his sixties with a room of his own from which he turned out a turgid and interminable stream of articles about pioneer families, for he was a dedicated snob, and was spurred by a fanatical desire to make of the State of Victoria, because it had had no convict settlement, the "superior" and aristocratic territory of the Commonwealth. He saw Melbourne as a kind of better Boston, spiritually ruled by a social aristocracy of antipodean Lodges and Cabots, who had mansions in Toorak and rich homesteads in the Western District, which his articles would delineate in much the same terms as modern guide-books might describe the stately homes and palaces of England. He truly believed that there was a racial distinction between the inhabitants of Melbourne and the people of Sydney or of Tasmania, whom he still saw as branded with the marks of manacles and leg-irons. Gunner Bannister also wrote ceremonial odes and sonnets for special occasions, and he was the author of a Saturday column which was erudite, immensely dull, and largely written in bad verse, of which he was a masterly exponent. Eventually he, too, died in his swivel chair, staring fixedly down at a half-finished parody of Keats, but in his case his death was quickly detected because a copy-boy distributing proofs observed that the old man was not twitching. (At the time of Mr. Farnsworth's death the very same copy-boy had continued delivering proofs to the chief sub's spike all through the afternoon without suspecting anything, so perhaps he had finally become suspicious of immobility.)

At any rate, being the youngest of the special writers, and the one most vulnerably placed, it was I who had to bear the brunt of the staff jealousies. My success at the *Morning Post*, although in a technical sense it had come easily, had not been achieved without certain personal frictions. The news reporters were always inclined to resent the special writers, and in my case there were some of the younger reporters who quite openly talked of personal favouritism. There was, admittedly, a certain validity in their charges, for Bernard Brewster had by this time become editor-in-chief, and as he continued to regard me as his particular protégé, this meant that rather special attention was paid to my progress. Certainly promotions seemed to come more easily for me than for the others, but I think what rankled with them more than anything was that I got an utterly disproportionate share of the choice assignments.

All the special shipping assignments naturally fell to me, and these were often glamorous and exciting jobs, like the annual cruise of the Government lighthouse-tender to the isolated lighthouses around the coast, or a foray into the Antarctic with a Norwegian whaling fleet, or the laying of a new submarine cable across the Tasman Sea, or naval manœuvres, or a hydrographic survey, or a " race " in ballast between two old square-rigged windjammers from Melbourne to Spencer Gulf. But Mr. Brewster also insisted more and more that I should handle the " atmosphere " or " colour " pieces on big general stories, often with a byline, and this was not always well received in the reporters' room.

There was a row about it one day between Brewster and Curtis Condon, who was the chief-of-staff and who detested me. Gavin Turley, who heard it all from his adjacent room, told me about it later.

" He's superficial . . . he's always skating on thin ice! " Condon stormed. " You simply cannot trust his facts, he just dabs things in to make the picture *seem* complete! He's never reliable! "

" Whether he is reliable or not, Mr. Condon, he happens to be the best descriptive writer you have on your staff," Mr. Brewster retorted. " The *only* evocative writer you have, Mr. Condon. He can make you see a thing. You read his piece and you are *there*, Mr. Condon. He has this trick of making you *see* what is happening, or what has happened. You *feel* it. You *smell* it. Sometimes you can *touch* it, Mr. Condon. You're not suggesting, surely, that this extraordinary knack he has for evoking the very essence of a thing is valueless? "

" I'm suggesting that one of these days he'll go too far," said Condon coldly.

" Indeed yes, he may go a great deal farther than either you or I can imagine."

" That isn't what I meant."

" No, but it is what *I* meant. If you are worried about his facts, Mr. Condon, send a hack along with him to jot down the corrective figures and statistics. But let young Meredith continue to supply us with the atmosphere and the colour and the *feeling* of things. He has attributes not at all common in this game of ours. I do intend to cultivate these attributes, Mr. Condon."

And since Mr. Brewster was, after all, the editor-in-chief there was nothing very much that Condon could do, except to bide his time and to nurture the deep personal animosity he felt for me.

Anzac Day was always one of the big "colour pieces" that fell to me after this, and this was one of the emotional setpieces that could always move me and embarrass me and upset me, and even wound me in some queer way, and to this day whenever I think of it I can smell eucalyptus and teaurns and salmon-sandwiches and the smell of beer and tobacco smoke at battalion reunions, and I can hear thousands and thousands of voices singing Kipling's "Recessional" and "Land of Hope and Glory," and a metallic amplified voice intoning to acres of hushed figures the last verse of Binyon's "For the Fallen," and the school children with their little square flags chanting:

> On the twenty-fifth of April, far across the sea,
> Our brave Australian soldiers stormed Gallipoli . . .

And all this is tied up with the dawn service at the Shrine of Remembrance, and then the great public march down along Swanston Street and across the bridge, and it was always, for me, a day of mixed feelings, but whatever I felt about it would have to be buried away in the stipulated chauvinisms of the story. Dad and Bert would always be there marching along in their old uniforms, which looked very shabby and far too small for them, with their big medals clinking on their chests, Dad behind the purple colour-patch of the engineers, and Bert with his old infantry battalion; and Paul Klein was a regular marcher, too, with the handful of veterans who had warred against the German Pacific Colonies, in a bowler hat with miniatures pinned to his navy-blue suit and carrying kid gloves, limping along as jauntily as ever and waving to me with his cane; and sometimes my mother would be in the parade, too. She would always appear in a thunder of hand clapping, because she would march with the little group of nurses and V.A.D.s who would push along, in wheel-beds and invalid-chairs, some of the hospital patients from Caulfield, and Mother always looked very small and round to me, with her long veils blowing and her medals bright on her starched bosom, and blinking around behind her spectacles as if she was not at all sure what was happening.

When any of the people who knew me came along towards the flag-draped saluting-post they would all begin to twist

their heads this way and that looking for the press-box to
catch a glimpse of me sitting up there among the generals
and the admirals and politicians and the city dignitaries,
wearing my brown pork-pie hat and a red paper Flanders
poppy in my buttonhole. If they caught my eye they would
call and wave, and then pull themselves together in time for
the " Eyes left!" of the salute, but after they had marched on
they would nudge those near them in the ranks, and they, too,
would turn to try to catch a glimpse of me.

I was always grateful that Mother seemed too bewildered
by everything that was happening ever to do this.

Curtis Condon was a quick-witted, formidable, irritable, intelligent man approaching his forties, with the sort of face
that never looked as if it had been young. He was a good
newspaperman and a frustrated writer—which is a bad combination—and he liked to consider himself a martinet. His
role in the Literary Staff was an important one, for he was
the executive go-between linking the management, the editor,
and the sub-editors with the working journalists of the
organisation. He marked out the daily duty-book, decided
assignments, forced cadets into shorthand tests, laboured
points of discipline, constantly contested overtime claims,
and believed in the sanctity of the *Morning Post* as if it were
the only true and established religion, and he, Curt Condon,
its high-priest. He was an old Public Schools man with a good
University degree (it was said that he had failed by a hair's-
breadth for a Rhodes scholarship), and I am pretty sure that
his dislike for me began as a resentment that I was the first
to have insinuated myself into the sacred precincts of the
Morning Post's Literary Staff with virtually no education at
all. (Thank heaven, neither he nor anybody else ever discovered about that Intermediate Certificate!) I think he
genuinely believed that I represented a lowering of standards
which in the long run could only bring harm to the newspaper and an undermining of all the traditions he believed in.
And, in a way, his fears were perfectly justified.

Condon's was a systematic and unrelenting chastening, and
always designed to make me feel slightly *persona non grata*.
It was not that I was to be made to feel actually objection-
able ; only that I was constantly and subtly to be reminded of

my social and intellectual inferiority. If he ever encountered me in the street it was inevitable that that afternoon I would be summoned to his glassed-in box to be privately reprimanded. " *Post* men don't slouch along the public thoroughfares, Meredith, with a cigarette drooling idiotically from their lips!" he would inform me contemptuously, or: " A gentleman, Meredith, does not loiter around street corners with his hands in his pockets. *Post* reporters are presumed to be gentlemen!" Or: " Do try to wear your hat like a *Post* man, Meredith, not like some cheapjack larrikin from Collingwood who doesn't know any better!" I knew that his charges were invented, and no more than expressions of a violent personal antipathy, but there was never anything I could say in rebuttal.

He had another little trick of writing out my instructions for some involved assignment, or querying some of my copy in proof, in his own advanced and faultless shorthand, knowing full well that I hardly understood even the most elementary Pitman's. Sometimes he would leave memoranda in my pigeon-hole with the point of the message written in Latin, so that I would have to try to look it up or be obliged to ask somebody to explain the meaning of it. But these, after all, were his petty goadings.

Our mutual enmity moved to a different plane on the night the *River Tamar* foundered.

She was a little coastal freighter of around 1000 tons that generally traded between Melbourne and Coff's Harbour, and she went down somewhere in Bass Strait on the first day of a tempest which eventually caused immense damage throughout Victoria. I had just been to the Marine Board offices to get the crew list, and in the lift going up to the third floor some of the night subs were just coming on duty, and one of them said to me, " What's the dope on that missing freighter?"

" She's gone down; she's lost," I said. " The Marine Board's just officially posted her."

" Any survivors?" he asked.

" No. Well, the posting is lost with all hands. Twenty-one including the captain."

" Great story!" he said approvingly. " We've got a cable-page lead then." And, as an afterthought: " Bad luck for those poor beggars, though. Twenty-one of them, eh? Heaven help the sailors on a night like this." They chuckled.

I worked through on the general story until after eleven, piecing the story together by phoning lighthouses and fishing villages and checking with other ships that had battled through the storm, and I had most of the conjecture and the few known facts assembled into a good, coherent story when Condon called me into his box and said, " Ah yes, Meredith, you do have the names and home addresses of all the ship's company?" I nodded, waiting; he knew I had because the list had already been set and proofs pulled, and one of the proofs was there on the spike right in front of his eyes, and it was distinctive enough because it was set in black and in a box. So I guessed he was up to something. " Where do they come from?" he asked.

"Williamstown," I said. "The captain from West Foot-scray and all the rest of them from Williamstown." The *River Tamar* had been a poor parsimonious little ship, but there were quite a few coasters laid up in those days, and beggars couldn't be choosers when you were as near the end of the road as the Williamstown slums.

" Ring for a taxi," said Condon crisply, reaching for his pad of pink cab-vouchers. " Grab a photographer and get out to Williamstown as fast as you can. I want concise, powerful little interviews with next-of-kin—widows, mothers, relatives, whoever you can get. Tell the photographer I want to run a strip of half-column blocks across five or six columns, with this human interest stuff below."

I waited a moment or two, and then, " I'm sorry, Mr. Condon," I said quite clearly, " but I won't do it."

" You won't—*what*?" He looked at me incredulously.

"I won't do it," I repeated. "You'll have to get one of the emergency men. I . . . I've put in the lead story, sir, and I think I've tied up all the ends. But I'm not going to do this."

"Would you regard it as an imposition if I asked way?" he said sarcastically.

" No. It's just that those people don't know anything about this yet."

" Is that *your* concern? They've got to know some time, haven't they?"

" Well, it'll be bad enough for them, anyway, reading about it in the papers to-morrow . . . because I don't suppose the Marine Board notifications will get to them until after the papers come out. But I know I'm not going out there in the middle of the night to knock at their doors to get them out of bed in the dark and the rain to tell them that their husbands or their sons or their fathers are dead. Drowned. Out there in Bass Strait in this sort of weather . . . I—I just couldn't do it, Mr. Condon."

" I hope you realise what this attitude of yours implies. This is a direct refusal of duty, and ——"

" But what would I *do*, Mr. Condon? Do you mean I should ask them how they *feel* about it? These people are very poor, Mr. Condon, and they live in a terrible part of Williamstown, the slummiest part, and they've had a rotten time already with the Depression, and this'll be the end for most of them . . . and I can't go out and tell them *that*. It—it just wouldn't be fair, Mr. Condon."

He looked me up and down as if I were some sort of strange, unpleasant animal, and then deliberately looked past me and called, " Strang! Dudley Strang!" and one of the cadets on emergency came running to the box, and Condon ripped off the taxi-voucher and tore the proof from the spike and shoved them both at Dudley Strang. " This is the *River Tamar*'s crew-list," he said snappishly. " This is a job for you, since Mr. Meredith here seems to have gone queasy on it. You'll find most of the victims come from Williamstown; the addresses are given there. Get a taxi. Ring Bailey for a photographer. Get out there smartly and bring back warm human interviews with all the next-of-kin you can run to earth. And photographs. Come on, look slippy now!"

" Yes, Mr. Condon," said Strang, and bolted.

Condon waited until he had left the reporters' room and then he turned to me. " You know, you'll never be a news-paperman as long as you live, Meredith," he said equably. " You just don't have what it takes, do you? Why don't you go back to your billboards and your jam labels? That's where you really belong, Meredith. It *is*, you know."

But the morning editions carried my lead and my story, practically word for word as I had written it, and there were no half-column blocks of the bereaved women nor any "warm human" interviews. I heard later that Strang and the photographer were working until one in the morning, getting women out of bed and breaking the grim news to them and popping flashlight bulbs in their twisted faces, but by the time they got back from Williamstown the first edition cable-page was already made up on the stone and old Farnsworth ruled that there was no space for special "angles." So it was all a waste of time, anyway.

The loss of the little steamer ushered in a very newsy time, for the storm grew in violence over the next few days, and rivers burst their banks and towns were flooded or threatened, and there was chaos everywhere and over most of the State great damage and a quite considerable loss of life. During nearly five days and nights I never got home at all, and in all that time I was able to snatch only a few hours of fitful and uncomfortable sleep underneath a leaking tarpaulin on the floor of an empty goods truck on a flooded railway siding somewhere down in Gippsland. Doing the "atmosphere" on these big news stories was not always a sinecure.

Before this, though, on a long-deserted beach on Phillip Island, on the far side of Seal Rocks, grey and wet under a scudding sky and hissing with the gravelly sting of windblown sand and the harsh rasp of the tossing marram-grass, I ran down the first clues that were found to the loss of the *River Tamar*. I had been sent to Phillip Island to check, and it was some sort of hunch that took me to this particular stretch of beach, although there was a certain logic, too, because I'd tried to work it out from what was known of the steamer's course and the prevailing wind and the set of the currents through the Bass Strait islands. Anyway, there at the edge of the wet sand one of the ship's lifebuoys was lodged in a tangled mat of kelp and bladderwrack and sea lettuce and old tarry slabs of cork. It looked quite fresh and new with the neat red lettering on the white round curve of glossy paint— *River Tamar—Melbourne*; at least it looked as if it could have *saved* somebody. This thought stuck in my mind, so that I didn't feel as elated about the find as I should have, and I remember trudging on along the cheerless, empty beach with a feeling of futility and depression, but past the next ridge of sand-dunes there was quite a lot of driftwood washed up with the storm-wrack. Most of it was sawn hardwood planking, which had probably been the ship's deck cargo, but among it I found the ship's clock, still screwed to a piece of smashed rosewood panelling, and stopped at ten-past one, and another lifebuoy and a chicken-coop and what looked like part of the wing of the bridge, and all this did make me excited, and then about sixty or seventy yards farther on I saw something big and dark and soft-looking that was rolling around in the foam on the slope of shingle where the seas would fan out and run back, just a little out of reach of the suck of the surf and the undertow.

When I got up close I saw it was the body of a man who looked enormously big but might have just been swollen, a man in black trousers and a blue jersey and one seaboot (the other foot seemed to be missing altogether), with a complexion that had turned a sort of glossy, bruised-looking purply-black. The body was bumping around, sliding this way and that in the shallow water beneath soapy clots of yellowish foam, underneath that raggedy grey wet stormy sky, and a drab canvas lifejacket was still attached to the man although not properly fastened, or maybe it had been fastened at first and he had tried to get rid of it.

I waded into the sucking hiss of the sea and grabbed at the arm that was flung out and sort of stiffly and spasmodically beating at the wet shingle, and I began to haul the dead sailor out on to the dryer part of the shore, but as soon as I exerted force the arm pulled right out of its socket, and I fell over backwards, still clinging to the corpse's arm, which had pulled away with the blue jersey sleeve and rotted threads and everything, and the stump of the limb was a ghastly transparent quick shimmer of sea-lice, that leaped and flickered and moved as if they were insane, and then I could feel them jumping and tickling all over my own hand, and I dropped the dead arm back into the sea and put my head down on the wet murmuring sand and vomited.

Yet from the newspaper point of view it was a good story, and exclusive to the *Post*, and it established the very time of the *River Tamar*'s sinking, and the Marine Board sent coast parties down and they eventually found eleven other bodies of the crew. (I never told anybody about the dead man's arm coming away in my hand.) With Condon this story more or less cancelled out my mutiny on the matter of the interviews, or I suppose it did, because he never mentioned it again, or perhaps he was exhausted himself by the long strain of those days and nights. All the complicated coverage had had to be organised by Condon, and he had scarcely taken a minute off, and his jowls had dropped and he looked unshaven and more piggy-looking than ever, but you had to admire him for the way he had done it.

On the night the storm ended there were about half a dozen of us still sitting around in our wet raincoats in the reporters' room at about half-past three in the morning, too exhausted, and too excited and overstrained in a way, to want to go home. The final edition had just been locked up and sent away, and the subs' table was empty because they were all upstairs in the cafeteria having snacks and coffee, and from the deep guts of the building we could hear the growling roar of the big Hoes running out the last of the country edition, and at this point Condon came out of his box, grey with tiredness and strain, and he went to every table in the reporters' room and examined each of the big pewter ink-wells, and they were all dry, every one of them, so he took them all to a central table and stacked them one on top of the other until he had a tall, wobbly column of pewter ink-wells nearly five feet high, and then he went to the corner lectern and took the big leather-bound assignment book and hurled it with all his force at the column of ink-wells, and sent them clattering and bouncing all over the room. I think every one of us liked Curtis Condon at that moment.

Mother had her sixtieth birthday not very long after these events—the storm and the loss of the *River Tamar* and the sailing off to Europe of the *Aller* with Johnny Drew and Noel Grantham aboard, but without me—and since I now felt, or had been made to feel, almost formally betrothed to Helen Midgeley, even though I was still not quite sure how this had happened, it seemed to me that this would be an appropriate occasion for her to meet my family. I knew that Mother's birthday party would be both festive and formal, with high tea in the front room and a general family reunion, and since I wanted to make Helen's début equally an occasion, I got Dad to let me have the car to pick her up and drive her home.

We had been lovers for nearly four years, yet this was the first time I had ever called for her. She lived in the old section of Brighton in part of a big, gloomy, decaying weatherboard house that seemed to be breaking apart at every joint: it was a gaunt, two-storied place with a slate roof covered in coloured lichens and hung with old swallows' nests, and it was remarkable for the things about it that were broken, because it had a broken tower with a broken clock-face and a broken staircase and a broken weather-vane and a broken dovecot and broken spouting hanging from the eves and a broken summer-house and broken swings in a rank, overgrown garden which at some time or another seemed to have included a tennis court and a croquet green. It was the sort of house which one always enters with the thought that somebody has just scuttled off to keep out of sight: you never quite *hear* anything or *see* anything, but there is always this absolutely distinct sense of having an emptiness where an instant before no emptiness existed. With me the vanished figure was always quite definite. She was a very tiny frail old lady with white hair and pale skin and pink-rimmed albino eyes, and she was supposed never to show herself to anybody, and she always wore an old Japanese kimono, faded to a sort of greenish-black, with a yellow crane embroidered on it. I never saw her because she never existed, but I seldom visited that house without imagining that I had just missed her by a split second, that she had vanished around the corner only an instant before with her eyes dilated and her fingers spread against her mouth. I always expected to find a thread of greenish-black silk caught on some obstruction, or an old tortoise-shell comb dropped in a passageway, but I never did. Still, that was the sort of house it was, and the tangled garden suited it.

The front door had enormous brass bell-pulls that didn't work and two massive lion's-head knockers which had got so rusty they were too stiff to move, and so you just had to beat at the cracked door panelling with your fists or knuckles. When the door was opened there was an awful jangling clamour because a huge bell was fastened to the inside of the door on a loop of spring steel. I never got used to this, and it always startled the wits out of me. Usually when this din subsided there was something else that was strange, because almost always you would hear, from some room high up and very far away, "Humoresque" being played very thinly on an out of tune piano. I never found out by whom. The albino woman, probably. . . .

Helen's mother had died some years before and she lived with her father, a nervous, shy mousy little man who worked as a tailor's cutter somewhere in the city (Leverson's, I think it was, who were the first to introduce the extra pair of trousers with the £3 suit), and a surly younger brother who was studying bookkeeping at Zercho's Business College. On this day when I first called for her I met neither her father nor her brother, because she must have been looking from a window waiting for me, and she opened the door with a wild clanging from the hidden bell even before I had time to work out the system of the exterior bell-pushes and knockers, and said, " I'm all ready, so let's go," and took me by the arm with a dazzling smile and twisted me round and walked me straight back to the front gate and the waiting car.

She had dressed herself very smartly in a suit of imitation Donegal in flecks of greys and blues, and the jacket was cut like an Edwardian Norfolk jacket with severe pleats and leather buttons. With this costume she wore gunmetal silk stockings, expensive matching shoes and handbag of some reptilian skin the identity of which I have forgotten, a mannish white blouse, frosty white gloves, and a strange soft little hat of blue felt. There was some strong masculine quality to it all that only accentuated her femininity and the shining gold of her hair. I felt intensely proud of her.

Driving back, I thought I should try to fortify her against any possible shocks or disappointments—she seemed in every way so superior to my own background, so utterly different in every imaginable aspect from my two sisters—and although I was relieved that I had no need to make excuses for our own house, so recently renovated and at least not disintegrating underneath one's eyes, I did say: " I'm afraid you'll have to take my people as you find them, Helen. Jack's a bit of a rough diamond," I said, " and Dad's a pig-headed old so-and-so and he can be difficult if he's in one of his moods, and Mother might seem rather . . . well, I don't mean she's ignorant about things, but she really doesn't take much interest in what's going on outside the home, and——"

" Darling, you *are* sweet," she said, and pushed her gloved hand affectionately between the car seat and the underpart of my thigh. " As if I care . . . I shall be very proud of *you*, and I'll adore them, you'll see. . . ."

The others were all there by the time we got to the house, and the place, rather to my consternation, seemed to be swarming with children, although there were really only six—Jean's and Bert's four sturdy boys, and Jack's two girls, Sharon and Kathleen, and Sheila, I saw, was well advanced into another pregnancy, and Jean always looked pregnant whether she was or not, so the impact of it all on Helen in the confined area of that little house admittedly must have been rather shattering. (Years afterwards, when we were separating finally, she evoked that day in a bitter recollection which startled me for the particular detail she had preserved of it. " The place stank of a shameless fecundity," she said. " That's what I really remember of it now, and I should have been warned then—damp patches on blouses and a stink of mother's milk and urine and soggy napkins, and children crawling around your legs and dribbling, and jelly stains on bibs. . . .")

Mother came to the panelled front hallway when we arrived, clearly a little over-awed, and startled too, I think, at how smart and mannish Helen looked, and quite obviously intimidated by her tallness, but she was very cordial and welcoming, and she held out her hand and this caused the first little contretemps of that very unsuccessful day, for Helen insisted on making an elaborate business of taking off her glove, and poor Mother was left with her hand sticking out and she didn't know what to do with it, and she looked embarrassed and blinked at me nervously as if I could instruct her, and then she wiped her hand on her apron and put it behind her back and finally got out of the situation by leading us both into the front room. " You'd better make the introductions yourself, Davy," she said, and hurried off to the kitchen in obvious relief.

They were all waiting there—Dad and Jack and Sheila and Bert and Jean and Marj ; and Little Jack, Jean's eldest, was belting out " American March Medley " on the pianola, and some of the other kids were crawling around the floor, under the table, or building walls out of the pianola roll-boxes, and

in the hush that marked our entrance—if anything could be
called a hush with " Light Cavalry Overture " continuing on
the loud pedal—I made the introductions and Jack at once
poured a tall glass of beer and handed it to Helen with a
pleasant welcoming grin.

Jean and Marj did the usual women's thing of smiling
watchfully over their " Pleased to meet you " and " How
d'you do," and of running their eyes up and down the Donegal costume, the sheer gunmetal stockings, the shoes and the
handbag, the blouse and the hair style, and after a few
moments they made their excuses and left the room, ostensibly
to help Mother bring things in from the kitchen, although it
was quite obvious they were really withdrawing for a com-
parison of opinions on Helen and her clothes and her
general appearance.

The room had been rather hideously decorated with twisted
paper streamers and coloured bells and lanterns of frilly
paper, and pleated collars of coloured crêpe-paper had been
arranged around the ferns and the flower-pots and what
Mother always called the " jarderneers," and in the centre of
the table was a frosted birthday cake with no candles but a
centrepiece of marzipan violets and a sugar " 60 " (later to
be preserved with all the other memorable fragments under
the glass dome on the pianola) and the words " Happy
Birthday to Mum " flowing over the almond-flavoured glaze
in pink hard icing; and Mother and Jean and Marj kept
coming up from the kitchen with still more dishes to add to
the prodigious bounty on the big table. My sisters, I suddenly
realised, must have been baking and cooking and preparing
for two whole days! There were dishes of cold chicken and
ham and corned beef and brawn and pork sausage, there were
salads and beetroot and radishes and spring opions, there were
sandwiches of cheese and of egg-and-lettuce and meat and of
lemon-butter for the children, there were plain scones and
fairy scones and sultana scones and date scones, there were
Banbury tarts and apple tarts and jam tarts and pikelets and
queen cakes and rock cakes and éclairs and napoleons and
lamingtons, there were sliced Madeira cake and sliced plain
cake and sliced caraway seed cake, there were mince pies and
sausage rolls and coffee scrolls, there was a plain cream

sponge and a chocolate sponge and a coconut sponge and an orange sponge, there were jellies and wine trifles and neapolitan blanc-manges and fruit-salad-and-cream, there were bananas and passion-fruit and pineapples, there were cheese straws, and there were milk arrowroot biscuits and rusks for the babies.

There was no organised point at which the party began, for in a sense it was a family gathering and not a party at all, but suddenly everybody was in the room at once, and seated, and passing dishes around, and Jack, the eternal barman, was pouring the drinks, and Jean was saying to her kids, " You just sit there where you are and keep quiet and wait till the grown-ups are served."

I think I saw them all more clearly on that birthday afternoon than I had seen them for years: I suppose it was that I was instinctively scrutinising them for the faults or merits that I felt Helen might find in them.

Mother and Sheila both sat back from the big table, Mother with her knitting and Sheila, her heavy rich ripe figure full and splendid in a grey linen maternity smock, relaxed in the big rocking-chair. The womanly things agreed with Sheila, motherhood and fertility and family devotion: to me she had grown much more beautiful since her marriage: her hands were clasped uninhibitedly across the swollen mound of her stomach, her pretty knees, as always, were exposed, her blouse was cut as provocatively as ever, the bold teasing wickedness was still there in her sharp quick Irish eyes . . . but now there were new and deeper qualities which enhanced all the younger attributes—a kind of mature vitality seemed to pump through her ; one sensed the subdued vigour of fulfilment tempered by a powerful and deeply-lodged serenity ; it was almost as if the fruitfulness of her womb was like some great riparian flooding which gave a renewal of richness to all the other humours of the body. It always astonished me that Helen should have so instantly disliked her. . . .

Mother, naturally, was knitting the baby's layette, because she had knitted all six of the babies' layettes, and for the rest of her life she would go on knitting babies' layettes. The bone needles moved with a magical flickering rapidity while Mother talked, watched, listened, smiled, blinked away behind her glasses, suggested a helping of chicken or of brawn, corrected a grandchild, or surreptitiously examined Helen Midgeley.

When she was knitting or crocheting, Mother almost never looked down at what she was doing, unless she was working on socks and had come to the turning of a heel or something like that, so that she gave the impression of being enslaved to a completely mechanical mannerism, but this knitting and the crochet had become, in fact, a quite crucial factor in her existence: through these tireless flickering needles she had been able to sublimate all her problems and re-establish the importance of her being. At sixty she seemed very diminutive and almost entirely spherical, for she also knitted everything for herself, usually on thick wooden needles, and she had knitted herself into what was very nearly a cocoon of gruel-coloured wool. She knitted herself suits, she knitted herself dresses, she knitted herself shawls and singlets and petticoats and stockings. Dad, too, was now almost permanently swathed in knitted singlets and undershirts and pullovers in heavy cable-stitch, and cardigans in moss-stitch, and mufflers to help fight his bronchial cough.

The reason for this was that in her pattern-books, in her bone and wood and metal knitting-needles, in her inexhaustible stock of coloured balls of Beehive Super-Fingering, in her crochet-hooks, Mother had found the symbols of a total security and had fashioned herself a kind of impermeable armour within which she existed absolutely safe from attack or doubt or harm. She had long since passed her change of life and had freed herself from the shackles of the flesh, and in the knitted self-sufficiency of a new benignity Dad was powerless to hurt or intimidate or frighten her. What she had done, of course, was to subordinate her own ambitions and desires to an undemanding state of identification with the happiness and the needs of others, and when the needs did not exist she simply invented them, and in the interminable clicking and flashing of these ever-restless needles she went on fashioning in purl and plain the palisades of her own composure and security—in bed-jackets, twin sets, suits and dresses, mufflers, shawls, pullovers, cardigans, sweaters, mittens and gloves, ties, socks and bed-socks, quilts, layettes, tea-cosies, doilies, pram-covers, table runners, even stuffed woollen toys for the children—knitted golliwogs and clowns and monkeys and lions and camels and giraffes and elephants. . . .

Where Mother had achieved a new and permanent kind of stability, Dad's grip on things had grown far more shaky, and he gave the impression that he was moving towards at least a partial disintegration.

I remember looking at him on that birthday afternoon and thinking of the thistledown clocks of our childhood. He seemed a little like a thistledown clock, with some of the seed-darts blown away by the first puff, " *One* o'clock!" and the breath already being inhaled for the second puff, " *Two* o'clock!" . . . He seemed shrunken and far more frail than one had realised, and his head was quite, quite bald, and flecked with little brown liverish blotches, and there was a sort of lost, uncertain, futile pugnacity about him, as if he still might try to force a pretence but knew really that all the foundations of his angers had been undermined. His claws had been drawn. He was like an old circus lion, grown mangy and a little smelly and with no appetite for his bones. Mother kept tossing him cable-stitch pullovers and new cardigans and thick mufflers, and he went on shrinking inside them.

Bert had aged, too, although he still had that fresh pink rustic complexion of a boy, and the same innocence of years before in his blue rather stupid eyes, but there were lines of pain and petulance scored around his cheeks and mouth, and all the collective suffering had knotted up his hands and wrists into an arthritic tangle of swollen veins and knuckles. A long series of amputations had taken his leg by this time almost to the joint of the knee, and he seldom wore an artificial limb any longer. He generally got about on one French crutch and a walking-stick, with the right leg of his trousers neatly pinned up, which, as he once pointed out, at least always got him a seat in a crowded tram. At this time he had a job driving one of the lifts in a big city insurance office, which was easier for him.

Bert had always been rather overshadowed by Jean's exuberant and more voluble personality, and what in earlier years had been only the shy taciturnity of a country boy had developed by now into almost a complete block so far as original conversation was concerned, so he seldom opened his mouth except to echo other people's observations, or to

repeat the points of jokes that somebody else had made,
which he would do very good-naturedly and with much
laughter and nudging and winking. (All Bert ever wanted in
his life, I think, was simply to be liked and approved: it was
only his dream of the unattainable that went beyond this,
where he was a brilliant original wit, a practical joker of
immense audacity, a debonair and flashy character whom
everybody talked about.) His one very earnest pursuit at this
time was an involvement with Dad in a series of complicated
projects for working out new betting systems which eventually were to make fortunes for both of them: he would come
across to our house after supper and they would spend hours
together compiling tables and statistics from the sporting
sections of the newspapers and the form-guides in *The Circle*
and *The Sporting Globe*. It had something to do with
" beaten favourites at last start," and was very involved, and
although practical tests were made each Saturday at Caulfield or Flemington—" two bob each way Dark Man " (Dad
also had a mystical obsession about any racehorse with a
name in which an " r " was the third letter), " all up, if any,
top weight in the last!"—no riches ever did come of it.

Bert was echoing Jack's jokes on this particular afternoon,
because it was Jack's personality and ebullience that were
dominating the occasion. He was a little drunk and merry
and spilling over with a flood of universal affection—and at
the beginning I could see he was trying very hard to see that
Helen fitted in—and he had already teased Dad by suggesting that they reverse the big, burdened table and play a
" hundred up " at billiards, and now he was making a comic
appreciation of Mother's massed oil paintings on the walls.
" But why should all these Old Masters just be gathering dust
in *this* place, that's what I want to know, when the National
Art Gallery could fill a whole bloomin' wing with 'em?" he
was saying. " Just think what the public's missing! What
you are depriving them of, Mum! That beaut snow scene
up there, for instance, with the steam roller chuffin' round
the bend and——"

" Oh you are a *fool*, Jack!" Mother protested, laughing.
" It's not a steam roller, it's a sleigh!"

" Or this one. Eh, now what about this one? This wonderful study of a bunch of . . . well, what *is* that a bunch of,

Mum? It can't be carrots, because I don't see how you'd have carrots all mixed up with a broken windmill and an old railway bridge, and it's too red for parsnips, but it looks more like carrots than beetroot, say, and——"

"You know very well they're not carrots at all, you idiot!" Mother giggled, delighted by the badinage, and playing up to him. "It's a sort of cliff, a rock formation coming down to that path there leading to the mill. And it's part of a water-wheel and nothing to do with a railway bridge at all, and anyone can see that who isn't blind or half tipsy." Having got that shaft home she turned to Helen and said, "You mustn't pay the least attention to anything this one says, Miss —er—Miss Midgeley. He's always acting the fool and trying to tease, and——"

"Are they really *your* paintings, though, Mrs. Meredith?" Helen asked, and there was something a little stiff and faintly disparaging in the way she said it—at least that was what I thought—and the whole conversation at once moved away from the plane of familiar, good-natured bantering that Jack had established, and Mother looked slightly uncomfortable and suddenly defensive, and I tried to save the situation on both sides by saying, "Helen used to be an art student herself, you see, Mother, and she knows something about painting," but Mother still looked very uncertain, and she flushed a little when she spoke:

"Well, most of them are just things I did when I was a girl; they're only copies, really . . . and these idiots are always making fun of them. They're not *all* by me, anyway. Jack likes you to think they are, but they're not. That big one over the fireplace, goodness only knows who did *that* ; we bought it at an auction sale the time we got that sideboard and the billiard-table, and it fits nice up there . . . and those two over on that wall in the carved frames, the autumn scenes, they're two that Davy did when he was still working at Klebendorf's. They're my favourites, really. . . ."

Helen gave a considered attention to the two Steiner tem-peras I had stolen and put my name to, while my stomach chilled with the shame of it, but she only said "Hmmm!" and nodded, and that made me feel worse than ever because even poor old dead Ludwig Steiner didn't get any praise out of it. . . .

This was the point when I suddenly began to realise that in some subtle and as yet unspecified way Helen and my family were not really hitting it off too well: more, I had the disturbing additional reflection that this fine sharp edge of incompatibility which had already been presented could never be withdrawn, and that, in spite of all Jack's good-natured efforts and Mother's innate kindliness, a sense of constraint would inevitably grow.

At once I began to study Helen's behaviour and reactions with a nervous, watchful concern, which, I realise now, doubtless communicated itself both to her and to everybody else. Watching her with this new vigilance it occurred to me that the stiffness that had been displayed in the tone of her voice was in fact only a part of her whole attitude. She was not comfortable. That was it—she was not comfortable. She even sat stiffly, with her handbag and gloves still on her lap, as if to imply that she would prefer not to stay for very long, and she was anything but relaxed as far as the swarming children on the floor were concerned, for she would instinctively flinch away and draw herself more tightly together when one of them crawled anywhere near her, and I think I realised the full measure of the tension that was gripping her when I noticed that Sheila was studying her from the rocking-chair with a kind of secret watchful amusement in her eyes.

Poor, simple, good-hearted Bert was hardly a help at this stage because he would insist on offering her dishes of food with a kind of forced ingratiating politeness, and she would keep refusing—" We had an absolutely huge lunch, and I'm honestly not a scrap hungry," she would say—and Bert in his innocent anxiety to please her and make her feel at home would promptly produce a dish of something else, and say, " But you've got to try one of these, though . . . they're home-made, they're my old woman's speciality . . ." and again she would refuse, and he would blunder on making the situation hopelessly worse, until her rejections grew colder and curter and edgier, and finally Jack had to say, " Oh for God's sake, Bert, why don't you *listen* to what she's telling you? She's not hungry. If she's told you once she's told you a hundred times! Why don't you offer *me* a sausage-roll? You won't catch me knocking back tucker like this!"

But then Sheila's baby, Kathleen, who was only at the crawling and the trying-to-stand-up stage, emerged determinedly from beneath a chair and before anyone could do anything about it she had grasped one of Helen's gunmetal-sheathed legs in her two pudgy, grimy little hands, and she drew herself wobblingly and uncertainly erect, and gooed at everyone, dribbling triumphantly through a paste of damp milk arrowroot biscuit and raspberry jam, and I could see the repugnance run like an electric charge all through Helen's body, and then Sheila leaned forward from the rocker and very gently disengaged the swaying baby and sent her crawling on her way, and murmured, " I'm sorry, the little devil seems to have left some of her jelly on the hem of your skirt. Here, I'll wipe it with this, it won't leave a mark."

I could feel the situation slipping distinctly out of control now, and at the same time becoming less diffuse. Mother had forgotten her momentary discomfort and was beamingly happy with everything, because Jack had insisted on giving her another glass of sweet muscat, and this had made her a little " wizzy," and at this stage Jack, I think, was still desperately trying to keep the harmonies intact, but the undercurrent of strain was becoming obvious in the room. Bert, still hurt by the impatient edge to Helen's last refusal of his offerings, and stung by Jack's rebuke, was rather petulantly taking it out on two of his children who were squabbling in the corner by the sea-chest, and crying children in a crowded room are seldom soothing to adult tensions. Jean and Marj had got to the stage of exchanging meaning glances with each other. Dad, stupefied by heavy food and too much beer, was half asleep in his chair, and belching softly. Sheila rocked herself back and forth and watched her husband.

I have not the faintest idea how the conversation ever moved to politics, although I imagine Helen and I probably began it out of some intuitive nervous desperation to re-establish our own rapport, but there we were suddenly discussing the Spanish Civil War and " Potato " Jones and Hoare and Laval and non-intervention and Fascist duplicity, and Helen was projecting herself a little, perhaps to establish herself on her own knowledgeable ground, and then quite suddenly, quite matter-of-factly, Jack was saying:

" Davy came to me with some cockeyed idea about going

over there to get into it, and I told him he ought to have his
bloomin' head read."

"And why do you consider it a cockeyed idea?" Helen
wanted to know. She put the question quietly enough, but the
antagonism and the challenge were there all right—she didn't
like Jack any better than she liked his wife—and Jack was an
old street fighter who could smell aggression in a syllable
and who knew a chip when he saw one on a shoulder, and he
was never anybody's fool about the way people felt about
him, so he knew what she was up to, of course, and he was
just drunk enough to want to meet the challenge, and that
was when the atmosphere began to change for the worse.
Permanently, as it eventually turned out. . . .

"Eh?" He ran his fingers through his thinning yellow silky
hair and looked at her in a measuring sort of way, and said,
"Well, don't you?"

"Of course not!" she said firmly, and for a disloyal
moment I found myself wishing she didn't sound so superior
when she really only wanted to be emphatic. "I think we
have to *believe* in things," she insisted. "We have to have
causes, and objects, and beliefs. And I don't think we should
just stand back and allow people to be trampled on. I mean,
what's democracy for, after all?"

Jack said, "Yes, that's all very well, but what I'm getting
at is, do you think Davy should've gone to Spain with those
two mates of his?" and Jean pulled a face and said, "Oh,
this is all way over *my* head!" and she made a signal to Marj
and they began to clear dishes away, and Bert sulked, and
Mother, reeking of sweet muscatel, had returned contentedly
to her knitting, and Dad belched again and mumbled something about the papers never printing the truth of things
anyway, and the children squawled and bickered, and I
realised suddenly that we were to be involved in antagonisms
that would never be forgiven, and that these antagonisms
would only concern Helen and Jack and me.

"No, not Davy necessarily," she said. "But that's only
because he's more valuable here, as a journalist. He can do
more for the causes here, more than he could by going over
there and perhaps sacrificing himself in a physical sense. But
that doesn't mean the others shouldn't have gone, those

friends of his . . . well, it doesn't matter about one of them, he was going to help the Fascists anyway, but——"

"Weren't they journalists too?" Jack asked.

"Yes. Yes, they were. But Davy is different. I mean he's not just a reporter. He can be very important here, writing things. But there are thousands of others who could go over there and give their help if they really wanted to, if they saw the need for taking up the challenge . . . well, if they think Fascism is something we have to destroy before it destroys us, and——"

"But that puts Davy in a pretty funny position, doesn't it?" Jack said. "Look, I don't read his articles so I don't know what he writes about, and I'm not too hot on this political lingo, Fascism and all that, but it makes a queer sort of a joker out of him if he's the one to stay back here simply because he's got to tell everybody else they've got to go over there to Spain and roll up their sleeves and start fighting! That makes him just a sort of an urger, doesn't it? You know what an urger is, don't you?"

"Oh, Jack, that's not what Helen means at all!" I began to protest, because the perils were all too obvious now, but Jack was just staring at Helen very intently, and he went on talk-ing as if I had made no interruption at all:

"Listen," he said to her, "why should Davy or anyone else out here get involved in a stoush between a bunch of wops and dagoes way over the other side of the world? That's what I want to know. Why? It's none of our business. People ought to fight their own battles, that's my rule. Just suppose there was some strife up north there in the canefields, between those dagoes who work the sugar around Innisfail and Cairns and Ingham. D'you think all those other dagoes from the Mediterranean are going to come rushin' all the way out here to take sides? Not on your bloomin' life they're not! Catch *them*! So why should *we* poke our noses into what's happening over there? If you want causes to worry about or to fight about, there's a whole bloomin' raft of things here, isn't there? You wouldn't call this flaming country a true and shining example of democracy, would you? There are plenty of things here anyone can have a go at, without an urger to push 'em into it. Have a look at the mines at Wont-haggi, or the timber camps at Powelltown, or walk along one of the Susso queues, or go down the docks on a wet morning and take a dekko at a wharfies' pick-up, or see the way they treat the factory hands in those sweatshops out West Melbourne way or Footscray. Why do we have to go fighting things in Spain, for God's sake?"

He paused and took a deep breath, and then turned to me suddenly, deliberately, I think, and said, "Listen, do you feel like watering the horses?" and I hesitated, and then nodded rather grudgingly, and we both stood up, and Jack said, with an apologetic grin, "All this beer, it goes right through you!" and I am sure he said it quite blatantly to shock Helen, and then we were both walking down the passageway together, and through the vestibule and out into the back yard, and we walked right up to the old sycamore tree before we spread our legs and undid our buttons.

"That's a bloody good-looking sheila you've got," said Jack, pissing a golden jet. "Bloody good figure, too. Bit on the skinny side for my taste, mind you, but she's certainly an eyeful!" He played the jet higher against the trunk of the tree and said, "Got a mind of her own too, eh? I mean, she's got pretty strong opinions about things, hasn't she?"

"What do you mean by that?" I asked suspiciously.

"Well . . . oh, nothing in particular. Gee! this is a relief, isn't it? . . . getting the old bladder emptied out, I mean . . . do you know I've been sitting there for the last half-hour with my legs crossed like a pair of bloody nutcrackers." He directed the jet at a knothole in the tree trunk and flushed a spider out, and broke wind and said, "Better an empty house than a bad tenant," and then, without any change of tone: "You serious about this sheila of yours?"

"Helen? Serious? Well, I'm probably going to marry her, if that's what you mean."

He shook himself and began to button up, and said, admiringly, "She's a good-looker all right. I'm not denying that. Dresses nice, too. And she seems pretty clever . . . you know, she's able to talk about things, sort of educated like." He paused, giving it consideration, then frowned slightly and said, "She seems to have pretty strong opinions, though, that's the thing that worries me, Davy. You *are* sure about this? I mean, well, you can tell me to mind my own business, but what I'm getting at is, marriage is a pretty serious affair . . .

it's the rest of your life, really, and it's having kids and all that . . . you know, it's quite a business. . . . And you haven't really knocked around much . . . I mean she *is* just about the first woman you've had anything to do with, isn't she?"

"What's all this to do with you?" I turned on him sharply, cold and angry and resentful.

"Nothing, Davy," he said with a faint smile. "It's to do with *you.* That's why I said you could tell me to mind my own business. No, it's to do with you," he repeated. "Whether you make a mistake or not, that's what I mean. People do, you know. You see, Davy, there has to be a lot of give and take in marriage. A hell of a lot. Even Sheila and me, well, we get on all right, but it's never all plain sailing, you know . . . there's always a bit of strife that's bound to come up, and sometimes the kids get on your nerves, or you might have been down the pub with the boys for a few too many beers, or you blue half your earnings on some bloody nag that runs dead, and you can get yourself into a pretty rotten mess unless you and your sheila have this thing of give and take with each other, and——"

"Yes, well I think we'd better be getting back inside," I said impatiently, and turned away from him and began to walk towards the house, but he called to me before I had reached the door:

"Hey, hold on a jiffy! No need to rush it. Why not give the women a chance to get together with each other? You know, I'd like Sheil' to have a bit of a talk with your girl." He had stopped half-way along the brick path and was staring at the squalid, scruffy little back garden. "Jesus, a lot of things have happened here, haven't they?" he said musingly, and put his hands on his hips and looked around with interest at the broken palings of the fence and the wizened fig-tree and the patchy unkempt lawn with the nettles and the clover coming through, and the tangled wire of the ruined fowl-house and the old wood-shed with the chassis of some ancient invalid wheel-chair rusting on its roof and the shabby privy crouched beneath its hump of honeysuckle, and the sycamore-tree that didn't seem anywhere near as big as it used to be and the messy thickets of the untrimmed shrubs. "Remember the old Dollicus that used to be here?" Jack said reminiscently, moving forward and rubbing his fingers across

the new wire screen of the sleep-out. "I miss that, you
know," he said. "I liked it better when that was growing here.
Oh, it's neater now, yeah, and a bloody sight cleaner, and I
bet it's got rid of all those bugs, but I sort of preferred it
the way it was. Inside the place, too, up there in the hall and
Mum's bedroom and the kitchen . . . I admit it's all nice and
up-to-date with that panelling they've put in and the new
paint and all that, but I still miss it a bit the way it used to
be. . . ."

I suppose it was the beer he had drunk and his emotional
concern for me and the sentiment engendered by Mother's
birthday that set his mood and brought it all back to him, for
he seemed to want to just stand there on the cracked brick
path looking at this shabby suburban squalor that surrounded him, this sad and pointless world confined within the
patched palings of the dividing fences and the red, ribbed
rooftops of the Gillons' bungalow and the dusty pepper-trees
that shaded Mrs. Hartrick's smelly hen-run, and seeing only
the flickering sequence of visions that his nostalgia evoked.

"Remember all those nights," he said, "when Mum was
hiding up there in the fernery, and the Old Man was out here
in the dark chargin' around all over the joint and waving that
whacking great pistol about and threatening to blow everybody's bloody brains out! Eh? He had another think coming, didn't he? Poor old bugger could hardly blow a candle
out now! And old Gran', remember the way she'd always
empty the pisspots up there under the fig-tree, and then Bert'd
get ropable at the smell of it because that's where he used to
like to sit waxing his thread and sewing soles and singing
those damned army songs. No wonder the tree looks so
bloody shrivelled up, eh? . . . although, come to think of it,
out the front there where we used to stand by the gate and
pee on the privet, that end always grew a good three feet taller
than the other end, and a thicker growth too, so maybe it's
coming out fresh that does it, and not being stale and out of
a jerry. . . ." He shook his head in a reflective pleasure at
this. "You know, Davy, we had a lot of fun here one way
and another, didn't we? Don't you reckon we did? Remember the punching-ball there under the trellis, and you and
me with the gloves on, and Jean tearin' in to tell Mum that
day I gave you the black eye, and when we put those live

crabs down in the socket of Bert's wooden leg, and d'you remember the tame magpie we had that used to pull all the pegs out of the washing and send Mum into a tizzy, and Dad swapping it for that bloody terrible cockatoo that moulted away until it didn't have one flamin' feather to its name, and——"

" I don't know about you, but I'm going back inside," I said, for I was in no mood for this maudlin flood of reminiscence, and Jack just shrugged and said, " All right, let's join the women, if that's what you want," and although he smiled it didn't quite conceal the trace of hurt in his eyes, but I shied away from that and deliberately walked in ahead of him.

It was like walking back into some staged dramatic tableau.

Helen was sitting rigidly in her chair, much as I had left her, but with a pale, set face, and Mother was flushed and kneeling on the carpet beside her rubbing at the Donegal skirt with a table napkin which she kept dipping in a shallow bowl containing some liquid, and one of Jean's kids was howling in a corner as if it had just been smacked, and Jean was standing over Mother with a nerve-blotched upset face and saying, " I tell you if you sprinkle ordinary salt over it and rub it well in it doesn't leave a mark at all," and Sheila, who was the only one who seemed unruffled, said, " Mum knows what she's doing, and even if it does leave a bit of a stain it can always be dry-cleaned, can't it?" and Helen looked up as I came into the room, and offered me, as if it were some gracious private privilege, a smile that was cool and brave, and the smile was like a net drawing me inexorably into alliance with her, into the isolation of her separateness, into the little enclave of our proven superiority, and she said, " Davy, darling, do tell them that it doesn't really matter at all, it's nothing, I can attend to it when I get home and you'll never see it, and . . ."—she broke off and turned quickly and touched Mother's shoulder lightly, solicitously, with her long, fine, aristocratic-looking fingers—" oh, please don't worry about it, Mrs. Meredith, you mustn't!" and Mother looked up at her and shook her head helplessly, and she was blinking away behind her glasses in that confused, beseeching way she had that could sometimes stab at me like real pain.

It was the combination of that cool and binding smile of Helen's and the look of baffled consternation on Mother's face that told me where I stood with a chilling finality. I realised that from the very first moment of our arrival at the house the visit had been fateful, that everything had been working towards this point we had now reached, momentous and irrevocable, where I had to choose between inflicting pain or suffering it, and the thrall of this cool and beautiful woman reached me like a command across the crowded tension of the room, and I realised that the price of alliance had been fixed and that it would have to be a continuation of the hurt I had deliberately given to Jack in the back yard, and that I would have to go on hurting and hurting and hurting, and that I was as totally committed to a proving of myself, just as imperative and just as wrong, as when poor, epileptic Harry Meade had blundered past me on the football field at school and I had had to hit him and hit him and hit him until he had fallen writhing and twitching at my feet, and it didn't matter any longer whether Jack was there to slap my face or not. We were men now, not children, and we were fighting for different things.

"What's happened?" I asked with a sinking heart, and Bert scowled and glared at the weeping child in the corner and said, "That damned clumsy brat of ours tipped a whole bowl of trifle and jelly all over Miss Midgeley's best suit!" and at this the offending brat howled all the louder, and Jean turned on Bert with a snappish, "Well, the child didn't do it on purpose, did he?" and Helen gave a deft, light underlining to it all with a dismissive, "But all this fuss is so silly, really. . . ."

"It's damned silly the way we put up with all these blasted children!" I said hotly. "Why the devil do they have to be under our *feet* all the time? Can't they go outside and play? God almighty, this is like living in a damned crèche!"

And then, deliberately, I turned to face Jack. He was leaning against the door-frame, and although there was no particular expression on his face I knew that he would meet it square on, without slapping my face perhaps, but without side-stepping.

"Well, what's a bit of jelly and trifle between friends?" he said quietly. "It'll clean off, won't it? The skirt isn't ruined."

"Yes, it's all very well for you to just stand there and shrug it off," I said angrily. "But why *do* we have to have these confounded kids swarming everywhere?"

"Because it's Mum's birthday. And these are her grand-children. And she's very fond of 'em. Isn't that right, Mum?"

"Then why the hell doesn't someone keep an eye on them?" I demanded, more riled than ever by a sudden dis-turbing realisation that, in his own way, he *was* about to slap me across the face, for in his eyes was exactly the same hard, set expression as when he had looked at me across the fallen figure of Harry Meade.

"What's got into *you*?" he said. "You're really trying to make something of this, aren't you? But you don't want to get above yourself, you know. Maybe Miss Midgeley would be interested to hear that when you were just about the same age as young Derek there we had a party in this very room, it was Pop's Welcome Home, the night he came back from the war, and you puked all the way from that end of the table to the outside vestibule door. You puked over aunts and cousins and neighbours and God knows who else . . . you've never *seen* such a mess! . . . and nobody thought a thing about it, they just rolled you up in an old quilt and put you to bed on that couch over there."

"Oh, for God's sake, keep your revolting stories to your-self! Helen's not interested, and neither am I. You're having quite a field day with your reminiscences, aren't you?" I added sarcastically, hoping to wound him again.

"Am I?" He gave me a long, careful look—that same measuring look with which he had accepted Helen's challenge earlier. "If I am," he said, "it might be because I'm trying to make you see a few things straight, like. This business I was trying to talk about outside just a while back. About give and take. That's one of 'em. But since you're the one who seems to want to make a first-class Kilkenny out of a little thing like a blob of jelly on a skirt, let me tell you something else. You seem to have got it into your head that you're a pretty superior sort of person—and maybe you are, for all I know—but it doesn't necessarily follow, remember, that we're not good enough for you. This is still *your* family. And kids are part of a family whether you like 'em or not. The Old Man there was one of nineteen, wasn't he? Don't you reckon they must have been a bit under each other's feet. Eh? Anyway, you were a kid yourself once, and *you* puked over people and *you* dribbled gravy and Mum had to sew a whole row of buttons on the sleeves of your jackets to stop you wiping your snotty nose there. So don't make the error of thinking yourself *too* superior, son! And if you and your sheila here are going to get spliced you might wake up to a few of these things. Like give and take. And realising that kids are kids."

"For heaven's sake stop this fighting, you two!" pleaded Mother, scared and anxious and still kneeling beside Helen with a stricken face, and Jean was standing very stiffly and gnawing at her lower lip, and Bert was looking down and rubbing at his knotty knuckles as if he'd just realised how nasty they looked, and I knew that Helen was trying to catch my eye but I wouldn't look at her, and Sheila had taken little Kathleen on her knee and was tweaking at her bare toes, and Dad lifted his head and for a moment seemed to sniff at the smell of hostility and conflict like some old war-horse, but then the belligerent fire faded in his bloodshot eyes and he hiccuped quietly and sank back into his pullover. . . .

"Who's fighting?" said Jack. "Stone the crows, Mum, this is your birthday, isn't it? This is a happy family gathering, isn't it?" He turned and his eyes met mine evenly. "Isn't it, Davy?" he said.

"And whose bloody fault if it isn't?" I snapped. "You've been spoiling for a fight ever since we came into the house! You've——"

"Don't, Davy," I heard Helen say. "It isn't worth it, darling, it——"

"What do you really mean, Miss Midgeley?" Jack said, turning on her swiftly. "What does *he* really mean? *It* isn't worth it, or *we* aren't worth it?"

"I mean—I mean all this fuss and anger over such a trivial little thing," she said, smiling at him, and detesting him.

"That's just what I think," he said. "It's what I've been saying. So suppose you ask *him* what else it is he's got stuck in his crop! You never know, it might just be this room that puts him on edge. First time he was ever in here he threw up. This is where he used to hide from his bogy-men, in that sea-chest over there. He never could stand the old women dying in here, or the coffins on the table. And now he can't stand the kids being here, his own nephews and nieces! All I can say is he seems bloody hard to please!" He looked across at his wife and said, " Soon as you're ready, Sheil', you'd better get your things, and I'll clean the kids up. It's time we were pushing along." He moved into the room and bent over Mother and kissed her on the forehead and said, " Sorry your party ended up in a yike, Mum. Never mind. The tucker was marvellous."

I drove Helen home in a cold and bitter fury. She was very quiet and she kept rubbing with her fingers at the big damp patch on her skirt.

It was *they* who had let me down, I told myself in raging indignation. The whole family! Every one of them! It wasn't just that none of them had approved of my choice, that might have been expected . . . but not a single one of them had had the ordinary common or garden intelligence to see that she was as different from them as chalk was from cheese. She had shown them all up, that was the blunt truth of it, shown them up in all their snide, shabby little pettiness . . . the whole bunch of them were just small enough and ignorant enough to realise that she was a cut above them, and to resent it! Well, I was a cut above them, too! I was just as different from them as she was, and that was something they were damn' well going to have to realise! I didn't belong to *them* any longer! They had no claim on me. I had fought my own way free of them—and without any bloody help on their part, by God!—and as long as I lived they were never going to drag me back again to their trumpery lives, to their uncouthness and stupidity and vulgarity and the crippling impossibility of that awful existence of theirs!

" To hell with them all!" I shouted aloud. I shouted it through the windscreen to the road down which we were driving, to a channel of asphalt that was grey and flat and treeless, like a dead drain running through a dead landscape, to the slithering flickering of the picket fences and the hedges and the lamp-posts and the neat letter-boxes and the names on gates.

Helen sat in silence, still rubbing at the damp patch on her skirt.

" I did warn you," I said. " When we were going out there

I told you they might be difficult. At least I tried to warn you."

She reached over and squeezed my arm.

We were married two months later. I had just turned twenty-six, and Helen was thirty. The wedding took place on the day that Guernica was bombed, although this had no connection with us, of course, and by that time neither Helen nor I had much real interest left in what was happening in Spain. It was the quietest ceremony possible, commensurate with Helen's insistence on wearing a bridal veil and a superb, sheath-like gown of ivory satin which she had designed herself, and the formal and unadorned service was held in the little Anglican church of St. Catherine's.

What I principally remember about it is that while waiting for the bride in the church vestry with Jerry Farley, who had been chosen by Helen to stand as my best man (his sister Moira being the only bridesmaid), I had the odd wish that something calamitous would happen, like the roof of the church falling in, which might bring to a stop, or at least to a postponement, a series of fantastic processes which quite suddenly seemed to me to be moving me against my will and better judgment towards a suspect destiny. Nothing so convenient happened. I cannot really claim this as any psychic presentiment, because my other memories of that wait in the vestry are equally ridiculous—the fact that one of Steiner's old calendars of years before was hanging there on the wall above the prayer books advertising Malvern Star Bicycles, that a fox-terrier dog walked in and lifted its leg against a chair and trotted out, that the vicar wore grey flannel bags under his surplice and had odd socks on, one brown and one black.

These absurd memories of then, of course, are in no way related to the perspective of *now*, when everything has long since run its course. On the much longer view I suppose one might claim that the odd little prickle of premonition was a sort of subconscious intuition that I was committing myself to a rash act of self-betrayal. Like the reassessment some military historian might make of a confused battle years after the smoke has blown away, it is often possible—sometimes, indeed, unavoidable—that one sees all the aspects of valour and of cowardice in a totally different way ; the heroic general whose equestrian statue is in the square is proved a blundering idiot, stark panic has been mistaken for reckless courage, gunpowder was wasted, and there was no justice in the awarding of the laurels. This is the tragical comedy that the historian defines as a re-appreciation. It is, alas, only possible to do this very much later.

So that now it is difficult not to feel some genuine sympathy, some stirring of compassion, for that younger David Meredith of years ago praying for sublime catastrophe in a church vestry, yet entirely unaware of the self-delusions that have placed him there. It is so easy to be wise after the event. . . .

As far as the wedding was concerned, it was Helen who supervised, with her customary neat efficiency, almost all of the planning and arrangements. It was she who decided on the church, the restricted list of invitations, the officiating cleric, the photographer who took our pictures, and the rather depressing hotel on the Esplanade at St. Kilda, in the " Blue Room " of which the stilted little reception was afterwards held. It was she, too, who, with scrupulous cordiality, won my family over to an uncritical if somewhat nervous acceptance of the situation, although there was still something of reserve and uncertainty in their attitudes towards her personally which they could never entirely conceal, and I think they realised this and it made them more uncomfortable than ever, and so none of them stayed for very long at the reception afterwards.

Only Jack, whose just and passionate spirit could never neglect a generosity, concealed his misgivings—if he still held them—behind the enormous festive sprig of orange-blossom he wore in the button-hole of his new navy-blue suit, and he kissed the bride as if he really meant it, and there was genuine admiration in his tone when he said, " He's always been the dark horse of the family, this one, and here he's gone and done it again, grabbin' the prettiest missus this side of the Black Stump!"

And then in an uncontrollable welling-up of clownish, affectionate exuberance, he was coming at me grinning on his nimble dancing feet, feinting short-arm jabs and uppercuts and right crosses and that straight left of his.

He had tied six old sea-boots to the back of the limousine

that was to take us to the railway station, but when we were
around the next corner and out of sight, Helen ordered the
chauffeur to stop, and made him get out and untie them and
leave them there in the gutter.

CHAPTER 12

If I recall nothing of our honeymoon it cannot be because it
was, as honeymoons go, a failure, for that would have had
immediate repercussions, and the first months of my married
life with Helen I clearly remember as being almost blissfully
satisfying.

I had the thrilling feeling of having finished a long and
difficult period of probation and come at last to the beginning
of real life. I was stimulated by that immediate consciousness
of maturity which the responsibility for a separate and personal establishment creates, I was relieved at being free at last
from the inhibiting background of my family, and I had an
almost intoxicating sense of delight that I was standing
finally on my own feet in a world which I believed to me
entirely mine.

A more intriguing factor of the changed circumstances was
the quite new and different emotional regard I felt for Helen.
It was much more than the intense and possessive pride I had
in a partner who was beautiful, intelligent, mature, and ad-
mirably presentable—here, I told myself, was the ideal companion for this new, modern, sophisticated, and challenging
world in which, ambitiously, I imagined myself cutting an
ever more important figure—but there had been a deep
change at the most intimate level of our relationship She had
become, to me, so much more valuable and desirable as the
public figure of a wife than she had ever been in the role of
the secretly cherished mistress: we were not blatantly and
unmistakably " in love," we talked and we behaved as lovers,
to the last cliché of endearment and as sentimentally as in the
popular songs, and in a way we had never been able to bring
ourselves to do in that long, curious, and incompletely casual
liaison we had shared in Perce Parkinson's library.

Perhaps one should have been able to see then beneath the surface of the sentimentality, for the physical act of love-making remained very much as it always had been—clean, neat, expedient, and somewhat passionless—but it was to be many months, under the balm of a romantic magic, before I even began to suspect either the true sterilities of our association or the trap which I had helped to fashion around myself.

I think that subconsciously it was the disparity between our ages that led me to entrust so much of the material construction of our new lives to Helen's decisions. On this question of our ages we had developed odd little tacit understandings: while the fact that she was four years older than I, for instance, was never directly stated we were in general agreement that women under thirty were almost certainly either "frivolous" or "immature." Helen, therefore, naturally assumed leadership on matters of taste and sophistication; where mature judgments were needed it was usually she who would make the decision. I admired her originality and vitality. I had unbounded confidence in her.

It was she who decided on the house in Beverley Grove, in a new "garden" subdivision in what at that time was considered a "good" suburb, and which placed almost half suburban Melbourne between us and the two old, shabby, antiquated houses where we had separately grown up. I am sure it must have been at least partly her violent resentment, and rejection, of the decay which had hitherto surrounded her, and the sordid dreariness from which she believed she had rescued me, that developed her insistence that we should begin our married life in a house so new that it seemed to me to have come to us still damp from the plasterer's trowel.

It was what at that time was usually described as a "double-fronted, ultra-modern, red brick, three-bedroom villa" and it stood on its sixty-foot frontage behind a low brick fence on its own small block of land beside a concrete drive leading to a separate fibro-plaster garage. It stank of cement mortar, raw floorboards, fresh paint, damp putty, and insulated electric wiring.

We were both of us inordinately proud of it, and on the day we signed the lease and were given the two Yale keys to the front door, Helen and I toasted each other in the empty "model" kitchen, which smelt of stainless steel and wood-shavings, from a bottle of Minchinbury Sparkling Hock I had bought specially for the occasion.

Beverley Grove, the house, the subdivision, the suburb, even that bottle of Sparkling Hock, were immediate tokens and symbols of social progression. Of an advancement in caste, even.

So were our neighbours in the new houses around us. Mr. Treadwell, our neighbour on the left, was a retired police court magistrate. Mr. Phyland, our neighbour on the right, was a chartered accountant in the city. Wally Solomons, who had the house directly opposite us and an indolent, soignée, highly sophisticated and very beautiful wife called Sandra, who spent most of her time in black slacks and boleros, smoking pastel-tinted cigarettes through a twelve-inch holder, was the head salesman in the main showrooms of General Motors. On the corner, where Beverley Grove joined Park Crescent (these names were incised in Roman capitals into the cement paving blocks), lived Dr. Felton Carradine, the dental surgeon.

The entire Beverley Park Gardens subdivision had been a big investment on the part of a building-contractor by the name of Bernie Rothenstein, who in the speculative days of Melbourne suburban estate development had a record for civic malefactions which was probably unmatched in the Southern Hemisphere, but which later won him a respected seat on the City Council and ultimately a knighthood: and although only three basic ground-plans were used for all the hundreds of houses in the subdivision, there were still no two houses in any one street, grove, crescent, drive, or avenue which could be said to really look alike. Each front elevation had its own distinct difference, in the design of the porch, the placement of the picture-window, the run of the paths and whether plain or " crazy," the position of the drive, the design of the chimney, the style of the front door, and so on, and even further permutations were possible, because there were three distinct ways in which the roofs of flat terracotta tiles could be pitched. The interiors of all the houses were virtually the same, of course, to the very inch in things like roof-area and the dimensions of rooms and halls and passageways and cupboard-space, and the immutable sameness of their inventoried fittings. (Not until long, long

afterwards did one pause to marvel at the deadening democracy of a system which could dictate, over nearly one
square-mile of human habitation, that no man should have
one more light-switch or power-point or water-faucet or
sliding drawer than any other!)

I was by this time earning a good salary at the *Morning
Post*, I had money in the bank and unshakable self-confidence,
my prospects were excellent: so it is not surprising that, with
the benevolent assistance of the hire-purchase system, we
committed ourselves deeply and eagerly to the panoply that
was in keeping with our new standing. For the virginal
garage I bought, extravagantly, a flashy and almost new
M.G., with wire wheels, Brooklands hubs, a throaty exhaust,
and a dashing finish in pillar-box red. Helen calculated, bar-
gained, and shunned excessive extravagances—for she was, in
fact, a dedicated home-builder in the best practical sense—
but she had set her heart on precisely the sort of home she
wanted, so the house was furnished in severely modern pale-
wood furniture, and she chose sophisticated Indian mats and
scatter-rugs instead of wall-to-wall carpets, and selected with
careful taste the folk-weave fabrics from which she made
curtains and drapes and the covers for cushions. She bought
for the walls reproduction prints of the right modern paintings, both the Van Gogh chair and his cypresses, a Matisse
odalisque, that Braque which is so suitable for modern
kitchens, and the Cézanne apples—but also, with an admir-
able subtlety, a Vlaminck and a Derain and a Bonnard—
and all of them were framed either in knotty pine or raw,
rubbed limewood. We had low twin beds for the front bedroom with parchment-shaded lamps and a white handset
telephone on the night-table between us, and it was Helen's
idea that the two spare bedrooms should, in fact, be used for
more practical purposes, so that one became my study and the
other her sewing-room. Here, too, there were tacit understandings that Helen did not propose to have children and
that there was little likelihood that we should want guests to
stay overnight. Her room went through a series of rapid
transformations. She made all her own clothes, so that the
sewing-machine which we bought on monthly terms was
really a very sound investment. To this was added a dressmaker's " shape " made exactly to her own measurements,

and then, when she went back to the fashion-drawing which
she had given up years before—mostly to design clothes which
she would make, or thought she might make, for herself—
first a drawing-table and then an easel were installed. The
consequence of this was that she began to paint, in water-
colour and gouache, in the beginning as a hobby but eventually with a quite zealous conviction of her own creative
ability. My study was another story . . .

To a very large degree it was Helen, also, who directed the
reorganisation of our social life. She adored entertaining, or
being entertained. In the cocktail parties which to me, until
then, had been only part of the unavoidable chores of daily
journalism, she found endless excitement and pleasure; she
adored gallery openings and the dull receptions given on the
maiden voyages of new ships and theatre parties and dress
rehearsals—any gathering, in fact, where she could meet
people. Her delight in these activities was genuine and dis-
arming, with the result that she made friends easily, and most
people seemed to like and to admire her. Well, she was an
extraordinarily attractive woman, she dressed smartly, she
had style and a gay, shallow exuberance and vivacity which
people found appealing. Certainly for a good long time she
had no admirer more devoted than myself . . . and, in that
misleading period of our social betterment, nobody more
proud of her. . . .

The companions for our leisure hours were chosen as conscientiously and with as much attention to taste and suitability
as she would select the picture for a wall, the guest-towels for
the bathroom, the mats for the dining-table, the tapestry
covering for a lounge chair.

The Farleys were quite suddenly our boon companions—
Jerry with his tidy little businessman's paunch and his Oldsmobile sedan and his membership in the Junior Chamber of
Commerce and his rather plain, scatterbrain wife Rene, whom
he had really married, I suspect, because her father was
someone important in one of the big stock-and-station
agencies and her uncle owned a wealthy grazing property
down Camperdown or Mount Elephant way—it was somewhere, at any rate, where polo was played—and the still
beautiful and now haughty Moira, with her dull fiancé Justin
Byrne, who was a teller in the head office of the E.S. and A.

Bank. The six of us were forever visiting each other, and on Sunday nights when I was not working we would make up gay, convivial parties at Mario's or the Café Latin, where we would sit by candlelight and eat minestrone or real Italian spaghetti or ravioli, and drink Chianti or Rheingold.

It was Helen's triumph that within a matter of only two or three weeks of our arrival in Beverley Grove we were also on the friendliest visiting terms with Wally and Sandra Solomons, who to this day occupy a rather special little niche in my memory as perhaps the two most stupid human beings I have ever known. But in those dazed months of bemused advancement, they were very much a part of Helen's chosen "set," and sometimes at week-ends we would all go dashing off in our cars on long, wild, exhilarating drives to Sorrento or Portsea, under enormous non-suburban skies that had the wind below the clouds, to frolic together over the measureless sand-dunes and scream our infantile challenges at the great strong beating sweep of the surf. Sometimes there are moments of splendour even in our stupidities.

The surprising addition to Helen's chosen coterie of intimate friends were Gavin Turley and his wife Peggy, who was a charming, pretty, and genuinely " social " girl who came from a well-off Toorak family, had " finished " in Switzerland and been presented at Buckingham Palace, and had met Gavin at the University (never referred to by Helen or her set as anything but " The Shop ") where they had graduated together in Arts. From the very beginning, Helen had been most sedulous in cultivating the more important or interesting of my colleagues on the newspaper—she was forever plaguing me to invite Mr. Brewster to the house for cocktails or for dinner, but I never did—and of those whose age qualified them for entry into Helen's group, Gavin Turley was certainly both the most important and the most interesting. His wife got on very well with Helen—they shared some mutual and esoteric passion about clothes and were forever shopping together and exchanging fashion magazines—but I know now that Gavin's liking for our company was based partly on the fact that he genuinely had an odd sardonic affection for me, which he continued to preserve for all the time I knew him, and partly because in his droll, analysing way he was always able to derive an infinite amount of whimsical and ironic amusement from our ambitions and our antics. He had an astute, observing mind which generally was allowed to operate behind a demeanour that was gentle, tolerant and only faintly quizzical, in much the way that his clever, lofty brow was always hidden under the dishevelled locks of fine black hair, worn very long, that seemed to fall at random all over his head. He was thin and tremendously tall—six-feet-six I think it was—and almost misshapen in his general awkwardness and the pronounced stoop which he cultivated. He had a long, thin, horsy face, which women found most attractive, a Ronald Colman moustache, huge square teeth which were discoloured by nicotine, and an almost faultless eye for human foibles. I never knew him to do an unkind act.

I still remember the first formal party he attended in the house in Beverley Grove. This was the " intimate " little function which Helen had substituted for the far more elaborate " house-warming " party she had at first intended to give. That idea had been quietly allowed to lapse after I had pointed out to her that such a party would of necessity mean the inviting not only of my parents and my sisters and Jack and Sheila, but of her own father, too, and her brother.

With Helen, there was to be no commingling of the old life and the new. There was, I believe, a certain forceful integrity about her determination never to return to the surroundings of her past in that she set herself just as obstinately against her own family and background as she did against mine. It was quite extraordinary after our marriage to observe the almost ruthless way in which she cast off everything that had gone before. Her meek, spineless little father called on us only once, and had almost nothing to say, and he never repeated the visit. After the day of our wedding I never saw the sullen, shadowy brother again. Helen seldom spoke of them afterwards. Her mysterious political friends vanished, the tennis club might never have existed, and apart from the fact that she would describe herself to my friends as having been a " librarian," Perce Parkinson's library and the Genoa velvet couch were not talked about any more.

One sees now that what was so sad about her, really, was that she never at any time saw any true and worthwhile goal

for herself, that once she had escaped she had no idea where
to go. Her ambitions had the impetus of desperation, and
no scale.

At any rate, instead of the "house-warming" we had
cocktails and a buffet supper for twelve more fastidiously-
chosen guests—the elect of Helen's new "set," the Turleys,
two other young reporters from the newspaper and the
assistant social editress, and one of Rene Farley's burly, polo-
playing cousins from the Western District, who was visiting
the city at the time on some matter concerning stud service
for a pedigreed Aberdeen Angus.

Helen went to immense pains to get everything right. She
was up at dawn and she happily worked all day with the same
unruffled and practical poise that she applied to almost anything she ever put her mind to, including copulation. She
spent hours in the kitchen, wearing the red rubber work-
gloves which had become almost a talisman of her domesticity
(she had a repugnance for touching raw meat or fish or any
tuberous vegetables, and, in any case, she always took the
greatest care of her fine and beautiful hands) indefatigably
busy and every now and then referring to an illustrated article
in the *Ladies' Home Journal* entitled "Sixteen Savouries With
a Difference."

The result of all her labours was lavish and striking.
Colour, she had decided, was to be her theme. I recall that
each person's table napkin and tumbler was of a different
colour, that colour glittered in gherkin parings and mara-
schino and pale cheese and purple olives and blushing carrot
gratings on the varied dishes of savouries (I suppose there
were sixteen of them; certainly they were all with a difference!); I remember mounds of grapefruit and oranges
curiously porcupined by coloured pickled onions stuck there
on toothpicks; there were oysters Kilpatrick and chicken
patties and bacon slices served with fried apple and baked
ham with grilled pineapple rings.

She must have known that she had carried off a real *tour-
de-force* when, in a wave of general compliments, Miss
Kirkwood, the gaunt and crane-like assistant social editress,
conferred on her the professional accolade of "imagination,
my dear, originality, and *excellent* taste." Helen accepted this
commendation with a composed smile and a winning, self-

deprecating little curtsy, but I knew that she really felt as if someone had pinned a medal to her breast.

I basked in my own pleasure for her. I saw her as the perfect hostess. I was gratifyingly conscious of how beautiful she looked. She was wearing a cyclamen chiffon cocktail dress with bare shoulders—the thin gold chain became an arrowhead pointing down to a slightly daring décolletage, and Sacco and Vanzetti were buried there behind a corsage of frangipani I had bought for her—and she wore her golden shining hair upswept and high in the Edwardian manner, which emphasised her tallness, her elegance, and the lovely bare shoulders. (Sandra Solomons, the week before, had given her the idea for the Edwardian hair-style, but on the night of this party Sandra had changed to a smooth and extremely attractive page-boy, which, a week later, Helen also copied.)

Gavin Turley, holding aloft a puce-coloured pickled onion on a toothpick, rather in the manner of a Regency fop with his quizzing-glass, stared intently at the wall above the lounge buffet, and said, " You know, that is a jolly good touch, that Vlaminck, I honestly have to admit it. It *is*, you know. In fact, everything is a jolly good touch, the house, this wonderful spread, our beautiful hostess, the hospitality. Simply superb! I must say you *are* doing fabulously well, Golden Boy, aren't you? " He looked at me mischievously.

" I'm glad you're enjoying it," I said.

" I am also admiring it," he said. " Brand-new house, guests guzzling a feast lavish enough for Lucullus himself, a gorgeous wife, this faultless décor—even including a not at all commonly appreciated Vlaminck—these prismatic pickled onions, a glittery little bawd of an M.G. parked out there in the drive next to that sad broken butter-box of a Baby Austin which is the best the poor old Turleys can ever run to. Great stuff, Golden Boy! Great stuff! " There was the same amused, faintly ironic gleam in his chestnut eyes as when he would slump back in his chair and spill cigarette ash all over himself and tolerantly listen to Helen's observations on politics.

" Here, this one is emerald-green," Helen said, presenting him with another onion on a toothpick. " It's only for the effect. The dyes are flavourless. They really all taste the

same. Tell me, why do you call David ' Golden Boy '?" she
asked. (She always referred to me as David now, never Davy
any longer.)

" Why? But, heavens above, why not? That's what he *is*,
isn't he? Ask anyone at the *Post*."

" I'm asking someone from the *Post*. I'm asking you."

" Well, simply look around you. Study your own mirror,
my dear Helen, if it comes to that. Or observe the chap himself. Look at him. A Simpson suit from Henry Buck's if ever
I've seen one. At more casual times Daks with Harris tweed,
suède shoes, hand-knitted ties. Regard this fellow as he
swings jauntily to the office each day, with the tiniest wing of
a humming-bird in the band of his snap-brim Borsalino, the
raglan topcoat, the pigskin brief-case, the smell of success he
carries with him like an aura, that indefinable air of the
coming man. Golden Boy, of course. Without a shadow of a
doubt!"

" I don't see you getting around in reach-me-downs," I said
good-humouredly. He wore all the same things himself, but
carelessly, even sloppily, and with an air that I had always
envied.

" Ah, but you do not see the shining elbows, the careful
darnings, the cobbled cuffs, the baggy knees, the gravy stains
that never *quite* come out. It is the difference, old man,
between your M.G. and my Baby Austin."

" Don't change the subject," said Helen. " I want to know
who calls David ' Golden Boy '."

" Well, everybody *calls* him it, although to tell you the
truth it was I who devised the name. You don't like it, my
dear?"

" I prefer David. And you haven't explained why they call
him this."

" Simply because he has merited it. It's justified. He *is*
Golden Boy. You see, Helen, I think you would have to know
the newspaper game to understand, but I'll try to explain. It
is a profession in which many are called but few are chosen,
and even among the few there is always *the one*. On each
and every newspaper this law will inexorably apply. Because,
you see, on any newspaper you will find there has to be a Mr.
Brewster, and there always has to be a Golden Boy for the

Mr. Brewsters just as there has to be a Susannah for the
Elders. My Biblical allusion I like, for there is in this
inflexible law of the Golden Boy something of the imperious
and unassailable quality of the rigid codes laid down by those
ancient, stern prophets of the desert."

"Oh, shut up, Gavin, you silly bugger!" I protested, laughing. "You've been whacking those gins too hard."

"You won't stop him," Peggy Turley said affectionately.
"The man is in spate. When he talks, he talks."

"If I am blind," said Gavin, "it is not from alcohol. More
likely it is from the prismatic rainbow shimmer of the pickled
onions."

"I'll never touch 'em unless I've got a packet of those
scented cachous in my pocket," said Wally Solomons.
"Sandra can't stand it when my breath smells."

Sandra, glassy-eyed and inattentive, stared blankly through
the smoke from a heliotrope cigarette.

"I don't mind 'em with beer," said the cousin from the
Western District. "Not these little cocktail ones, but the big
brown ones you get in those glass jars in the pubs."

"Yes, well, may I be allowed to continue my little disserta-
tion to Helen?" asked Gavin politely. "I was about to point
out certain salient significances concerning David's role as
Golden Boy. This is what he is, and this is what he must
inescapably continue to be. The point, you see, which I had
intended to make is that on a newspaper there is also, among
those who are above us, always Romantic Man and Practical
Man. In our case, we have Mr. Bernard Brewster representing the former, and Mr. Curtis Condon representing the latter.
Now, Mr. Condon would, I think, have his happiest moment
if he were carrying through the streets of Melbourne the head
of David Meredith on a pike. Mr. Brewster, on the other
hand, regards this same David Meredith as the apple of his
eye. He sees in him an Oliver Twist, a David Copperfield, a
Pip. And Mr. Bernard Brewster is, after all "—he bowed
slightly in mock reverence—"the editor-in-chief of the
Morning Post."

"Aren't you jealous then?" Helen asked.

"Jealous! I adore this brumby of a husband of yours. I
study his progress with the same intensity and enthralment

and excitement as Koch or Ehrlich studied the behaviour of bacilli under their microscopes. Oh, one has certain little wistful regrets about it, yes. All of us. But we make our obeisances, bow ourselves out, climb into our failing Baby Austins and chug-chug somewhat spiritlessly to our shabby little dens, and there perhaps the more sensitive among us may shed a single silent tear for languished hopes and dusty careers that have been filed away."

"Gavin just happens to be the best writer the *Post* has," I said, turning in explanation to the others, although, apart from a persisting interest in Helen, none of them seemed very attentive. "What he is——"

"Without question," Gavin agreed cheerfully. "Certainly I am the better writer. But *you* are Golden Boy." He fixed his gentle brown gaze on Helen. "My dear Helen," he said, "have you never paused to consider what an extraordinary partner it is that you have chosen for this game of life? Do you realise that in this terribly chummy, hand-picked, gentlemanly club we have which is called the *Morning Post* Literary Staff, this husband of yours is the outsider, the maverick? Last month, on the day of the public schools boat races, here were all the young gentlemen in their old school ties, and wearing their partisan silken favours and rosettes from their lapels almost to their navels—dark-blue for Grammar, sky-blue for Geelong, red-and-black for Xavier, and so forth—and I must admit that I rather loathe this sort of thing and therefore waived the purple-and-gold of my *alma mater* in favour of my black-and-blue tie of The Shop—who were not rowing, of course—and here was David in the middle of this ridiculous schoolboy Mardi Gras being sneered at by all these privileged young pissants because no rosette was pinned to his lapel, and the tie he was sporting seemed to me to be of the Coldstream Guards but was probably only the stripy colours of his University of Hard Knocks."

"Oh, *do* shut up, Gavin!" I pleaded.

"Why should I shut up? The point I am about to make is vital. Here am I, five years older than your husband, Helen, and tucked away in Mr. Brewster's back room with old files and the *Enclycopædia*. Under intellectual duress, as it were. You might even say I *am* old files and the *Encyclopædia*

Britannica! The years I spent at Wesley College were valueless except in that they took me to the University. The years
at The Shop gave me nothing except a worthless B.A. and the
privilege of being thrown into the University lake on one
occasion in defence of the statements of Bertrand Russell.
David here spends the same years in his University of Hard
Knocks, in dreary dockland, comes in like Oliver Twist, and
before you can say Jack Robinson, here he is Golden Boy.
Remarkable! Don't you agree? Yet—would you believe
this?—on this day when he is being baited by these nincom-
poops in the reporters' room, I find this chap in the toilet on
the third floor chewing his lip and almost at the point of tears,
because—isn't this *fantastic*?—because he feels himself
slighted and shamed!"

"But David never told *me* about this," said Helen.

"Yes, and I remember what you said to me," I said, feeling
myself choking up, knowing I had to tell about it. "I
remember your very words. You said, 'David, old cock, go
and have a look at a Test cricket match. England and
Australia. Observe the English team, the way the Gentlemen
emerge from one exit, the Players from another. Glance at
the scoreboard. The names of the Gentlemen are there with
their initials, the poor Players have only their surnames. The
game begins. And it is the Gentleman who is back in the
pavilion for a duck, the Player who knocks up that double
century. And remember also, old boy, that Australian teams
do not have Gentlemen and Players, only players, without a
capital P.' That's exactly what you said, and I've never forgotten it because——"

"I think it's you, old boy, who is getting a bit pissed," said
Gavin, and Helen looked at me and said, "He never told me
a word about this," and I turned away and said, "I'd better
mix up some more of that gin squash."

But he really *was* in spate, because as I was squeezing the
lemons he was still going on about it to Helen, and what he
was saying came to me disjointedly through the conversation
of the others, who had long since lost interest in the discussion, but I remember him saying, at the end of it:

"We may respect him, admire him, even be intrigued and
puzzled by some mysterious fallibility that is in him . . . it
may be *this*, you know, that makes us not envy him . . . but

I'll tell you one thing you should know and always remember, Helen. There is no guarantee in him, my dear. There is no guarantee."

Family visits were very different from the gay, glittering little parties Helen loved to give, but she devoted to them a formal attention which was impressive. Being quite secure in her ownership of me, she was friendly, polite, amusing, and hospitable—even especially considerate to any of the children who were brought—and she would go to almost as much trouble in the preparation of drinks and savouries, or in seeing that the house was at its best—as for the Saturday night parties attended by our real friends.

There was awkwardness in these visits, of course. Dad would fidget around, sitting bolt upright on what he clearly regarded as a very strange chair, looking as if he didn't know what to do with the ash on his cigarette. He could never quite bring himself to meet Helen's eyes directly. He would study the exotic savouries that were offered to him with a dubious look, as if he suspected strychnine. After ten minutes or so of this discomfort he would take himself off and prowl morosely around the garden, poking at the seedlings, or he would call me out to talk about the car. Mother would stay on in the lounge, knitting furiously, and smiling with a blank eagerness at Helen, and nibbling at things that were offered to her and then nodding her head quickly in automatic approval, but there were times when I would catch her warily eyeing the furniture or the pictures, as if she half-expected some unfamiliar object to suddenly snarl and spring at her. They called only on Sunday afternoons and never stayed for very long.

They were impressed by my new surroundings, yes, there was no doubt about that—Helen set out, I have thought since, to impress people rather than to please them—but I always had an uncomfortable feeling myself that Mother was forever awaiting an opportunity to get me away from somewhere by myself and quickly to whisper something to me very urgently from behind her hand, but I could never decide what it might be that she would want to say or to know.

Although Jack and I remained the best of friends—our quarrel at Mother's birthday party was never mentioned

again, and we would meet often in the city to have a few
beers together at one of the pubs—he visited the house in
Beverley Grove only once that I remember. He came alone,
bcause Sheila had just been delivered of the new baby.
Another girl. " I read in a magazine¹ somewhere that it proves
the male dominance," he said, with a rather wry grin. " Ah,
well," he said philosophically, " if at first you don't succeed.
. . . They reckon even now I hardly give the missus time to
get her clothes back on," he said cheerfully.

When he arrived at the house I was disappointed that Sheila
was not with him, not only because of my fondness for her,
but because I had rather wanted to show things off to her, but
Jack had not been in the house for very long before I began
to change my mind about it. Jack examined everything with
great interest and a certain curiosity, but he made no bones
about the fact that he was far more taken by my M.G. than
by any single aspect of Helen's home-making.

In fact, when we were sitting together in the lounge just
before he left he suddenly began to chuckle and I asked him
what the joke was and he said, " Nothing. It's just this funny
furniture. To tell you the honest truth, it gives me the creeps
a bit. I get the feeling that if I take my eyes off it for a jiffy
it'll just get up and start walkin' around the room on its
own! "

We all laughed at this, but I could see that Helen was not
amused.

Even so, the first misgivings I ever felt about my new condition arose not from these family visits but from my developing friendship with Gavin Turley.

It occurred to me quite suddenly one day that the Turleys
were the only ones in our new gay social group whom I
really liked, and the only ones who interested me, and I began
to wonder what the connection was between them and the
dull Solomons couple, or the Farleys, or the infinitely boring
Justin Byrne. The thought, once implanted in my mind, was
quite insidious. I would find myself, at the early stages of
some soirée or other, feeling flat and bored and empty, and
I would know that it was because I was only waiting for the
Turleys to arrive. And the trouble about this was the Turleys
were the least ubiquitous of our guests, because it was not

often that Gavin and I would have our nights off together, especially at week-ends, because he was at that time, among his other specialisations, dramatic critic for the paper.

His absences from the group began more and more to unsettle me, and this would lead to an increasing impatience with Helen's other friends and the pompous inanities or the repetitive observations about nothing at all that passed for social chit-chat among them. Gavin Turley, I began to realise, was the only one among them who *had* any conversation, or any ideas about things, or anything to contribute, and even though his intellect was considerably sharper than mine, it began to be equally clear to me that I had nothing in common with them either! Why then did we go to all this bother? Why were Helen and I acting as some sort of social solder to make an amalgam of such utterly incompatible people? What the hell, I began to ask myself in the moods of irritation and depression that were coming more frequently, *was* it all about?

It was quite some months, now that I come to think of it, before the Turleys asked us to their own place to dinner, although before this they had entertained us occasionally in restaurants in town.

They had their separate apartment in one wing of the huge old dilapidated Turley mansion in Toorak, which had been built some seventy years before when old Sir Luke Turley, in his retirement, decided on something a little more substantial than the Colonial residencies which, in various pink sections of the Imperial map, he had for decades inhabited.

We arrived there in the appropriateness of a late afterglow, and went through great creaky wooden gates hung from square stone pillars and into a dusky jungle of a garden with black thickets of azaleas and the biggest rhododendrons I ever saw in my life until years later when I looked across at the crimson forests buttressing Tibet from the Katmandu side, and there was a weird tangle of gigantic creepers and those huge leafy things that we always called elephants' ears and fat cacti standing on enormous thick hairy prickly stems like mammoths' legs. Curving through this dense wilderness of darkness and damp, decaying smells there was a crunchy gravelled carriage-drive scattered with fallen leaves, leaves that were long and stiff and curled-up and cardboardy, which

had dropped from two tremendous Moreton Bay fig-trees that
blocked out all the gloomy sky above us, and the leaves in
the evening breeze were moving around with a dry, scaly,
scurrying sound.

It was quite a walk up to the massive old entrance with the
name of the house, *Bangalore*, chiselled in stone above a
heavy, panelled door which had massive lion-knockers and
big brass bell-pulls which, coming after the tangled garden,
sharply reminded me of the old house where Helen had lived.
This one, although in much the same condition of disintegration and neglect, was a stone house that had once been very
grand and so it had more solidity and dignity, of course, and
even a sense of some continuing splendour in its decay. But
Helen must have been struck by much the same feeling, and
perhaps felt an uneasiness about it, because this was one of
the few occasions I remember when her cool poise seemed to
be shaken by a disturbing breath of something, like super-
stition or an almost atavistic fear.

Or it might have been the Turleys' apartment itself that
unsettled her. Their section of the old house comprised one
huge high-ceilinged room which they used as a combined
living-room and dining-room, and a small kitchen, and a
bathroom which had cracked porcelain fittings with blue
Victorian floral patterns in the glaze, and one of those antiquated geyser bath-heaters which stood threateningly at one
end like an upended Napoleonic cannon and which burned
wood chips, and the kindling was there alongside it in a
clothes-basket of battered unravelling cane, and on the lino-
leumed floor there was a drift of spilt wood-dust and tiny
chips, and a brownish-yellow stain ran down the side of the
big enamel bathtub where the water from the geyser dripped.
If it went on, one thought, a stalagmite would form. There
was also a study for Gavin and two bedrooms. (It was some
years later before I was really able to understand how it was
that two people like Gavin and Peggy, who were so obviously
devoted to each other, should want to sleep in separate bedrooms.)

They both came to meet us at the door, and Peggy took the
coats away while Gavin showed us into the main room, and
this was just about the most extraordinary mix and clutter
and congested mess of a room I had ever seen. It had once

been stately, and probably had been used for receptions, because the moulded ceiling was superb and there were marble pilasters on either side of the fireplace and above the ornate carved mantel a huge and magnificent French Renaissance looking-glass in bad repair which gave back a mysterious muddy reflection such as one might get from a stagnant pond, and from the ceiling-boss still hung the heavy gilded chains which must have once supported a chandelier. The immensely tall windows were hidden behind tarnished velvet curtains hanging from sagging pelmets, and there were damp mildewy stains down one wall, where the plaster moulding was broken away, and alarming cracks in all four walls, and the carpets on the floor were very thin and faded out, like old flowers found pressed between the leaves of a book, and tattered at the edges.

The room was furnished in the most astonishing jumble of good antique pieces and second-hand junk which had been rather amateurishly painted, and there was a great quantity of *chinoiserie*, lacquered screens and cloisonné vases as tall as an adolescent child, and jade pieces and a gong, and books and gramophone records scattered everywhere, and a mad proliferation of bric-à-brac, and a litter of papers and magazines, and more pictures on the walls than we had had in the front room at Avalon: great yellowed early Colonial landscapes of the Buvelot School, and dingy portraits staring out from their frames behind dark glassy varnish like night intruders peering furtively in through windows, and some works that were identifiably very good—a pair of lovely tiny Hilder water-colours, and a very good Elioth Gruner and a Heysen and a marvellous Tom Roberts—and in the very centre of all this incredible confusion was a gorgeous round table with a surface polished to the feel of soft old silk and on it were places set for four and white candles in Georgian candelabra.

"I'm afraid it's only the four of us," Gavin said apologetically. "To tell the truth, neither Peggy nor I really care much for big dinner parties. Or big parties of any sort, for that matter. Four's always fun, I think."

"Oh, but that's splendid!" Helen said brightly, although the uneasiness seemed to cling to her, and she looked very slightly at a loss and not quite herself, or perhaps she *was* disappointed that there weren't more people—possibly even Mr. Brewster!—but I know his words gave me a sudden secret pleasure, because I saw it as proof that he did share my thoughts about our other sterile friends, and there was also this sense of privilege that it was only Helen and I who had been asked.

It was a very simple and wonderful dinner, a clear soup, and then a huge steak-and-kidney pie that was brought to the table in its blue enamel baking-dish, and a chocolate mousse to follow, and dry biscuits with Camembert and Gorgonzola. I remember being surprised at how heavy everything was, not the food, but everything else—the weight of the old thick china plates and the heavy crystal goblets and the solid Georgian silver and the massive, beautiful serving things, and there was even a great rich satisfying feeling of weight to the big square table napkins, which were of spotless white damask with the neatest tiny patches of darning here and there and stiffly heavy with starch.

The steak-and-kidney pie had a cockled crust with crimped edges and a big pastry rose right in the middle, and Gavin served the pie from his place at the table and passed the plates along for Peggy to add the potatoes and the broccoli, but before he began to serve he detached the pastry rose from the crust and put it carefully aside on his own plate and grinned rather sheepishly and said, " Excusez-moi. But I always do take that bit for myself." And then he cut down into the pie and the steam came and the rich baking smell, and it went inside my head like an ecstatic drug, and for a magical instant I was back in the old kitchen, with Mother and Jean and Marj all baking away on a Sunday morning and Dad with his violin out fiddling away at Irish jigs in a stink of flying resin.

It was one of those very warm and very easy dinner parties from which one recollects almost nothing of the conversation. I remember he encouraged Helen to talk a good deal about books from her experience as a librarian, and he contributed a little himself, but modestly, and when the meal was over Peggy and Helen took the dishes into the kitchen and then went into the bedroom to look at dresses and patterns, and we sat on at the table for a while smoking and talking about Munich and the Anschluss and the European crisis generally, and I asked Gavin if he really thought there might be war, and he said, "I can't possibly see how it's to be avoided."

"Helen seems perfectly convinced there won't be," I said. She had been quoting something from some book during the meal.

"But in this case Helen might conceivably be wrong," he said quietly. "Like a good many other people, I think she doesn't want to believe there'll be a war simply because she does not *want* a war. But I think it's on the cards, you know. I really think it's on the cards."

" And do you think we'd be involved?"

"Who knows? England seems awfully dicky about it all. And after all we *are* a long way away." He began to push his chair back, and said, "You know, those two women will be stuck into those French fashion magazines for hours. Would you like to come into my sty and have a brandy?"

The study, because it was so much smaller, seemed even more of a clutter than the other room, if that were possible. Mostly, perhaps, because of Gavin's incorrigible slovenliness. There were pictures on one wall above a rather crude-looking trestle work-table, on which was a portable typewriter and a goat's nest of books and papers and folders and pipes and dust and note-books and things clipped together with bull-dog clips and overflowing ash-trays, and there were three waste-paper baskets under the table, but all three were stuffed with crumpled paper which had spilled out all over the floor. One never doubted that in this room no woman was ever allowed to tidy up. The three other walls were books from floor to ceiling.

"Sorry about the mess," he said, without any real apology, and motioned me to one of two shabby but comfortable arm-chairs, very deep, with the leather covering worn to the softness of chamois. "It's the only way I can work, really. All of it's mostly my doing . . . I hammered up those shelves myself, but the confounded books keeps swamping me. I get all these damned review copies, you see, and I do sell a lot to a tame dealer I've got in the Eastern Market, but there are always quite a few you feel you want to keep, and they mount up and . . . well, there the bloody things are!"

We had brandy, good brandy, Courvoisier I think it was, in big balloons, and I looked at the wall above his desk, at the paintings, a few bold, explorative abstracts of his own, not bad, and a good sanguine drawing of a nude which I recognised as old Barnaby Stanton's, and another compelling oil-painting of a carnival scene, clowns and pierrots and masked figures, very vivacious and strong and forceful, which troubled me for a few moments, and then I said, "That's one of Sam Burlington's, isn't it?" He nodded. "Yes. A jolly good one, too, I think. How did you pick it?"

"Well, I should know," I said. "He was my best friend at the Gallery. In fact I lived with him for a while. I ran away from home once, when I was beginning to write for the *Post*, and I went to live with Sam in that studio he had in Spring Street."

He studied me with quizzical, amused interest. "You know you really *do* spring the most surprising things on people," he said. "So now we learn you ran away from home . . . you lived with old Sam Burlington! Bloody fantastic is all I have to say! Because I never knew this, you see. Sam and I were pretty good mates once . . . he grew up just around the corner from here, and we were at Wesley together before he went to the Gallery school."

"It's a wonder I haven't brought it up before," I said. "Because at times you remind me of Sam a bit . . . the way you talk, really . . not always, but when you're trying to get at somebody, like trying to explain me in the character of Golden Boy, for instance, the way you did at that party of ours. Then you talk just the way he used to."

"I wish to Christ I'd been able to *paint* the way he used to," Gavin said, staring up at the picture. "In me, alas, you find a frustrated Royal Academician." His eyes moved critically to his own paintings, still on canvas that was tack-spiked from the stretchers and just fastened to the wall with drawing-pins. "If I had had just a half of Sam Burlington's talent ten years ago, you wouldn't find me stuck there now in old Brewster's dugout! Sam was the best of them all, you know. He should have won that Travelling Scholarship and shoved off to Paris. Bloody tragic that awful rotten business, and the way it all worked out for him."

"Oh, but I was involved in that, too," I said. "Right up to the neck! They even came down from Russell Street and practically put me through the third degree! They grilled me for hours about it." I sipped at the cognac in appreciative reminiscence. "Well, I knew the poor girl, of course, and I was Sam's particular friend, but there was nothing much I could tell them. Nor would have."

"You don't have any idea where he is now, or what the poor bastard's doing?" He looked again at the picture on the will, this time rather sadly. "You never hear from him?"

"No," I said. "I don't think anybody does."

I got up from the arm-chair and took my brandy across to the trestle table. Beside the typewriter there was a new copy of Faulkner's *The Unvanquished* stuck with torn strips of paper as markers, and an unfinished review in the machine, and a stack of other review copies of books pushed to one side. I said, "I see you don't work at a desk."

"Jesus, *no!*" he said fervently. "I like a long table, plenty of room to mess up the way I want it. I made this one myself, you know," he said with some pride. "I knocked it up out of an old door I found in the stable-loft."

"I worked on a table like that before I got married," I said. And then I turned and said, "Gavin, while we're just here together, there's something I've been meaning to ask you. One night at our place I overheard something you were saying to Helen."

"Yes?"

"What you said, I think, was that there was no guarantee about me. Something to that effect."

He looked up at me very carefully. "Yes?" he said.

"Well—well what did you mean by that?"

"Just what I said, old cock. There is no guarantee about you. In proper context, of course, what I was saying was really to Helen. I was indicating that she would be unwise ever to entirely rely upon you . . . for you to stay put, was what I meant . . . for you to remain quite fixed in the role she seems to want for you."

"Oh, I see. I thought you were referring to me as a writer."

"Well, it would apply to that, too. They *are* part of the same thing, I think. Don't you feel this yourself?"

"Look, Gavin, I'm not even sure I know what you're driving at," I said helplessly. "You're saying in effect that I'm unreliable, or unstable, or . . . I don't know. . . ."

"No—not quite." Again he gave me that long, considering look, and tugged at his lip and rubbed his finger against his big discoloured teeth. Then he seemed to come to some sort of a decision with himself and said, "Condon dislikes you, admittedly, but he talked to me about you some little time back, and he referred to what he called your 'flashy unreliable brilliance.' All right, concede the prejudice, but Curt Condon's no fool, you know."

"But this is what I said. Unreliable."

"Just wait a moment. To be perfectly candid, I've always thought there is a grave fallibility in you, David. And I told Helen as much, too, if you want to know. Your brilliance, I think—and you have brilliance, don't make any mistake about that!—lies in the fact that you possess what I consider to be certain remarkable flairs. You have facility, adroitness, an almost unbridled imagination, a quite fantastic celerity in getting your stuff written. You know the old adage, 'Don't get it right, get it written!' Well, I think it would be a bit harsh to apply that to you, but at the same time you do, I suspect, have tendencies towards the slightly unscrupulous. Probably your best talent at the moment is for polishing things to the highest possible burnish. You really *do* keep coming in with the shiniest apples for the teacher!"

"The teacher being," I said with an edge of tartness I could not quite control, "Mr. Brewster?"

"There you are, you see—another talent! Acumen. Great acumen!" His grin softened it, but the remark still hurt a little. "Listen," he said, "whatever is the name of that very odd bird—is it a creek-runner or something?—that seems to flit along on the surfaces of streams, gobbling up the midges and things as it darts about? No, wait a minute, better still . . . let us take those pond creatures—insects, are they, or beetles or bugs or what?—the tiny collywobble things that go skittering around on the surfaces of ponds. I remember them as a child when I've been yabbing. Well, do you know, David, I think you're a bit like these collywobbles. You rely on surface-tension. If the surface-tension broke *you'd* drown! At least I *think* you'd drown. Now, that's one of the troubles about you, you see—one invariably finds oneself hedging. Almost every time one finds oneself having to qualify the observation about you, because deep down one can never be quite sure. That's rather strange, isn't it?"

"Well, all I can say is that without qualification it all sounds as if you don't have much of an opinion of me as a writer."

"But are you a writer?" he asked earnestly. "A *real* writer?" He rubbed quite vigorously at his teeth. "I honestly think—no," he said at last.

"Well, that makes two of you," I said with a note of bitterness. "It's also Condon's opinion. He told me to my face, months ago."

"Yes, but I believe Condon and I are talking about different things, really. What I mean is this—I think if you ever wrote a novel and I had to review it, I honestly believe I'd have to slam it pretty solidly."

"Then neither of us has any worries. I'm not writing a novel."

"No. Do you write anything at all now, David? Outside the office, I mean."

"There isn't all that much time, is there?"

"There never is all that much time, no." He uncoupled his awkward spidery limbs and rose gracelessly from the arm-chair, shedding a grey pollen of cigarette ash, and moved stoopingly to one of the bookshelves, and took down a slight small book and passed it across to me, rubbing the teeth again rather nervously. I opened it at the title page and read: *D. H. Lawrence in Australia*. A Critical Study. By GAVIN TURLEY.

"But I never knew *you'd* written a book!" I exclaimed in surprise.

"You are with the great majority, old boy. Very few people do know. It sold less than three hundred copies and was then remaindered for sixpence on the stalls in the Eastern Market. Rather a shame, really, because it has one or two quite interesting little things to say concerning Lawrence. Never mind. I'm working on something much more ambitious now," he said—rather ruefully, I thought. "I'm trying to do a critical biography of Henry Handel Richardson. Been at the bloody thing for two years already. But, as you say, there isn't all that much time. Still, one has to have a

go at these things. Take that copy along with you if you'd
like to. I'd be overjoyed to have just one more reader."

"I'd love to have it. You'll write something in it?"

"I've written everything that *is* in it, old cock. Nothing to
be added. And if it was just the usual crap to be scrawled on
the fly-leaf, for you it would have to be something appro-
priately sinister like 'Beware the ides of March' or '*Mene
mene tekel upharsin.*' And that might put the mozz on you.
Best if you just take it as it is, old boy, and admire the prose."
He went back and awkwardly refolded himself into the arm-
chair, limb after limb, like the same great spider returning to
the centre of its web. "David," he said, "shall I sum it all
up for you in one crisp sentence? I am safe, and you are
not."

"Far too crisp," I said. "You'll have to elaborate."

"You have no guarantee, David. And I have. Simply that.
After all, what is a guarantee? An insurance policy, a doctor's
diploma, a fixed superannuation, a certificate issued under the
Pure Foods Act. Security. You see, I shall always play it for
security and safety . . . for the cosy niche right next to Mr.
Brewster's handsome office, for respectable advancement, for
the occasional editorial praised in the House, for the just
review, for the slim critical volumes appearing at intervals
under my name, for the modest *succès d'estime*, for the grati-
fying half-inch in *Who's Who in Australia*, for the intellectual
warmth that I can wear like an undervest, next to my B.A.
And I can go on and on doing this and die at the end of it
full of years and respect, like poor old bloody Farnsworth
sitting at a desk staring at a spike, with rigor mortis setting
in!" He seemed to be smiling at himself with the irony that
was usually in his eyes for others, and his hair had fallen
across his forehead like a golliwog's mop, and he rubbed at
his moustache with a nicotine-stained finger.

"And what about me?" I asked him gently.

"You are quite different," he said. "You have neither the
desire for this, nor the credentials with which to accomplish
it. In a way, David, you are like some queer, strange savage
who has journeyed a long way from his own tangled wilderness, and you look down on the palisades of the little settlement, and you wonder how you will pillage it and what
trophies you will find. You can be sure of nothing, of course,

because you carry with you no guarantees. And *we* cannot be sure that you will even try your wits against that particular stockade. It is, in fact, a thing we *feel* rather than a thing we know. We feel that you will have to go on and on in your own strange solitary way, too far from your own wilderness ever to go back to it, beating and bashing and cheating and striving towards some goal which up to now, I swear, you have never yet glimpsed!" He gave me a quick, slightly embarrassed glance and squirmed deeper into his chair. "That's why I sometimes think," he went on in a tone which was deliberately more matter-of-fact, "it would really pay you to set yourself to this business of becoming a writer. In depth, I mean. A *real* writer. You see, one day that surface-tension will break, or you'll just get fed up with being a pond-skimmer, the fastest collywobble on the pool. And you'll have to learn some other way of getting around. Or you really *will* drown!"

When we were driving home Helen suddenly began to laugh, and said, "And there was I thinking the Turleys would probably have a butler! David, how *can* people like Gavin and Peggy live in such a shambles! In that *midden*! Goodness! wouldn't you just love to put a vacuum-cleaner through it?"

I only grunted, and pressed down harder on the accelerator of the little red M.G., and drove faster and faster through the night-shrouded suburbs, for all the world as if I had a desperate anxiety to get back to my own home.

CHAPTER 13

The next morning was a Sunday, and after breakfast I went in to my own study, with the pretext that there were some letters I wanted to write, and I closed the door on myself, and, like Carl Sandburg's fog, every doubt crept in with me on little cat feet and moved noiselessly around on the burgundy-coloured square of feltex, and I think I stood there for a long time just looking at it all.

I can see it even now to the last detail of all its imprisoning shamefulness, as vividly as I must have seen it on that

despondent morning when I stood there, tense and wary as a
trapped animal, with the Sunday morning sounds drifting to
me through the thin brick walls, of Beverley Grove awakening to the active pursuits of its day—the snarling chirrup of
its lawn-mowers and the hiss of garden hoses and the snipping
of the sécateurs and the idling cough of the cars coming out
of their fibro-plaster garages for the ritual washings. . . .

It had been Helen who had decided on what she had called
the " motif "—flattering to me, she had reasoned, because of
my interest in the " old days of sail "—and on the granulated
plaster walls that even yet retained the smell of the cream
eggshell-finish paint were only two pictures, big expensively-
framed reproductions, one of Turner's " The Fighting Témér-
aire " and the other of Somerscales' " Off Valparaiso "—and
although I had looked at this last one a hundred times it was
only then at this moment of troubled self-examination that I
found myself remembering that it was from Valparaiso that
they had shipped Jack out as a D.B.S.—and there was a decorative circular waste-paper basket covered with a lacquered
reproduction of Spurling's painting of the famous clipper
Cutty Sark, and on the desk a pottery ash-tray in the shape of
a lifebuoy and a miniature binnacle and steering-wheel that
was really an ink-stand and a cigarette-lighter.

But there was no ash in the ash-tray. There was no
crumpled paper in the waste-paper basket or on the floor.
There was no ink-mark on the handsome leather-cornered
blotter stamped in gold with my initials. The sleek new
Royal portable typewriter which had supplanted the cumbersome Remington hid chastely beneath its shiny dust-cover.
No loose papers or scattered books marred the bevelled glass
top of the angular modern desk of waxed light-oak ; nothing
was there save the handset extension telephone, serviceably
black, and a little copper bowl for pins and paper-clips, and
the queer-looking draughtsman's work-lamp, a mad flamingo
of a thing spindly on tube-legs of adjustable metal, and a
leather-covered book embossed with the words *Where Was
It?* There was no clutter anywhere. There was *nothing*
anywhere. . . .

Behind the desk, which was centred on the square of Feltex
—the room, I suddenly realised, had the horrible proportions
of an exact cube—was an arm-chair of stout stiff leatherette

on a chromium tubular frame and alongside this comfortless monstrosity stood a chromium pedestal reading-lamp with a witch's hat of pleated wax-paper. Across from this, in the middle of one wall, stood the book-case, in light-oak to match the desk, with dustproof doors of sliding glass, and the books were arranged on the shelves in tidy little platoons according to their bindings or their authors. The curtains, of the same colour as the floor covering, exposed my one small window, and looking out I could see, through the faint green diffusion of the fly-wire screen, the top of a paling fence, part of a red brick wall, and the plumbing outlets from the Phylands' bathroom.

The window of Gavin Turley's study, I reflected, would open on to the rank vegetation and the mysteriously splendid decay of that old garden, with perhaps a piece of broken statuary strangled by the vines. Once, through fly-wire, there had been the Dollicus. . . .

" You *will* be washing the car, darling?" Helen called to me from the corridor, and through the closed door I called back, " No!" and she said, " What?" and I said, " Later. I'm busy now. I'll do it later," and I prayed that she would not come in, and so I stood there, quite tense, listening, until I could hear her singing to herself in her sewing-room. . . .

I realise now, as I try to reassemble in my mind the incidents of that Sunday morning and of what followed from it, that this was the precise point where my injustice to my wife became a deliberate, planned thing. I was at bay in my privacy and I wanted no intrusion, yet until that moment Helen had always been coming into the room, and I had liked her visits and had encouraged them. I had not sought privacy then, I had preferred to be sharing things with her, I had enjoyed her frivolous, inconsequential half-flirtations when she would be there, sitting on the edge of the desk, swinging her long beautiful silken legs and chattering gaily to me about the arrangements for some party she was planning, or the new " outfit" she was making, or some scheme she had just devised for rearranging the dining-room furniture, or an idea she had had for a new painting she would like to do, and what did I think about this detail of the composition? Both of us had enjoyed the very particular camaraderie that was associated with " the den," so she had got into the habit of using the telephone on my desk rather than the one in our bedroom for her social calls to her friends or when she was going over her shopping-list with Cullingford the grocer.

And now, quite suddenly, all this had changed. "For Christ's sake go away and leave me alone!" I said savagely under my breath, and that was when I began my attack.

I opened the desk drawers first because this was where everything I had brought from the old house had carefully been put away, and there it was, or what was left of it, the strivings and the absurdities and the lost adventures, and I took it out, bit by bit, and strewed it on the Feltex—the glossy postcards of old ships bearing the stamp of the Nautical Photo Agency, the ones I had preserved for God knows what reason, and the drafts of never-finished articles and the outlines of stories, and several carefully trimmed clippings of "The Glory That Was" by Stunsail fastened together with a brass clip, and the sad, dog-eared manuscript of *Pearls of Maïeta*, and the old exercise books scrawled with embarrassing Viking sagas, and the big spiral-bound sketch pad in which so laboriously I had practised the bizarre hieroglyphics of Ancient Egypt, and I held this in my hands for a long time, marvelling at the hours of patient and meticulous and wasted work that had gone into the now pathetic and rather ridiculous affectation of the cover, for I had treated this as an exact facsimile of part of an inscribed wall on the temple of Queen Hatshepsut's temple at Deir-el-Bahri with each of the hundreds of hieroglyphic characters shaded and high-lighted as if incised into the stone itself, a copy far more remarkable in its way than the forged painting of the *Grafton*. . . .

Yet there had been adventure then, and excitement, and strangeness, and challenge, a sense of struggling through *towards* something, and even the failures and the affectations were not without a certain brave significance . . . and Sundays then had been days to wander solitary along South Wharf or Victoria Docks groping for some identification with beauty and mystery and poetry, and one then would gather together the few bright grains of it that one had been able to pick up, like the glittering dust of hard-won gold that had been in the aspirin bottle Jack had brought back from Berringa, and this would be carried home very carefully, like treasure, to be examined and admired in privacy and seclusion. There *had*

been privacy and seclusion then, and in an old room with a
crude work-table that was littered with papers and books and
the urgent waste of reference, and important things were
pinned up on walls, and hopes were there, spilled in the cluttered tangle, and beliefs too, and there had been shelves that
I, also, had hammered up against a wall to hold the books I
felt I had had to keep, and through the window of that room,
with its fly-wire screen, there had been a fernery and a tangle
of dusky vegetation that had hidden my mother on occasions
and could at least hide the dividing fence and the plumbing
outlets of the house next door. . . .

I got up then from the floor litter and pushed the desk all
the way back against the wall, shoving against the tenacious
cling of the Feltex, because I could only work facing a wall,
and it had to be a blank wall, and that was when I tore the
two big pictures down from their hooks and flung them with
the other things on the floor, and after this I turned my attention to the book-case because I realised that I hated books
behind glass anyway, and there were all the books so treacherously imposed—the ordered required reading specially selected
by the " librarian "—in the stipulated dosage of necessary
culture, and I began to shovel them out on to the floor and
then one of them was in my hand and I was looking at it and
it was Ibsen's *The Master Builder*, and the whole spurious
futility of it all burst in a fury of choking, impotent rage, and
I hurled the book at the wall with all my strength and at the
top of my voice I shouted, " And I don't even *understand*
Ibsen!" and then I turned wildly and kicked a hole clean
through the *Cutty Sark* waste-paper basket, and that was
when Helen burst in and cried, " David! My God! What in
heaven's name is going on?" and I turned to face her in a
gasping spasm of rage and hatred that left me empty of words
and I could only stare at her and shake my head.

"What are you *doing*? What *is* this?" she cried, aghast,
and she was frightened by the look of me, I could see that,
but when I still made no reply she took one step towards me
and said, " What is it all about, darling? . . . tell me for God's
sake." She stared around helplessly. " All this stuff on the
floor . . . and . . . the pictures pulled down. And why
is the desk over there? . . . it—it spoils the whole look of the
room. David, darling, for heaven's sake *what is the matter*?"

I took a long deep breath. " I am rearranging my study,"
I said stiffly. " That stuff on the floor's only junk and I just
felt I wanted some rubbish to put in my waste-paper basket."

" In that?" she said numbly. " You've broken it."

" I'll get another. I might even get two or three. Plain ones.
I've pulled the pictures down because, frankly, I'm sick and
bloody tired of them. And the desk is over there because I
don't like a desk that's out from the wall. In fact I don't
like desks. *That* desk especially. I'm going back to a work-
table."

" But the books! Just look at the books, for heaven's
sake!"

" Oh, I'm cleaning out the book-case too. This is a real
clean sweep! I think I've decided I'd rather have open
shelves. Besides, there's only one book I want at the moment," I said, and I went over and very deliberately put the
little volume entitled *D. H. Lawrence in Australia* exactly in
the middle of the bare top shelf where the " classics " had
been arranged.

" What was that you were shouting about Ibsen?" she asked
nervously.

" Nothing."

" I distinctly heard——"

" Nothing!" I repeated harshly. " I have nothing to say
about Ibsen. Except that I can't bloody well read him, that's
all."

" You're in a very queer mood, David," she said. " You
are. You're strange. I . . . I've never seen you like this. I'll
. . . I think I'd better go and make you some coffee."

" I don't want coffee. Just go away. Just please go away
and leave me to my rearrangements."

The quick hurt in her eyes told me how badly I was behaving—sullen, defiant, vindictive, like some rebellious child—
and I was aware that she was behaving, and would behave,
better than I : yet with a deep and passionate certainty I knew
that I was right and she was wrong.

She did make coffee—I think she retreated to the kitchen
really to pull herself together, and because she did not yet
know what to do about the confusion in the room—but her
being in the kitchen had the effect of sharpening the hostility
I felt towards her, for it made me think of the steak-and-

kidney pie at the Turleys', and she was out there and there were no smells coming from the kitchen, no food smells, Sunday morning smells, and I thought of all the meals we had eaten together that had had no smells, all the clever exotic imaginative tasteless plates of nothing that we had eaten by the refined glow of coloured candles.

When she returned with the coffee she brought much of her composure with her. I knew that she was still scared underneath and upset and bewildered and hurt, but she dissembled it well, even with a slight air of conciliation, as if she had decided that with a little patience and a little tolerance it would all be explained. And she sat on the desk in her yellow house-coat, swinging those gorgeous legs of hers above the mess on the floor as if it wasn't even there, and she gave me a gentle, understanding smile as if she wanted to reassure me that she had no intention of condemning me or punishing me: but she had not visited her hairdresser during all that week and for the very first time I noticed that there was a dark discoloration at the roots of her hair, not grey really, but dry and dull and flaky, like the ashes of a fire.

"I did put the car things out for you earlier," she said. "At the top of the drive. The buckets and the sponges, and that new polish you asked Wally to get. There's a new chamois if you want it in the kitchen cupboard."

"I'm not cleaning the car," I said. "I'm taking it out. I'm going for a drive."

"On Sunday morning? Where would you go on Sunday morning?"

"I don't know. I haven't decided. Anywhere. I'd just like to get out of the house, that's all."

"Yes, I think that might be a very good idea," she said carefully. "If you *are* in this strange, funny mood it——"

"I might call in on Mum and Dad. I want to ask about that old work-table of mine, anyway. Or I might even go on down to see Jack and Sheila and the new baby. I'll decide when I'm out on the road. I'll find somewhere to go."

The telephone rang then and she took the call, saying, "Speak!" the way she always did, then, "Oh, it's you. We're fine, yes. No, of course we hadn't forgotten. I'm just doing crumbed cutlets to-day anyway, so between twelve and half past would be perfect." She put her hand over the mouthpiece and turned to me. "It's Sandra," she said. "So don't go too far, David, will you? You hadn't forgotten that we promised to pop over there before lunch to try that new Pimms' drink that Wally's been raving about."

"How could I ever forget that?" I said as I went out the door.

I did clean the car the following Sunday morning, though, and altogether there were seven cars out along Beverley Grove, all being hosed or polished or rubbed at, and Wally Solomons came across from the big cream company Plymouth he had taken out for the week-end, with a handsome yellow polishing-cloth of a new sort, impregnated with something or other, which he presented to me because General Motors were sending them out with their country salesmen as a little goodwill stunt, and he said, "It's this chemical stuff that's in the cloth, it just shifts the road-scum like that," and I said, "Oh?" and he said, "It's windscreens and hub-caps that give the final touch to a polish job, you know, if they're not sparkling the whole vehicle looks like nothing on earth." And under my breath I said, "Go and get stuffed."

And then Phyland the chartered accountant came up from his neat black Hillman wiping the dipstick on a clean pull of cotton-waste, Phyland the accountant with his pale, pinched-up little widowed woman's face, the sort of face, I found myself thinking, that he must take out from a locked filing-cabinet each day and put on very carefully and accurately like a company audit. Solomons showed him the new impregnated polishing-cloth and explained it, and Phyland said, "By Jove, that sounds pretty good," and Solomons promised to try to get one for him too, and then for five minutes they just stood there beside the red M.G. discussing whether Karkleen Rapid was a better polish than Caldwell's Hi-Glass, and I thought of the balanced, audited Phyland turds flowing down the plumbing outlet outside my study window, and under my breath I said, "You can *both* go and get stuffed," and turned my back on them and pretended to be busy on something to do with the front-suspension. But even from there I could see old Treadwell pottering among his dahlias, and looking rather critically across the dividing fence at Helen's cinerarias.

It was worse the Sunday after that. Two days previous to

this the van had delivered our new console-radio, which Helen and I had chosen after hours of poring over catalogues, and which had been delivered from the same company which had made my desk and much of the furniture in the house. Although the wood was plain and waxed and solid, the contraption was deceptively elaborate, for in addition to the sunken wireless it contained a record-player and a compact cocktail-cabinet with a coloured cut-glass set for twelve, and I hated it from the moment it was delivered to our house, although I had thoroughly approved of it at the beginning and had signed the time-payment agreement without a qualm.

On this Sunday morning I had to get up on the roof to fit the stubby tubular mast which would take the new long aerial, and it had to be made fast to the chimney with the bolted metal straps which had come with the set, and for this I borrowed the Solomons' ladder. When I had finished the job—which didn't take long because the pamphlet which had come with the radio gave detailed illustrated instructions for fixing what was called the Quicktite Patent Antenna Clamp, and added, "Even a child can do it!"—I stayed up on the roof, sitting on the sloping, terracotta tiles with my back wedged against the chimney because for the first time in weeks I had an odd feeling, not only of being alone and away from everything, but of being in some way unassailable as well, and I had not been up on the roof of a house since the time, more than twenty years before, when I had looked down in the rain on old Grandma Emma raging around the back garden brandishing the castor-oil bottle.

This second experience was even more terrifying, in a different way, because my elevation provided me with the first opportunity I had had to look out over all the Beverley Park Gardens Estate, and there was nothing all around me, as far as I could see, but a plain of dull red rooftops in their three forms of pitching and closer to hand the green squares and rectangles of lawns intersected by ribbons of asphalt and cement, and I counted nine cars out in Beverley Grove being washed and polished. In the slums, I reflected, they had a fetish about keeping front door-knobs polished, but here in the " good " respectable suburbs the fetish was applied to cars and to gardens, and there were fixed rituals about this, so that hedges were clipped and lawns trimmed and beds weeded, and the lobelia and the mignonette were tidy in their borders, and the people would see that these things were so no matter what desolation or anxiety or fear was in their hearts, or what spiritless endeavours or connubial treacheries were practised behind the blind neat concealment of their thin red-brick walls. The door-knobs and this more elaborate ritual were part of a similar thing, of course, the public " front," but it occurred to me suddenly that the door-knob people might be a worthier tribe, really, because they still grappled with existence where audacities were possible, and even adventure.

I stayed up on the roof because once I had worked this out a great many other things began to follow. Strange things. Terrifying things. Wondering things. (I could even stay up here for years, I thought, like some Stylite of the suburbs, on terracotta building tiles in place of a Syrian pillar, and ruminate on all the problems of the world. The ancient Stylites had liked desert places for their meditations.)

The realisation that I did not love Helen, and never had loved her, came to me quite dispassionately at first; so dispassionately that I was able to examine the revelation with a kind of clear careful logic, and find it sound, and put it aside for later. " Later," of course, would be another thing altogether, when I would want to blame *her* for the predicament we were in, and then passion and anger would need to be invoked. But not yet.

Still, it was the thought of Helen, busy at her casserole in the kitchen, that diverted my reflections at once to all the disturbing little problems and quandaries which up until so recently had baffled and troubled me—politics and Spain and the German ships and the interviews on the liners—because I saw that I had been wrong to allow Helen to work these things out for me. I should have seen for myself that a lot of the dissonance of the world had nothing whatever to do with " downtrodden masses " or any of Helen's other clichés, but was there because half the world lived in mental deserts very much like the Beverley Park Gardens Estate, and that the real enemy was not the obvious embodiment of evil, like Hitler or his persecution of the Jews or the Russian purges or the bombs on Guernica, but was this awful fetish of a respectability that would rather look the other way than

cause a fuss, that hated " scenes," that did not *want* to know
because *to know* might somehow force them into a situation
which could take the polish off the duco and blight the herba-
ceous borders and lay scabrous patches across the attended
lawns.

But there were gradations of this respectability—this was
the next thing I worked out as Meredith Stylites of the Garden
Suburb—and I knew that there had been more things of true
value in the shabby house called *Avalon*, from which I had
fled, than there ever would be, or could be, in this villa in
Beverley Grove. This was where my meditations began to
turn in and maul me. I stared around over the whole of the
sterile desolation, and I realised with a start of panic that I
had got myself into the middle of this red and arid desert, and
there was nobody to bring me water.

I had chosen it, of my own free will. I had planned for it,
approved of it, connived at it, worked for it, and paid for it.
But no!—I winced as the mauling became more brutal—the
whole point was that *I had not paid for it*! Oh no, I had not
paid for it, not yet . . . I had mortgaged my life and my
career for years ahead simply for the privilege of living between Mr. Phyland and Mr. Treadwell and directly opposite
Wally and Sandra Solomons!

And the console-radio, the hated new acquisition of the
console-radio, inclusive of the Quicktite Patent Antenna
Clamp against which my back rested, was another seventy-
five pounds, thirteen shillings and elevenpence to be added to
all those other precise and handsomely-printed documents
with which the top drawer of my study desk was stuffed. My
guarantees! Diplomas! Some of them even looked like
diplomas, with their Old English type and the copperplate
flourishes and the big red impressive seals. Diplomas conferred in testimony of some inalienable right to live on in the
soft warmth of these empty plains where heads could always
be hidden in the comforting granular sand of an unimpeachable respectability. Gavin Turley's guarantees. . . .

(This was the point where Meredith Stylites of the Garden
Suburb abandoned his red brick chimney-pillar and eased
himself down the pitch of the tiled roof, and was transformed
into the qualified Meredith, Bachelor of Deserts, Doctor of
Sterile Studies, Master of the Empty Soul, by the time he

reached the point where the borrowed Solomons' ladder poked
two rungs above the eaves, and there he sat for a few more
minutes with his long legs dangling over the guttering, staring
around at the desert of his choice as if he might memorise
forever its every shade and contour, and this was when the
really forceful realisation came to him. . . .)

There was not one tree on the whole estate.

Yet there must have been trees once, I thought, because
when you closely examined the layout of the estate there were
little folds to it and faint graceful rises and declivities, not
anywhere near definite enough to be thought of as hills or
gullies, but the place was not really *flat*, that was the point,
and at one side, a little distance beyond Dr. Felton Carradine's
house, there was almost a real knoll. Once—I felt absolutely
sure about this—there would have been trees growing here
and there, and I pictured this knoll as having two or three
good sturdy blue-gums or stringybarks on the crest, and slopes
brown with bracken, and some sandy chewed-out patches
where rabbits would have made little squats scattered with the
liquorice-black pellets of their droppings and where they
would have hopped about at dusk, flickering the pale cotton
tufts of their tails. The place could have been really beautiful
at one time in a tranquil sort of way, I thought—before
Bernie Rothenstein came in with his bulldozers and graders
and grubbed out all the trees and flattened everything out so
that the subdivision pegs could be hammered in and his lorries
could move about without hindrance—because there was a
blur of higher ground much farther out, and beyond that the
bluish bulk of the Dandenongs sat up there against a good
bright sky in nice shapes and colours. And now there was
nothing but a great red scab grown over the wounds the
bulldozers had made, and not a single tree remaining, because
by no stretch of the imagination could anybody count the
spindly little sticks which had been stuck in at intervals along
the footpaths, because they really were only sticks, and too
hidden behind their ugly little tree-guards for anyone to
know whether they were leafing or whether they were dead.

I climbed down the Solomons' ladder at once and went
straight out to the car and just drove off. It was only about a
mile to Goodenough's Nurseries, and we had bought our
seedlings there so I knew he stayed open on Sunday mornings,

because that was when a lot of suburban gardeners who were tied up at their offices through the week would come to pick up shrubs or seedlings, or to arrange for top-dressing, or to discuss pruning or spraying, or just to talk with him or his gardeners about mulching and tilth and compost-heaps and reinvigoration of their lawns and beds.

I parked the car outside and went in through the gate beneath the painted sign that simply said GOODENOUGH NUR-SERIES—Jos. Goodenough, Prop.—Est. 1907, and there was Jos. Goodenough himself standing beside the potting-sheds, looking square and reddish and sort of flatly cut out against the slow cool sweep of the sprinklers over the flower-beds, like the Jack of Hearts in a pack of playing cards, and I felt renewed at the very sight of him because there was something earthy and true and reliable about his presence as he stood there in the smell of damp loam and blood-and-bone manure, with a felt hat on his head, his Sunday hat, and his thick braces up over his grey flannel undershirt, and I remember that his braces were striped the way men's winceyette pyjamas used to be and the words POLICE AND FIREMEN were stamped on each of the little metal clips that adjusted them, and I have often wondered since what sort of a guarantee *that* was supposed to be.

I told him I wanted to buy a tree, and he rubbed at his nose and said, " Well, mister, that's a bit broad and sweepin' like, ain't it? You know, a tree. Which district do you live, can you tell me that to give me an idea?" So I told him and this brightened him up, because at once he nodded knowingly and said, " Beverley Park Gardens, eh . . . yeah, well up there they're goin' in fer the more decorative type of thing, aren't they? You know, the camellia, like, or the hardier sort of hibiscus, or gardenia, even a good well-developed double-fuchsia. Or some of the nice ornamental shrubs an' that."

" No," I said. " A tree. I want a *proper* tree. Something that'll grow into a real tree very quickly."

" Well . . ." He went back to rubbing at his nose, harder than before. " It wouldn't be something like a decorative cypress you got in mind, one each side of a front entrance porch, like . . . although they *are* pretty slow comin' on, you know, they do look well in the long run but they're slow old growers."

"Listen, Mr. Goodenough," I said patiently. "It's quite simple. I want something you can put in the ground now and look at it in, say, two years' time and say, 'There, that's a real bloody tree!'"

He had both hands busy now, one scrubbing at his nose and the other scratching pensively at his backside.

"It ain't a *gum* you got in mind, is it?" he asked at last, rather dubiously. "One of them quick-growin' eucalypts . . . you wouldn't be thinkin' of them, though?"

"Why not? Do they grow quickly?"

"Some of 'em. Some of 'em shoot up like billy-oh. The sugar-gum 'ld be about the best taker, I'd say. The sugars won't get to the size of some of the others, mind you, not at the mature growth, but in the early stages I reckon it's the sugar'ld give you the best show. Oh, I reckon you could get a tree say thirty foot high or so within a couple of years if you gave her a bit of encouragement early. Maybe even up to forty foot if the spread's there for the roots."

"But that sounds exactly what I want."

"Sugar-gum, eh?" He scratched away at his bottom and shook his head. "Yeah, well you're the customer, mister, an' if that's what you got your mind set on. . . . Matter of fact, I got a pretty fair sort of a sapling round behind the sheds there—I keep a few of 'em on hand just in case there's a call for wind-breaks, you know. I c'ld let you have her for six bob. I wouldn't like you to regret it later, though, mister, and be complainin' so I better warn you. Plants an' trees are just like anythink else, you know, an' you can't never expect anythink to come on well unless it's at the expense of somethink else, an' these gums they do tear a pretty solid amount of nourishment out of the soil. I mean you'd have to expect strife with your lawn growth and your flower-beds."

When I got back to Beverley Grove I dumped the sapling on the drive near the front gate and went through to the kitchen, and Helen said, "David, where on earth have you been? You didn't say you were going somewhere. I thought you were still up there on the roof, and when I went to call you for your cup of tea——"

"I went out and bought a tree," I said.

"A *tree*?"

"A tree for the garden. I drove down to Goodenough's Nurseries. Only six bob," I added proudly.

"David, how marvellous!" she cried. "Where is it?"

"Out the front. Come and see."

Her expression changed when she did see it, and admittedly it did look rather scruffy and limp and drab with its roots packed up into a big shapeless pudding of wet hessian.

"Yes, but what is it?" she asked. "It—it looks like a gum-tree."

"It *is* a gum-tree. It's a sugar-gum."

"Oh," she said, and for a moment or two she looked blank, and then, "Where are you going to put it?" she said. "I mean, where do you want it to grow?"

"There." I pointed. "Right there, smack bang in the middle of the lawn!"

"Oh!"

"Why do you just keep saying 'Oh'?"

"No reason . . . I mean, well, do you really think that's the place for it, David? I mean, if it's to be there, right in the middle of everything, I would have thought something smaller, or even——"

"What's wrong with a gum-tree?"

"Well, if you want to know, darling, I personally think they're rather *ordinary*. They're so drab, David. I'd honestly prefer something decorative, especially for there, right in the front of the house, some nice flowering shrub, or camellia, or mock-orange. What *would* look lovely would be one of those Japanese dwarf-maples."

"Not on your sweet life, my dear! No dwarf anythings! I want a tree. A proper bloody tree! Do you realise," I said, "there's not one tree growing in this whole damned street . . . on the whole estate if it comes to that? And this is a *grove* we live in, darling. It's printed on the footpath at the corner. Beverley Grove. Don't you know the definition of a grove? We've been letting them pull the wool over our eyes. The Beverley—Park—Gardens—Estate." I spaced the words with careful sarcasm. "It isn't a park and it isn't a garden and this isn't a grove. They've got us here on false pretences. They can't bloody well do that to *us*! Besides, this is our chance to be original. Let *us* be leaders of fashion, Helen.

And let me point out—because old Goodenough told me this himself—that that thing you're turning up your nose at—all right, I admit it *does* look a bit scraggy at the moment—but he assured me it'll grow into a tree forty feet high in two years. A *real tree*! And what this damned place needs is a good firm far-sighted policy of reafforestation!"

I went round to the shed in the back yard then and got out the pick and shovel.

I think there are more people than will admit it who are inclined to force their big issues on trivial things, rather than face up to the basic problems full on, and certainly this was the way it worked with me. It was this six-shilling sugar-gum from the Goodenough Nurseries that was to become the bone of contention between Helen and me, and ultimately the hammered-in wedge that split us apart. Yet I have often wondered since how many marriages there are that seem to founder on the dramatic reefs of adultery and illicit liaisons and eternal triangles and paranoiac pressures that are really scuttled long before, cravenly and treacherously, with the trivial little augers of spite and resentment and camouflaged incompatibilities and petty prejudices. Marriage is an institution not notable for the big-mindedness with which it sees its failings and its hazards.

From that moment of revelation on the roof of the house I was in conflict with Helen, but there was no open declaration of hostilities. Subterfuge, rather, was to be the pattern. In this I was entirely to blame, for Helen had had no similar revelation, had found no reason whatever for conflict or enmity. My turning against her in the way I did was treacherous, deliberate, and very cruel. One sees now, of course, that the destruction of individual character is never the sudden dramatic fracture: it resembles more a slow poisoning: it begins with the smallest indifference, the littlest act of cowardice, the tiniest of compromises, and the toll it takes is slow and deadly.

She continued to behave well. But I watched her now, surreptitiously, in much the way I had watched her at Mother's birthday party, and I detected changes in her—changes, I think, that were perceptible only to me. Outsiders, I think, saw no ruffling of her composure, no weakening of her poise,

no wavering in her affection for me or in her sedulous attention to the building of a pattern of life which she desired and
which she honestly thought was what I desired also. Yet
changes were there all right: *I* could see them, like the
shadows of unknown things glimpsed beneath the surface of a
running stream—little subdued fears, anxieties, uncertainties,
mostly a desperately baffled desire to find some reason behind
the subtle changes in my temperament, the moods that would
take me, the studied little injuries I would inflict, the moments of polite coldness, the resentments hinted at yet never
quite declared, this secret enmity that now lay hidden beneath the surface of our relationship. I knew all this, but I
would not confront her. I see now how cruelly difficult it
must have been for her, because she had no back-reference
to which she could refer that did not disclose my own choice
of and admiration for everything which I seemed now to
resent.

When I could I evaded the issues in the privacy of my study.
I would spend much time there, with the door closed, and
sensing my almost childish sulkiness and my need for evasive-
ness, she would come to the room now only when it was
unavoidable. She had gone back to doing her telephoning
from the bedroom. The study remained very much as it had
been. Helen had tidied up. My flare of revolution had won
me only paltry gains. The desk, it is true, remained where I
had pushed it against the wall, and there was a new waste-
paper basket, a plain one of wicker, often filled with
crumpled paper now—the desperate calculations I would
make of the money we owed and the instalments due, which
I would work out from the handsome diploma-forms stuffed
into the top drawer. The books were back on their shelves
behind the sliding glass. The pictures had been returned to
the walls. There were times when I realised that it was a
strange privacy I had won for myself, morose, embittered,
doubting. I did no writing.

It was from the tree that I derived a sort of spiteful comfort. Old Jos. Goodenough had been right—it took astonish-
ingly. One could almost see it grow. At some stage I must
have accepted that the tree had become very much more than
merely a symbol of protest against suburban values. If I had
not, in fact, planted it with malice aforethought, I very soon

began to be aware that I was using it as a weapon with which
to force a situation which I was not prepared to attack
directly. I gave it much attention, forking, watering, manur-
ing,—far more attention than I would give to the now-hated
flower-beds which were Helen's pride and joy. (One was
always on the prowl, of course, trying to sniff out other
sources of resentment.) It even came to the absurdly childish
point where I would water the tree copiously and, in the case
of a eucalypt quite unnecessarily, and deliberately neglect
those beds which I had come to detest because of the little
wooden label-stakes which Helen had lettered herself so
neatly. I think I really hated them because of the affectation
she had perpetrated in using only the botanical names for her
flowers, and I would stalk the hated beds at dusk, spitting the
words out under my breath: *Phlox Drummondii, Tropæolum,
Arctotis, Myosotis dissitiflora, Antirrhinum!* God! what was
wrong with forget-me-not or snapdragon?

As it worked out, it was neither Helen nor I who forced the
issue in the end, although Helen was obliged to act as the
intermediary. It began one evening at supper, which we were
eating in the dining-room, and she had gone to some trouble
preparing a menu of what she called " Chinese chow," and
there were *dim-sims* and spring rolls she had bought from a
Chinese restaurant in Little Bourke Street, and she had made
the soup and the sweet-and-sour pork herself, and the candles
were green, and from the radio-console in the adjoining room
a record was playing " Selections From The Great Operas "
and *La Bohème* had just taken over from *Madame Butterfly*
when she said, " David, I'm afraid we'll have to do something
about that tree in the front."

" Do what?" I asked.

" Well, what happened is that Mr. Treadwell from next
door dropped in here this afternoon. He's complaining about
it."

" He's *what*! It's not *his* bloody tree!"

" He insists you'll have to dig it out. The roots are getting
in under the cement of his drive."

" Oh, bollocks!" I said. " His drive's thirty feet away
from the tree! Do you mean to tell me that roots can go
thirty feet underground in a few bloody months!"

" *I'm* not telling you anything, darling. I am simply repeating to you what *he* says. Treadwell is a perfectly nice inoffensive little old man, and he's not a fussy neighbour, and he was most polite about it all. But you know he is a very keen amateur gardener himself and——"

"Well, the old bastard's got nothing *else* to do, has he? He's on a Government pension. He doesn't work. And what the devil has that got to do with our gum-tree?"

"Because he also claims that a tree like that takes the good out of the soil, too—our own lawn *is* getting awfully patchy, darling—and if the roots get near his dahlia beds he——"

"Oh, go to blazes with his dahlia beds. And what's wrong with some upended cement slabs? The place is too damned neat as it is. It's—it's like having some damned woman walking around after you with an ash-tray in her hand, or plumping up the cushions the minute you stand up. My God! I'd like to have two whacking great Moreton Bay figs like those at the Turleys', and then we could tip the slabs up the whole length of the street! Which might be a bloody good thing! And I think I'm going to plant a huge black Dollicus outside my study window, did you know that? I would, too, if I knew what the real name of the thing was." I looked at her deliberately. "You're rather set against this tree yourself, aren't you, my dear?"

"I've never liked it particularly," she said quietly. "You know that. I think it's rather dreary, and it does spoil the whole look of the front of the house."

"I happen to place a great importance on that tree," I pointed out stiffly.

"I know you do. I've simply conveyed what Mr. Treadwell said." She met the challenge with cool dignity. "That's all. And you're working yourself up to another of those moods, aren't you?" With that she got up from the table and left me, and I went out to the front garden and gave particularly solicitous attention to my sugar-gum.

Two weeks later she was invited into the Treadwell garden to examine the unevenness of the drive. Quite probably there was neighbourly collusion, but a few days after this Mr. Phyland also complained about the tree. I bought a bag of superphosphate and forked it well in around the healthy-looking trunk.

Some little time passed before Helen reopened the issue.

" I'm sorry to bring this up," she said very quietly. " It's the tree again, I'm afraid. Mr. Treadwell and Mr. Phyland intend to make an official complaint to the municipal council if you don't do something about it. Now wait, *please* David, it really has to be taken seriously this time. There *is* something in the council by-laws, and they can bring a lawsuit against you . . . they have perfectly good legal grounds, it seems. And don't forget Mr. Treadwell was a magistrate, and he has quite a lot of pull and——"

" So I should dig it up, eh? Is that what you think?"

" It's your tree, David," she said evenly. " You're the one who's been so obstinate about——"

" I asked you a simple question. You think I should root the bloody thing out?"

" I see no point whatever in upsetting all the neighbours, darling. Not just for a tree."

That was when I saw red I knew, of course, that I had been defeated by the forces of conformity. Yet, in its way, the tree had served its purpose. And it was still a weapon to be used, a weapon that would hurt—that would inflict pain—that might even kill. . . .

" Not just for a tree," I repeated bitterly. " God! you just can't afford to be different, can you? You always have to conform to their rotten dreary suburban sameness. If Sandra Solomons has a page-boy you've got to have a blasted page-boy! If bloody Phyland plants out antirrhinums *we've* got to plant out antirrhinums. If we all do everything exactly the same none of us will upset the other, will we? We can die for air in their suffocating bloody sterility, we can die for water in their barren bloody desert, but we mustn't cry out or make a scene or protest about it! All right. *Let's* conform! Let's be just the same as they are. I'll dig out the blasted tree. And we'll fill the bloody hole with antirrhinums! and let's go the whole hog, shall we, and give a name to the house? What would you like, my pet? Nothing banal, like *Emoh Ruo* or *The Nest* or *Nirvana*. No, something original and imaginative, like your damned dull little parties! *I'll* do it! I'm very expert at painting signs for front gates. How does *Valhalla* appeal? No, no, we can do better than that. Not *Avalon* or *Bangalore*, they're out, they've been used. Something sentimental, like *Guernica*, say, to remind us of our

wedding day? Or how about *The Masses*? Or better still—
here's a beauty, a real original—suppose we call it *Sacco and
Vanzetti*?"

I had broken her at last. All her defences had collapsed,
the poise and the coolness and the composure gone, and
there she was standing before me in her neat smart clothes,
stricken and trembling, hopeless and bewildered, and afraid of
me, and she looked older than her thirty-one years, and her
fine thin face was ravaged by a flood of tears, and because this
was the first time I had ever seen her cry I brought the razor-
strop down again across her back to punish her for the crimes
she had never committed, and I said, " You've asked for this,
you know. You've been told there's no guarantee in me.
And there isn't, by Jesus, there *isn't*."

There was no finality in it, then or later, it just went on,
dragging, drifting, and there was a wall between us that could
never be scaled again, and yet she still tried—I swear she did
—but the parties went on, and the cleaning of the car, and a
mock-orange was planted where the sugar-gum had grown,
and then it was the morning of September the fourth, and the
bedroom telephone rang to awaken me barely half an hour
after I had dropped off to an exhausted sleep. It was Jack,
and he sounded very excited.

" Nipper? That you, nipper? Listen, are you going to be
in it?"

" Be in what?" I said, yawning through the daze of sleep.

" Why, the *war*. There's a war. They've declared war."

" I know," I said dryly. " I've been up all night. I just got
to bed five minutes ago."

" I woke you up, eh? You're going to be in it, aren't you?"

" What are you talking about? Be in what? England's
declared war, Jack. Parliament hasn't even met out here. *We*
aren't at war."

" Ah, we *will* be, though Everyone knows that. But I just
thought I'd make sure you intended to be in it. That's all."

" But why wake me up to talk about that now?" I said
wearily. " There's plenty of time, for Christ's sake. Don't
you understand, if we do go in with Britain it's going to be
weeks and weeks, months even, before anything will be teed
up. Recruiting. They've got to have camps. Uniforms.

Millions of things. So go away, will you, and let me get back to sleep."

"Keep your shirt on," he said cheerfully. "As long as you're going to get a guernsey, that's the main thing."

"Jack, please piss off. I'm nearly dead."

"Davy?"

"Oh dear God, what is it *now*?"

"Listen, be sure and give me the drum if you hear anything at the office. You'd know about things before they get into the paper, wouldn't you? I mean, about enlisting and that. I'd like to be in there and sign on the dotted line early, you know. So give me the drum, Davy, won't you? And I'll be in it like a rat up a rope. Well, both of us, eh? We could——" I yawned and put the receiver down and cut him off and dropped my head back on the pillow.

CHAPTER 14

The time of war began as sometimes a storm begins, with nervous little gusts and flurries of excitement rising and dying away, veering this way and that, dropping altogether into waiting gaps of brief calm: and indeed the very air in that opening fortnight of September seemed charged with something of the electrical apprehension that forebodes the tempest: and then all would fall still again, as it often does, deceptively, in advent of the fiercest hurricane, and the storm was still there pushed away behind the hills, waiting. And of course it was spring, and the wattle yellow along the Yarra, and the high air charged with restlessness anyway.

This queer trenchant time, stimulating yet frustrating, eager yet balked in some way, had, in Australia, I think, an effect on people peculiar to the nature of their environment and to the odd quirking elements of their character—which were part of the same thing, of course—and the words that Gavin Turley had used months before, "And after all we are a long way away," derived a different intonation from the long remove of our involvement.

Parliament had met and we were, unanimously, in a declared state of war with Hitler's Germany: as in the past there

would be discipline and organisation, but no compulsion—
the Australian Expeditionary Force to fight overseas would
follow the established tradition of being composed entirely of
volunteers. The system had worked well enough for the Boer
War and the First World War, and nobody would have had it
any other way.

Jack's almost passionate response to the new situation was
typical enough of many Australian young men at that time—
he was roused very probably by the same pull which a quarter
of a century earlier had taken Dad away, and Bert, and had
made Mother leave her small children and go to France—yet
he could not have made articulate the reason for his excited
eagerness. It was not patriotism that lay behind it nor any
particular political feeling. He was not drawn by causes—I
doubt if he ever questioned the rights or the wrongs which
were involved: others more qualified, the " brainy jokers,"
had decided the justice of the decision (for justice, whether
consciously or unconsciously, always *did* concern him): the
pull, I am inclined to think, was almost mythic, and dictated
by the land in which he lived.

I have thought about this thing very often during the years
of my explanation, and I have concluded that there *is* the
substance of myth in the very insistency with which this call
towards the distant adventure is repeated to generation after
generation of my countrymen. Myths do grow out of the
eternal earth, this much is certain: and this Australian myth
seems to derive from something primal, an earth-challenge.
The continent is cruel and pitiless, four-fifths of it uninhabit-
able. The vast dry heart of the land is dead, and it is on this
intractable central grimness that the teeth of adventure have
long since been blunted. Here journeys have ended, the pion-
ering flame has guttered and failed, hopes and ambitions lie
buried beneath the blowing sand. It is the one challenge from
which the adventurous Australian has always had to retreat,
back to the narrow, safer skin of his coastal holdings, and
he has been forced to turn his back, because he must, on the
invincible wilderness that lies behind him. So he has been
obliged to look elsewhere for the great adventures, the necessary challenges to the flesh and spirit. This is why his wars
must be fought for other causes than his own—and often for
strange ones—and always in faraway places. He is, because

the merciless quality of his own land dictates it to him, the soldier of far fortune. This is why his armies which are sent to these faraway places are always of volunteers, for there is never any lack of young men of eager spirit willing to respond to the far call. I have been with the armies of many races, but I have known no other soldier with such pure and passionate regard for the adventure in itself.

Jack's tragedy was that he was such a one. The myth was lodged and burning deep inside him.

So there must have been for him in those jaunty jangled days of a September spring in Melbourne the charged atmosphere of a time that was opening to the promise of splendid adventure like a slow-blooming flower. The old women were out along Flinders Street with their baskets of spring blossom and sprigs of golden wattle, and the smell of brown boronia was in the streets, and men's faces were eager over newspapers in trams, and the girls seemed prettier than one had ever realised, and vivacious, quick-tapping on their high spike heels, showing lots of leg that year, and London-tan and teal-blue were the colours, I remember, and the hair was worn in a page-boy and covered by a snood, so that the girls moved in the streets to the lively rhythm of those pretty coloured netted bags of hair lifting and falling, lifting and falling, as if to the measure of a conductor's baton. And sometimes at a city intersection a tram-driver, exuberant in his cabin, would tintinnabulate his bell in a mad, irresistible tattoo, a reveille, a tinny pibroch of the times.

But it was an unresolved time, too, and slow in developing. One noticed that the flags were up, brave and bright in the equinoctial winds, but nothing was happening. We were in a state of war, and there was no war. An urgent patriotism would seem to flare up and then die in embarrassment. Hearts would kick with a queer compulsive excitement at the sight of some staff-car moving from Victoria Barracks with uniforms inside it and polished badges, but there was almost no khaki in the streets, and no posters that appealed for sacrifice, and no bands playing. At the far fringes of the world areoplanes were dropping bombs inside the walls of old medieval cities, but they were dropping leaflets too, and even where buildings were falling in flame and rubble there was no way of grasping with any sense of belief the fact that death and captivity

was also a part of war, because all the names were bizarre
and unfamiliar, even unpronounceable, Warszawa and Lodz
and Cracow and Grudziadz, and we were, after all, a long
way away.

Nobody stopped to consider that the other names that were
familiar to every schoolboy, the names I had grown up with
—Gaba Tepe and Gallipoli and Villers-Bretonneux and Vimy
Ridge and Passchendaele, even the earlier names of Mafe-
king and Spion Kop and Ladysmith—had once seemed just
as alien and unreal. Familiarity with the words that were the
fingerposts of wars had had to be learnt, that was the point,
and would still have to be learnt, and blood was the only
adhesive that might stick them into the native lexicon. It was
too early then, in those impetuous, stalling September days,
to realise this, of course, for this was only the dawn of the
distant adventure, and there were a hundred names for the
later lexicon—Tobruk and Bardia and Kokoda and Merjiyun
and El Alamein and Monastir Gap and all the others—that
nobody had even heard of then. . . .

This state of uncertainty, as it went on, had no appeal at all
to Jack. He grew nervous and impatient and angry, and
never a day passed without his telephoning me. " Listen,
Davy, haven't you heard *anything* yet?" he would say,
bitterly aggrieved. " What the hell are they up to? Look,
there's a joker here in the factory, and he's a pretty brainy
bloke, he's well up on these things, see, and he was saying only
half an hour ago he reckons the bloody war will be *over* in
six weeks! At the *outside*, he says! I mean it, it'll be over
before we're even bloody *in* it!"

I had little time to be concerned with Jack's distress. Gavin
Turley and I were frantically busy trying to explain it all, and
we would be on duty fourteen, even sixteen hours at a stretch,
monitoring the overseas radio broadcasts and churning out
special articles of background and interpretation, half-buried
in files from the morgue or reference books from the library.
Mr. Brewster had detached us from all other duties so that we
might concentrate, in the words of his rather flamboyant
memorandum, " on all aspects of the military situation, both
at home and abroad." Our two typewriters seemed to be
endlessly chattering out hasty pieces to meet editions, and
special editions were coming off the presses at all hours of

the day and night—biographies of the German generals, comparative military strengths, assessments, speculations—what we called "situationers" and ' 'ink-pieces "—the significance of air power, of naval strengt , of armour, whether the sinking of the *Athenia* would bring America in, the background of Poland with its absurd and baffling names. . . .

There was a topsy-turvy quality about it, too, of Europe's day being our night, for we usually worked through from dusk until dawn, and would sleep when we could with blinds drawn against the sunlight and the bakers' carts delivering along the suburban streets. During this hectic, exhilarating, unbalanced time I saw very little of Helen, and the house in Beverley Grove was no more than a place in which to sleep. This was a great relief to me. It removed my despair, it eased the surface tensions that existed between Helen and me, it staved off any need to make, or to evade, a decision. The long remove, the voices heard through the night-crackle of static, the happenings of far away, once more seemed to offer me an avenue of escape, or of postponement, where before there had been only a cul-de-sac.

In the end Jack did volunteer for the Army on the first day that recruiting finally was opened, and was accepted, and although he was not, after all, the first to get there he was among the first fifty, and perhaps he would have been even higher up the list had he not stopped on the way to telephone me.

"You coming along, nipper?" he said briskly. "To join up, I mean."

"Not a chance," I told him. "I've got an article I have to finish. Besides, why all the rush?"

"Rush? Oh, don't come *that*! Jesus! how long is it now we've been just sitting on our backsides, chewing our fingernails, waiting?"

"Why be impetuous? There'll be plenty of time. The way the Germans are going there'll be years and years to get into it. Anyway, didn't the announcement say single men would be preferred? You've got a wife and three kids, remember."

"What odds? That'll only bump up my pay. Christ, Davy, I wouldn't miss out on this if I had fifty bloody kids.

Listen, I can't waste time. I've got to scoot. If you can't come, you can't. I'll keep you a place, though."

They took the first of the recruits out to the showgrounds and issued them with giggle-suits and kit and palliasses and Jack was among those quartered in the Pig Pavilion, in a pen marked LARGE WHITES, and later they were all moved to the big training camp at Puckapunyal, sixty miles or so north of Melbourne, and it was some weeks after this that Mr. Brewster sent me up there to do some articles on the training of this first brigade.

I saw Jack the following morning. He was with a battalion on a route march along the old Seymour road, and they were marching at ease in the new columns of three with their rifles slung, slogging along through the hot dry yellow dust underneath big, scraggy, olive-drab gum-trees, and although he didn't see me because I was in a staff car with the brigade-major, it gave me a queer feeling to see him there because the column was just passing the old Seymour camp where the soldiers of the First World War had trained, and I realised that Dad and Bert must have slogged along this very same road on route marches, too, through the same dun dust under the same trees, and although this new generation of Diggers wore khaki shorts and white gaiters over their socks and not the old baggy trousers and puttees, and they were singing "Waltzing Matilda" instead of "Tipperary," the same rifles were on their shoulders and the faces must have looked pretty much the same under the same broad hats tipped up at one side with the rising-sun badges glinting there against the pleated white of the puggarees.

I spoke to Jack that evening in the camp canteen in a roaring crowded atmosphere of tobacco smoke and beer fumes and singing and raucous horseplay, and they were talking a new slang and the bawdy jokes had the flavour of a novel topicality, and I could tell right away that Jack was a very popular figure with his own particular group, especially when he had his mouth-organ out. but after a time he took me aside to one end of the long, makeshift bar, and we just drank beer and talked together.

I was intrigued, and impressed, at the change in him. He was so darkly sunburnt that his hair seemed almost white, and he looked tough, hard, and very fit. I could not decide whether he looked older or younger, but certainly he looked different. In the open-neck shirt and the shorts and the white gaiters and the white webbing belt, there was a look of absolute *rightness* about him—I had forgotten his strong, graceful boxer's legs, a deep brown now and dusted with a thick gold down of hair. What had changed about him, I began to realise, was both subtle and profound: it was almost as if he had been fined down to the " essential Jack," as if this was what my brother really *should* look like, as if all his growing and maturing had been working towards the presentation of this man in this exact appearance at this precise time. Even more than this, for I saw that this was not only that he looked as *Jack* should look, but he looked as a proper *man* should look. As he talked to me—and his talk was the talk of the old Jack I had always known—I began to sense something that was in him that had not been there before, the quiet authority of an absolute conviction . . . something like that . . . there was an impalpable feeling about him, almost an emanation, that here was a man totally sure of the rightness of what he was doing. I felt good for him, and yet it disturbed me strangely. . . .

" Listen, Davy, what's been holding you back?" he said. " You know, each day I've been expecting you to jump out of one of them trucks with your kitbag and all that. Although you've been doing all those write-ups, haven't you, about the war?"

" Yes, they've been keeping me pretty busy," I said.

" Well, you don't have to worry about it, you know. There's a new lurk. I got the drum about it from one of the officers. I mean, when you *do* join up, don't you worry at all about what unit they shove you in. I'll tell you why. I found out. An elder brother's got the right to claim a younger brother, did *you* know that? Get him into the same unit, like, You know, so he can look after him, sort of. Well, I mean, don't go and join the Air Force or the Navy or anything like that! It's got to be the Army. Then it's simple as shellin' peas. All you do is let me know what unit they've put you in and your VX number and that, and I do the rest. I just go to my C.O. and claim you, and he makes out the form, and they transfer you right off to my unit. Fair enough, eh?"

They were in full cry behind us, around a tinny upright piano, singing, "Roll Out The Barrel." He took it absolutely for granted that I would be volunteering. I said, "Do you really like it here?"

"My oath! It's all right by me, *this* life! Oh, we all grizzle, you know, I do it myself, but this'll do me. Tucker's pretty fair, and plenty of it. They look after you. And it's not a bad mob of blokes, taken all round. You know, they yell, 'You'll be sorry!' and all that, but nobody takes much notice of the bullshit. Well, you look at it this way, Davy, I reckon half the bastards here, this is the first regular job they've had in their whole bloody lives. I mean, blokes who came out of school smack into the Depression and never knew where their next flamin' meal was coming from . . . well, this is just a real bloody picnic for *them*, isn't it?"

"I suppose it is."

He laughed. "Tell you something funny," he chuckled. "You remember when we were kids those larrikin gangs, the Grey Caps and the Bludgers? You know, and how they always wanted me to join 'em? Well—this'll root you!—I bloody *have*, sport. Half the bastards are here, marching around with .303s on their shoulders instead of those fence-pickets and chunks of road-metal they used to throw around! You wouldn't read about it, would you?"

"You mean ones we knew?"

"Bloody dozens of 'em. All those Susso-workers from the council drays. That little bastard Dud Bennett, remember him? . . . he's in *my* platoon! Oh yeah, and you'd remember that big prick I had the fight with at school—you know, when Mum laid around with the umbrella!—Snowy Bretherton, well apparently he had a Chocko commission, and he's a flamin' *captain*! They don't go for him, mind you . . . he tries to chuck his weight around, and he's always buggerising about with that goon-stick he carries . . . and the blokes in his company they all reckon he'll go. They'll dump him over the side of the troopship on the way over. When he's taking parade, you know, there's always this whisper that follows him along the ranks, 'Shark-bait. Shark-bait!' Yeah, they reckon he'll go all right."

He smiled at this, but almost immediately his face was anxious and serious. "Davy," he said, lowering his voice, "do you get any buzz about anything down there at the Barracks? Where they're going to send us, I mean. Up here, you go barmy trying to sort out the furphies that go around. One day it's France and the next day it's Palestine, and it's England and Egypt, and then it's South Africa. South bloody Africa! What the hell would we do *there*? Have a go at the Kaffirs again? Don't you hear *anything* from down there at the Barracks?"

"The same sort of rumours, that's all. My own guess is it would be England, most likely, then over to France. That's where they're building up."

"Well, they'll let us know in time to catch the ship, I suppose. Tell me about things at home. Sheil' writes every day, of course. She tells me the Old Girl's up to her eyes in it."

"Mum? Yes." I laughed with him. "She's always knitting those damned balaclavas. Did you know she's organised her own Red Cross auxiliary! Some of the old women from around the neighbourhood and the wives of a couple of chaps in the lodge . . . they meet in the front room each day, about a dozen of them, for Mum's sewing-bees and knitting-bees."

"Don't tell *me*!" he snorted. "I get about three bloomin' parcels a week from her. Half my platoon's wearing Mum's socks and Mum's pullovers. That reminds me, when you see the old chook you might tell her—do it gently, for Christ's sake, because all the blokes reckon she makes a bloody superior type of sock, you know . . . and that issue stuff is murder, you get blisters like bloody soup plates!—but just tell her, tactful like, it's been a hundred-and-bloody-three in the shade here, and there's not all that much call for mittens or balaclavas!"

When I left he said, "Drop in and see Sheil' and the kids if you get a chance, Davy. Tell Sheil' I'm very appreciative of the cakes and things and tell her I'm fit as a fiddle and having a bloody wonderful time."

I heard a little more about Jack in the officers' mess the following day just before I left to go back to the city. Jack's company commander was there, a young captain who'd been a farmer at Porepunkah, and the brigade-major, who in civilian life had owned his own electrical business in Essendon.

" That's a jolly good type, that brother of yours, Mr. Meredith," the captain said, topping up my glass of beer. " You couldn't persuade him to try for promotion, I suppose? He's good N.C.O. material, you know."

" We tried to put it to him that he should have a stab at N.C.O.'s school," said the brigade-major. " Wouldn't have a bar of it. Said he'd rather stay with the boys."

" Well, that's Jack, I'm afraid," I said.

" Pity in a way," said the captain. " You know, he's got the real good solid Digger look about him. He seems a straight sort of a chap . . . I mean, I like the way he meets your eyes, square on. Right from the jump I've felt he'd be a handy sort of a bloke to have around you in a fight."

" He's always been able to take care of himself, I know that," I said.

" Well, Captain Jackson here can keep an eye on him," said the brigade-major. " We've got a lot of training time ahead of us yet. We'll have another shot at him. I think he'd make a first-rate W.O. Possibly even get a commission in the long run. I mean, it's always on the cards with that sort of chap, and this is a crazy democratic army we've got. In 2nd/6th Battalion C. Company, Mr. Meredith, there's a grazier worth half a million quid if he's worth nine bob a day. Geelong Grammar, University degree, and he's still a private and flatly refuses to be anything else, and his own station rouseabout is his platoon commander! Would you believe that? In your brother's company there's a bank manager who gets kitchen fatigues from one of his own clerks, who happens to be a lieut. It's a bloody funny way to go to war."

Going back in the train from Seymour I had much to think about, and mostly it was about Jack. His well-being, both physical and spiritual, had impressed me in a way which I found strangely disconcerting. He had unsettled me, that was the plain truth of it. I saw him suddenly as a kind of sunburnt Icarus, a free man, buoyant and soaring in his own air, in the clear and boundless space of an element familiar and yet new. It was not only as if he had been born for this realisation of his true self: it was almost as if the whole baffling pattern of world events had been in conspiracy to fulfil it. I envied the profound certainty there was about him, when I was so uncertain.

The train clattered to the southward through the brown burnt rushing world, the wheels nickerty-nattered on the rails, the water sloshed in the carafe below the luggage-rack. From the corner of my eye I was aware of the leap, sag, flow, and kick of the telegraph lines. I saw sheep like scattered knuckle-bones in the purple pools of tree-shadow, a herd of Herefords slow on a brown hill, the red-painted iron roofs and the faded weatherboards of towns. And I thought uneasily of Beverley Grove and of my wife Helen.

Even Beverley Grove had grown disconcerting, I realised, looking back on it. The war had not been two weeks old when Phyland from next door had appeared in uniform, and with three pips on each shoulder and a Sam Browne belt— mobilised for some headquarters administrative job on a reserve commission which I had never known he had—and with the same familiar brief-case under his arm had vanished into Victoria Barracks. And not more than a few days after this Wally Solomons had been mobilised, *Major* Solomons, to organise some base transport section. Oh yes, that had been disconcerting, too! And Helen? While the train rushed south I thought of Helen . . . of a way of escape . . . of the free and buoyant air. . . . Tempting thoughts.

I saw Mr. Brewster in his office that night. He was sympathetic and understanding, and quite firm.

" Don't think I don't realise how difficult it must be for you, David," he said. He had grown rather fatter, but otherwise had changed little from the time, more than eleven years before, when I had first met him. He no longer sat at his desk in shirt-sleeves and thin coloured braces, but his heavy, dewlapped face was as ruddy as ever, his mane of hair as white and silky. His neat chubby fingers still fidgeted with things, the edge of the blotter, his calendar pad, a pencil, a spike of proofs: he still had that trick of looking down at his thighs or up at the ceiling, and meeting your eyes only at moments of emphasis, as if vision was an exclamation-mark. " With your brother in, yes, it's hard for you," he said. " And I know your mother and your father were both in the first show. As *I* was, you know. Don't forget that. Don't think I don't understand. But it is a question of *value*, you

see, David. There is always a good sound truth buried in
every cliché, you know, and what you have to realise is that
the pen *is* mightier than the sword. In your case, that is. For
the time being, at any rate." He folded his hands across the
dome of grey worsted that hid his paunch and gloomily
examined the ceiling. "You and Turley are doing a most
vital and important job. War is a very complex and confus-
ing thing. It has to be interpreted, explained. There must be
instruction, elucidation, a channel for the spread of informed
and accurate information. You two chaps form a critical
link between our war effort out here, the military situation as
a whole, and the general public. It is the fundamental duty
of a newspaper to *serve* the general public. The people have
every right to know what is going on. As the situation stands
now each of you is worth a whole battalion of troops. I am
not exaggerating, you know. Always remember, David, that
propaganda is one of the most powerful weapons of war."

"Yet, I still have this feeling that I should be in it," I said,
but rather half-heartedly.

"You *are* in it, boy. You're up to your neck in it. You are
doing an excellent and an invaluable job for the war effort.
In any case, you know perfectly well that the War Cabinet has
classified certain reserved occupations. If you did enlist we
should simply apply for your withdrawal. They would have
to release you. They would *want* to release you. Your stocks
are very high down at the Barracks, you know, for the job
you're doing. It is as much in their interests as in ours that
you should continue to do precisely what you are doing. You
are pulling a good stout oar in this war effort, David. Don't
have a conscience about it, boy."

I accepted his ruling almost with relief. Again the decision
had been taken out of my hands, and again I could go back to
my work as if nothing had happened. Although one could not
but be aware that something *had* happened. The office,
especially the reporters' room, was beginning to be very
strange. Curtis Condon had long since gone to some censorship job at the Barracks. Familiar faces were missing from
many of the desks and scarcely a day seemed to pass without
one of the copy-boys coming round with the "whip-round"
list of names, asking for subscriptions towards someone's
going-away presentation. There were quite a few women and

girls in the reporters' room now, brought down from the social staff to replace the men.

Even so, Mr. Brewster's talk had effectively stilled any conscience I might have had, and I gave the problem no further thought until about a month later, when I walked into the subs'-room and there was a group of sub-editors and reporters surrounding Gavin Turley, and Gavin was wearing a khaki uniform with grey-bordered colour-patches at his shoulders. He cut the most ludicrous figure. The uniform was sloppy and still creased and rumpled from the quarter-master's issue-store, the sleeves were too short by four inches for his long spidery arms, the trousers were half-mast, and one bootlace was untied. His neck, pink and bulging at the Adam's apple, seemed to extend endlessly from the high coarse collar with the rising-sun badges like a long fleshy worm wriggling from a clod of dry earth, his mop of long black hair had been cut off and was now slicked down and parted at one side. With his immense skinny height, his awkward look, and this shoddy, ill-fitting uniform, he was a memorably lamentable figure of a soldier.

" Good God!" I gasped. " What in the name of——?"

He grinned. " You do not perceive my field-marshal's baton, old cock? Is that it? I keep it in my knapsack." He turned to a copy-boy hovering at the fringes of the group. " You have Mr. Meredith's name there on the whip-round list? Put him down for five bob. No, make it ten bob, the same as the executives." He turned to me again. " I know one should not take this direct role in ones' own farewell presentation, but I'm deathly afraid they'll give me an entrée-dish, and I'm trying to get the total up to a tenner. I've rather set my mind on something more martial. A small cannon, say."

" But you mean you——?"

He spread his arms in rueful display. " You have only to observe," he said, " this rare shade of shit in which they've robed me to know that I have joined what are euphemistically called ' the colours.' On battlefields—they assure me of this —it is the most neutral tone. Chameleon Turley they will call me."

" Yes, but damn it all, Gavin——"

" Why, you ask? Simply because I felt I needed a rest.

They have been working me too hard here. I'm looking for
the easy life." He grinned again. " Ha-ha, now *you'll* have to
take your finger out, won't you, Golden Boy? The whole war
effort on *your* slender shoulders now, old cock, eh? It will be
nice to know, though, that I shall have you here to background my intrepid exploits."

It was an illogical anger that took me this time to Mr.
Brewster's office. I felt as if a moral prop had fallen. I felt
deceived, betrayed, tricked into something against my will.

Mr. Brewster was imperturbable, and this time sentimental.

" You told me," I said, " that Gavin and I were classified
as reserved occupations. You insisted that——"

" Reserved occupations? The term is loosely defined." He
looked at me blandly. " And *we* must apply for withdrawal.
The onus is on *us*, you see."

" But you said Gavin's work was absolutely vital, and
that——"

" David, let me explain. Turley was very insistent about it.
I did not feel that we had the right to hold him back while we
have you here. I realise this will mean more work for you, a
greater responsibility will have to fall on your shoulders. It
will——"

" That's not the angle that upsets me, Mr. Brewster.
Excuse me, sir, but I *have* to say this. Gavin and I were doing
the same sort of work and——"

" I tried to dissuade him. I honestly did. I told him very
much what I told you, David, when you were in to see me
several weeks back. He was quite immovable. He has some
sort of ' call,' you might even say, some visionary thing
about it all." He gave a slight shrug, almost, I could not help
thinking, as if to imply that he had washed his hands of
Gavin Turley. " I cannot convey to you his obstinacy," he
said. " There was simply nothing I could do. I *did* make sug-
gestions, once I knew the chap was set on it. I would have
thought a commission, with his background . . . some useful
role where he could avail himself of his technical accomplish-
ments—censorship, say, public relations, even military intelligence. He would have none of that. It seems he must go
into the ranks. Well . . ." The slight, dismissive shrug was
repeated, and he put his fingertips together and stared down
at his desk. " David, this is a total war," he said very seri-

ously. "Every civilian organisation must make its sacrifices
in the cause. Let me say to you then, as man to man—and in
the strictest confidence—that if there has to be a question of
sacrificing Gavin Turley or of sacrificing David Meredith,
then we have no hesitation. To the *Morning Post* you are by
far the more valuable writer. To the overall war effort you
are the far more valuable asset. So there it is . . ." He looked
at me and smiled. "And since Turley's heart is set on it, well
. . . some rough campaigning might not do the chap all that
much harm, you know."

"Yes, but I think it still makes my position rather invi-
dious, and——"

"Nonsense! Why should it? Heavens above, boy, these
are early times yet. We've years ahead of us. Our own A.I.F.
has not yet fired a shot in anger. There'll be plenty of time for
you. But for the time being you are needed *right here*. Again
in the strictest confidence, there are things brewing for you.
Important things. You may be interested to know that your
name was mentioned only yesterday by the Chief of the
General Staff. There are things in the wind, David. Big
things in the wind."

He looked at me very carefully, as if waiting for me to say
something, but I remained silent. I felt intensely curious,
and I felt reassured, and I was no longer angry.

"David, my boy," he went on in a softer, mellower voice,
" do believe that I am acting in your interests, that I am doing
the best that is possible *for* you. I have a great personal fondness for you—I'm talking as a man, now, as a friend, not
merely as your editor . . . David, how long is it now . . . ten
years? . . . heavens it must be even more . . . that night when
I looked up from my desk to see some hoary old shellback
and there he was, this sixteen-year-old Ancient Mariner blushing to the roots of his hair, this Stunsail "—an affectionate
chuckle exploded from his bulk—" yes, there he was, a raw
lad, and I think I sized you up instantly, David. I do, you
know. I believe that from that very night I saw you as . . .
well, almost as my own protégé. And you can't say that I
haven't looked after you since then, can you? I have never
let you down, have I? And I shan't let you down. This you
must believe, my boy. You have come a very long way, you
know, since those Stunsail days. And you have a very long

way still to go. You could have a brilliant future. You could, one day, be sitting at this very desk. We have plans for you, David. *Great* plans. Don't worry, my boy. I shall never let you down, you can rely on that. And there will be all the time in the world for you to find the more obvious outlets for your patriotism. Great patriots have worn mufti too, you know."

I left his office with all my doubts allayed, and I was walking along the corridor to my room—I had my own room now —when one of the copy-boys came panting after me.

" Mr. Meredith," he called. " I took a phone-call for you while you were in with Mr. Brewster. I typed out the message," he said, handing me a slip of copy-paper with a few sentences of typescript amateurishly picked out on one finger. I took it from him and read:

10.12 p.m. Memo. Mr. D. Meredith. Your sister-in-law, Mrs. Sheila Meredith, telephoned to say your brother was seriously injured in an accident at camp. He was transferred to Caulfield Military Hospital. He is in Ward 12-F. Mrs. Meredith says it is serious but not critical.

In spite of my Defence Department special pass they would not let me see him that night, and all I could find out was that he had been brought down from Puckapunyal by ambulance, that the final medical report was still not in, and that it was " something to do with his leg."

Sheila was already at the hospital when I got there next day, sitting beside his bed in a long cool ward that opened on to a screened veranda. Jack's left leg was a hard bolster of plaster slung at an angle of thirty degrees from a scaffold-like contraption at the end of the bed. He looked cheerful, rueful, rather drawn, and happy to see me.

The accident had happened quite absurdly, it seemed, during a mock air-raid alarm two nights before, and Jack had been jumped on in a slit-trench by a crowd of other soldiers.

" So I've done my femur—that's the thigh-bone, isn't it?— although it's only a simple fracture, nothing complicated, they reckon, and then there's something about the pelvis . . . nothing broken, but cracked or something, they think, but I haven't heard about the X-ray reports yet. What a way for a bloody thing to happen, eh?" he said disgustedly. "Wouldn't it! You know, I've always said, haven't I, that if they sawed Mae West in halves I'd be the poor unlucky bastard who'd get the half that talks! And, do you know, Davy, I swear it was that little prick Dud Bennett that done it to me. On purpose, I mean. He's been dwelling on it for years, just to get me. They all came into that trench arse over tip, and then that Bennett came down on me like a bloody ton of bricks. He's been dwelling on me, I'll bet you a quid!"

"Well, a broken leg's not serious these days," I said comfortingly. "It'll take a bit of time, that's all."

"Yeah, that's all very well, but there's been the buzz around Pucka for days now that our pre-embarkation leave's due to come up any minute . . . five days they reckon, and then off."

"I haven't heard anything." I said this, too, to comfort him, because it was a lie, and I *had* heard.

He was probably in quite a bit of pain, because as he talked he would wince a little every now and then, and once Sheila reached over and took his hand and said, "Is it hurting, Jack?" and he grinned at her and said, "Only when I breathe."

Perhaps he sensed her anxiety and concern because he deliberately changed the subject, and began to be nostalgic about the old hospital. "You know, Sheil'," he said, "Davy might've been a bit small to remember this, but when we were little nippers we used to come here on Sundays to flog postcards for the Red Cross. We'd go all round the wards—you know they don't look much different now from the way I remember 'em—and all the visitors would sling us trey-bits and zacks and lollies . . . you'd remember those lollies, Davy? . . . the nullah-mullahs and silver sammies and liquorice-straps, and those violet crumbles you used to go for, and sometimes we'd get a whole box of columbine caramels. Cripes! we used to have a marvellous time here. Davy," he said, turning to me, "do you know there are blokes still here from *then*. There's a couple of old jokers in this ward, up that end there, they've been stuck in this place twenty-bloody-two years! And do they *perform*! Talk about a pair of bloody prima-donnas! They nearly drive the rest of us barmy. They never stop grizzling and whingeing, and they howl all night, always screeching for the bloody sisters or something, or they can't find their bedpans, or there's a draught blowing down their necks. They're a real bloody circus, those two!"

Mother, he said, had been to visit him before anyone else. "I hadn't been here half an hour and she comes puffin' in—well, she just lives down the road there, of course—and the funny thing was she was so bloomin' *embarrassed*. That's what tickled me. Just sat in that chair there knitting away like mad, and anyone comes near she's bobbin' up and down like a yo-yo, and going red as a beetroot and I tell you straight I thought she was going to curtsy to the ward orderly! Can you understand that? Sheil', Mum used to *run* this joint . . . she *did*, I tell you, she *ran* the bloody place! She was in there sawing off blokes' legs and arms, and lugging 'em home to stay, or what was left of 'em, I should say! No, she ran the whole bloody joint! Min the Merciless!"

His last comment was to Sheila. He gave a long, rueful look at the suspended plaster bolster and said, "Couldn't get me leg over you now, Sheil', could I? Looks as if you might be safe for the duration, eh? Righto, Jackie Meredith, hang it up in the rack there with the other old cues!"

I left with Sheila and offered to drive her home, but she said, "Thank you, Davy, if you could just drop me off at Saint Teresa's, that's the Catholic church down——"

"I know it," I said. "Jump in." We began to move off, and I said, "Well, what do you think of it all?"

For an appreciable interval she looked straight ahead through the windscreen. She was gripping the clasp of her handbag very tightly. "I'm pleased for me, of course," she said at last. "But I hate it for him." I studied her sidelong in the rear-vision mirror. Time was touching her, too, I saw . . . lightly yet, but there were little brushings of silver in the black, black hair, and there was something rather sweetly housewifely about that added matronly roundness that three children had given her, and about her simple serviceable clothes, too, and her shoes and her handbag and the rather shabby gloves she carried. I thought of Helen and her smartness and that slightly lacquered look she was beginning to get, and these two women were much of an age and yet so totally

different, and Sheila was still very pretty and not at all smart
—just a very pretty housewife in her thirties . . . and, in a way,
another reason to envy Jack, too.

" Davy," she said, " he's not going to get away, is he?"

" Now then, now then! " I reproved her lightly. " Careless
Talk Costs Lives. You've seen the posters. Troop movements
come very strictly under military security." Then I became
serious and said, " No, Sheila, not this time. Not with his
own crowd. That buzz he heard wasn't just a rumour ; they'll
be going any day."

" It'll break his heart when he knows," she said.

" Nonsense. He knows already that he can't possibly get
away with the first lot now. But there are other divisions.
There are three more forming right at this moment. Good
God, Sheila, they couldn't keep *him* out of it with wild horses,
you know that." I paused. " It isn't going to be easy for you
when he does go," I said gently.

" Oh, don't worry about me," she said. " I'll manage."

I let her out at the church, but I didn't drive off straight
away, and she turned and waved to me from the top of the
steps before she went into the dim, candle-lit interior, and I
drove off slowly, thinking what a warm, loyal, wonderful
woman she was, and I knew that I had been a little bit in love
with her ever since I had met her, and I knew that I would
be for as long as I lived.

CHAPTER 15

Helen took contagion from the war in her own special way.
The change in her was neither sudden nor really profound: in
fact, when you come to think about it quite dispassionately,
she grew to the fulfilment of her true role as *rightly* as Jack
had to his. It was and always had been her nature to be the
sort of woman she eventually became.

The first year of war, with its excitements and distractions
was important to each of us ; avoiding any open engagement
we were easing out of an uncomfortable situation with as
little fuss and friction as possible, dividing our unity almost

as a single-cell animal divides, by natural processes, without particular effort, without any declaration of intentions. We allowed ourselves, without resistance, to be parties to an applied pattern of change, and if it was protracted at least it was fairly painless.

She became in the end a very typical woman of the war. Later, on my journeyings, I was to see them everywhere: indeed, so alike did they seem, so interchangeable, from city to city, even from continent to continent, that I am inclined now to visualise them all in the exact image of Helen herself.

Always a woman in her early thirties, extremely attractive, fashionably dressed, groomed in a fine polished lacquered way—one always felt there had been a visit to the hairdresser that very afternoon, that the cosmetics were expensive and the lingerie glamorous, that the elusive perfume would have to be Chanel No. 5 or Schiaparelli's Shocking—invariably encountered at smart bars or in hotel lounges, in a beautiful suit and perhaps with a padded pompadour, with a glass in her hand and heavy bracelets jangling at her wrist. Always wearing a wedding ring, *always*. . . . And inevitably with officers in uniform. Gay, charming, vivacious, laughing—to cover some emptiness within? . . . one never really knew. . . .

Helen's transformation towards this sort of woman began quite early, about the time Wally Solomons went into khaki. Almost at once the parties she gave or attended were bigger than before, with a special titillation to them—she drank more than she had previously—and increasingly sprinkled with uniforms, mostly Wally's officer friends. But there were some surprises, too. Jerry Farley wangled some sort of commission and appeared as a lieutenant: the dull Justin Byrne, like many another bank teller, volunteered for the Air Force. After Gavin Turley had gone into camp at Darley I was the only one of the old set still wearing that Simpson suit and the Borsalino hat.

In my relationship with Helen it was inevitable, of course, that certain curious undertones should develop. I had never at any time discussed with her, other than superficially, the attitudes which either of us took towards the war, because to a very marked degree she seemed to have become almost apolitical, and appeared to have little or no interest in the developments in Europe. It was almost as if *her* war was confined to the Barracks, to familiar faces in familiar uniforms, to the heightened social gaiety which the times had forced. The question of whether I should or should not enlist was never debated between us. I think I felt that on the whole she was very content to leave things exactly as they were: she had a certain definite social standing as the wife of a journalist whose work was being talked about, whose name was appearing practically every day over important articles, and whose salary permitted her the parties and the clothes and the visits to the beauty parlour which were becoming increasingly necessary to her enjoyment. Even more so after Gavin's enlistment when, because of the extra work and responsibility, Mr. Brewster saw to it that I was promoted to the status of what used to be called a " super-senior," which meant that not only was my salary greatly increased, but it came now in the form of a monthly cheque paid into my banking account, and I no longer had to go to the counting-house every Friday and sign for a weekly envelope. Status has many symbols. Helen now had her own cheque-book. And since because of my work I was heavily involved with military staff-cars and taxis and trips away, the little red M.G. virtually became hers. Certainly *she* applied no pressure on me to enlist in the A.I.F. and begin the life of a zealous patriot at nine shillings a day. Yet there were times, I think, when she could not quite resist—perhaps because of her own new passion for uniforms—trying to score a little off my continuing civilian status.

I remember returning from the office one night to find Jerry Farley sitting in his shirt-sleeves in the lounge, and Helen in her sewing-room with his officer's tunic over her knees stitching new colour-patches to the sleeves.

" Why *you*?" I asked. " Can't Rene sew?"

She laughed softly. " It so happens he likes my needle-work," she said.

I was never really affected by any of her attitudes. In an odd way, our relationship had drifted back to something not unlike that which we had shared at Perce Parkinson's library, when I would join her for the almost casual affections and comforts and be both oblivious and heedless of any other exterior life which she might be leading. She continued to be perfectly agreeable and conscientious in carrying out all her wifely duties: if I was to be home for dinner it was always prepared and pleasantly served: if I sought the conjugal pleasures of the bedroom, she was willing, submissive, and as efficient as before. No more than that—but no less, either. . . .

But as time went on the situation took on queer little tones of surprise, especially after Wally Solomons went away. He was posted to the A.I.F. and went overseas in that first convoy that should have taken Jack—long afterwards I heard at the Barracks, that he became a full colonel in Palestine or somewhere, and they spoke highly of his brilliant organisation of desert transport—and after he had gone Helen and Sandra Solomons—and the red M.G.—were almost inseparable.

During this period I was usually working very late at the office, and was often away on trips for days at a time. It was odd to come home to Beverley Grove after midnight to find some hilarious party in full swing, with Sandra and Helen and young officers from L.H.Q. or the Navy or the Air Force, and young women I had never seen before: there would always be an embarrassing, halting moment when my appearance would be taken in critically, almost as if I were an interloper—and a sober one at that, and in civilian clothes!—and then Helen would run to greet me, and take my hands most affectionately, and make the introductions.

Still more surprising was the curious and often repeated experience of my chancing accidentally upon Helen and Sandra in the lounge of one of the smarter city hotels, Menzies or The Australia or the Old Treasury.

These were two distinctly beautiful women, and each time I saw them they seemed to have grown a little lovelier, a shade smarter, more "groomed," more sophisticated—both had acquired that bright almost indefinable air of women bent on gaiety and pleasure—and the usual admiring young officers would be with them. If I was beckoned over to join the group—and sometimes I was not—I would have the feeling of being almost a stranger—a stranger, I mean, to Helen—and the young men in their uniforms would be guardedly patronising because, I suppose, they could not be quite sure how important I was, or how influential with their superior officers at the Barracks, but also because of some uncertainty

they must have had about the personal situation that existed
between Helen and me.

To this day I do not know whether these gay encounters of
Helen's were innocent or guilty, because it never bothered me
to try to find out: an occasional little thought concerning
Jerry Farley would sometimes trespass, to be soon dismissed.
One thing I know—Helen always did seem very proud to
introduce me to her friends, so I suppose that was something. . . .

I was, in fact, more concerned about Jack than I was about
Helen.

He was not discharged from hospital until several months
after his division had sailed for overseas in the *Queen Mary*,
and although he was then declared fit for active service and
drafted to a base reinforcement camp, two more infantry
divisions went abroad without him, one to fight in Syria, the
other to be overwhelmed by the Japanese in Malaya. He
was constantly applying for a definite overseas posting, but
somehow he was always passed over. Then two months later
he was back in hospital with some complication concerned
with the pelvis injury.

When I visited him there he seemed cheerful enough, and
confident, and his talk now was all about tanks: he had
heard that Australian armoured divisions were being formed:
he would wink at me and hint at the " strings " he was pulling.
But his second discharge from hospital I think must have
carried with it evidence of some dubious medical risk, because
this time the Army seized upon his previous civilian employment as a factory storeman to transfer him to Base Ordnance
Stores. He had been promoted to the rank of corporal, and
he still wore his grey-bordered overseas colour-patches, and
although he was angry at delays and " Army red tape " he
was still perfectly confident of getting away. He had become
almost fanatical about his fitness. He had rigged up a
punching-ball in a corner of one of the ordnance depots, he
did special exercises which some physiotherapist in the hospital
had told him about, he dosed himself with tablets of calcium
and phosphorus because he believed it would help to strength-
en his bones. The armoured division was formed and left
him in the ordnance stores.

I am sure he was having more trouble with that game leg of his than he would ever admit, because he suffered some injury later when moving heavy ammunition cases, and was taken back to hospital again.

At the time this happened I was away on a very special assignment—a 15,000-mile tour of the entire Australian defence effort organised at the personal request of the Chief of the General Staff (the first of Mr. Brewster's "big things in the wind"), the object of which, in a long series of articles and a published book, was to stimulate recruiting. It was an assignment I greatly enjoyed and for which I have ever since been grateful. It is a good thing to have the privilege of discovering one's own country before seeing other parts of the world, the size of it, the loneliness beyond the cities, the beauty and the savagery, that frightening and desolate heart that is the well-spring of the myth. When I flew back from Darwin the newspapers were full of the first Australian victories in the Libyan Desert. And Jack was back in hospital.

He gave me a crooked little smile when I went to see him, and said, "So they took bloody Tobruk without me, eh? Those Grey Caps and Bludgers! You wouldn't read about it, would you?"

He did not seem quite as cheerful as before, and there was a sort of self-consciousness about him, as if he was embarrassed at my finding him in a hospital bed again, or because I thought him guilty of a physical weakness.

"It's all this bloody Army red tape!" he said with some heat. "There was nothing wrong with me all that time they kept me down in that reinforcement depot. There's nothing wrong with me *now*, if they'd only wake up to themselves! Jesus, you should've seen some of the bastards they sent away! I wouldn't have given 'em a gun to shoot wooden ducks in one of those Luna Park places! They shoved *them* off to North Africa, though."

I tried to cheer him up, and I told him something about my trip, especially North Australia and the Centre and the great military road they'd made running up from Alice Springs.

"You're a lucky bastard, seeing all that," he said. "I'd like to have a go up there myself one of these days. You

know, you're getting to be quite a big shot, aren't you?" he
went on. " I mean, all these trips you make, and those whacking great articles you write. The blokes here in the ward talk
about your stuff, you know. And they did down at the ordnance place . . . not only the boys, the officers too. You're
getting quite a reputation, aren't you?" He thought for a
while, and then he said, " Davy, doesn't it worry you a bit,
though? I mean, I know this stuff you're writing is important
and all that—well, people talk about it and it *is* for the war—
but like this trip of yours, going around the camps and
garrisons and things, doesn't it sometimes make you feel you
should be in it yourself?"

" Sometimes," I said.

" I mean, I'm not saying you're an *urger* or anything like
that, but this recruiting stuff, well, it *is* sort of urging in a
way, don't you think?"

" It has to be done," I said. " *They* want it. And somebody's got to do it."

" Oh, I know. And I realise it's bloody important and all
that. It's just . . . well, the way you feel about it yourself is
what I was thinking of."

" It doesn't worry me, if that's what you mean. This last
job, for instance, was practically under military orders. It was
the Chief of the General Staff himself who asked for me to do
it."

" Yes, I see what you mean." He nodded, although I had
the feeling that he didn't think his question had been
answered, and then he grew thoughtful, and seemed to hesi-
tate, and then, " Davy, there was something I was going to
ask you," he said. " You knowing all the brass-hats and the
skulls down at the Barracks, and that. I mean, I don't suppose you could pull some strings for me . . . to get me overseas, I mean? You'd have influence down there, wouldn't
you? That's all it would need, you know, I'm bloody sure of
that." He glanced at me quickly, and there was a tiny glint
of desperation in his eyes. " You see, they'll be shoving me
out of here next Monday," he said, " and I'm dead scared it
might be that ordnance thing again unless . . . well, you
know. . . ."

" Well, I'll see what I can do," I said.

I did nothing about it, though. I suppose I could have

tried to pull some strings, but somehow I thought it would be futile, and I was not entirely confident of my influence *within* the military structure, and anyway I had more important things to do. Jack went back to the ordnance depot.

I saw very little of him in the months that followed. A great many things were happening—defeat in Greece, defeat in Crete, the besieging of Tobruk, Syria, and there were a good many Australians there in the Battle of Britain—Justin Bryne among them—and the newspapers were filling up with casualty lists, and it was a war now, a real war, there was no doubt about it, and the hospital ships were coming back, and one began to remember again the things in our old hallway and in the drawer of the big wardrobe and the group snapshots on the front lawn and the mask of Gabby Dixon's face faint in the room-shadows and this was when the guilt began to creep in, not too disturbingly at first, but with a cruel stab to it in the office one night when there on the long spiked proof of one of the casualty lists from Greece and Crete, there was the name—somebody had ticked it with red ink— TURLEY, Lieut. Gavin J., with his VX number after it, among fifty or so other names listed under the cross-heading " Missing in Action."

I telephoned Peggy at once. She was crying. She was killed three weeks later when the Turleys' shabby little Baby Austin rammed a parked lorry in Brighton Road. The cadet-reporter who was covering the City Morgue on the day of the inquest told me that the pathologist's evidence made it unmistakably clear that Peggy had been very much the worse for drink, and there must have been some doubt in the coroner's mind because he brought in a finding of death by misadventure. The real tragedy of it all was that Gavin's escape from Crete was reported in the papers later that very same week.

These were the things that hurt, but the months dragged on and I still procrastinated with myself. There was a smell of defeat and disaster in the air—so soon, it seemed, after the Libyan victories, and deep down inside myself I was a prey to all the dark fears of my childhood, and I thought of death and of maimings and of ruined faces, and more and more I came to dread the prospect of being involved in it, and if conscience would stir or guilt prick me—without any sense of

duty or of patriotism, though—I would find myself resenting
the way I thought people were looking at me in the street, or
the innuendo I suspected in a conversation. It was, for me, a
restless, troubling, morbid time, and I was still unable to
bring myself to any point of decision that might force me to
exchange for uncertain jeopardies the security and the importance of the role I had. Even when the Japs came in and
the war moved closer, I could still not make up my mind.

In the end the problem, as usual, was taken out of my
hands. And again by Mr. Brewster.

The *Morning Post* had decided to appoint its own war correspondent, and I had been chosen for the job. "We all know,
David, how desperately you've wanted to get into the thick of
things," said Mr. Brewster with a pompous sincerity—he
even had his hand resting on my shoulder as he spoke—" and
your chance finally has come. We're sending you to New
Guinea. You must be ready to leave within forty-eight hours.
We've teed up everything for you . . . shots and vaccination,
kit and uniform . . . you have to report to the Barracks,
Room 27, Block J, for credentials, cap and shoulder badges.
. . ." I only half-heard what he said: I was stupefied by a
kind of raging, confused panic, in which relief, uncertainty,
fear, and despair were all present, and fragments of his conversation were woven without connection through a whirl of
thoughts gradually coalescing into a realisation of a fateful
finality . . . "need your measurements . . . tropical-weight
officer's uniform . . . in the event of your falling into enemy
hands you have, under The Hague Convention, the same
status as a major . . . you will be unarmed, of course. . . ."
Only his final remarks do I remember clearly:

"I'm confident this will be the beginning of a really
brilliant period for you. The war won't only be New Guinea,
you know. We've other irons in the fire, too. You'll travel.
You'll see things. You'll meet people. And it will be *after*
the war when you will really come into your own. So always
remember, David, that the only good war correspondent is a
live one. You'll be there to report the war, not to fight it.
Don't be impetuous or foolhardy. We want you back, you
know. We've plans for you."

The war correspondent badges were green-and-gold and

looked like pickle labels. I took them with the tropical-weight officer's uniform to Helen in her sewing-room.

"I like your needlework too," I said.

There was a coral reef outside the harbour, and a wrecked ship on it, and there were coconut palms growing here and there, but Port Moresby was drab, squalid, hot, and dusty, no more than a depressing suburb of the true tropical jungle. It had already been bombed pretty heavily by the time I got there, and the town itself had been abandoned and the liquor stores looted, and there were pieces of twisted corrugated iron and splintered plaster and smashed timber all over the main street, and the garrison was scattered and dispersed through nineteen miles of dreary scrubland.

The smell of defeat and disaster was much more pungent here, and I suppose this was understandable enough, for the place was undermanned and poorly equipped and a brooding sense of hopelessness prevailed everywhere in the heavy humid air.

I needed no infection from it, for my own mood was depressed, fearful, and demoralised enough. I felt myself to be an unwilling observer of an inimical situation in a hateful place. And I was deeply conscious of how inexperienced I was. I suppose it cannot but be disturbing to be the unarmed man among armed men, the untrained among trained men, the amateur among the professionals, to be a thing apart from the esoteric community, the outsider, the separate being.

They gave me quarters in a native hut with the Signals Officer, in a small clearing in the dusty scrub near the Military Intelligence Section, not far from a ravaged airfield littered with the burnt-out carcasses of planes. The garrison had virtually no air support whatever and only a few batteries of anti-aircraft guns, and the Japanese bombers would come over by day or by night almost without impediment, and we would scatter, cower in slit-trenches, hide in the undergrowth, cringe against the earth, and hate it.

At the beginning one was very conscious of being a nuisance, too. I am sure they tried very hard not to show it, but in the provision of quarters, a chair in the mess, the issue of some tropical equipment, there was a faintly grudging quality,

as if they resented having to do it for a non-combatant, a
civilian masquerading in khaki, an incubus forced upon them
by superior orders. Yet there was also an almost pathetic
desire on their part for the right sort of publicity, a wish to be
seen by the people " back home " not in the true sad hopelessness of their situation, but as men almost of heroic stature,
up against it, certainly, but steadfast and staunch, doughty
defenders of their native land.

It was not until much later that I realised how ideally fitted
I was for the role that had been forced upon me, for the
temper of the times, the machinery of military security, the
very atmosphere of New Guinea in those early, desperate,
embattled days, called for a deft duplicity. I was the perfect
person for the job that had to be done—a writer with what
Gavin Turley had defined as " flairs " and with tendencies
towards the unscrupulous. From the very beginning one was
committed to journalistic chicanery whether one wanted to be
or not.

Yet as one looks back on it now and very clearly sees the
difference between the picture as it actually was and the somewhat glorified picture that was conveyed back to the people
in mainland Australia, one also sees how desperately necessary the dishonesty was.

To Australians in those first two months of 1942 this was
no longer the mythic far adventure. The seemingly invincible
Japanese were swarming through the Pacific, bombs were
actually falling on Australian soil, and war was at the very
threshold. The mood at home, under the threat of that
Yellow Peril that had haunted the minds of three generations
of Australians, was very different from what it had been in
the earlier, brave, audacious days of the challenge from far
away, and darkened by the realisation that the country's best
fighting men—the hand-picked, the well-trained, the battle-
seasoned—were all still overseas, ten thousand miles away. . . .

It would never have done to have admitted the truth of
things, for the times were desperate and demoralising enough,
and New Guinea was the only bastion against invasion, and
so one painted a picture in vivid colours and larger than life
of this little tropical fortress of heroes, brave and unflinching
and undismayed under the blows of the arrogant, advancing

enemy. One did see heroic actions, of course—and in later months one was to see immeasurably more—and one did see bold efforts to cope with a situation which seemed hopeless and impossible and almost defeatist, yet the dispatches that went back under my name and the sweeping dateline of " Somewhere in New Guinea " gave only a false and highly tinted version of the truth. For morale at home and for security in the field there was, admittedly, nothing else that one could have done, but the falsity I built, or allowed to be built, around myself is perhaps less excusable. I wrote copiously and I wrote brilliantly and I wrote with all the practised " flairs " for which Gavin Turley had commended me, and I skulked and I dodged and I was desperately afraid, and I wrote myself into my own lie, the lie I had *had* to create, so that it was taken for granted that I was there, *right there*, in the thin red line of heroes, and gradually I picked up all the tricks of evasion and avoidance and wove them into an almost fool-proof pattern. I suffered nothing more than a spurious self-inflicted heroism. One has sometimes wondered since about the real truth of other Omdurmans and Agincourts. . . .

Towards the end of February I got a letter from my brother Jack :

Dear David,
  I am dropping you a line from Civvie Street just to let you know how all of us down here keep thinking of you in these difficult times. We read everything you write in the paper, and it seems you must be going through a pretty rough time up there. Sheil' burns a couple of candles for you every week at Saint Teresa's. (I don't know what good that's going to do you ! ! !) I just keep my fingers crossed and we all hope the Japs don't come down from Rabaul to have a bash at the place. I would give almost anything to be in it up there with you, but the trouble is my last medical board turned out pretty rotten for me and they say that for the moment I have been classified as unfit for overseas service. However, I have got two officers pulling some strings and I am confident that all will be well. Anyway it looks as if the thing

will be going on a good long while yet, thanks to our little friend Tojo, so while there's life there's hope and I keep up the old exercises like mad.

On the family front, you will be interested to know Bert is back in the Army again, driving a lift in a new building they have taken over for part of L.H.Q., with that old leg of his pinned up. Dad is trying to wangle himself into the V.D.C., that's this Home Guard thing they have started, and he might pull it off. Mum's Red Cross auxiliary has got so big they have moved into a church hall. Jean drives a staff-car for some brass-hats down at the Barracks. Marj has got herself engaged to a Navy chap in one of the corvettes, the *Bendigo*, I think. He seems a quiet decent sort of a chap. Reading back on this makes it sound as if I am the only drongo in the family, doesn't it?"

Incidentally, I just stopped Mum in time. She was sending some of those blessed balaclavas up to you and I told her you were practically sitting on the equator and she said yes, but it must get cold at night. Isn't she a real old card?

Sheil' is well, and the kids. We don't see much of Helen, but you would hear from her anyway. Well I believe that is about all the news as it leaves me at present. You take care of yourself. We are all very proud of you being up there in the front line of things. Even Dad does a bit of a skite about you every so often. So keep smiling, nipper. We are all with you in spirit, and I myself would give anything to be with you in the flesh too. We all send our love.

> I remain,
>> Your affectionate bro.,
>>> *Jack*

The letter had come in the dusk plane from Townsville, and after I had read it I went out into the little clearing between the huts and tents. The moon was up above the squat hills on the far side of the Seven-mile Airfield, a full moon, the bombers' moon, and there was a still, silvered, waiting look about everything, and even as I stood there I heard from the listening-post on the airfield the three repeated rifle shots which was the air-raid alarm because we had no sirens at that time.

The shots were taken up from hill to hill and through the scatter of the camp areas, and when the echoes of all these fusillades had died away I could hear the high faint whiningly uneven drone of the Mitsubishis coming closer above Laloki Gorge, and then the searchlights were cutting blue-white channels in the dark sky, stretched right out up towards the sound, arcing, swaying, searching, probing, meeting and parting, meeting again, locked at last on a moving silver glitter like a single trapped insect. Then other searchlights came in, and the glitter became a triangle and then a diamond, a cheap bauble of costume jewellery, of marcasite, pinned to the purple velvet of the sky, and ruddy hard flashes were shuddering along the hills as the 4.7 Militia batteries opened up, and rubies pricked the sky sharply around the high inexorably moving lozenge lodged in the holding beams of light. There were other dronings coming in from the reef and over the stilt-village of Hanuabada, and from the west too. It was to be a big raid. Behind me I could hear the boots pounding in the huts and the clink of steel helmets, and dark figures were scurrying everywhere in the scrub, running for the slit-trenches.

I had Jack's letter crumpled in my hand, and for some reason I didn't want to go back for my own steel helmet, and I didn't want to run for the shelter of the trenches, and I just wanted to stand there watching it all for the great and terrible beauty that was in it: because I wanted Jack to be there in my place, not from cowardice this time, but because I felt he had earned the right to it and I had not, and I found myself wishing suddenly that a younger brother could claim an older brother.

The dronings had become a roar now, throbbing and terrifying, and the salvoes of the batteries were slapping at the air, and I heard the thin tight whistle of the falling bombs, and I was running, falling, crawling, pressing my face against the earth and the twigs and the soft damp leaves, and some dry scaly insect scrabbled against my mouth then burrowed away.

CHAPTER 16

I stayed in New Guinea, on and off, for about a year longer, evading or avoiding when I could, getting back to the comforting fleshpots of Townsville or Brisbane whenever the chance offered. (Correspondents' dispatches then were always datelined " Somewhere in the South-west Pacific," so nobody could be really sure *where* you were writing from, and I know of many a jungle skirmish that was covered vividly from the bar of Lennon's Hotel, in Brisbane, nearly two thousand miles away!)

It was a pretty savage year of war for the fighting men, though. The veterans of the Expeditionary Force came back from North Africa—those who were still alive and not in prison camps—and they changed their uniforms from desert-khaki to jungle-green and were thrown almost at once into the tangled rain-forest of tropical, mountainous New Guinea to try and halt the Japanese advance towards Port Moresby. Air support did come eventually. The Americans sent squadrons of Kittyhawks, and when they were wiped out they sent squadrons of Marauders, and when they were wiped out they sent squadrons of Lightnings, and they sent Flying Fortresses and Liberators and Mitchells, and although there were a lot of Americans and Australians who were dead at the end of it, the Japanese were finally beaten in the air.

And Guadalcanal was fought and the Battle of the Coral Sea and the bitter, brutal campaign of the Kokoda Trail, and the beaches were swept clean at Buna and Gona, and retreat became victory and for the first time the Japanese were being beaten back and back and back. It was a costly and merciless war in that jungle-fighting year, but victory did come out of it—and so did a greatly enhanced reputation for David Meredith.

From the hindsight of a much wider experience I suppose now I would classify that David Meredith of the New Guinea days as middling honest, as war correspondents go, and perhaps no more cowardly than a good many others—

there were really brave ones too, of course—and perhaps there are extenuating circumstances in this curiously isolated role which the unarmed, non-combatant, untrained reporter has in war. He is, after all, a free agent: he is under no direct orders, he may come and go more or less as he chooses, pick his own vantage-points, decide the measure of his involvements. I have wondered sometimes since if all soldiers, however gallant, would remain in their positions, fighting back, if the choice to be there or not to be was in their own hands. . . .

At any rate, I looked after myself as carefully as I could, and if there were unavoidable little periods of direct involvement I sedulously tried to observe Mr. Brewster's instruction, and I stayed alive. I never walked the Kokoda Trail, although I did walk some of it: I saw something of the fighting at Buna and Gona, but my visits there were short. In a sense these were no more than the necessary skirmishes made to pick up the vibrant colour, the human textures, that would be woven into the more detailed and more comprehensive pictures of the struggle which could only be done competently—or so I was able to convince myself—from some base headquarters far behind the fighting front. I remember that once Gavin Turley's words recurred to me: "You will wonder how you will pillage it and what trophies you will find. . . ." Well, I raided my little settlements and by the time I returned from New Guinea my reputation stood higher than ever before. My dispatches were admired, syndicated, published abroad. If you are given the privilege of having your name in the papers every day, and on your own terms, deception and self-aggrandisement are easy arts to practise.

Coming south through the cities again was a strange experience. So much had changed in that time I had been away. One saw women in uniform everywhere, and Americans in their thousands, and one could pick the men back from New Guinea by the atebrin-yellow of their complexions, and the taxi-drivers had grown ruder and more unscrupulous and shopkeepers greedier, and black markets were booming everywhere, and yet the very air was alive and vibrant and charged with presage. It was not the same as the atmosphere of 1939, for it seemed to me that there was some sense of innocence lacking, and yet there was another dynamic element in it of success and accomplishment, and a rapidity about everything that had not been there before, as if the coming of the Americans had somehow quickened the tempo of life.

Mr. Brewster had arranged certain engagements for me before my return—guest speaker at a Rotary Club luncheon, an important dinner at the Constitutional Club, a meeting with Legacy, some morale-building lectures to home defence units organised by the Army Education Service.

Helen, as might have been expected, had a party to celebrate my return, at which I had distinction now, even among her officer friends, most of whom were of an older group than before, and of higher rank. There were quite a few Americans among them, most of them Air Force although one was a colonel of Marines.

I noticed that she smoked only American cigarettes now, and there was a good deal of American idiom in her speech, and this made me wonder a little because in the letters which she had sent me every week during my absence—always affectionate and sometimes even tender—she had never mentioned having American friends. The party was lavish, with lots of bourbon and rye and Scotch, and it occurred to me that Helen had probably suffered very little from the rationing and the war-time austerities because her officer friends would have been generous to her, and I remember that Sandra Solomons was brought to the party by an American lieutenant-colonel from MacArthur's staff, and she was not brought from the house opposite us but from a flat in St. Kilda Road. Wally was away in North Queensland somewhere, and I was only in Melbourne for a week and I never found out whether they were divorced or had separated or what. Much later, when the war was over, other people were living in the house across from us in Beverley Grove. And I don't think I ever did bother to ask Helen what had happened.

On the following day I took Jack and Sheila to lunch at The Australia.

Sheila was as pretty as ever, and neat in her " best black," and again a little older, and there was some look about her that made me suspect she might be pregnant. It was Jack who had really changed, though. He no longer looked *young*, that was the first thing I noticed, and there was a sort of shamed, almost furtive look in his eyes, and lines around them that had not been there before. He wore sergeant's chevrons on his tunic now, but I noticed he had taken off his overseas colour-patches. He had given up rolling his own cigarettes and he chain-smoked full-strength Capstans from the brown packets, and he smoked them very quickly and nervously, almost tugging at them. We were not done with the hors-d'œuvres when I began to understand the rage of desperation that possessed him.

"Now listen, Davy," he said, leaning across the table at me, keeping his voice low and taut, "this time you've got to do something, sport. By Christ you *have*! You can pull some strings, you know you can!" He was suddenly aggressive and accusing, and Sheila looked nervously from his face to mine and moved her hand across as if to pacify him, but he shook his head quickly, without looking at her, still fixing me with stern, blaming eyes, and said, "No, I'm going to say it. Been bottling it up too bloody long as it is. Davy, you could have done something that last time I asked, you know you could, and I don't think you did, did you? I could have got away to New Guinea if you'd only tried for me. You were up there, for Christ's sake, you must have seen some of the drongos, the Chockos, they *did* send, that time when the Japs were pushin' through. You know——"

"Jack, I did what I could!" I protested. "But it isn't for me to decide who——"

"You can't say I haven't *tried* to get away, can you?" he demanded angrily. "Do you bloody well realise what my VX number is? Jesus, I was there on the first day, wasn't I? And I've sat here on my arse in Melbourne ever since! Three whole bloody years! Do you know how many days there are in three years? One thousand and ninety-bloody-six! . . . I've counted them and there was a Leap Year in that and I've counted that one in too! And what do you think *I* felt like down here during that Owen Stanley thing? . . . shovin' off the stuff for them—Owen guns and Sten guns and Brens and bloody ammunition and mortars and shells and things! And look where they've *been* while I've been sitting on my backside down here wrappin' up parcels like some flamin' counter-jumper in the haberdashery at Myer's! They've been all over bloody New Guinea and they've been to Syria and Greece and Crete and Abyssinia and Malaya and Java and

Timor, and El Alamein and Bardia and Derna and Benghazi and Tobruk! Jesus Christ, Davy, a little squirt like Dud Bennett got himself *killed* at Tobruk, didn't he? While I sit here on my arse for three flamin' years——"

His voice had risen in his passion and he stopped suddenly, flushed and aware that the waiters and the people at the other tables were turning and looking. " Excuse me," he mumbled awkwardly, and pushed his chair back, and rose. His face was crimson and there was a nerve twitching in his cheek. " I got to go and splash the boots," he said. " Be back in a jiff."

I watched him go through the tables, tall and loose-moving in his khaki uniform, and then I turned and I saw Sheila, with the tears pouring down her cheeks, not even trying to hide them, and her fingers trembling on a wadded handkerchief.

" In all my life I've only loved this man," she sobbed in a choking whisper, " and I can't *bear* it, Davy! I can't bear to see him ashamed! Jack! Jack of all men to be *ashamed*! You have to try for him, Davy! You *have* to!"

" But, Sheila, I——"

" You *must*, Davy!" she insisted. " This time you've got to try for him. He . . . I think he'll go mad if you don't."

I realised that for once Sheila could *not* manage, and perhaps that was the most heartbreaking thing of all. . . .

The thought of Jack haunted me for the rest of the afternoon, and a curious little coincidence occurred to sharpen it all up, because I was committed to one of the Army Education lectures which Mr. Brewster had arranged, and the staff-car came and I was driven to an anti-aircraft training camp, and it was on the golf links where Jack and I had played as children, and the actual gun-site was located around that very mound where the two of us had once pretended to be Everest mountaineers.

The top of the mound had been scooped out and sandbagged to make instrument pits, and arced around were the four big gun-pits with the lean long graceful 3.7 barrels nosing up, and beyond that was barbed wire and outside the wire were green level patches where some late-afternoon golfers were playing. From the instrument pits cement steps led down through sandbags to the plotting room, a strange

science-fiction cave buried deep in that unimpressive little
knoll whose rough skin of onion-grass and dandelions had
never betrayed even the smallest hint of its future to the two
small boys who had rolled and climbed on it so many years
before.

The funny thing was that the unit was composed largely of
women, the A.W.A.S., who were taking over home defences
at that time so that the men could move up to the forward
areas, and this was the first chance I had had to really look at
them, and I remember being amused at the way they deliberately copied the loose, lounging look of Australian soldiers,
and at their strained overalls and casual battle-blouses, and
at the obvious suspicion with which they, as gunners, regarded
me. After I had given my talk the battery commander took
me on a tour of inspection.

He was a lieutenant, only lately promoted from W.O., not
quite young, with a long pale sheep's face and fair woolly
hair like unscoured merino clippings, and mournful yellow
eyes. There was a shamefaced, diffident air about him. I
could not decide whether he really did want to get away to
the war—he kept telling me this—and accordingly resented
the job of having to train these women, or whether he just
thought there might be something disgraceful to be discovered
if he didn't keep his distinguished visitor on the move.

At any rate, he kept talking quickly and nervously as he
walked me around, and then we came to Number 3 gun-pit
and surprised five girls cleaning ammunition, and I said to
the lieutenant, "Well, it's nice to see that a woman's place is
still with a duster in her hands!" but even as I spoke I was
conscious of a pair of marsh-green eyes, cloudy and a little
scornful, and of a grubby hand pushing a book surreptitiously
between the grass and the sandbags, and I knew that the
lieutenant was just as aware of the eyes as I was, and more
nervous than ever in case his awareness should be detected. I
suspect, anyway, that this prompted him to seize upon the
excuse of an old D.C.3 coming in from the east towards
Laverton to insist upon a mock "action" for my benefit.

The alarms shrieked and men and girls came scrambling
from everywhere, and the girl with the green eyes grabbed a
tin hat from the sandbags and legged it out of the gun-pit and
up the rise to the instruments, and I reached over and took

the book out from behind the sandbags to see what it was. *Tristam Shandy*. I put it back in its hiding place and followed the lieutenant to the top of the mound.

It was a good, efficient demonstration as demonstrations go, although it was very odd to hear the clear young girl voices calling the old familiar action cries that I had heard in quite different circumstances. *On* target! . . . height-finder on *target* . . . a lapse, a frantic traversing of the predictor, the telescopes elevating, the lean gun-barrels following the predictor telescopes, swinging ahead of the lumbering D.C.3, the triumphant yells: *On target . . . predictor on target! . . . Fire!* And I saw that the sheep-faced lieutenant could not keep his eyes off the girl on the Number One telescope and that her bottom was fairly jiggling. *Tristam Shandy*, I thought, and suddenly I wanted to laugh out loud.

I watched the girl and I watched the lieutenant watching the girl with his lugubrious yellow eyes, and thought how transparent the poor bugger was, and he said, " Did we get him, Gunner Morley?"—speaking almost in spite of himself, as it were—and she said, " In *flames!*" and added, " Sir," as if it were an afterthought, and there was still this incredible sense of excitement about her, like a child playing at soldiers, and I found myself thinking that she might break into a jig at any moment, and only then did it occur to me that she was showing off a little, and for my benefit, and I realised that she was eyeing me obliquely and that there was a speculative smile touching her wide silky mouth and that she was the youngest thing I had ever seen in my life.

" Well," I said, taking advantage of my V.I.P. standing, " that was a very efficient show, Gunner——?"

" Morley, sir!" she returned briskly. " Instrument specialist "

" And does Gunner Morley, instrument specialist, also happen to have a first name?" I said, deliberately teasing her.

" Yes, sir," she said, and her eyes were as cool and deep and clear as the reef seas and her mouth lifted its wide ripply corners, almost tremulously, as if she might really burst into laughter from sheer happiness. " Cressida, sir," she said. . . .

Cressida Morley, there in a gun-pit on that same scraggy little hill where I had come as a child looking for adventure

. . . another of life's strange tangents. I have a snapshot that
must have been taken of her at about that time, for in it she
is still a gunner and the instrument specialist's badge is there
on her sleeve, but I hardly need it to remember that first
meeting, although it does confirm the thought I did have
then, that all her features were too big for her, as if she had
not really grown into them yet. (She was only a couple of
months past eighteen at that time, and in fact she did not
realise her full beauty until she was almost thirty.) Her
broad, sun-freckled brow looked too wide, her cheekbones
too heroic, and she wore her extraordinary mouth and eyes
like finery she was not quite sure of and was trying to be
nonchalant about. Nor, in those days, was anything quite
under control, neither eyes nor mouth, nor the contralto voice
that was also too big and with a husky lilt to it, nor the body
in that ridiculous stained battle-dress, still with a child's
gawkiness about it . . . she seemed to have no breasts at all,
but her shoulders were broad and her hips lean, and with the
gawkiness she had a certain quick, boyish grace. Boy's hands,
too, square and brown and muscular and grubby. And even
if nothing of all this was under control then, there was a sense
of vital power about her, as if she were practising with
everything all at once and on any person available. The
sheep-faced lieutenant, for instance. And certainly me!

Perhaps he sensed this, because he dismissed her rather
peevishly, and I said to myself, " You poor devil, she's going
to make mincemeat out of *you*!" and at once the thought was
followed by an absurd little twinge, almost of jealousy, as if
that might be a fate unique, and even enviable.

She saluted with an exaggeration of smartness and gave me
one great green luminous glance and turned smartly and
marched off, and her bottom wiggled impudently, and for a
moment I honestly expected her to turn and put her fingers
to her nose and then run for her life.

" Well, that certainly is a pert, efficient young lady . . ." I
began tentatively, but the lieutenant had grown morose and
wouldn't rise, and he just grunted and led me off and we had
a drink in his quarters before the staff-car came to take me
away. Outside a team of men was playing basketball against
a team of girls. She had taken her battle-dress off and was

leaping and running, quick and skilful, in a khaki shirt and shorts. She did have breasts after all, like little muscles high on her broad boy's chest. . . .

Colonel Brindsmead, the headquarters medical officer, was waiting for me in his office when I called next morning, tall and brown-skinned, with a clipped grey moustache, and blue overseas service chevrons on his sleeve and the 8th Army clip on the ribbon of his Africa Star, and he shook hands cordially and came directly to the point.

" Sit down, Mr. Meredith," he said. " I sent for his files after you phoned me, and I have gone through them, and we shouldn't have to waste much of your time." He put his fingertips together and looked at me across them from steady steely eyes. " In a word," he said, " it's hopeless."

I stared down at my own hands, not quite knowing what to say, and he waited a moment or two before he spoke again. He opened the pink folder on his desk first, and moved his fingers through some papers.

" This VX number he has, can that be right?" he said.

" Yes," I said. " He enlisted on the first day."

" Hmmm! It *is* very basic, I must say. Which makes it all the more bloody for him, I suppose. Unfortunately, it's perfectly obvious from these histories that not only is overseas service quite out of the question for your brother, but that strictly speaking he should be out of the Army altogether."

" But he's been trying to get away since 1939 and——"

" He *can't* get away, my dear chap! He's not fit. We only give the privilege of dying to the physically fit, Mr. Meredith."

" It's not a question of dying, Colonel. There are safe places in operational areas, ordnance bases, stores, L. of C. units, all——"

" Mr. Meredith," he said patiently, " you telephoned to ask me to find out whether I could help this brother of yours. I have gone into the matter thoroughly. *And* sympathetically, Mr. Meredith, I assure you of that, because I was away with the Sixth Divvy and I believe I know exactly how he feels. And there is nothing that can be done. Simply nothing. I am very sorry, but there it is."

"Going through those records of his, was there any point where he might have got away?" I asked.

"In fact there was, yes. I made some jottings." He took up a small scribbling-block. "He could have got away right back there in '40," he said. "After his first discharge from hospital."

"Then why was he kept here?"

The colonel shrugged. "There could have been many reasons. Drafts may have been filled. He was in a reinforcement depot, not on a divisional strength. Just overlooked, perhaps. And don't forget there's always an invisible question-mark over a chap just out of hospital, however clean his papers." He consulted the pad again. "Remember, also, that during this time we embarked three other infantry divisions, *and* corps troops, within the space of only a few months. Easy enough in that confusion for one solitary private to be mislaid. Incidentally, he could be jolly thankful he *didn't* get away, you know. On the dates and figures he would almost certainly have gone with the Eighth Div. And nobody knows what's happened to those poor devils, what? We hear these frightful stories from Malaya and the atrocities along this Burma-Siam railroad. Probably never see any of those poor bloody wretches again. I take it, Mr. Meredith, you would hardly wish that sort of fate on your brother."

I shook my head. "Was there any other chance for him? . . . I mean, I thought you implied——"

"Yes, there was. His *best* chance oddly enough. I say that because this was when his medical classification was definitely below par . . . that would have been any time, say, between latish '41 to the middle of '42, at the time of his last re-transfer from hospital back to ordnance. Well, the Japs were pressing us, we were desperately short of trained man-power, a chap didn't have to be a hundred per cent then to be thrown in to hold the fort. It was a very sticky time, and one was obliged to wink a blind eye at certain breaches of conventional procedure."

"Well, in this case, couldn't that be done again?"

"It would be more than my job was worth to even suggest that your brother was fit for active service, Mr. Meredith, let alone to recommend it. Because this is not a matter merely of *now*, you see . . . the future is involved, pension claims, repatriation, all manner of things that are quite outside my province. I am terribly sorry about this, but absolutely nothing can be done."

"Are you the final arbiter on this, Colonel Brindsmead?" I asked.

"What do you mean?"

"I mean, supposing I were to go to . . . well, to a higher echelon, let us say, and——"

"And what, Mr. Meredith?"

"And get an order that said Sergeant Jack Meredith, A.I.F., was to be posted to an operational area regardless of all other considerations," I said. I was really an urger now.

He looked at me for a long time with no expression on his face. In the end he said, "I could oppose the order. Or being a soldier, I could obey it, coming from a superior officer. But I'll tell you this—I should make perfectly sure that I had several copies made of that directive, and I should very carefully file them away against any possible future contingency."

I did go to my higher echelon—some articles of mine had helped him very much during a certain earlier crisis in military politics—and before I left the Barracks I rang Jack and suggested that he meet me at the Saracen's Head, in Bourke Street.

He was already there by the time I got to the bar, in a blue haze of cigarette smoke, with the two pots of beer already lined up on the counter.

"Hallo, nipper," he said, trying to sound casual. "How did you go?"

"I wangled something," I said, "but I don't know how you'll like it."

"Yeah?" he said, almost as if his lips could hardly move in the stiff face watching through the blue haze of smoke.

"It's not what *I* wanted," I said defensively. "I pushed all I could for New Guinea, but they just won't come at it." I lowered my head, fingering the froth off my beer, because I could not look at him, knowing that he could have been in New Guinea had I tried for him when he had first wanted me to. "You know, your medical record is really pretty bloody wobbly. So New Guinea's out."

"Well, thanks for trying." His words were toneless, like a

man speaking from a trance, his face was set and waiting and coiled around with smoke.

"Anyway, you wanted me to pull strings, and I did," I said, almost aggressively. "I went right up top. To the Deputy C.G.S., if you want to know. I'm well in with him. So. Well . . . the upshot is you're to be posted to Northern Territory. Darwin. It's a job of salvaging army vehicles that have been left behind, getting them into a central transport pool and all that." I was talking quickly, talking down at the pot of beer, afraid to look up and face the disappointment in his face. "I know it's not an operational theatre any longer, but it's a wonderful bloody place, Jack, and you'll love it up there, I *know* you will. And you'll be up and down the North-South Road . . . you'll see Alice Springs and Barrow Creek and Bonney's Well and the Devil's Marbles and Tennant and——"

I had to turn and meet his eyes then. They were shining.

"And north from Birdum, that's marvellous country, Jack!" I hurried on in a sudden welling of relief and enthusiasm. "You'll get to the big cattle stations, and there's Adelaide River and the Katherine and along the Roper . . . and Darwin itself, of course . . . that's a fascinating place."

"Oh, I know! Darwin, yeah . . . well, they were pretty badly bombed up there . . I mean, they were *in* it, weren't they?" He was all smiles, radiant in his mist of smoke, and his air of desperation had vanished and his eyes were the eyes of that younger Jack, the eyes that had always met things square on. "*Jesus*, I'm grateful to you, Davy," he said. "You know, you doing this for me. . . ."

"Well, I would have preferred it to be New Guinea, of course, but——"

"Oh, balls to *that*! Christ, you don't have to worry about that, nipper. I mean, once I'm up *there*, well that's more than half the battle, isn't it? I mean, it's a jumping-off place . . . well, you're practically *there*. There'll be lurks, you'll see. . . . I mean it's only a hop-step-and-a-jump from there to New Guinea, anyway, and I'm a pretty good sort of a lurk-merchant, you know! Christ, if I can't find some strings to pull once I'm that bloody close well my name's not Jack Meredith! Davy, I can't tell you how bloody grateful I am. . . ."

And suddenly he was shuffling around me, shaping up, sparring, in that crazy little parody of a boxing bout, feinting and jabbing, just as he had on my wedding day—only a shade more stiffly now, I thought—and then he stopped suddenly and slapped me on the shoulder and burst into laughter, and said, " Those army quacks ought to have a talk to Sheil'. I mean, she's up the duff again, you know. Why don't they go and ask *her* what's wrong with that pelvis of mine!"

And then he was away again, moving back on those quick nimble feet of his, feinting a right, tilting his head to dodge an imagined left hook, then coming in at me with a tattoo of short-arm jabs.

I had gone from Melbourne within twenty-four hours, and it was to be more than two years before I saw Jack or any of them again.

Mr. Brewster insisted on taking me to lunch at the Savage Club for my final briefing, and it was funny to be walking up with him past the old factory of Klebendorf and Hardt's. One frontage was boarded up and it was in process of demolition, and there was a big sign on one wall that said WHELAN THE WRECKER IS HERE. There were only some iron girders where the old studio had been but one of the retaining walls was still standing, and where the wallboard hadn't torn away the old posters were still there, York Minster and the Brangwyn bridges and even a part of Jane Avril's leg. . . .

I was to go first to the United States, because Mr. Brewster had arranged for me to get a general accreditation to all theatres of war, and this had to be picked up in Washington, and he said, " We want you on the move, David, watching events, meeting people, absorbing background. Getting around, David, that's it. *Getting around!* Don't hurry out of the States, mind you: that's more and more becoming the vital nerve-centre of the whole global picture. Make contacts. Yes, *contacts*, they'll be priceless later. You'll be getting directives from us from time to time, of course, but very often you will have to be your own judge of where to go, what to cover, who to see. We want the war, of course—those vivid descriptive pieces of yours, that human interest stuff you do so brilliantly, but now your canvas, David, is to be the whole world at war. Not just New Guinea, but *the whole world.* I told you this long ago. And I have not let you down, have I? I said there were big things in the wind for you. And now to my final point—and this, in many respects, is the most important aspect of all—you must always bear in mind that we are far less interested in your day-to-day reporting than in the background which you will bring back for later. After the war is over we want you back here, David, as our first-hand reference—on places, on people, on events, on political situations . . . our chart, you might say, for the historic currents of our times. We are putting a good deal of our future into you, young Meredith."

I carried out his mandate. I flew across the Pacific to San Francisco, and then on to New York and to Washington, and I followed his advice and I didn't hurry out of America, because I found it a pleasant war there, and I had two or three affairs with attractive and accommodating women, and I was able to get a book finished and published successfully enough for another to be commissioned, and even when I finally did pull myself away my luck stood by me.

I left Norfolk Roads in a convoy which was supposed to take me across the North Atlantic to the Oran landings, but a hurricane caught us the second day out, ships and escorts were scattered, two vessels foundered in the storm, and the freighter I was in was damaged and we had to put into Guantanamo Bay, in Cuba, and after this a Dutch corvette from Curaçao took me down to Panama, and in a bar in Cristobal one night a genial American tanker captain who was taking his ship to Venezuela suggested that I come along so I went to Caracas just for the fun of it. It was all more colourful and exciting—and safer, of course—than the North African landings turned out to be, although in this case that hurricane had been to blame and the evasion was not deliberate on my part. The interlude enabled me to get the second book finished, and when it was published later it was quite a success.

I did travel widely once this first adventure was over, both to the obvious places and to the not-so-obvious places, because by this time it *was* pretty much a whole world at war, and if colourful copy was wanted and Mr. Brewster's " background " for later, then there was almost nowhere that you could not go. So I was in the obvious places, like

London and Rome and Athens and Cairo, and all over the
Near East, and Iran and India and Burma and Ceylon and
China, but I fitted curious illogical things in too, like being
in Katmandu and looking at the rhododendron forests, or
watching the camel caravans from Bokhara and Samarkand
on the Old Silk Road coming through the Gobi Desert with
sacking bales ridiculously stamped USE NO HOOKS, or riding
in a jeep out beyond the Khyber Pass on the road into
Afghanistan, or talking to old Amami the ivory-planter in a
splashing courtyard in Isphahan, or watching the Russians
occupying an airfield in Rumania, or riding in a junk through
the Yangtze gorges. And when I could I fulfilled little secret
private missions, too, and I went up the Nile just to see that
great temple of Queen Hatshepsut, the inscriptions from
which I had once traced so meticulously on the cover of a
sketch-block, and I marvelled at the mysterious beauty of it
against those huge fissured sandstone cliffs, although it sad-
dened me a little that I could no longer read the hieroglyphics.

There were battles that I saw, too—the " Box " at Imphal,
and the crossing of the Chindwin with the Indians and the
British, the assault beyond the Salween with the Chinese, the
fighting for the Ledo Road in North Burma with the
Americans, and with the Americans again and the New
Zealanders in the struggle for Florence, and with the Gurkhas
at Mandalay, and as I set it down it all sounds that much
more intrepid than it really was, for these were my skirmishes
too, and there was more of the " getting around " that Mr.
Brewster wanted than there was of shot and shell, and more
luxury hotels or comfortable officers' transient quarters than
camps and bivouacs, and far more bars than battles.

One learned much in the bars, in fact, and I was able to
sharpen many fine professional skills through my meetings
with other correspondents, some of them the ones with the
really big reputations, bigger reputations, in fact, than the
generals had they wrote about and called by first names—the
men of great standing who had written books and graduated
beyond mere eye-witness demands and who sat in bars with
the impassive majesty of Buddhas in temples, big and intimidating, buying highballs and signing chits, and sucking brains.

I met them and learned from them, and I met Prime
Ministers and Presidents and great generals and admirals and

statesmen and leaders, and I walked in the rain with Gandhi under a black umbrella, down to the white-robed hordes on the banks of the Jumna, and I met film-stars and the figures of popular excitement, and I met eager unstable women in flirtations and brief liaisons and quick hot affairs, and I met Helens everywhere. . . .

It was queer about these Helens, these facsimile substitutes for my own wife, for in meeting them I began to realise how very pleasant she must be out there in faraway Australia for the bright and momentary company she would offer: and they kept occurring and recurring with me as my staging-posts to somewhere—at the garden bar of Maiden's in Old Delhi or the Galle Face in Ceylon, in the smart street cafés along the bright curve swinging up Vittorio Veneto, at Groppi's on Melika Farida, at the Savoy Bar in London—and they were the same women, really, as the ones I had met in the cocktail-bar of the Pierre on Fifth Avenue or at the Twenty-one or at the Statler in Washington. I drank with so many of them, and I laughed with them, and was refreshed by the undemanding vivacity of their companionship, and I saw how essentially these Helens were a part of war. I slept casually with a number of them, and always after I had done this I would go to one of the smart shops, or to a bazaar if it was in the East, and I would buy some special present to send to Helen—a length of silk or of brocade, ear-rings perhaps, or a bracelet of black silver. . . .

Through all these experiences I could feel my own growth, a development, a new sophistication, so that the casual conquests were never difficult. I saw that the very singularity of the uniform and the badges *did* give a special sort of glamour (it was a word much in use at that time), the very fact of separateness, of not belonging to the unified structure of things, a kind of adventuring and different individuality. But this isolation from the corps, the organised unit, the cohesive groupings of war, created periods of oppressive loneliness, too—of birthdays and anniversaries and carnival moments uncelebrated in impersonal hotel rooms in friendless places, of dull waitings on alien airfields, of sad and solitary debauches in strange bars—and there were many times when I thought this romantic world-wandering life was in some way very like those lonely Sundays of my early youth when, solitary and unsure, I would wander around the Melbourne wharves, searching for the bright little fragments of beauty and of colour, and I imagine this must have been the mood that was on me on that afternoon when I landed on Capodochino airfield, coming in from Bari, with a black storm boiling over Vesuvius, and it was too late to get on to Rome and the tempest, anyway, was raging all the way along the Apennines, and so they quartered me for the night in the transient billets, which were at Caserta, in the palace of the old Kings of Naples, and they gave me a splendid room with marble walls and a marble floor which was ice-cold as a tomb.

I stayed there only that one night, frozen and sleepless, and so I remember it only sketchily. The room was very much in the grand manner of the Bourbon Baroque, and it was sixty-eight feet long and thirty-six feet wide—I paced it out as a way of keeping warm—and the ceiling was wholly and floridly frescoed with Tritons and Dryads and allegorical figures in golden breast-plates and plumed helmets, and there was a bad lithograph on one wall of some obscure Neapolitan saint, half out of its frame and with the glass broken, and some earlier lonely transient had drawn moustaches on the saint's face, and a huge and magnificent mirror of ormolu above an ornate mantelpiece, and nothing else except a creaking camp stretcher with one grey army blanket.

I spent the night in my greatcoat smoking cigarettes through chattering teeth, and it was perhaps the very absurdity of my opulent discomfort that turned my thoughts away from the physical state of my loneliness and misery, and into my mind crept that more poignant and still indefinable sense of loss which more and more frequently was beginning to assail me in the solitude of these foregn places. And it occurred to me again how strange it was that in all my travellings, in all the mélange of races and places that had come to be the new reality of my own experience, I almost never encountered my own countrymen any longer. For them the far adventure was over: they had all gone back and they were fighting from their own land now through the tangled pattern of the islands.

I sat huddled on the edge of the camp stretcher with the army blanket wrapped around the greatcoat and thought about this. I knew that on the following day I would be in

Rome, and that the New Zealanders, at any rate, would be there: but they were not the same, any more than their hats were the same, because theirs were the flat-brimmed, three-dented hats of a lifetime before—the hats that Stubby and Aleck had worn for snapshots on the front lawn—and I thought of the bush-hats the British had worn in Burma and they were not the same either, nor the hats of the Gurkhas with their pleated puggarees—and suddenly I resented other people wearing hats like that! And the very curious thing is that I believe this is the precise moment—in this quick, unreasonable, ridiculous little flare of prejudiced nationalism —when I began to expatriate myself.

It was an awakening feeling much stronger than the mere fact that during my travels I had seen many places which had made me make the mental note that one day I would have to come back and examine them again, and more closely, and in different circumstances. (It is significant, I think, that I never visualised myself as coming back in the company of Helen.) It is not just curiosity that makes an expatriate, there must also be something that happens in the very soul of him. Gradually I began to sense that already, and delib-erately, I had begun proceedings of divorcement from my country and my people, and it was at this point that I got up and walked down the room to the huge baroque mirror at the far end, and the glass had the same cloudy, muddy opacity of the mirror in Gavin Turley's house, and I stared very intently at the indistinct reflection that looked back at me through the clouded darkness and the pin-spots of time. I saw change in it at once. I saw it as older than I had realised, and becoming a little world-weary, and a shade too cynical around the deep-set eyes, and then I looked closer and I realised that it was not at all the same face as those other faces under the broad-brimmed hats . . . not the same, for instance, as my brother Jack's face. A difference had grown into it, or developed out of it. I turned my head this way and that, studying it, and suddenly I realised that there was a sort of calculation in it, that this was a face watching for opportunities, that what was lacking in it was the truth those other faces had for the passionate regard for the adventure in itself, and I knew then that I was not quite one of them, that I never had been, and that I never would be. Yet I went back to the camp stretcher still wondering why this had come about. . . .

I went north to Rome next day, and up to the Hotel de la Ville, on the via Sistina, where the war correspondents stayed —no heating and frigid marble again!—and mail was waiting there for me, and among it a letter from Jack scrawled over with three different re-addressings.

This was only the third letter Jack had ever written to me, and it was the last. He has never written to me in all the years I have been away—although Sheila always keeps in touch—and perhaps he felt afterwards that there was never really anything more to say. I thought at the time that it was the saddest letter I had ever received, and I think in some ways it still is.

I went into the bar to read it, because it was a little warmer there, and I ordered a double brandy and sat beneath the coloured bottles.

Along the bar from me a very distinguished war correspondent, grossly fat and unfit-looking in his dark officer's blouse, was closely questioning a New Zealand infantry lieutenant about the street-fighting in Florence and making notes on a paper table-napkin. He kept saying, " Yup, that's swell. Keep filling me in, boy." There was a blind-eyed marble bust of the Emperor Hadrian on a pedestal just beyond his shoulder. I opened Jack's letter first, and began to read:

Dear David,

This APO number thing seems a very funny address they have given me, but I take up my pen to write hoping it will find you in due course. After all the great trouble you went to on my behalf I am terribly sorry to have to inform you that circumstances seem to have been against me once again, so I did not get overseas in the end, and I am now back in Melbourne. What happened was that a command-car I was taking up from Larrimah rolled over in the mulga and the old leg went on me again. They flew me back here to hospital (not the old one but a new one at Heidelberg which is very swanky ! ! !) and when I was discharged they scrubbed me finally for any active service. I have now faced up quite realistically to the situation (at last ! ! !) and any-

way I did have a good few months up there in the
Territory and loved every minute of it and would give
anything to get back there when the war is over. There
is some talk now that it might be declared as an area
for the 1939-43 medal, so I might even get one ribbon
to pin on the old chest and that will be something, anyway.

"Yup, that's dandy!" the war correspondent was saying,
"but what was this Texas outfit doing *outside* the mine
tapes? Let's get the picture right, then we can peg the detail.
Just keep filling me in, boy."

I am a staff-sergeant now and I have been transferred to
the Pay Corps, which is just about the softest job you
ever saw, and Sheila likes it of course because she has
me home every night, and I don't mind it all that much
myself although we are in the same building where Bert
drives the lift and that is sometimes a bit hard to take.

"It's very difficult," the New Zealand lieutenant was explaining. "I mean in all that rubble, with the fronts of the
buildings demolished across the streets, and the taping of the
minefields was very rough, you know . . . well, half the time
I wouldn't know what the next platoon was doing. Thanks,
yes, a very short one . . . lots of soda. . . ." The correspondent
poured from the black Haig and Haig bottle, and he sat
there on the high bar stool like some great tarantula, and the
white sightless eyes of Hadrian stared right through him.

However as long as one of us is over there in the thick of
it I have no complaints, and I must say that it is with
very great pride that we read about all your adventures.
You certainly are getting around!!! Sheila says we
should have a big map of The World up in the kitchen
with those coloured pins to mark your progress. We
never know where you will turn up next!!!
   I have left the most important item of news until now.
Sheila had another baby and this time it was a BOY. His
name is Jack of course!!!! I am naturally tickled pink.
Sheila and I have always had an understanding that she

can have the three girls for the Pope, but the boy is mine. I mean I would like to bring him up in my own way. Since he came along I have been giving a lot of thought to these matters, and I have come to the conclusion that education is the main thing. As you are aware, we did not have very much of a chance ourselves in this respect, and that is why I would like to say here and now how much I have admired the way you have battled it out for yourself and risen to the position you occupy to-day. I remember how I used to poke fun at you always stuck in that room with your books and those " sonky mates " of yours, and never going out, but I must admit that events have certainly proved you right. In fact nothing would please me more than if my nipper Jack turned out as good a man, and as brainy a one, as his Uncle Davy. Sheila is in complete agreement with this statement, but then you have always been very popular in that quarter.

I put the letter down and asked for another brandy, and I found myself desperately wanting something to intervene between me and Jack's letter and between me and the fat war correspondent with his thirsty, sucking eyes, and the exhausted battle-wearied face of the New Zealand lieutenant, and the war correspondent was saying, " Yup, well just keep filling me in, boy. I can work it out," so I went back to reading Jack's letter because there was nothing else I could do.

On the physical side, of course, I am confident that I can handle him O.K. He looks pretty good material to me, and has a nice promising reach and a quick look about him. I would not want him to take after *you* in this respect!!! You were never much of a one in a scrap, were you? A good southpaw can sometimes be tricky, but a bad southpaw like you is an offence to the Noble Art and is always just asking for trouble. Still, in your case brains have proved more than brawn, haven't they? Which is the main thing.

We are all well here, and as proud of you as all get out, and we sincerely trust we will all be safely and

happily reunited when this other business is over, so I
will close now on this note with much love from all of us
back here in old Aussie.

                    I remain,
                        Your most affectionate bro.
                            Jack Meredith, Sr ! ! !

There was a postscript added after that mad neat copperplate
signature:

P.S. We dropped in at home last week-end and Dad, who
as you know is back in the colours, and a lance-corporal
now! ! ! gave me a message for you. His V.D.C. squad
was being given small-arms training some little time
back by a girl N.C.O. from the A.W.A.S. who apparently
knows you. I wrote the name down. Bombardier Morley. She asked Dad to pass on her very best regards to
you if someone was writing. I nearly split my sides
laughing at the thought of the Old Man being trained in
small-arms by a girl soldier. How are the mighty
fallen, eh! ! !

The war correspondent said, " Yup, boy, now we're really
getting somewhere," and the New Zealander pensively stirred
the soda with a swizzle-stick and I stared straight at the
marble eyeballs of the Emperor Hadrian and I thought of the
greenest eyes I had ever seen. *Bombardier* Morley now.
Tristram Shandy was getting on in the world. . . .

CHAPTER 17

I did not see Cressida Morley until a little time after the fall
of Mandalay. Once Fort Dufferin had been taken I flew from
Burma to India then up to Assam and across to China, and a
recurrence of malaria laid me up for a few days in Chungking, and there seemed to be nothing much doing anywhere,
so I cabled Mr. Brewster asking permission to return to
Melbourne for a short leave. He agreed, so then there was
the wearisome series of flights back, from Chungking to

Kunming to Assam to Calcutta and down to Ceylon, and then across the Indian Ocean to Exmouth Gulf, and the whole width of Australia, and one saw how far away it really was, and I think I must have been very tired and dispirited by the time I got back home.

I remember being shocked and startled by the changes which I felt had taken place in my absence, although had I paused to look I would have seen much the same things going on everywhere else, and anyway I had not taken into account the changes in myself. The Germans had been defeated and the Japanese beaten back almost to their own islands, and there was this distinct feeling of the war drawing to its close, and the feeling seemed to hold all the city in its grip, as heavy in its portent as the autumnal weather. It was as if all the people had sensed this and were uneasily conscious of the imminence of other problems which soon would have to be faced, and very often these were deeply personal problems which they kept stalling at, as if they wanted more time in which to think about them. The air of excitement and jubilation in victories and the satisfaction of achievement was there too, of course, but the underlying feeling, the true spirit of the times, as it were, was not like this at all. It is a curious reflection on human attitudes that man moves from peace into war in a state of buoyancy and exhilaration, and from war back to peace with a melancholic and fearful anxiety. Perhaps too much had intervened, in time and events and change. . . .

For it was not only the physical things that arrested one's attention, like people having to share taxi-cabs, or that rackets had flourished and manners deteriorated, or that shiploads of " G.I. Brides " were leaving for the States, or that one had to buy queer-smelling South African cigarettes, or that there was a slightly frenzied edge to the hilarities, or that the slang in common usage was almost more American than Australian, or that a whole pattern of new caste-snobberies—and animosities—seemed to have been built around military exploits which had once been sufficient in themselves.

The city to my vision seemed to be gripped in an atmosphere that was tense and quick and brittle, not quite panicky but feverish in a way, and I detected a kind of rapaciousness almost everywhere, as if people wanted to squeeze out the last of the juices before it was too late. They seemed nervous and in some way unsatisfied, as if a sixth sense was warning them that their own values were being melted away in the climate of victory. I came back to my own city with a sharp consciousness of things splintering and breaking and falling to the ground.

Probably I read much of my own personal dilemma into the general situation. Even though I knew I would have to go back to it, for Mr. Brewster had allowed me only one week, I was quite certain that the war *was* hurtling inexorably towards conclusion. (Within less than six months of that visit I had walked the ghastly fused earth of Hiroshima, and in Tokyo Bay I had stood on the deck of the battleship *Missouri* and watched the Japanese bow before MacArthur and sign unconditional surrender.) And I knew that the time was drawing ever closer when I would no longer be able to push my own problems aside.

My reunion with Helen, although on the surface warm and affectionate enough in a well-rehearsed way, inwardly left me dismayed and apprehensive. The drift had gone too far, and suddenly I could see our relationship in all its barrenness, our posturings as no more than a game of charades that had been played too often and for too long and had become tiresome. Perhaps too many other substitute Helens had intervened, but the feeling she evoked in me now was only a desolate despair.

I saw that she had only grown older in the time that I had been growing different. She was thirty-seven now, and there were clear hints of desperation and uncertainty in her gaiety, and somehow this filled me with a bitter sense of exasperation. She had formed no permanent liaison during all my absences. She still frivolled with her officer friends, who were always Americans now, but they were always changing, because this was a time when everything seemed to be working to a series of quick, spasmodic changes. The time for constancy, or even the possibility of constancy, had already passed. She had missed her opportunity.

It was this harsh and bitter reflection that made me realise the final resentful truth of the matter: almost throughout the entire war, and certainly during all the time I had been abroad, I had been subconsciously hoping—even expecting—

that she would take the decision into her own hands, that she would find her own way out and relieve me of the necessity for action. But she had just gone on—on and on and on, skimming the shallow surface of her social revels. She had let me down, I told myself angrily. God knows, I had given her all the liberties in the world! Endured my own humiliations, suffered the boredom and the condescension of her friends, just so she could continue the gay, smart, meaningless life which she desired. She had had any number of opportunities with her endless, ever-changing court of admirers, her gay majors and handsome colonels! And she had let me down! Heavens above, countless thousands of *other* Australian marriages had been broken into smithereens by war-time absences and the romping hysterias of the times . . . why, her own best friend, Sandra Solomons had flown the roost, hadn't she? . . . why should Wally Solomons have all the luck, and poor bloody David Meredith be the one to get the short end of the stick?

And what if nothing *did* happen? This was the deadliest thought of all. Was I to be expected to go back to that life in Beverley Grove? To resume everything as before, as if there had been nothing in between? To have travelled the world as I had only to have to drop back again into the mundane horrors of the Beverley Park Gardens Estate, and Helen's bright parties? Yet what was quite certain was that this more desperate Helen, moving towards the treacherous quicksands of her forties, was hardly likely to relinquish me willingly. Oh no, she would clutch and possess this husband of hers who had already achieved some distinction, who provided her with security and the established social standing, who would emerge from the war with reputation and a great potential—the coming man . . . even perhaps the heir-apparent. . . . There were quicksands for me, too, I began to realise.

On the Sunday I was escaping from both Helen and this desperately troubling issue, and I found it very lonely walking the streets of my own city in a soft pale drizzle of rain, and I was quite uncertain of what I wanted to do or where I wanted to go—excepting that I had the strongest feelings that I had nothing at all to go back to at Beverley Grove—so I just went on despondently walking around until the dusk became night and the street-lamps were blurred and blobby through the fine slide of rain, and the spires of St. Paul's shone against the street-glow like the points of licked lead-pencils, and the coloured tram-tickets at the street corners had been trampled and muddied into patchy little Braque-coloured collages, and I had the oddest sensation of being nowhere at all, or anywhere, because I had flown all the way from the province of Szechwan in West China and I had brought myself· and my loneliness and my solitude all that way with me in the same uniform and with the same badges, and if I wanted to I could find a nice smart bar somewhere, or a night-club, and the vivacious undemanding companion-ship of some other Helen with a bracelet of black silver heavy on her wrist, who would smile at me across her glass, and there would be a slightly tired terror in her eyes, too, for the curtain falling on something that had never quite added up to what it might have been. . . .

And then I remembered it was Sunday night, so I turned and began to walk up towards Mario's, because there would be wine there and Continental food, and there would be a guitar and a mandolin and an accordion, and Italian singers among the waiters who would sing " Sorrento " and " Santa Lucia," and they would sing the new nostalgia back into me, the nostalgia to be somewhere over there, thousands of miles away from the emptiness of here.

And the marvel of it was that as I was climbing the stairs to Mario's upper restaurant I met Cressida Morley coming down.

There was a little interval of non-recognition for both of us, and for my part this was understandable enough, for she looked tall in her beautifully-tailored officer's uniform with the carefully scoured buttons and the Australia badges and two pips on each broad shoulder, and artillery patches on her sleeves and the tunic pockets lying almost as flat as a man's so that she seemed to have no breasts, and the soft brown hair was not tousled now under a tin hat but pulled back into a sleek chignon, and she was not a child any more and immensely beautiful, but it was I who spoke first because I knew that there could be no other eyes in the world quite as green as these.

" Well, hallo!" I said. " You have come up in the world!"
" Oh, that," she said, and smiled her recognition and

pleasure and a kind of diffidence too, and I saw that she also
had grown different as well as having grown older, and her
"older," after all, was still so breathtakingly young. "It's
war-time," she said. "Things happen."

"Thank you for your message, by the way," I said. "I got
it in Rome."

Her mouth lifted a little. "Oh, that," she said again. "I
wondered if they'd pass it on. Your father was one of the
nicest of my Sunday gentlemen. He talked often about you."

I hesitated, then said, "You wouldn't be alone, I suppose?"

"Here? Hardly!" But she still lingered on the stairs,
young now and shining in a way and delighted.

"Pity," I said ruefully. "Because I am, you see."

"Actually I'm here with my boss," she said, and now the
smile was all over her face, mischievous and speculative.
"Why don't you join us? I am sure—I am absolutely perfectly sure—he would be very happy. Truly."

"Well . . ." I shrugged and followed her, and walking into
the crowding, buzzing, candle-lit room, I thought her back
seemed to be shaking with laughter. She was threading her
way through to a table in the far corner, and sitting there was
a thin, shaggy-haired officer with a major's crowns on his
shoulders, and one sleeve, the left, emptily pinned up above
the elbow, and an expression of incredulous recognition
already breaking over his long horse face.

"My darling Cress!" he cried, and he seemed to uncoil
from his chair, rising like a cobra emerging from its basket,
pushing out the one arm he had. "You merely said you
were going to the loo! And you come back with this . . .
this Troilus."

"Jesus Christ!" I gasped. "Gavin Bloody Turley!"

And the girl was there between us, radiant and glimmering
in the candlelight, laughing.

"Well . . ." I said, and I was laughing too, and then I
broke off the laugh because of the pinned-up sleeve and the
major's crowns and the ribbons on his tunic—that silver 8
again on the Africa Star and the white and purple bands of
the Military Cross, and there was a silver rosette on that, too,
and it all came back to me quite suddenly and I said, "I was
very upset about Peggy, Gavin. I was terribly sorry."

"So was I, David," he said. "Thanks, cock. Well . . .

well, now let us . . . umm . . . let us arrange ourselves comfortably and get some more grog and another glass and start in to natter. My darling Cress, since you are the most eye-catching thing here, do be useful and catch a waiter's, will you?"

I glanced at him gratefully for getting us over the moment, and then I said, "How the devil did you pick up Tristram Shandy here?" They looked at me blankly, so I smiled, possessing her in a way, and said, "When last *I* saw her she was very grubby and she was sitting in a gun-pit on a golf links reading *Tristram Shandy*."

"How did you know that?" she gasped delightedly.

"I have my sources," I said. "I am a newspaper man. But you still haven't told me. How?"

"She is, in fact, my military compensation," Gavin said. "The ways of the Army are mysterious, as no doubt you have discovered. When I got back they shoved me into Military History and Information, which is a kind of knacker's yard for the no-longer-serviceable longhairs like myself, and as a sort of a sop, shall we say, my darling Cress here was given to me for an offsider. You will remember Ben Johnson's observation on Shakespeare that he had little Latin and less Greek: well, Turley's observation on Lieutenant Morley is that she had little History and less Information, but on Military she has acquired some considerable breadth of knowledge. Field-rank and above, usually. Isn't it a briggy who's chasing you now, Cress?"

"He's fat," she said. "He'd have to run a lot harder than *he's* capable of doing! Do you want me to pour you some wine?"

"Bless you," he said, and patted her hand affectionately. Her hands were no longer grubby, I saw, but still muscular and brown, and looked after. "Pour some for old Golden Boy, too. How *bloody* good to see you, old cock!" he said in an exuberant rush of pleasure. "Marvellous! Cress dashing off and simply conjuring you out of the loo or somewhere! As David Meredith said to Churchill . . . 'Winnie, old boy, the essence of victory is in surprise.' And the honour for *us*! How does it feel, Cress, a mere lieutenant, to be sitting here not only with a distinguished major but with *the* distinguished war correspondent? Don't just sit there with that minx expression in your eyes, girl, be over-awed. To have him *here*, as one of us! We do read all your dispatches, David, don't we, Cress? And now we are waiting with bated breath—bate your breath, Cress—to hear some-thing off the cuff or on the record, the inside story, the informed summing-up, the word from the unimpeachable source. When, for instance, is this bloody war going to be over?" I saw then that he was a little drunk, and with a pang of compassion I realised that he would often be a little drunk now.

"God only knows," I said. "Sooner or later." Sooner, I thought . . . the decisions, the commitments, the readjustings, the end of easy evasions. Helen. Beverley Grove. But no Peggy for Gavin, and no pie with a pastry rose on top. I looked at the girl and back at Gavin, and I wondered, and a little current of uneasiness stirred inside me. Could this one cook?

"No worries for *you*, though," Gavin said. "You'll be right. Old Brewster genuflects even now at the golden ring of every syllable of your byline. You're tipped as the heir-apparent, did you know? You jolly well are! Which reminds me, when the sceptre does fall into your little hot hand do reserve a tiny cubby-hole for me, wont you? Nothing fancy, just a bark lean-to somewhere for your old mate."

"Oh shut up, you silly bastard!" I said.

"You just wait and see. You'll never believe this but I bumped into old Curt Condon a few weeks back and he told me he bought your last book. Actually *bought* it! Thought it was first rate, he said. Doubtless he'll want you to scribble something endearing on the fly-leaf. You know—but for whom. . . . I told him your next one was to be entitled *Famous People Who Have Met Me*."

"There is no next one," I said, laughing.

"Really? How sad! I had planned to keep feeding you your titles. *Inside John Gunther* was one that rather pleased me. But seriously, David, how on earth have you managed all this?"

"I simply followed your advice, Gavin. I sharpened up the flairs. Polished the apples. Preserved that precious little asset of the unscrupulous. Learned several more very useful

tricks from the Great Masters—like it not being necessary to
have actually *been* there. For example, did you know I
escaped from Crete on your raft? You don't mind, I hope?"

"Not in the least, old cock. It's just that I have no idea
what you're talking about."

"It's a game I play with other correspondents and people
gullible enough to believe that I escaped from Crete on a raft
. . . on *your* raft. It's a sort of intellectual exercise on seeing
how far you can go and still get away with it. You would be
amazed how many people there are eager to believe anything
that sounds adventurous. I covered Spain, too. I was at the
bombing of Guernica. I saw the Anschluss. Aren't you proud
of me, Gavin?"

"My dear chap, if we weren't so crowded in here I'd be
kow-towing!"

"No doubt I would have used that arm of yours, and that
M.C. twice over, had I only known the details."

"Too sordid," he said. "The arm, I mean. Trampled
underfoot in a brothel in Alex during a surprise raid by
M.P.s. I never like to talk about it in front of the child
Cress here."

"And the gongs?"

"Influence," he said, with his big soiled toothy smile.
Only then did I realise that he no longer rubbed at his teeth
with his fingers, so probably it had been a mannerism of his
left hand. It was curious to think of a mannerism being
blown off as well as an arm.

"Vicarious identification with other people's adventures,"
I said. "Surely that's essentially part of our trade too. Well,
just that, really, and deciding on the stockades that *can* be
raided, then whipping in and pillaging and grabbing the
trophies. Oh, yes, I came out with my trophies all right!"

He gave me a long considering look, and that old familiar
quirk of irony was in his face as he said, "You know, David,
it's possible I may have guessed the wrong fallibility in you,
after all. I do believe you're beginning to acquire an odd,
indeed a most peculiar, sort of honesty. Watch it! Because
that, old cock, could be the stone end of *you*!" He paused
and looked at Cressida, who through all this conversational
back-and-forth between us had listened with a still, intent
sort of pleasure with her strong boyish hands cupped around

her wine-glass, and his glance was like an understood signal, because she lit a cigarette for him and refilled his wine-glass, and he turned to me again. " Some of your stuff has been very, very good indeed," he said. " Was that in spite of yourself? "

I didn't have to answer because this was when the waiters bustled in with a flapping of long white aprons, an interruption of flurrying activity like an unexpected gust of wind billowing out a curtain, and there were platters of cannelone and ravioli on the red check of the cloth, and bread rolls in a wicker basket, and two more flagons of Chianti, and crumbs and white napkins, and the candles seemed to be almost jumping out of the wax-dribbled Vat 69 bottles. I had a heightened awareness of all the smells of wax and candlewick and food and smoke and wine and perfume, and of the dove-grey steam from the food that was different from the cigarette smoke, because cigarette smoke when it was exhaled was a kind of dirty yellowish-grey and it only turned blue when it wreathed up and joined the flattened cloudy bars hanging below the ceiling like soiled silk ribbons. There was a waitress, an Italian girl, moving between the tables playing " Santa Lucia " on an accordion, and the people all around were swaying their heads to the rhythm and singing, and quite suddenly I knew that I had no nostalgia inside me. No nostalgia at all. And I was not lonely any longer. And nothing of the packed restaurant or the singing had done this, because in all this noise and crowding and confusion it was just the three of us isolated around a table under a canopy of smoke. The candlelight seemed to jump everyhere, without the discipline of light, making rainclouds-and-rainbows and runny oil whorls on the mother-of-pearl decorations on the accordion, and jerking the grooved pained lines on Gavin's dark face as if someone with a carbon pencil was tentatively sketching them in, looking for the right place to make an expression, and the flickering light played in the girl's eyes like seaweed moving in the shoalwater tides, and I didn't want to be anywhere else in the world but here. And I was just like the sheep-faced lieutenant on the gun-site, because I could not keep my eyes off her. . . .

And I saw that she broke his bread roll for him, much in the way she would pour his wine or light his cigarettes, and

there was some obvious warmth and tenderness in these
small solicitudes that linked them in a kind of unique communion, for I knew instinctively that she would be one of
the very few people, perhaps the only person, whom Gavin
would allow to do such things for him, and this disturbed me
in a queer way, and then Gavin said:

" It's Venezuela, you know, that *really* intrigues. I mean,
I am quite aware that the rear is the rear, and that very often
much valuable bumph is to be picked up there, which is fair
enough, but how could anything in the war—global as it might
be—be quite so rear as *Venezuela*?"

So I told him about Venezuela, and I told him about the
Old Silk Road, and about some of the other odder places, and
even as I talked I knew that I was showing off a little to
impress her, as she had showed off to impress me on that gun-
site more than two years earlier, and I saw with a little surge
of triumph that she *was* impressed. And everything I was
saying was being painted against the grey of smoke and the
black-and-white of waiters coming and going and I saw two
empty flagons of Chianti moving away and two full ones
descending in their places, and Cressida just kept watching
my face as I talked, and finally I was saying, " So, you see,
Gavin, it really isn't Golden Boy at all. It's Little Jack
Horner. Who sat in his corner, eating his Christmas pie.
And he put in his thumb, and pulled out a plum. . . ." I left it
at that and his long face glowed in delight.

" And I'll bet you that every time you got a plum you
said, ' And look what a good boy am *I*?'" Pleasure almost
seemed to bubble out of him, and I wanted all three of us to
burst into laughter, and I realised that I was getting a little
drunk too, and suddenly I wanted to bring it to an end and
talk about something else, or just give attention to this girl
between us, so I put on a serious tone and said, " All right,
Gavin, now you tell me what you would have done in my
place," and he met me on that level, quite sincerely, and
said, " Exactly the same, I dare say. But not half as well."
And it was at this point that Cressida said, " I am going to
Venezuela after the war," and she said it with an absolute
conviction in that husky voice that was now a little blurry
with wine. " I *am* going, to Venezuela and to New York,
and London and Rome and Paris. The Old Silk Road, too, I

think. And places where other people *haven't* been. Like
Timbuktu."

"Yes, you must, Cress," Gavin said soothingly. "It will
brush up your geography." He patted her hand as he said it,
but I could see that he hated to let me go, because he said to
me, "And to-morrow, I read in the popular press, the
curtain-raiser to the big parade is to be none other than *our*
David Meredith delivering a patriotic exhortation from the
top of a tank in Collins Street!"

"What odds?" I said. "I have made a speech from a
captured midget Japanese submarine in Times Square at seven
o'clock on a Sunday evening. What's a tank to me?"

"I am going to Times Square too," said Cressida. "Nobody listens to a word *I* say. I keep telling everyone that I
am going to Venezuela after the war, and to——" and Gavin
picked up her hand and kissed it lightly, and, ignoring her, he
said, "I *am* an impolite bastard, David. How is Helen? I
should have asked . . ."

"Oh, you know Helen," I said easily. "She has her
friends. . . ."

"This *bloody* war!" he said.

"I think we should listen to Lieutenant Morley on her
future Odysseys," I said lightly. I didn't want to talk about
Helen, and I didn't want to even think about her, and I was
sorry he had mentioned her name. "We two have hogged it
long enough," I said, and I looked across at her and in the
jump of light little beads of gold slid along her cheekbone,
and that same tremulous childish eagerness gave a curious
mobility to her wide mouth, and again I was aware of that
unsettling impression she gave of only awaiting some clue to
release the strong latent forces she was holding back, of joy
perhaps, of excitement, of some pure intensity of living.

One of the black-and-white waiters was on the platform,
fat, with a sweat-glaze on blue jowls that gave a mackerel
look to his complexion, and he looked like the old stiff photographs of Caruso which they still sold in the back streets of
Naples except that he had a table napkin over one arm and
a white apron taped across his paunch, but the stance was
the same, and the cocksure Neapolitan tilt to the curly head,
and he cleared his throat and plucked at his Adam's apple as
the instruments began on the opening bars of "Sorrento."

"Let us then consider Lieutenant Morley," Gavin said, and he pulled a comic judicial face, then examined her intently as if he found it difficult to get her in focus, and a little unsteadily, as if his long shaggy head was suddenly insecure on the thin stalk of his neck. He was having difficulty too, it seemed, in fixing his feelings, because interest, affection, irony, possessiveness, and a kind of sadness all moved across his long lean face like the shadows of drifting clouds. "My darling Cress," he said at last in a kind of soft wondering admiration. "You have here a savage, David," he said, talking to me, but still staring at her as if searching for something in her that might surprise him. "An authentic savage. At least as authentic, old cock, as those fuzzy-wuzzies and Hottentots and *kuku-kukus* which *you've* been chucking in for colour! Consider her beginnings. She is born on a barren mile of Pacific beach. Not a soul goes there. Nothing but sand-dunes and sharks and kelp. Oh, a log or two of driftwood, perhaps. And our Cress. . . ."

It was perfectly and absolutely *right*, of course! It had to be—that was where her eyes came from, out of the ocean, out of the endless Pacific depths. And that was precisely what she was—a savage, a pagan, an authentic something that was quite different from anything else . . . and she was only twenty now, and she would have gone from her long lonely beach to a gun-site and from a gun-site to Gavin Turley, and she would never have known a suburban street in her life, or a garden subdivision, and she wouldn't know an Antirrhinum from a Phlox Drummondii or a mock-orange if one fell on her! And of course she would go to Venezuela, there was no question about it. . . . I was absolutely perfectly sure. That was what she had said on the stairs . . . absolutely perfectly sure. . . . I was probably almost as drunk as Gavin now, because I had a whole lot of thoughts suddenly mixed up together . . . that bottom-wiggling, grubby gamin of the gun-site, and that in some way was tangled with the mound and Jack and I playing there as kids, and I saw suddenly that there was something about her, some absolute and perfect directness that reminded me of my brother Jack . . . she was not the same sort of person as Jack, no, but she was the same sort of *thing.* . . . That was it. . . . Gavin said, "Never wore a pair of shoes until she was thirteen. Isn't that so, my darling Cress?"

"Well, not quite. But I know you like to think so." The smile she gave him indicated such rapport between them, so close and so tender a bond, that I felt panic lay a light finger on me.

"Like Christopher Robin, she still has sand between the toes, David. Important to remember this. Bless you for your sandy toes, Cress."

The fat waiter had come down and was singing through the tables and the girl with the accordion walked behind him, and a man with a guitar behind her, and they were moving towards us through the black and white and the smoke and the dance of candles, and the song came towards us growing from the clear high tenor voice and the folding and unfolding pleats of the accordion and from the throats all round the room, and Cressida Morley said to me, "Have you been to Sorrento too?"

"Yes," I said.

"That's another place I am going to," she said with husky determination.

We were *all* drunk, I realised, the three of us.

"Why don't you take her, David?" Gavin said, and his face as he turned to me seemed twisted in the candle-flare, as if there was a sudden sharp twinge of pain he was trying to screw out of himself. "Now there's a challenge," he offered thickly. "A *real* challenge. She has no guarantee either, did you know that? Down at the Barracks there is talk of striking a decoration for personnel game enough to take on our Cress. You take *her* to Sorrento, Little Jack Horner! *If* you're game!"

"I don't know about Sorrento," I said, parrying him, "but I would like to take her to dinner to-morrow night. Before I go back again to the intrepid life."

"On your last night?" he said, raising his eyebrows.

"Why not?"

He looked at me. "This would be without my tagging along, I assume?"

"Naturally. I'll be gone the day after to-morrow. You'll have her for the rest of the war." I turned to her. She was holding Gavin's hand. "Will you?" I said.

"Thank you. I'd love to."

It was Jack who had suggested the visit to Port Melbourne. "They've been extra good to me at Klebendorf's," he said to me. "You know, they make up some of the army pay so Sheil' can get along a bit better with the kids, so I pop down and see 'em every now and then. You know, keep in touch. They like that. And they'd *love* to see you, Davy, they really would. They're always asking about you."

The new factory was very functional, concrete and saw-toothed roofing and steel-framed windows, all on one floor and covering about two acres, and it was in a part of Port Melbourne just up from the old pier where the *Ceramic* had come in after the First World War.

It was Werner Klebendorf who greeted us in the front office, treating Jack with affectionate familiarity, and me with such respect that I felt for a moment as if I were the Governor-General, and I half expected him to bow. He had aged quite a bit and grown grey and stout and was beginning to look very much as his father had looked, which struck me as rather odd because there was nothing of the German thick-ness in his speech, and his accent, in fact, was rather culti-vated and clipped in the public school way. He was bursting to show me over the new premises.

As we went around I began to realise that he was almost as proud of showing me off to his employees as he was of showing the factory to me. What with time, change, and the war, there were very few familiar faces, and the factory itself, which seemed enormous and efficient on its vast cement floor, was so utterly different from the old factory that the machines were almost unrecognisable and I could hardly believe it was the same business and I expected the big presses to be turning out canned food or aeroplane parts instead of printed sheets, and I suddenly remembered Jane Avril's shoe still kicking beneath the wrecker's sign and I had a surge of nostalgic sadness for the old place with its dust and dark corners and collected smells.

Down one side of the factory were five big enclosed rooms flickering with blue light behind frosted glass, and Werner explained to me with great enthusiasm, " It's all photo-litho-graphy now, David. Photo-offset's the shot, and we're into it

up to our eyeballs. Hand-lithography's almost out. Thing of
the past." That made me wonder about them all, and so I
asked, and he chuckled and said, " Oh, you'll see your old
boss in a minute or two," and then he told me about the
others.

Paul Klein, it seemed, was in charge of a Red Cross unit
somewhere up in the Philippines, and Barney Druce was now
head-artist with a rival firm, and Tom Middleton was with a
camouflage section in Dutch New Guinea, and Young Joe
had been caught in the crossfire of two of those heavy Juki
machine-guns and shot to death on the bank of the Gerua
River.

His father had a room all to himself now on the side of the
factory opposite the photo-litho rooms, and unlike the rest of
the factory it was a cluttered place and hung with things
pinned up. We stood at the door looking in for quite a time
before he realised we were there. He looked shrunken and
very old, and he was on one of the high stools crouched over
a polished oatmeal-coloured stone, and he was working in
the way old Fritz Richter had always worked, with the fine
camelhair brush underneath a magnifying-glass.

" Practically no call now for the fine hand-work," Werner
said, almost in a whisper. " So we just keep old Joe on that."
I saw that the Bavarian stones—or those still preserved, for
there seemed fewer of them than I remembered—were stacked
along the wall, still numbered and dusted down, and as we
walked in I could not resist running my fingers across the
surface of one, just to feel the cool sweet silkiness again, and
then old Joe Denton was rising and staring, and blinking his
eyes back to a longer focus, and then he seemed to give a
funny little hop and he was trotting towards me with quick
little jerky steps, and he grasped both of my hands in his and
shook them up and down furiously and said, " Bless my soul!
Bless my soul! Bless my soul!" There were tears in his eyes,
perhaps from the strain of the fine work he had been doing,
and he looked incredibly old, as old as Steiner had looked
and Richter had looked, and just as much of an oddity, a
survival from some other thing that had long since vanished.
" Bless my soul, David!" he said, and shook his head very
quickly, blinking away like mad.

Werner and Jack went away to look at some new equipment in the paper store, and left me with him, and he took me along to his work-table and made me sit on the tall stool while he perched himself on a great stack of *Penrose Annuals*, and we talked about all sorts of things, about his dahlias and Gilbert and Sullivan and poor old Richter and about Paul Klein's walking-stick, and neither of us said anything about Young Joe, and I leaned over to look at the stone and saw the meticulous neatness of the gumming-out and the hairline precision of the register-marks and beautifully modelled on the pale sleek stone was a toned patch of the finest, finest stippling that would make the flushing ripeness of a peach on some fruit label. He smiled when he saw me looking and said, " It's the third colour, the light-blue. It's for Ardmona. They're submitting a range of their products for some international trade show, and they want specially handsome labels. Nine colours *and* gold-embossed." He nodded his head admiringly. "They don't often go to such pains nowadays," he said. Behind the shaggy, snowy fall of his hair I saw the things on the wall, the templates and the colour-wheels, and the proof sheets with their improbable blobs of pink and blue and scarlet and yellow, and the key drawings on transparent paper, and a French curve, and a tracing of an initial letter for an illumination, and a calendar advertising Wimble's Printing Inks.

He walked all the way up the factory with me when I was leaving, and when he shook hands with me he said, " It was so nice of you, David, to drop in like this. I *have* enjoyed it. I sometimes think "—he chuckled and squeezed my arm— " yes, I sometimes think you're just about Klebendorf's proudest product, you know."

When we left I suggested to Jack that we walk down to the sea-front, and I went to the end of the pier and sat on a rusty old bollard, and I stared out across the blue dancing bay to Williamstown and the Gellibrand Pile Light, and after a time I said to Jack, " You know, this is about the first thing I ever remember in my life, this pier here. It's where the *Ceramic* pulled in when Dad came back from the war. Do you remember? We came down here with Mum and old Gran."

" Do I remember?" He laughed. " And the Old Man picked you up and you howled like a stuck pig! Jesus, eh . . . that's a long time ago, isn't it?"

I thought of the bands playing and the flags and the triumphal arches, and the putteed legs and the thick boots pounding on the planking, and Jack said, " Someone was telling me they hardly use this pier any more. It's been condemned or something." And I could smell the rank iodine smell of the seaweed rotting underneath the piles and I thought to myself, The Glory That Was, eh, Stunsail? The glory that was. . . .

I don't know how long it was that I sat there staring out across Hobson's Bay with the marching feet pounding inside my brain and there was a gull in the sky slanted on the wind like a lick of white paint, and Jack was walking along the pier kicking at the splintered wood, but then he was tapping me on the shoulder and saying, " Eh, no time for day-dreaming, sport. We better get cracking. You've got that speech to make, and you've got lunch with your boss, and then you've got to meet me for the march. So come on, let's go." We walked over to the tram stop and while we were waiting he said, " Jesus, they were tickled pink to see you there at Klebendorf's, weren't they? Eh? I'm bloody glad you did it. I'm very grateful. I've been promising 'em I'd try and get you down. They all think the bloody sun shines out of you."

I was not the only one to give a speech from the top of the tank, because the Defence Minister was there and a man who'd won the Victoria Cross and a radio comedian and there was a musical comedy star who sang " Wish Me Luck As You Wave Me Good-bye " and " This is Worth Fighting For," and I made my little patriotic exhortation—rather self-consciously, because Gavin Turley was there, overtopping everyone in the crowd and grinning up at me. It was something to do with the opening of a new War Loan drive—they called this one the Victory Loan, I remember, and after the speeches I joined Mr. Brewster and Helen at The Australia. Helen, having got Mr. Brewster at last, seemed less excited than she should have been, and for a time in the dining-room she seemed to pay more attention to acquaintances at other tables, waving and smiling and patting at her hair, which I remember was not golden-blonde any longer but tinted Titian. I also remember wanting to kick old Brewster under the table, and kick him hard, because he kept telling Helen how proud she should be of her husband and what a splendid future there was in store for him—because this did seem to quicken her interest considerably—and I might even have strangled him when he said, " I am sorry, Mrs. Meredith, that we have had to cut his stay to short, but I know you don't have to be told how vitally important his work is. After the war is over, of course, it will be different. You'll be able to share things. You'll go abroad with him. You'll see these places too. Just bear with us a little longer, my dear, just until we see the great task through." Under my breath I said, " Pompous old pissant!"

The only real pleasure I got out of the luncheon was in making an excuse as we left the table and going discreetly to the head waiter and ordering my table and the wines for dinner, and I had a momentary little flurry of self-esteem as I walked off to catch up with Helen and ·Mr. Brewster, not only at the discretion with which I had done it, but with the way I handled waiters now, or selected wine, or ordered food, and of course the head waiter's air of deferential respect had pleased me too. . . .

The march was by one of the good A.I.F. divisions, which was going away somewhere or had just come back from somewhere, I no longer remember, and I left Helen and Mr. Brewster, and I met Jack, and we found a good position in the crowd, almost on the barricades up near the top end of Collins Street.

It was the usual patriotic thing—there were other units in the march, and half a dozen bands, and W.A.A.A.F.s and A.W.A.S. and some garrison units and contingents from the Air Force and the Navy, and it moved along to the jumping bursts of applause and showers of torn paper and the waving of little flags, but the big thing—and you could hear it coming by a growling, rolling, thunderous note in the cheering—was the march past by the fighting troops.

I am sure my mood must have been deeply affected by the visit to Klebendorf's and the old pier at Port Melbourne, because the thick boots were still trampling and trampling inside my brain, and a kind of panic clutched at me as I remembered the black mirror in the freezing room in the palace at Caserta, and I was almost afraid to see them again after not having seen them for so long, but I was craning my neck like all the others, craning through the tumult and the frantic shimmer of the little flags and the overhanging foliage of the plane-trees, and I heard the shrill pipe of the whistle and the slow nasal wail and bark of the order, and my stomach seemed to cramp into a hard knot of pain as I saw them wheeling at the top of the street within the thick green frame of the trees, the first ranks of fifteen thousand fighting men, swinging on the inside man in the steady slow up-and-down beat of the white gaiters and then rising to the forward stride and coming down, marching nine abreast, with the rippling blue flash of the fixed bayonets on their shouldered rifles. They marched as they liked to march, in their slouch hats with the grey-bordered colour-patches on the bleached-out puggarees, in khaki shorts and their open-neck shirts with sleeves rolled up above bunched brown muscles, and the white wide belts and the white canvas gaiters over the brown boots, and on practically every chest were the multi-coloured campaign ribbons of the deserts and the jungles and the mountains and the islands and the beaches, and they came towards us behind the colour-party with the drawn swords and the hoisted flags and the brave emblazonings of the old-familiar and the new-familiar names. And I had to blink and gulp and fight with the emotion and sentiment and pain that racked me to the very guts.

They were going past now in the rhythmic thunder of the boots, with the clip of metal in the sound, beating through the roar of cheering, and they marched, not like Guardsmen, but in their big loose straight easy way, the hard brown faces under the tipped-up hats, lean faces with the chin-straps taut and shining on the harsh slanting planes, and the strong brown downy legs above the socks and the white gaiters, the men of the far adventure, the soldiers of far fortune. And the anguish inside me had twisted and turned into an awful and irremediable sense of loss, and I thought of Dad and the putteed men coming off the *Ceramic*, and I thought of Jack when I had seen him at Puckapunyal five long years before, looking just like these men, hard and strong and confident and with his brown legs planted in the Seymour dust as if the whole world was his to conquer, a man fulfilled in his own rightness, and suddenly and terribly I knew that all the Jacks were marching past me, all the Jacks were still marching. . . .

I have no idea how much time passed before I turned to him and said, " Do you want to see the rest of it?" and he looked at me for a moment and said, " Oh, no, not if you don't want to. I mean, well . . . these shows do turn me up a bit, you know . . . I thought *you'd* like to see them, that's all."

" I've had enough, I think," I said. " Let's push through."

" Righto. We could go up to the Royal Empire and have a grog. Some of the boys are bound to be up there."

I turned, and behind me they were still marching and marching and marching, and as we shouldered our way out through the press of people I heard someone say, " *Psst!* Look. A war correspondent!" and we went down to Exhibition Street to get out of the crowd, and the parade had emptied out the whole street and as we turned up to the north through a flurrying shower of rain I noticed for the very first time that Jack walked with a slight limp. The realisation made me study him more closely and I saw that he no longer held himself quite so straight and there was a hint of heaviness around his hips, so that I looked leaner than he did and two inches taller. He seemed older and different somehow and there was a plain L.H.Q. colour-patch on his sleeve above the crown and the chevrons, and he walked with a limp and the screw turned tighter as I realised that he had given up. . . .

" They looked good though, didn't they?" he said. " They looked bloody fit."

" Yes," I said.

" I don't go for these parades much, as you can imagine, but they do march well, don't they?" I just nodded. They were still marching, marching inside my brain, marching through my whole life. Jack said, " I'm glad we cut out of it early, though. I told the boys in my Pay Corps section I'd try to get you up for a beer or two. They're all dead keen on meeting you." A heavier squall of rain flurried across the street and then it stopped quite suddenly and the surface of the asphalt turned pale and cloudy like a drying slate.

There were seven or eight of them already there, waiting in the bar. They were all in uniform, but not impressively so:

there was a rather timid, quiet, unsoldierly look about them in spite of the khaki and the slouch hats, and two of them wore spectacles.

"Well, here he is," Jack said with a flourish. "Told you I'd bring him, didn't I? This is my brother Davy; these are the jokers from the section I was telling you about. This is Bill here, and Steve, Harry, and Tom over there, this fat bastard's Alfie. . . ." He made the introductions like an entrepreneur presenting his great celebrity, and they shook hands one by one almost with the deference the head waiter had displayed, and then there was an eager rush among them to be the first to buy me a drink, and it was a young pimply-faced lance-corporal who won the honour and he handed me the glass, and said, "Did you have a look at the march, sir?" And Jack said, "Eh, chop *that*! You don't have to pull that sir stuff, Sid! He's only a civvie, you know." But Jack said it with an immeasurable pride, and there was a good-natured, understanding burst of laughter . . . and the screw began to twist tighter. "He gets about, yeah," said Jack, "but he's still only a civvie, after all . . . I mean he hasn't got the burden of the war effort on his broad shoulders like us bunch of old-and-bolds." Again they all laughed, and each one of them seemed anxious to catch my eyes and be the one to be laughing with me, but at the same time this made them seem more at ease with me and they became almost excessively friendly, and none of them would even hear of it that I should pay for a drink, and Jack was standing back with a pot in his hand, pleased as Punch and beaming with pride, and then he fixed his attention on a thin and sallow private at the far end of the bar and said, "Well, go on, don't be a bloody drongo! He won't *bite* you! Go on, Tom, hand it over, he'll be tickled pink." And Tom rather shyly took up a newspaper-wrapped package from the bar counter and unfolded it and took out a book, and there was a photograph of me on the back of the dust-jacket looking rather intrepid in front of a Burmese temple, and Jack said, "Old Tom's the great fan of yours, and when he knew you were coming he bought a copy of that last book you wrote, and he thought you might write some . . . well, you know, some affectionate epistle in the front of it. For crying out loud, pass it *over* to him, Tom! I mean, it was you who *bought* the flamin' book! He makes a bob or two out of you, doesn't he?"

Tom handed me the book, and three other men were offering me pens, and Tom said very respectfully, " I've started it already, Mr. Meredith, and I like it very much. I read everything you write in the papers, I have for years . . . Jack's right, you know, I am a bit of a fan, and . . . well, you know I'll treasure this book now . . . I mean, having met you in the flesh and all that. . . ."

"Christ!" I said to myself, "when is the pain going to stop?"

But I stayed on with them because I couldn't let Jack down now, and others came in, wet from the rain, and had to be introduced, and someone went off with a message and that brought Bert down on his crutches with his leg pinned up, and he told me with a grin that he'd put the OUT OF ORDER sign on the lift, and he had two quick schooners before he had to go back, and every now and then Jack would say, " Go on, Davy, tell the boys about some of your adventures over there . . . you know, this is an opportunity for *them*, isn't it? . . . I mean, getting it straight from the horse's mouth . . . tell 'em about Churchill, or that hurricane you were in. Fair dinkum, he's got a thousand bloody stories, this young brother of mine," he said to them. " No, I've got it, Davy—tell 'em about that time you broke the jeep record for the Burma Road—he *did*, you know, you bastards, it's true! . . . he had a date with some Chinese sheila who stood him up. Go on, tell 'em that, Davy. It's a bloody good story."

There he was in the haze of cigarette smoke, the genial entrepreneur, managing his famed celebrity, his eyes shining, wrapped in the delight of his own inexhaustible pride, and the slouch hat was nonchalantly tilted back on the broad freckled brow and there was the same thin fair receding hair and I saw suddenly how exactly he looked as Dad had looked on that day the *Ceramic* came back, and I seemed to be drowning in a chaos of disordered time, because even the smells were the same, damp serge and tobacco and beer, and there were explosions of laughter, and the strong brown boots were still beating and beating through my brain, and suddenly I knew with the last final excruciating turn of the screw that I had become surrogate for my own brother. He had given up, and he limped, and he had invested all his brave pride and passion and purpose in me. I had become *his* vicarious adventure. I was *his brother Davy*!

I stared around at the slightly rumpled uniforms, the lounging unsmartness, the unsoldierliness of them all, the spectacles, the not-quite-fitness, the Pay Corps . . . at the respect and admiration in their eyes for me . . . at the expansive good humour of the entrepreneur who had scored a bull's-eye. And they were all triers, and I had never really tried, not in five whole years . . . I had only grabbed at the opportunity whenever I saw it. . . .

" Listen, Davy," Jack was saying eagerly, " when we break it up here what about coming up to our place, and we can soldier on a bit up there? It's just half a block around the corner. I mean some of the other jokers can't get off duty, and they'd like to meet you too. I mean, we've got a place there . . . well, it's not a mess exactly, but it's a nice big room and we've got a wet canteen and there's a piano. We could have a bit of a sing-song." The others were nodding and smiling their eagerness for me to accept.

" The trouble is, Jack, I have a date at six," I said regretfully. " I have to meet someone at The Australia."

" Ar, that's bad luck. Well . . ."

I hesitated. " Afterwards perhaps?" I suggested. " I mean, how late do you go on?"

" Well, not *too* late. I mean, most of us are family men, you see . . . and, you know, there's wives and kids. But we could stay on, of course . . . I mean we'd hang on if we knew you *would* be coming. . . ."

" I'll try and make it if I can," I said. " I don't know how tied up I'll be, though. It's my last night, you see. So you mustn't wait on my account . . . I mean I *will* try, but I just can't promise. . . ."

I was more than ten minutes late in getting to The Australia because I stayed on with Jack and the Pay Corps men until closing time, and I half-thought she might not be there, and a little flurry of panic made me take the steps two at a time. But she was there, sitting on the curved leather lounge, polished shoes demurely together and gloved hands resting on a brief-case, and she seemed quite unaware of the nine wolves in various Allied uniforms who were circling her with intent.

As I walked towards her through the crowded foyer I was a tangle of violent emotions—it was my day for violent emotions!—and if some were unlike anything I had ever experienced before and therefore not to be recognised, it must have been because I had never been in love before. In the confused whirl of these feelings there was wonder, and terror, and something magical, and there was certainty and uncertainty, and most of all a sense of hurtling willy-nilly into something so extraordinary, so risky, and so filled with a potential of pain for me that for an impulsive instant I wanted to turn around and run for my life.

But she had seen me and was rising to meet me, in the well-tailored uniform and the felt hat with the rising-sun badge set square on the broad brow, and with that smile already touching the wide corners of her mouth, and she might laugh in a moment, I thought, from the sheerest pleasure in herself and in David Meredith coming towards her across the foyer in a war correspondent's uniform, and I remember thinking then that there was more life in the corners of her mouth than other women had in their whole bodies. But I remember realising also that she was more dangerous than a bomb, and more risk than I had ever taken in my life, and that I would have to go back to the war to-morrow and that there was not enough time for anything, and it would be more sensible to leave her to the wolves than to even attempt whatever it was I would have to attempt at the risk of the pain and despair I had always wanted to avoid or evade.

And at the expense of Jack, too, because Jack would be up there waiting, expecting, hoping that I would return to that mess that wasn't quite a mess, with a wet canteen and a piano for a sing-song. Jack was still haunting my mind, and I wanted desperately to go back to him and try to explain to him what it was all about, but I was looking down into the welcoming eyes and it was too late and I was drowning in their cloudy marshes. . . . Yet there was still time. There was still time, and it was the easiest thing in the world. I need only say to her, " Look, it's pretty early to dine. Would you like to come with me for an hour or so and meet my brother

Jack? He's a staff-sergeant in the Pay Corps and they've got
a kind of mess in that L.H.Q. building up the top of Swanston
Street. He's a very good chap, my brother. . . ."

But my hand magically was under her firm young arm and
we were going through the glass doors into the carpeted comfort and the white napery and the glitter of glass and silver
and the coloured bottles along the cocktail-bar, and the head
waiter was bowing his deference and smiling his pleasure,
and already I was planning my assault on the fortress to
which I had fallen captive and I told myself that I was, after
all, five years younger than Gavin Turley and I had both
arms and I *could* offer her Venezuela, and Gavin, anyway,
was far too honourable a man to contest an issue so much to
the girl's advantage . . . and then I was taking her brief-case
and handing it to a bowing boy in a short white jacket, and
through the parrot-chatter all around us I seemed to hear
Jack's voice, loyal in protest against the tinny tinkling of an
out-of-tune piano:

" Oh, give him another ten minutes or so, you lot of bloody
whingers! He's a pretty important character, you got to
realise that, and he told you this was his last night. He just
got caught up in something. And it's not all *that* late, anyway. He'll be along. Here, let's have another go at that
mouth-organ. After all, he knows we're waiting here for
him, doesn't he? My brother Davy's not the sort of bloke
who ever let anyone down, you know. . . ."

THE END

Fontana Australian Novels

My Brother Jack   George Johnston
'Enthralling . . . entertaining . . . vividly original . . . Mr.
Johnston knows Australia and can write about it with
passionate sincerity.' *Melbourne Age*. 'One of the most
profoundly moving and disturbing books that I have ever
read.' *Illustrated London News*

Clean Straw for Nothing   George Johnston
'Even better, more poignant, than *My Brother Jack*. Here is
one man baring his soul as no Australian has ever done.'
Melbourne Sun. 'A deeply moving novel of a kind that one
would guess had taken not merely years of agony to write,
but years of agony to live.' *Sunday Telegraph*

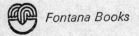 *Fontana Books*

James Jones

A Touch of Danger
A superb first thriller by the author of *From Here to Eternity* set on an Aegean island where the sun and sex are corrupted by violence and drugs. 'A believable private eye at last—not too tough, not too lucky—and a plot built with loving care.' *John Braine, Daily Express*

The Thin Red Line
His novel of the Marines on Guadalcanal—a gory, appallingly accurate description of men at war. 'Raw, violent, powerful and terrible, the most convincing account of battle experience I have ever read.' *Richard Lister, Evening Standard*

From Here to Eternity
The world famous novel of the men of the U.S. Army stationed at Pearl Harbour in the months immediately before America's entry into World War II. 'One reads every page persuaded that it is a remarkable, a very remarkable book indeed.' *Listener*

Go to the Widow-Maker
A superb novel about the war between the sexes, set in the world of rich men and those who cater to them. In Jones's tale of dangerous living, love is for men and women are for sex. 'Jones is the Hemingway of our time . . . There is savage poetry in his descriptions of spear-fishing and treasure-hunting.' *Spectator*

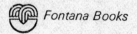 Fontana Books

Howard Spring

In 1938 his most famous book, *My Son, My Son*, was published; it was a world-wide success. Since then all his books, without exception, have been best-sellers and have earned Howard Spring a high reputation as an author of universal appeal.

'He is not afraid of stark drama, and he writes with real feeling.' *Sunday Times*

Time and the Hour

All the Day Long

Fame is the Spur

Rachel Rosing

Shabby Tiger

I Met a Lady

A Sunset Touch

Winds of the Day

These Lovers Fled Away

My Son, My Son

There is No Armour

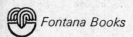 *Fontana Books*

Fontana Paperbacks

Fontana is a leading paperback publisher of fiction and non-fiction, with authors ranging from Alistair MacLean, Agatha Christie and Desmond Bagley to Solzhenitsyn and Pasternak, from Gerald Durrell and Joy Adamson to the famous Modern Masters series.

In addition to a wide-ranging collection of internationally popular writers of fiction, Fontana also has an outstanding reputation for history, natural history, military history, psychology, psychiatry, politics, economics, religion and the social sciences.

All Fontana books are available at your bookshop or newsagent; or can be ordered direct.